THE ROOMMATE MISTAKE

AN OFF-LIMITS RUGBY ROM-COM

PIPPA GRANT

Editing by Jessica Snyder, HEA Author Services
Proofreading by Emily Laughridge & Jodi Duggan
Cover Design by Qamber Designs
Cover Image Copyright © Wander Aguiar

1

Holt Webster, aka a professional rugby player ready to start the next phase of his life

An unfamiliar car is parked in the loading zone.

THAT'S the text message waiting for me when I pull into the staff lot behind the Copper Valley Aquarium.

I don't work at the aquarium, but I do occasionally moonlight as private security for a high-end catering company that often does after-hours events here. And one of the staff I know has texted that they're worried about the black Kia sedan blocking the oversize garage door behind the building.

Loading zone's for the catering vans.

That car shouldn't be there.

I text back that I'll check it out, pocket my phone, then brace myself before opening my Jeep door and stepping out into the parking lot.

Not just hot this summer. It's fucking hot. The kind of hot that makes you expect that the soles of your shoes will melt into the pavement if you don't walk quickly enough, which you don't want to do because the air is so thick, it's like walking through a wall of swamp water.

I'm sweating by the time I get close to the loading dock, where two more things strike me.

One, the car's running.

And two, there's a person in the driver's seat.

Bonus—I'm pretty sure it's a rental.

This isn't a *go inside and find out whose car this is* situation.

It's a *question how the hell someone in a rental car got a pass to get into the staff parking lot and why they're sitting in the loading zone* situation.

I'm three steps away from the driver's side door when I realize there's one more thing completely wrong about this situation.

The driver is hunched over and gnawing on—what the fuck is that?

Is that a cake that she's eating with her whole face?

A massive sub sandwich?

No, it's—are you serious?

It's a rotisserie chicken.

Isn't it?

I squint harder, and yep.

That's exactly what it is.

The white woman parked in the loading zone is gnawing on a rotisserie chicken. The kind you get at a grocery store deli.

But she hasn't picked a leg. Not a breast. Or a wing.

It's the whole chicken.

She has the *whole chicken* in her hands, and she's going to town on it. Large bites right out of the breast area. And—

Is she even chewing?

Or is she swallowing every bite whole?

Wild.

She's barely pausing. Just diving in for one bite after another as if she hasn't eaten in a week.

Or more.

I mentally sigh.

Been doing security in my off-season for extra cash and to keep me occupied for a few years now, but this is a new one.

It's going to be one of those nights.

But at least she's alone.

I draw in a deep breath, almost choke on the humidity, and rap my knuckles against her window.

Wide blue eyes meet mine as she shrieks loudly enough for me to hear the muffled reverberations through the glass.

But it's not the shriek that has me ducking.

It's the fact that she's throwing the entire chicken at me.

One moment, she's cavewomaning the bird, the next, she's winding up and launching it like she's a weekend quarterback.

I'm halfway to the ground, out of range of the chicken, when I remember something important.

Her window's up.

Her window's up, and the chicken's bouncing off it back into her lap, leaving a greasy smear all over the window.

And that's why it takes me a second to realize the next thing.

She's choking.

She's choking on the forty-one bites of chicken that she's

hoovered into her mouth in the thirteen seconds since I spotted her.

Fuck me.

I straighten, grab the door handle, and yank it open. The scent of roasted chicken spills out of the car and joins the aroma of sweaty asphalt.

Chicken spills out of the car too.

"Swallow," I order.

She lifts a finger, then manages a feeble cough.

Dammit, Webster. Way to go.

Good news is, if she's coughing, she's not choking.

For the moment.

"Are you okay?" I ask.

She nods, still coughing.

"Do you need help?"

Head shake.

She does not.

"What are you doing here?"

She looks over at me and hacks again. Wide, wary blue eyes connect with mine.

I tap the private security logo on my polo. "You can't park here. Private property."

She coughs once more, shakes her head, and then looks down.

Outside the car to where the whole goddamn chicken minus half a breast that she's been gnawing on has flopped over onto its back, legs spread, wings looking a little worse for the adventure.

"I can't eat that now, can I?" The statement is a whole mood. Melancholy and desperation with a touch of *three-second rule.*

And I feel a familiar punch to the gut.

Caden would've laughed his ass off about this.

If I could tell my brother that I found a woman going full predator on an entire rotisserie chicken in the loading zone at one of my shifts, he would've congratulated me on meeting my soulmate and asked when the wedding was.

I would've flipped him off.

He would've told me to bring popcorn the next time I wanted to talk about my future wife.

Fuck, I miss my brother.

He was funny as hell.

"Your digestive system, your choice, but you can't eat it here," I reply.

She eyes me.

I eye her right back.

There's a ring of grease around her plump lips and a bit of chicken on her chin that wobbles as she mutters something to herself.

The ghost in my head is right.

There could be something here.

She's fucking adorable.

And I'm leaving the country in five days and not coming back. Ever.

"Ma'am, this is a private parking lot—"

"You're security?" she interrupts.

"Yes, ma'am."

"ID, please."

The authority in her voice doesn't match the way she's using the edge of her T-shirt to wipe a streak of grease off of the steering wheel, and it momentarily catches me off guard as I peek beneath her T-shirt.

Blue.

She's either an alien with a blue stomach, or she's wearing an undershirt.

Alien with a blue stomach?

Christ on a cracker.

It truly will be one of *those* nights. I should've said no when the call came in.

And missed meeting the lioness? Caden's voice says in my head.

I instruct myself to unclench my jaw. My work ID is attached to my hip, which she could clearly see if she'd look down. But she doesn't, so I unclip it and show it to her.

She leans in, squinting at it while she angles her body just outside the car enough to reach for the chicken.

Like she's being subtle. Like I won't notice that she's trying to grab the poultry on the pavement.

I sigh and bend to grab it for her but pause when she straightens.

"Oh. *You're* Holt." Her wide blue eyes light up as if me being Holt is the best news she's had all day, and her smile—

Fuck me.

That smile says I'm better than the chicken.

And given the way she was eating it up—literally—the thought has me temporarily disoriented.

Soul. Mate. Called it.

My brother's been gone for almost nine months, and much as I miss him, his memory still manages to annoy me sometimes.

She starts to extend a greasy hand, looks down at it, and pulls it back into the car. "Hi. I'm Ziggy Barnes. The new sommelier? Brydie said I should find you to help me unload the wine. And here you are."

My left eyelid twitches.

I started doing security one or two nights a week while Caden was sick to get out of the house in the off-season. Theoretically to make a little extra cash too, since rugby in the US doesn't pay a lot. The Pounders' owner hooked me up with a company he uses regularly. This is the kind of catering company that handles events for the bigger teams in the city. Political events. The most exclusive weddings for the richest of the rich here.

And their new *sommelier* is sitting outside her first event, gnawing on a whole chicken. Wearing sweatpants and a T-shirt and a ring of grease around her mouth. In a rental car.

Definitely a rental. The paperwork is sitting in the cupholder.

There's a story here. Likely a fascinating story.

A fascinating story that's none of my business. Work and pleasure don't mix.

It's a rule. A good one at that.

I clear my throat. "Didn't know we were getting a new wine person."

"All I know is that Michael is no longer with the company. I didn't ask questions."

I don't know if I believe her, and I don't know how much of my doubt is because she's pretty and how much is because it's been months since I've thought a woman was pretty so I don't trust my own gut.

"What's with the chicken?"

She grins again. "I was hungry, and it sounded good."

"Normal people use forks and plates."

"Why be normal when you can trap yourself in your car without napkins on the first day of a new job?"

"How'd you get into the parking lot?"

That bright, sunny smile finally drops away.

I feel like I've kicked a puppy.

Shit.

"Brydie gave me a pass. My uniform is in the back seat, and all of the wine for this evening is in the trunk. I was told you wouldn't be here until five, which would've given me plenty of time to finish my dinner in peace instead of being judged for it. Would you like to call Brydie to confirm that I'm supposed to be here, or would you like to continue glaring at me like my very existence is giving you constipation?"

Did a woman with a fleck of chicken breast on her nose just attempt to give me a smackdown?

Yep.

She did.

And once again, I get that gut reaction that I can't wait to tell my best friend this story—once it's funny—and then the subsequent punch at remembering he's not here anymore.

I miss that fucker.

Especially in the rugby off-season.

Solo training doesn't work off the same level of frustration as full-team practices with scrums and rucks and tackles.

I pull my phone out with every intention of calling Brydie, the lead caterer, when a text lands from her.

Brydie: In case nobody told you, Michael was let go yesterday. We have a new somm coming in. Super fancy lady. Very pretty. Her name's Ziggy Barnes and she should be here by five with all of tonight's wine. Can you please help her bring it in? Did I mention she's very pretty?

Brydie clearly hasn't communicated Ziggy Barnes's

arrival to the rest of the staff, or I wouldn't have that first text about this unfamiliar car.

I lift my phone, snap Ziggy's picture as she's once again leaning over, reaching for the chicken, and send it back to Brydie.

Me: This her?

The message gets read, but not answered immediately.

Not on text anyway.

The back door of the aquarium swings open, and Brydie herself leans out the door, squinting at both of us in the sunshine. She's a white lady in her late fifties and her favorite pastime is showing everyone pictures of her grandbabies.

Ziggy leans out her window. "Hi, Brydie. I'm early."

"Is that a grocery-store chicken?" Brydie says.

"I got hungry."

"Honey, that's been on the ground. Do you know what falls on the ground outside a loading dock at an aquarium? Leave it to the birds. We'll feed you inside."

Ziggy gestures to me with her thumb. "Is this the guy who's supposed to help me carry in the wine?"

Brydie beams at me. "That's him."

"Why isn't the wine already on the catering truck?" I ask.

"Michael," Brydie replies.

I scrub a hand over my face.

This is not my circus.

Not really.

It's an easy-ish job that pays as well as playing rugby in the States and gives me something to do outside of my house a few nights a week.

Until I leave for Europe in five days.

Going back to where rugby's more common. Where selling out stadiums means a paycheck orders of magnitude bigger than what we get here. Where we can't go out in public without getting recognized.

Unlike here, where I've quit correcting Brydie every time she tells someone I play lacrosse, because here, if it's not football or hockey or baseball or basketball, it doesn't count.

"Pop the trunk," I tell Ziggy.

I don't like her.

Liar, Caden's voice whispers.

Fine.

I don't *want* to like her.

She's new. I don't know where she came from or what her qualifications are. It's not normal to gnaw on a whole chicken inside a car. And said gnawing doesn't match the *super fancy* that I was told to look for.

Though she *is* pretty.

Gorgeous, actually. Round cheeks that have a glow. Those bright blue eyes. Soft pink lips. Brown hair just the right kind of messy to give a guy ideas about gripping it while—

Fuck it.

Maybe she's up for fun before she leaves.

Why not? I haven't thought another woman was pretty in months, and who can be attractive while devouring a full bird the way she was?

Plus, while work and fun don't mix, I'm quitting.

This is my last shift before I leave.

The attraction I'm feeling here is either *it's been too long* catching up with me, or there's something innately appealing about her.

Brydie strides down the three short stairs to join us and hands Ziggy the towel tucked into her apron like it's normal for a new somm to show up with chicken grease all over herself.

"Ziggy ran all over the city today buying replacement wine for tonight," Brydie tells me. "Saved the day. Oh, honey, you missed a spot. Here."

She takes the towel that Ziggy's using to smear chicken grease worse over the driver's side window and rubs Ziggy's nose instead.

Ziggy shoots a wary glance at me.

"The trunk?" I repeat.

"Don't mind him," Brydie says to her. "He doesn't like the heat."

"Who does?" Ziggy finally pushes out of the car as I head to the back of the vehicle. "Holy hell, who turned on the ovens in the parking lot?"

"Global warming," Brydie says. "Was it not this hot in Europe?"

My head jerks back to look at Ziggy.

Europe? She was in Europe recently?

She grins, but it's more guarded than it was before. "Just because I eat my rotisserie chicken like a rabid toddler doesn't mean I haven't seen other parts of the world, Mr. Security Man. Who's ready to carry wine?"

She pops the trunk.

"Vacation?" I ask her.

"Work."

"Chicken-tester?"

She smiles again. "Yes. I worked for a luxury cruise line in the Med making sure all of their chicken was properly edible. Five stars on this one, by the way. Hints of rosemary and thyme on the nose, a bold, full-bodied poultry grease mouthfeel, and a delightful *I'm going to have indigestion* finish."

I was out with my teammates right after the season ended for us one match short of the championship last month, and I watched one of the younger guys fall hard for a woman at the bar who kept smearing ketchup on her mouth every time she had a fry.

I didn't get it.

Now, I think I do.

And because I haven't been out in the hooking-up or flirting or dating game since my first attempt after Caden died ended like shit, I don't actually know what to say back.

Or if I want to.

Don't need another stalker leaving cheese in my mailbox with sticky notes attached insulting my character.

Not that she'll have access to my mailbox.

I'll be in Spain. Long way to get to my mailbox.

I grunt and push the trunk open, then grab a case of wine.

Ziggy steps beside me and reaches for another case but gets shooed by Brydie, who whispers something about her *condition*.

Condition?

Like a blood sugar condition? Does she have scoliosis? Is there some underlying condition that the average human wouldn't recognize that she's dealing—

Nope.

Stop it, Webster.

Got enough on my plate being captain of the team and keeping all of the young guys—and often the not-as-young guys—out of trouble.

My job of playing full-on caretaker ended when Caden died.

I don't have to care about strangers and their situations.

Even when they're pretty and funny and intriguing.

And even when I'm lying, and I still watch over my teammates like I'm their big brother. My neighbors like I'm their nephew. My coworkers like—

You get the idea.

Leaving the country will be good for me in every way that counts.

"Go on, go in and get changed," Brydie repeats to her.

Ziggy rubs her eye as she nods. "Okay. Thank you. I'll be ready in ten minutes."

She switches course and grabs a suit bag out of the back seat, but when she bends to retrieve her chicken, a large black bird swoops in and buzzes her.

She shrieks.

I drop the wine and lunge for her, steadying her before she topples over.

Honey.

Her hair smells like warm honey, and her body is soft as it presses back into mine, her ass curvy against my thigh.

I could absolutely see myself going home with this woman tonight.

Blow off steam.

Have fun.

Make a nice memory before I leave for Spain.

"So I'll leave the chicken for the birds." She's not struggling to get out of my grasp, and her voice is high-pitched and unsteady.

Attraction?

Or fear of crows or ravens?

Shit. I don't know what she's feeling any more than I know what kind of bird that was.

"I'll get it away from the door," I say.

I don't let go.

She doesn't pull away.

"Shoo, shoo," Brydie says. "You'll get your food, but you have to wait three minutes. Didn't your mother teach you any bird manners?"

The bird screams at her.

Okay. Time to let go.

Ziggy's here all night.

I'm here all night.

I'll get a chance to talk to her again without the danger of bird attacks.

Honey and vanilla. There's definitely a subtle vanilla scent in her hair too. But you have to breathe deep to notice it.

She straightens.

I drop my grip on her. "In you go."

"We've got the chicken," Brydie says. "Oh, good, none of these bottles broke."

Ziggy tucks a stray wisp of hair behind her ear. "Thank you," she says to Brydie without looking at me.

"Of course, sweetheart. You go in and get ready. We're right behind you."

Ziggy beelines for the door, head down.

"She's a really sweet girl," Brydie says to me after I toss the chicken over the back fence and into a weedy area for the birds. "Such a sad situation that brought her home."

I almost ask, but I don't.

Not my business.

Not when *sad situation* says everything I need to know.

Ziggy Barnes comes with complications.

And I don't want complications.

Even for just one night.

2

Ziggy Barnes, aka a woman who's sure that her gloomiest days are over and she's back on a positive life track

THE CHICKEN by itself was a bad idea.

It looked good in the moment.

It smelled good in the moment.

It did not settle well though.

I'd say it's morning sickness—which is totally misbranded, by the way, because it happens all damn day—but I suspect I'd be sick tonight even if I wasn't pregnant.

Why?

Because my first night at my first job after unexpectedly moving back home when I decided that I wanted to carry and raise this baby involves serving my former best friend's father-in-law and brother-in-law.

Abby Nora Ewing—now Abby Nora Ewing-Harrison—saved my life when I was thirteen.

While I wasn't in physical danger, my mental health and

self-confidence weren't so great. My mom had raised me solo since my father died when I was too young to remember him, but when I was thirteen, she married Roland Keating, one of the richest men in Copper Valley, and we moved into his mansion in his fancy upscale neighborhood.

And I didn't belong. I felt so out of place.

But Abby Nora—the girl next door—took me in and made friends with me and didn't mock me for my lack of knowledge about makeup and fashion and what the symphony was playing this season.

We started high school together. We planned our class schedules so we'd have as much overlap as possible. We went to football and basketball games and dances together. After graduation, we went to culinary school together.

We both sobbed until we couldn't sob any more when I left the East Coast for sommelier training and my subsequent first job in Napa. And then we texted constantly and talked on the phone at least once a week.

It slowed down when she met Josh, her future husband, but we still talked all the time.

She got engaged. Then married. And until two months ago, when she didn't realize I'd called in over video to her baby shower and said some highly unflattering things about me while I could hear, I thought we were still besties.

She made it crystal clear to everyone at her baby shower that we are not, in fact, *besties*.

And tonight, her in-laws are among the guests I'm serving on my first shift.

This.

Is.

The.

Absolute.

Worst.

Event.

Ever.

Sad, really. The aquarium is beautiful. We're in the ocean room, a viewing area with a cavernous floor-to-ceiling window into a wide, deep, seemingly endless pool, where sharks and stingrays and schools of fish and even the occasional whale shark float by. The water casts a blue glow into the room, creating an ambiance that the cruise line I used to work for tried to recreate in one of their dining rooms.

The ship's Blue Lagoon restaurant came close, but this has a magic that can't be emulated.

I'll have to come back another day to truly enjoy it though.

Tonight, the only magic I want is for my former BFF's family to continue to either not recognize me or continue to pretend they don't.

I manage to keep the chicken down most of the evening, but when I'm finally done explaining the final wine pairing of the evening to the guests, I bolt to the bathroom and let the chicken go.

You'd think this is when my evening would get better—when my stomach is no longer angry, when the guests are relaxed and full and slightly tipsy, when the security guy is on higher alert because of the alcohol consumed so that I can keep stealing surreptitious glances at his gorgeous face—but it is, in fact, the start of something even worse.

Because when I leave the bathroom, Eli Harrison is hanging out in the short hallway, blocking my exit.

Abby Nora's brother-in-law.

He might not recognize me.

He might not have heard from Abby Nora about what

went down at her baby shower several weeks ago, before I came home pregnant and homeless and jobless, which I sincerely hope she hasn't heard yet.

Or he might not care.

Not only is he blocking my path back to the main event room, but now the man is trying to convince me to join his vitamin-selling pyramid scheme.

"If you talked about our vitamins the way you talk about wine, we'd be unstoppable," he's saying.

Seven years of working cruise ships in Europe, mostly on the Med, trained me for situations like this. Flat smile. Minimal eye contact. Call them *sir* or *ma'am* or their chosen honorific if they provide it.

"I'm sorry, sir, I need to see to the other guests."

"No, see, these vitamins will change your life," the tall, bulky man says.

It seems unlikely that he recognizes me from Abby Nora's wedding. Could be the wine.

Could be his "vitamins".

No telling.

But I do know he shouldn't need to sell vitamins. His family is in real estate, and if they don't run at least half of the vacation rental homes in the city, they're close. They're here tonight for a community service awards banquet because of how well they do with their local empire.

I continue to smile with bland professionalism while my stomach rolls over. It's been hard enough being home, moving in the same circles where I know I'm likely to run into Abby Nora and having to play *that* game where we both pretend we're still friendly.

But tonight? Right now, with her brother-in-law trapping me outside the bathroom?

18

No matter how excited I am about my own pregnancy and the new opportunities here at home, I wish I were still in Europe. "I'm sure they're wonderful. If you'll excuse me, I need to get back to the bar."

"These vitamins, they're not like normal vitamins. They're like vitamins that take vitamins to be better vitamins. Get it? Vitamins on vitamins."

He chuckles at his own joke, making the melting ice in his rocks glass rattle as his hand shakes along with his chuckle.

"Drink service closes in fifteen minutes, sir, and I need to be available for all of the guests." I angle to sneak around him, but he shifts once again, trapping me in the small hallway outside the bathrooms. While it's not as dimly lit here as it is in the ocean room, it's not as brightly lit as I'd prefer.

And we're completely out of view of the other guests.

None of whom have needed to come down the hall to the bathroom.

This isn't the first time I've had to extricate myself from a situation like this, and I don't expect it'll be the last.

The guest is always right. Don't make a scene. Defuse with firm politeness.

When the guest is related to the woman I thought was my best friend until she told the attendees at her baby shower that I'm a selfish cunt who uses people, and when my stomach is knotting itself tighter at that memory bubbling to the surface over and over and over again all night, I wish *firm, polite professionalism* involved a wee bit of violence.

Eli rubs a spot on his red cheek while he looks down at his rocks glass. The man's more than a few glasses deep and his complexion shows it. "You know what? We should go into business. You and me. We'll put my vitamins in your wine and make it *healthy*. Call it *winetamins*. Heh. And you can be the face because pretty girls always sell things better."

He winks, then gives me the wiggly brown eyebrows of *yeah, you're cute, and yeah, I've noticed*. Probably some *come on, flirt back with me* in there too.

I hope I'm staying blank-faced in response. The last thing he needs to know is that I'm ready to panic.

Why aren't any other guests coming to use the restroom? Or the staff? Where's security? "My current contract prevents me from going into alternate wine-related businesses," I tell him as I try again—unsuccessfully—to ease around him.

His chuckle makes my arm hairs stand on end.

"Oh, I can take care of that."

My brain does that thing it's been doing since the day I video-called in to Abby Nora's baby shower to witness her full opinion of me, and it starts spinning out of control.

No one's coming.

I'm stuck here forever.

I need to puke again.

If he hurts my baby, I will hunt him to the ends of the earth and make him pay.

If this is another elaborate ruse by Abby Nora's family to make me feel like someone who doesn't belong in my own life, I'll—I'll—

Fuck.

I'll cry.

That's what I'll do.

I'll cry because it hurts, and then they'll know they hurt me, and I don't want them to know they hurt me.

I want to move on with my life.

Hunt for a house that'll be perfect for me and my own baby.

Get a dog.

Start a garden.

Plant grapes.

Study for my level three certification.

Have lunch with my mom and stepsister.

Take a chance at trusting people to be my friends again.

"There's nothing my family can't do in this town," Eli Harrison says. "I'll take care of your contract."

My feet ache and my stomach is doing that uncomfortable grumble that's been my constant companion for the past month, but worse, because *anxiety*. "Excuse me, sir, I need to return to the bar to help the other guests before drink service closes."

Wonderful. He's frowning now. "I'm a paying customer too. They can wait. Do you take vitamins? I don't sell them because I need to. Clearly. I'm here getting an award for how I use my millions, aren't I? I sell them because I believe in them. And you're pretty, but you could be prettier on vitamins. You join my team, you'd make enough that you wouldn't have to work second-rate jobs as a bartender either."

If I were on the ship, someone would've come to check on me by now. My colleagues and I—especially the other women—had a system. We watched out for each other.

No one is watching out for me tonight.

Ever since Abby Nora told everyone at her baby shower that the only reason I worked cruise ships was so that I could talk about *living on the Med* like I'm better than I really am, I don't know who I trust to have my back.

I can't even trust myself at this point.

21

I'm the one who buried my grief in ouzo and a one-night stand with unexpected consequences.

Mostly good, but being home again definitely has its struggles.

And now I'm getting pissed that I need someone to protect me tonight. What about the rest of the staff? Have I failed at keeping an eye out for them?

Oh god.

Am I a shitty coworker who hasn't been caring enough for my fellow staff?

I square my shoulders when I'd really like to barf again. "I enjoy my job, sir. Thank you for the offer, but I don't think it fits my life plan right now. If you'll accompany me to the bar, I can refill your drink for you."

"You know, your life could be longer if you took the right vitamins. I take them every day, and look at me. Yeah? See? Look at this." He flexes his arm. He's tall—at least six feet— and broad like a former college football player, and when he flexes, he takes up the entire hallway. "Solid as a rock. Here. Feel it."

"It's against the rules for me to touch guests, sir."

The asshole angles closer. "C'mon, honey, you know there's more here than just *guest* and *bartender*."

Anxiety is giving way to anger, and neither is good for my stomach. "Sir, if I've given you the wrong impression, I apologize. I—"

"She doesn't apologize," a voice interrupts from behind him. "Stop harassing the staff and return to your table."

Goosebumps race over my arms and up my neck as Holt, the security guy, muscles his way around Eli.

If I were letting myself contemplate men right now— which I'm not, but if I were—Holt is exactly the type of guy

I'd stare at from across the bar while debating how to best make my move.

Okay.

Okay, *fine.*

I've been staring at him at every opportunity since he interrupted my chickenfest.

Where Eli Harrison is tall and thick, Holt is taller and thicker.

Holt's nearly black hair is neatly trimmed but still falling over his forehead. His deep-set brown eyes telegraph *danger* and his square jaw and the way his biceps are testing the limits of his polo sleeves promise that he can back up any threat he makes. And when he turns around—just *holy hell.*

An ass like that should be illegal.

The relief that he's here to help me mingles with carnal attraction and makes my belly flip for a different reason.

"You spilled my drink," Eli growls at Holt.

In my fantasies, this is where the hot security guy pulls me to his side, growls back *and you made my girlfriend uncomfortable,* and carries me past the man who's harassing me, apologizes for calling me his girlfriend but says he was going nuts trying to find me, and then we kiss dramatically, and—

And nobody wants a single pregnant woman and I need to get a freaking grip.

Holt stares Eli dead in the eye. "Does your wife know you're hitting on the staff?"

And while my fantasy wasn't the right way to defuse this situation, neither is that question.

Eli's jaw visibly clenches. The ice in his empty glass rattles while his knuckles go white. "Watch yourself, you little pissant. I can get you fired with one phone call."

"Ziggy, go back in the bathroom," Holt says.

Defuse defuse defuse.

It's ingrained in me after seven years of close-quarters hospitality service.

Even when the vengeful parts of me want to see someone in Abby Nora's family hurt the way she hurt me. "Oh, look, the whale sharks are at the window." I can't see the whale sharks from here, but the question should distract them both. "Is there a magic show tonight? I heard a magician was making a surprise appearance. We're not missing it, are we?"

"Shut up, you little whore," Eli says.

"And we're done here," Holt says. "Ziggy. Bathroom. Sir, you have ten seconds to leave on your own before I make you leave."

"You can't make me do a goddamn thing."

"You're harassing my staff. The exit is behind you."

"She's hitting on me. Little cunt knows—"

There are approximately five words in any of the three languages I know that will set me off.

And that one?

After Abby Nora used it at her baby shower, that's the biggest trigger of all.

I elbow my way around Holt and get up in Eli's face. "What did you just call me?"

He leans into my face with his whiskey breath. Holt grabs my arm and tries to tug me back while shoving between us.

"I said, you're a little cunt. You know you want me."

My brain fills with memories of that video call in to the shower.

Oh god, don't say her name. I'm so glad she's not here. Such a cunt, thinking she's better than the rest of us because she has a fancy job on some cruise ship. She shits in an airplane toilet on fish piss water all day, but ooooh, we're supposed to lick her feet because she knows all about wine and sails around the Mediterranean. Whoop-de-fucking-do.

They hate me. They all hate me.

Such a cunt, and I don't call people cunts.

Everyone in Abby Nora's circle thinks I'm a terrible person.

Cunt! Cunt! Cunt!

I have to make this stop.

You guys... Ziggy's on the phone. She can hear you.

I don't know where I am, and I don't care.

All I know is a blinding hot rage at being called that word *again*.

Does he know who I am? Did Abby Nora tell him I'm *one of those?*

Is that why he's using it?

Better question—do I care?

"Ziggy," a voice says beside me.

I don't listen.

I'm *beyond* listening.

I don't want to fucking *defuse*.

"Ziggy—" Holt repeats as I duck around his attempt to push me behind him once more.

I have to get up on my tiptoes to get even partially close to Eli's face, but I do it. "You're a rude, uncultured waste of oxygen who can shove those vitamins that you bought with your daddy's money right up your ass."

His cheek twitches and his lip curls. "Someone needs a lesson in where her place is."

"Ziggy." A firm hand clamps down on my left arm.

There's no universe where I'm stronger than Holt.

Until adrenaline and pent-up grief and rage get involved.

25

And that's exactly what I'm feeling as Eli sneers at me. "*Ziggy*. That's such a whore name."

I'm only partially in control of my body. There's a whisper in my head saying *don't do it* but a bigger voice chanting *show them they can't use you as a punching bag.*

Show them you're done with their shit.

Show them they can't talk to you like this.

I'd like to tell you that it's the voice that propels my fist into Eli Harrison's nose.

But that's not what happens.

What happens is that all of the turmoil inside of me decides to depart on its own, in its own fashion, and I haven't been paying close enough attention to know that I should've done exactly what Holt told me to do and gone back into the bathroom.

I don't feel my mouth open, but I see what comes out of it.

And lands square in the middle of Eli Harrison's chest.

All over his arms.

In his rocks glass.

Splatters up to his chin.

I finally feel the heave in my stomach. Taste the acid in my mouth. Notice the hard grip on my arm.

Oh, shit.

Shit shit *shit*.

Eli screams. "You *cunt*, this is Armani."

He lunges for me, but there's no impact, because a large man in a black polo and khaki uniform pants is tackling him to the ground.

I'm going to puke again.

This time, I turn and dash for the bathroom.

"Get the fuck off me, you asshole," Eli's yelling as I push into the ladies' room.

"Maybe next time you'll think twice before trapping a woman in a hallway, you fuckwanker," Holt replies as I dash into a stall.

I'm fired.

I am *so* fired.

This is exactly why I'm not on the ship anymore.

Because you don't puke on cruise ships.

And you don't puke when you're working with a catering staff either.

I want this baby.

I do.

Even if this isn't where I saw my life going immediately. It wasn't in my plans so soon. But I'm choosing this.

Not because Abby Nora's pregnant and I want what she has.

Not because my mother is thrilled to be a grandmother.

But because *I want this*.

This baby is the new start to my life after the most significant relationship I've ever had fell apart.

But why does it have to be so hard?

3

Holt

THIS IS the worst idea in the history of terrible ideas.

This is a fucking awesome idea, I can practically hear Caden reply. *Got my popcorn and a beer. Let's do this.*

And that's why I'm here.

Because since Caden died, I haven't taken chances. I haven't put myself out there. I haven't *lived*.

Yes, I've played a successful season of rugby.

Yes, I've had fun with my teammates off the pitch.

But it's been motions.

Not *feelings*.

Today?

Today, I have some feelings.

I fucked up last night, and it got Ziggy Barnes fired.

I should've noticed faster that she wasn't at her station. But I didn't because I was feeling a little like a creeper for looking her way too often, so I made myself ignore her.

Wasn't getting the *yeah, you're hot, I'm hot, let's be hot together* vibes off of her, and I knew I needed to cool it.

But the minute I finally got a grip and quit staring, *the incident* happened, and I wasn't there to stop it soon enough.

And after *the incident*, Brydie told me Ziggy's been living in a hotel since returning to the States because living with her parents was, and I quote, *not ideal*.

Know a thing or two about *not ideal* parents myself.

See also, they're both still alive, and they weren't invited to Caden's funeral, nor were they asked for help when he was sick.

I shake my head.

Not what I need to concentrate on now.

When I stopped in at the catering office this morning to turn in my gear and my uniform, I heard they'd fired Ziggy because of last night's unexpected turn of events.

So I did what I always do, and I stuck my nose into someone's business when they're down, and I told Brydie that I'd help Ziggy get a new job. She gave me a copy of Ziggy's résumé, and I'm looking it over once again while I remind myself that this is not me taking responsibility for a random woman's life, but instead, offering her an opportunity that will be mutually beneficial for both of us.

Even with the *I'm not into you* vibes.

That's not why I'm doing this.

I'm doing it because it's the right thing to do. The fact that she's pretty and I could listen to her talk about wines for hours despite not liking wine at all is irrelevant.

Beyond the fact that her résumé is impressive and makes her look like a potentially good candidate for what I need.

Or at least not a bad candidate.

It doesn't actually matter to me that she went to culinary

school in New York and has a level two sommelier certification. Or that she's done continuing education, studying Spanish and Italian—makes so much sense now why I couldn't understand what she was muttering when I went to check on her after I escorted the fuckwanker who cornered her out of the building—or that she spent seven years working for Lusso Cruises.

Despite my first impression of her last night with that chicken, she's elegant and sophisticated and way out of my league.

Knew that as soon as she stepped out of the restroom ready for work—black pencil skirt, white blouse, black apron, makeup fixed and curly hair tamed.

And then she stood in front of the roomful of Copper Valley's richest residents, hosting an awards banquet to congratulate themselves for donating to various charities over the year, and she described every wine in a way that made my balls ache and put me under a goddamn spell of wanting to ask questions just to hear her say things like *Rhone Valley* and *hints of tobacco* and *ashy soil* and *particularly good crop that year*.

She's fancy as fuck.

And now unemployed as fuck.

The unemployed part is the main reason I'm sitting in the parking lot of her hotel, next to her rental car, waiting for her to come out.

I'm not a total creeper—I got her number off her résumé and texted her to ask if we could talk.

Told her it had to be in person because I need to see for myself that she's okay after letting her down last night.

After it was my fault she got fired.

Partially my fault. Not all my fault. Partially. But a crucial part. I should've gone looking for her sooner. When I found her, I should've told her someone needed her help.

Not gotten my boxer briefs in a bunch over watching a guy hit on her and make her uncomfortable.

Though it was satisfying to tackle the asshole.

Little gross too, given Ziggy's method of trying to get him to back off, but satisfying.

It's a good thing I'm leaving the country soon.

Probably a bad sign I'm still attracted to her despite what she's demonstrated she's capable of doing when she's not interested in a guy.

And there she is, stepping out of the hotel lobby, pulling a suitcase, looking fucking gorgeous.

Her face twists up in an *I'm going to puke* expression that has me wondering again what's going on with her.

But it could be the weather.

Hell has nothing on the temperatures in Copper Valley today. Whoever gave July permission to exist is an asshole.

I climb out of the air-conditioned interior of my Jeep and grimace myself as the heat smacks me in the face.

Ziggy spots me, and her face goes blank. More pink rises in her cheeks. Much like when I found her in her car last night, she's in cotton shorts and a casual shirt, though today's is a pink tank top instead of a T-shirt. Her curly light-brown hair is tied up in a loose bun with wispy, frizzy little hairs standing up all over her scalp.

Ziggy's hair, zero. Humidity, one.

I take a hit to the chest where my heart lives.

What is it about this woman?

What is it about her that makes me want to put myself out there again?

"Good morning," she says in a pleasant tone that doesn't match her wary eyes as her sandals tap the pavement.

I hate wary.

I hate that she has any reason to be concerned.

If I'd done my damn job better, she wouldn't need to worry.

"Morning. Feeling better today?"

"Yes. Thank you."

I angle another look at her suitcase as she approaches her rental car. Black. Simple. Small. Not much bigger than my overnight bag for away matches during the season.

"You checking out?"

Her nose wrinkles briefly before she blanks her face. "Sometimes smart financial decisions have to be made."

"Moving in with your parents?" I ask.

She sighs. "Naked Tuesdays, here I come."

"Naked Tuesdays?"

"Forget I said that."

No chance. And now I'm imagining Ziggy naked. Maybe she has a secret tattoo. Birthmarks somewhere. Are her nipples light pink or a dusty rose?

Not the time, Webster.

I clear my throat. "There's not a person on this earth who could forget you said that."

Her wince is wincey enough that I feel it in my own face. "Please don't take this the wrong way, but why are you here?"

"To apologize."

"For what? You didn't do anything wrong. Except possibly judge me for how I ate my chicken. Which, clearly, was a bad idea. I should not have had that chicken. And I will likely never eat chicken again."

Oh. *Food poisoning.* That makes sense. Shit. Been there. I

32

should've checked in with her last night. When I didn't have her phone number. "I should've noticed the situation with the dick-nugget sooner."

"You're supposed to be some kind of superhero, tracking everyone at every single minute?"

"That actually *was* what I was supposed to be doing. It's the job."

She slides me a look as she pops her trunk. "That's an impossible task."

"Still mine to do." I snatch her suitcase and lift it in for her.

She's traveling light.

And there's not another suitcase in the car. No boxes. No bags. Not even the empty cloth grocery bags that everyone I know carries in their car these days.

Maybe she's not checking out.

Regardless, she's crossed her arms and is frowning at me. "It's hot, so excuse me for being short, but you don't need to feel any obligation to apologize to me. Or feel any shred of responsibility on my behalf. What happened was entirely my fault, and you don't need to worry about me. I'll be fine."

"I don't know you well enough to feel obligations or responsibilities to you."

Those wide blue eyes telegraph *if that was true, you wouldn't be here.*

It's like she knows I agreed to take in my neighbor's dog despite the fact that the dog hates me. That I make an effort to have dinner with even my most annoying teammates regularly in the offseason to make sure they're doing okay physically and financially. That the schools hand out my address for every fundraiser since I can't tell random kids no when they come to my door.

Or possibly those wide blue eyes are telegraphing *that was an asshole thing to say.*

Shit.

I'm usually good at this.

I shift on the pavement. It's so hot the soles of my shoes are heating up. "I mean, I know I can't stop shitty people from doing shitty things every minute of every event I work, but it's human and natural to feel bad when you could've made a situation better instead of worse."

Do I sound like a blabbering idiot, or am I being extra hard on myself because I want to impress this woman and I want her to like me even if I never see her again?

Both.

Definitely both.

And I'm making her uncomfortable.

The wary is back in her eyes.

As it probably should be. A guy smaller than me cornered her and made her feel uncomfortable and then called her names when she wasn't interested, and now here I am, bumbling through offering to help her.

She probably thinks I'm here to ask her to get involved in my protein powder pyramid scheme.

"You didn't make it worse," she says. "What happened was...inevitable. And had nothing to do with what you did or didn't do."

"It was inevitable that a guy would corner you like that?"

"No. It's not—actually, yes." She sucks a breath through her nose and squints up at the sky. "Yes. Let's go with yes."

I know women get the shitty end of the stick when it comes to dealing with some guys. That's a big reason my offseason job exists—to handle what happened last night because it happens too frequently.

But I get the impression there's more to Ziggy's story than *when you work with the public, it's inevitable that a guy will push boundaries he shouldn't.*

And the regrets at how I handled last night are getting heavier. "Sorry. Again. That I didn't get there quicker."

She shakes her head. "It's fine. It ended fine."

"You got fired."

"Probably shouldn't be working events right now anyway."

"So you know, I quit."

She presses her hands to her cheeks. "Oh my *god.*"

"Not because of you."

If I hadn't met her while she was shoving a whole roasted chicken in her face, the dead-eyed *get to the point* look she's giving me now would probably intimidate at least some small part of me. Maybe an eyelid or one of my pinky fingernails.

I'd enjoy it too.

Not immune to teacher-librarian fantasies.

Fuck, it's hot out here. "Last night was already scheduled to be my last night."

"Oh. Good. Then I hope your next job is less exciting."

"It's overseas."

The corners of her mouth tighten. "Did Abby Nora send you?"

"What?"

"Never mind. Enjoy overseas."

She was overseas. Wonder if she misses it.

I miss it. Been a long five years since I left the league in the UK to come home and take care of Caden. "I will, but that's why I'm here."

She glances down and seems to realize I'm holding her résumé in my hand.

I get another look.

A *what the fuck is going on?* look.

"I need a dog sitter," I say quickly.

She speaks Spanish.

Don't want her thinking I need a personal translator.

Wait.

Did I tell her I was going to Spain?

No, I just said *overseas.* She'd only know it was Spain if someone told her, and I doubt Ziggy got specific, *accurate* information about me from anyone last night.

If she asked.

Which she probably didn't.

She stares at me blankly. "Have you looked at pet-sitting websites?"

Fuck.

She's probably not a dog person.

"I was going to board her, but she's not the type who will like that."

"Is this a thing where you assume that since you saw me eating chicken like a dog would *one time,* that I must want a second job as a dog sitter?"

I'm the goddamn captain of a rugby team. I'm the *wise* one. The guy who solves other people's problems. The guy that the other guys come to for advice. Advice on women. Sports. Buying a car. Picking jobs in the off-season.

And I can't spit out what I actually want when I'm standing in front of Ziggy Barnes.

"Watching my dog comes with staying in my house. I'm offering you a place to stay while I'm out of town if you'll watch my dog."

"That's very kind of you—"

I hate that phrase. *Hate* it. "Why'd you leave the cruise line?"

"Because when you're puking every day, the guests get concerned about norovirus."

"You puked every day for seven years?"

"Okay, near-stranger in the parking lot, what did you do, hire a private investigator in the last twelve hours? Where did you get my résumé?"

"Brydie."

"She doesn't have boundaries, does she?"

"No, but once you have her chocolate lava cake, you don't care anymore. Stuff's next-level delicious. Totally worth letting her pick apart your private life to get another slice. If you were seasick, how—"

"Pregnant, Holt. I got pregnant, and then I got morning sick, and when I decided I wanted to keep the baby, I had to come home. That's why I puked on Vitamin Man last night. Chicken and baby didn't mix. Not right now anyway."

Oh, shiiiiiit. Didn't see that coming.

Also—*fuck.* I got a pregnant woman fired.

And I'm standing here thinking about her naked.

While she probably has a boyfriend or a husband.

No ring though.

And she's living in a hotel and talking about moving in with her parents, and *shiiiiit* again.

This just got a lot more complicated.

She lifts a hand. "Don't. Do *not* look at me like I'm a pity case. I'm perfectly fine. I'm looking for a house of my own, my parents are excited, I'll find another job, and I'll be fine. Thank you for—"

"So you *are* moving back in with them."

Her eyelid twitches. "Likely for a short time. If I can survive doing my laundry at their house today."

"And this Naked Tuesdays thing...?"

"I didn't say that."

"You very clearly said that."

"And I also very clearly asked you to forget you heard it because I didn't say it."

Huh.

I'm smiling.

I'm smiling at a woman because she's funny.

And someone in my head is whispering *that house needs babies after everything it's seen.*

Fuck.

Fuck.

It does.

That house needs new life in it.

"I'm gone for at least six weeks. Have a few contractors coming in and out. Could use someone to keep an eye on them. And walk my dog. If you're a dog person."

"I appreciate the offer, but—"

"You prefer Naked Tuesdays."

"You're a complete stranger."

"My neighbor's a doctor. The kind that delivers babies."

"How convenient."

"Kitchen renovation is done. Brand-new appliances. Granite countertops. Built-in step stools hidden in the lower cabinets so short people can reach all the way up to the highest cabinets safely."

That gets her attention.

Can't miss the way her pupils dilate.

Getting her résumé was an excellent move.

"Are you selling me your house or asking me to house-sit?" she asks.

The question makes my brain hiccup.

It's Caden's house.

I can renovate it.

But I can't sell it.

If I sell it, whenever I finally end my career and come home from Europe—and I am *definitely* getting a spot on a team somewhere overseas before training camp is done—I want to come home to Caden's house.

I want to still have that part of him.

Even if I move to Milwaukee or settle in San Francisco or become a hermit in the Pacific Northwest, I want to know I can still see Caden's final chosen home.

Ziggy fans her face. "Thank you for the offer—"

"I leave in four days. If you want to see the house, text me. If not, I have friends who will check on it and I'll board my dog."

She flinches.

Not a little flinch either.

This is a whole-body, *warn me before you slap me next time* flinch.

This woman is a puzzle box of puzzles, and I'm so fucking curious right now.

"Well, I'm happy for you," she says shortly. "Please excuse me. I have a meeting with a real estate agent and my mom. I hope you enjoy your trip."

"What did I say?"

She shakes her head while she moves to the driver's side door. "It's not you."

"Offer stands."

"You don't know me. *At all.* You watched me throw up all over a man last night—"

"He deserved it."

He did, but she keeps going like she didn't hear me. "—and otherwise, all you know about me is what's on my résumé. Why would you ask a complete stranger to house-sit for you? I might be the kind of person who throws ragers. I might be a terrible dog sitter. I might paint the exterior an awful color for fun and sell all of your appliances for cash."

"You saw things working on that cruise ship, didn't you?"

She does a slow blink, and then the most magical thing happens.

Ziggy Barnes cracks, and she starts to smile.

I saw her smile last night.

It's glorious. Like a sunset over the mountains. Rain in the desert. A great white breaching the ocean surface when you've given up hope of spotting it.

"I did," she says. "I heard things too."

"Would you destroy my house?"

"No."

"Your baby daddy in the picture?"

She shakes her head.

Fuck yeah, we have a chance.

And I need to shove that voice in a damn box.

I'm not asking a morning-sick pregnant woman who's all alone if she wants to get naked before I leave and maybe never come back.

"My dog's not the kind that'll be happy being boarded," I tell her. Pretty sure I already said that, but it's my best card right now.

I don't add *she already hates me, and this will only add fuel to the fire, especially since I don't know if I'll need to find her a new home or move her overseas with me when I make a team after camp.*

I'm struggling enough with that.

I don't let people down. I take care of them.

I moved here to take care of my brother. I take care of the guys on my team. I take care of my neighbors. I water their gardens. I mow their grass. I take in their pets when they die.

And Ziggy seems like a person who just needs a break. A person who needs a break because I was doing a shitty job of being the security guy last night.

"I'm still a stranger," she says.

"Hard to feel like someone's a stranger after what we went through last night. I wore your body fluids."

She flips me off but also fails miserably at suppressing the laugh she's clearly trying to hold in. "You're a dick."

"Stage two of not being strangers. You've seen me for who I am. A huge dick. That's as low as I go, by the way."

"Thank you for the apology." She opens her car door, grimacing and retreating a step, which I assume is due to the extra heat rolling out of the car. "It was unnecessary, but thank you."

"Four days if you change your mind."

"I won't."

"Good luck with everything. You seem like a nice person who deserves good things."

Her eyes meet mine over the top of her car, and she blinks hard and fast like I've said the exact wrong thing. "Thank you. You too."

I nod.

She nods.

She climbs into the car and cranks the engine.

I don't wait to feel the heat off of it before I get back in my Jeep, which has also gotten hotter in the few minutes I've been outside.

I leave first.

It's a rule. You don't follow a woman you barely know out of a parking lot, so you do your damnedest to leave first.

Only you could find a single pregnant woman in need of a home on your last night working in Copper Valley.

Swear I can hear my brother cracking open another beer in my head too.

Too bad you're a creeper and you fucked this up, but it was always a bad idea.

I puff out my cheeks, blowing out a breath as I steer my Jeep out of the parking lot.

This might've been a terrible idea.

But I made the offer.

And now I'll never see Ziggy Barnes again.

4

Ziggy

You know what's more awkward than failing at adulting?

Keeping the extent of your failures a secret from your parents.

Thanks for lunch at your club, Mom. Also, you know that company Dad got me an interview with? Welp, that's over now. Funny story. Abby Nora's brother-in-law was there, and he was harassing me, and I tossed my cookies all over him, and so I'm fired. But don't worry. I don't have to move back in with you. The security guy from last night offered to let me house-sit for him. I can probably squat there for a while. Oh, by the way, Abby Nora hates my guts now.

I stab another rosemary potato cube on my plate as I sit with my mom and her real estate agent friend at a table in the opulently appointed Heartwood Valley Owners Club dining room. If I say anything beyond *thanks for lunch*, the rest of it will spill out.

Telling my parents I accidentally got pregnant and I want to keep the baby?

Easy.

Telling my parents it happened because I had a grief-fling with a random guy in a port in Greece the night after I found out Abby Nora wasn't the friend I thought she was is completely different.

They think we're still besties. That I've seen her since I got back and that she's thrilled I'm home again. That I'm not telling her about my own pregnancy yet so that I let her finish out hers with all eyes on her.

Every time I start to tell my parents what actually happened with Abby Nora, I get a knot in my gut and my legs quiver and I break out in a sweat.

They will be so disappointed.

It was easier to tell them I'm pregnant and can't find the father than it will be to tell them I had a BFF breakup with my longest-standing friend.

My soulmate friend. The sister of my heart who knew all of my deepest fears and secrets.

The bestie who was drifting away.

How did I not notice?

How did I not realize that I was the one who initiated every text conversation and phone call for the past few years, and that she shared less and less of her own personal life every time we talked?

Mom waves a ring-covered hand in front of my face. "Sweetheart, you haven't touched your chicken."

"My stomach is off." It's an easier answer than *I told you I didn't want the chicken today.*

Mom means well. But she doesn't listen sometimes.

Other times, she listens very well.

"Oh, honey. I can imagine. Jet lag can do such terrible things to your stomach." She smiles at Niki, the real estate agent who's joined us with a tablet to show us houses that she thinks would be a good fit for me. "When I was jet-lagged with Ziggy, I wanted avocado and peanut butter almost every day. The peanut butter, we could afford. The avocados, not as much."

Niki, a kind woman in her mid-forties, blinks slowly at Mom but doesn't question why *jet lag* would cause stomach problems and cravings. Or how one can be *jet-lagged* with someone else.

It's a rule in places like this.

You don't question what the eccentric rich lady says.

Right now, I wish Mom wasn't the eccentric rich lady. I wish we hadn't moved into Roland's swanky Heartwood Valley mansion. That I hadn't met Abby Nora. That Mom and I still lived in our one-bedroom apartment in the Warehouse District.

But wishing Roland out of Mom's life is awful and makes me feel guilty.

He makes her happy. Their life together makes her happy.

Just like I get to find what makes me happy.

Maybe I don't need a house.

Maybe I need a one-bedroom apartment in the Warehouse District.

"I was on an overnight flight once where beets caused a large problem," Niki says.

I've asked my family to please not tell *anyone* about my pregnancy until I'm at least into my second trimester, and yes, I continued the excuse of letting Abby Nora have the pregnancy spotlight as the reason. *Jet lag* is Mom's code word today, and Niki clearly thinks we're actually talking about travel.

Necessary.

She runs into Abby Nora's in-laws all the time. Real estate circles and all that.

Mom swirls her chardonnay and smiles at Niki. "I love beets. We used to grow them in a community garden."

Niki turns to me. "Do you have any interest in gardening, Ziggy?"

I swallow another potato.

Why do rosemary potato cubes taste like heaven? I'm not even jealous that my mom is having wine and I'm not. That's how good this potato is.

"I have interest, but I don't know if I have the time or energy."

"That'll come and go for the next few years." Mom's face freezes. "As you get over jet lag."

This was a terrible idea.

"It's a lot of work to start over when you have big dreams," I say. "Even when you have support."

"Yes! That's what I meant. You'll have a lot on your plate the next few years while you pursue your...big dreams." She fiddles with one of her earrings as she smiles at Niki again. "We should make sure to limit our search to the Belmont District or here in Heartwood Valley. Guaranteed yard space for gardens for when Ziggy has the energy and time for it."

A blond head catches my eye behind Mom, and I flinch.

Abby Nora's here.

Here.

With her mother.

Being escorted to a table near the windows overlooking the golf course lake.

It's the first time I've seen her in person since I was home on a break in early January, and the grief hits me hard and fast at knowing I can't leap up, run across the room, and hug her like I used to.

My former best friend is in a navy-blue dress that shows off her baby bump, doing the full belly-waddle of an almost-nine-months-pregnant woman. Her due date is early August, but she's far enough along that she could give birth any time now.

And I won't be among those getting a baby announcement. I won't be among those taking her meals so she and her husband don't have to think about eating like my mom used to for new moms in our old neighborhood. I won't be dropping by to offer to watch the baby so she can take a nap in the middle of the day.

She doesn't want me to.

And not because I have little firsthand experience with babies myself.

But because I did something wrong or we grew apart while I wasn't paying attention or because we were never as close as I thought we were in the first place.

That last potato suddenly isn't settling so well either.

Dammit.

I jerk my attention back to Mom.

She's staring at me.

So is Niki.

So much for them not seeing me flinch.

I stab another potato. What were we talking about?

Chicken. Avocado. Beets. Right.

Gardening. "I don't even know if I want to garden yet. And there are community gardens all over the city. I'd rather focus on finding a low-maintenance house that I can afford right now."

Mom sips her wine while she studies me. It's a young chardonnay from Napa. Probably has notes of peach and hibiscus. Likely on the drier side.

Probably delicious.

And all I want is a Tums.

She sets her glass down and looks at Niki. "Ziggy's father and I will be *happy* to give her a down payment. Let's not limit things yet."

"Mom, you don't have to do that. I have a nice nest egg. I can afford to buy a house on my own."

"Sweetie, your life is about to be hard enough. With your —erm—dreams. Let us do this one little—oh, look at *that* house."

That house on Niki's tablet is big enough to justify a moat and a drawbridge in the surrounding acres of the yard. I shake my head. "That's so much more space than I need."

"But what if you want a home office one day? And a play —*art* room. My baby definitely needs an art room. I know how much you love to…art."

If Niki hasn't figured out yet that I'm pregnant, she will in the next five minutes.

And I don't know if I care anymore.

I should.

The biggest reason I'm not talking about my *delicate condition* is that I don't want Abby Nora saying I only got pregnant because I was jealous of her and wanted what she has.

And does it matter?

Does it?

Actually, yes.

Yes, it does. I don't want Abby Nora knowing anything that she could use to hurt me. Directly or indirectly.

Would she mock me for not being married before getting pregnant?

Probably.

She talks—*talked* to me constantly about Josh being the thing that completed her life. She thinks marriage is the best.

I stab a potato and don't look in Abby Nora's direction. "I can find a studio if I want to *art*."

"But do you want to go to that effort, sweetheart?"

"Art studios will have other artists that I can ask for advice since I'm out of practice at arting."

I don't think *arting* is a word.

Though, if I switched into Italian, they might have a word for—no.

Nope.

No switching to Italian words.

Then I'm *showing off*.

"We can look for a house that has an art studio and public gardens nearby," Niki says. "I showed a lovely four-bedroom south of downtown just last week that had a ladies' paint night shop just a few blocks away. And I heard they're expanding to offer pottery wheel classes."

"I'm sure there are plenty of options for what I want in a city this big," I say.

The hairs on the back of my neck rise like someone's watching me, and it takes every ounce of determination to not look around the dining room to see if Abby Nora has spotted me.

"The sooner you find it, the better," Mom says. "I'm worried about you in that hotel. I wish you'd move in with us while you look for a house."

I lift my brows at her.

She blushes.

We both know what else I won't say out loud in front of Niki today.

I don't move in with people who walk around naked every Tuesday.

I've heard people say Mom married Roland for his money, but it's not true.

Whenever anyone implies that in my presence, I promptly inform them she married him for his dick just to make them uncomfortable.

But the truth is, she found the love of her life when she met Roland. She would've married him regardless of the size of his house and bank accounts.

If anything, the money made her more uncomfortable at first.

It would've made me more uncomfortable if I hadn't had Abby Nora.

And now my throat is getting tight. *Dammit.*

"I'm used to living in a cabin the size of a dorm room," I remind Mom and Niki. "With a roommate. I don't need a big house. I just need a house that feels right."

"Don't discount that a house with room to grow could feel right. What if you want more—art hobbies? Art. Hobbies. Collections. What if you want a dog? What if you open a catering company and you need a good home kitchen before you have the cash to buy an industrial kitchen?"

"Then I'll move."

Mom sighs.

I sigh.

My phone buzzes, and I subtly check the text message under the table while Mom and Niki ignore me to discuss the benefits of a large house in one of Copper Valley's most expensive neighborhoods.

It's Miranda, my stepsister.

When I came home last summer, Mom and Miranda and I took a trip down to Charleston and toured the city and had a spa day and ate amazing food and shared a vacation rental house and laughed and talked for hours.

Miranda was six to my thirteen when Mom married Roland, and we only saw her every other weekend and a few weeks every summer, so we weren't tight before I left for culinary school. She graduated college right before our trip last year. It was fun to reconnect and spend time getting to know her as an adult, and we've texted and kept up on socials more in the past year than we ever did before. We even started talking about a vacation, just the two of us, or Miranda flying to Europe and coming on one of my cruises.

And now, the baby has changed everything.

Clearly, Miranda isn't coming to the Med. Mom's not talking about girls' trips with both of us. She's not talking about her ladies' club and their volunteer activities. She's not even talking about introducing me to her book club.

She's talking about diapers and cribs and playrooms and how stressed I'll be without any time for myself.

She's talking about buying me a mansion so that I'll never have to worry about running out of space.

And all I want is a girls' trip to make me feel normal.

Like I haven't completely upended my life.

Like I still have friends I can trust in my life, even if they're related to me and I don't want to live with one of them.

Call me when you're done, Miranda's text says. *We'll get ice cream and I'll tell you all about our parents' plans to build a little carriage house at the back of their property so that you and the baby are always there.*

I eye my mom.

Then Niki, who's one of Mom's friends from her garden club.

My phone buzzes again.

Miranda: *In case you missed the subtle hint, once you check into the Parental Unit Hotel, they're never letting you leave.*

Miranda isn't saying anything I haven't known on some level. It's the bigger reason I got a hotel room instead of staying with them when I got home.

I know my parents love me. I know I'm incredibly lucky to get along with both my mom and my stepdad. I didn't take his last name, but I do call him *Dad* when we're together, and it fits.

He took me to dance classes. He showed up with Mom at nearly every one of my high school plays. He taught me to play chess and drove me to school early so I could take extra language classes—my choice—and he had more patience than my friends' parents when I was deep in the throes of puberty with mood swings and breakdowns.

Miranda says he handled her teenage years well too, even if he was overbearing about her boyfriends, which I also experienced firsthand.

But despite me leaving home at eighteen for culinary school and moving to Europe at twenty-three with my first cruise line contract, my parents are struggling with the idea that I'm a grown woman who can choose to raise a baby on my own.

They've convinced themselves I was at sleepaway camp when I was working onboard and that I'm still a teenager.

I want my parents to once again be who they were when I was an actual teenager.

Except for the overbearing with the dating part.

I could do without my stepfather staring silently at every boy who came to pick me up for a dance or a movie or a picnic.

I'm not good enough for your mother, so how do you expect me to ever believe any of these immature balls of hormones are good enough for you?

It was endearing once.

By the time I left home, I was thrilled to not have to introduce dates to my parents.

Not that I dated a lot.

I'm apparently *too picky*. Abby Nora called me that once and I thought it was funny.

Now I wonder if she's right. And also if it was meant as an insult.

I grab my water and don't look in her direction.

"Ziggy, we'll add this one to the tour list." Mom shows me the mansion in Heartwood Valley that's on Niki's tablet again. "Ooh, the dessert tray. How does dessert sound? Do you feel like dessert?"

My stomach clenches. "I do not, thank you. Excuse me. I need to use the toilet. *Ladies' room.* I need to use the ladies' room."

I retreat to the restroom, where something worse than morning sickness is waiting.

That something is a massively pregnant blonde in a navy dress with a diamond ring the size of a quarter sparkling in the lights as she messes with her hair in one of the individual mirrors over the row of white marble sinks.

My eyes meet hers in her reflection as I freeze in my tracks, stifling a good *fuck* that I want to utter in Italian.

Abby Nora stares back at me.

She's such a stuck-up cunt.

It's impossible to see her and not hear her words in my head.

I should've done a sweep of the room before I came in here.

I should've made sure I knew where she was.

But I didn't, and now we're face-to-face for the first time since before I witnessed her telling everyone at her baby shower that I'm a *stuck-up cunt.*

"Ziggy." She stutters like she, too, can hear her words echoing off the restroom walls, even though nothing echoes off the demure ivory wallpaper in here. "Oh my god, it's so good to—"

"Great to see you too," I blurt.

She stares at me as she reaches for a cloth towel from the basket between the sinks.

There's no warmth. No true *it's good to see you.* No regret or apology.

Just awkwardness.

And I don't think it's because she's heard what I did to her brother-in-law last night.

He didn't recognize my name from her wedding, so I'm pretty sure he didn't recognize me. Him calling me a cunt was probably because it's a favorite word in their family. There's a solid chance that he'll never tell about last night because he doesn't know he's supposed to.

And I suspect she would definitely want him to.

54

I start to turn around to leave—I'd rather go puke in a bush outside—but then I stop myself.

I square my shoulders.

And I make myself turn around to face her again as she finishes wiping her hands, which she shouldn't need to do after messing with her hair.

One more clue she's nervous.

"Why?" I say.

She blinks. "Why what?"

"Why don't you like me anymore? What did I do?"

Her nose twitches as she makes eye contact with my chin. "What are you talking about? Of course I like you. Duh. We've been friends forever, haven't we?"

I swallow. "Right. Forever."

I've had two months to fully accept that Abby Nora doesn't want me anymore.

And I need to not care as much as she doesn't.

But here I am, my stomach in knots just from seeing her, my bruised heart bleeding again, letting her see how much she's hurt me.

I don't want her to know I'm hurt.

Except she's the one person I could always go to whenever I was hurt before.

"You should've told me you were coming home. Honestly, I'm hurt you didn't." She drops the cloth towel into the used basket and rubs a hand over her stomach. "We should do lunch before the baby's born. You know. Make it up to me."

"Right. Lunch."

"It'll be so fun. Like old times."

"So fun."

"Call me. But do it quick. Before baby." She laughs.

It's fake.

It's so fake.

I will not get sick again. I will not get sick again. "Of course."

She pushes out of the restroom without a hug, without another glance back, but with the fakest smile I've ever seen on her face.

A toilet flushes, and I realize what's just happened.

We aren't alone.

She knew it.

And now whoever is in there can tell people that *I'm* the problem. That I'm making up drama where there is none, and poor Abby Nora is dealing with her best friend going crazy while she's so heavily pregnant, and isn't that the last thing any woman needs?

I dash into the nearest stall, sit, and breathe as quietly as possible.

Breathe. Breathe. Breathe.

I can get through this. My stomach is fine.

The bottle of Tums I'm keeping in my purse is half-empty. Constant companion these days, but they help.

What would help more would've been not running into Abby Nora.

Is it bad that I don't want to live in Heartwood Valley or the Belmont District so that I can establish a social circle for myself that definitely won't intersect with Abby Nora's social circle?

The sink turns on.

"Grow a pair, Ziggy," I whisper to myself under the noise of the running water.

I was so distracted by defending my honor against a man last night that I didn't even realize I was about to puke on him. You'd think I had a pair.

Apparently not.

I pull up my text messages as soon as I'm sure I don't need to toss my lunch.

Miranda's sent another message, and so has Francesca, my former roommate from the cruise ship, but my shaky finger accidentally hits the message beneath hers, and I'm instead looking at the other conversation I've had over text today.

Holt: *This is Holt Webster. Security guy from last night. Brydie gave me your number. Wanted to talk for a minute. Can I stop by? Best in person.*

My stomach clenches again.

I don't like Holt.

To be more precise, I don't like the way my body responds when I'm around him.

The man had the absolute audacity to be leaning against a Jeep in four-hundred-thousand-degree heat in a backward baseball cap, a faded gray Crow's Nest Bakery T-shirt, and jeans.

Jeans.

In this heat.

Without a visible drop of sweat on him.

And for a split second when I spotted him, I thought, *wouldn't it be nice to always have a friend with a great ass who can tackle people who are mean to me and who says "Don't worry about it" when I apologize for the mess all over his clothes?*

Or something like that.

Maybe something a little dirtier.

Especially when he started talking about his kitchen.

Not that I'm in any position to explore anything with him.

He's leaving the country.

I'm pregnant.

He probably has a girlfriend. Possibly one here and one there.

I'm pregnant.

He very likely doesn't want to be the person who would've come barreling into the bathroom and rescued me from that awkward moment with Abby Nora.

I'm pregnant.

Brydie told me he plays lacrosse professionally, which explains the muscles. I know even less about lacrosse than I do about rugby. Dad bought his rugby team after I moved overseas, and I haven't been home during the season, ever. Mom calls it his little retirement hobby, even though he's not retired yet.

Not by a long shot.

Hence *hobby*.

And speaking of Mom—I only get so long in this bathroom before she comes looking for me to make sure I didn't throw up and pass out, so I need to quit breathing and overthinking everything and finish up in here.

I switch back to the message with Miranda and make myself be normal.

Me: How did you get out? Of living with them, I mean.

Bubbles pop up telling me she's texting me back nearly immediately, and then—

Miranda: I wasn't carrying their grandbaby.

Me: I fucked up, didn't I?

Miranda: You fucked something.

I snort in the bathroom, hear it echo, and freeze.

No sounds.

I think whoever was in here has left.

I hope.

I'm very grateful for you, I text to Miranda.

She's the only person I've told about Abby Nora's baby shower outside of my friends on the ship. So she's the only person here at home who knows.

Miranda: Aw, I'm grateful for you too. Also, in case your mom hasn't told you, they called your hotel this morning to pay your bill.

I cringe.

Me: Do they realize how controlling this looks? Mom's trying to convince me I need to let her buy me a house in Heartwood Valley.

The response is quick enough that I guess she's doing voice-to-text.

Miranda: I had a ton of fun with you at lunch yesterday and definitely want to do it again every week, so I hope you understand how much it costs me to tell you that I think your only option is to run away to Canada but tell them you're in Napa.

I completely relate to what she's saying.

I hesitate just a moment, then reply.

Me: I loved spending time with you too, and I need you to know I'd say that regardless of how many other friends I do or don't have here. You're not a consolation prize, okay? You're pretty damn awesome.

Miranda: *Oh, I know. You're very lucky I find you tolerable.*

I crack up again because I can picture her grinning as she says it.

I send her a heart emoji, then pop over to my hotel app.

And—yep.

She's right.

My credit card has been replaced by a number I don't recognize with my mom's first initial and last name attached to it.

On the one hand, I'm grateful that my parents care and want to help take care of me.

But on the other, I already feel like a fuck-up for losing one job because I'm pregnant—which happened during a one-night stand that turned out to be a poor coping mechanism for losing my bestie—moving home, and then getting fired from another job.

There's nothing wrong with accepting help.

But I don't *need* help.

And I don't want the complicated feelings of obligations to go with it.

Especially because I *do* sometimes feel like I had an unfair advantage when Mom married a man who paid for culinary school for me, then pulled some strings to get me the interview with Lusso Cruises.

I want to visit my parents because I want to see them. Not because I need things from them. Not because I want to use their connections. And I don't want those lines to get blurry.

But they know everyone. And anyone they don't know would recognize their names.

And that's what has me returning to the message from Holt.

He doesn't know me. He doesn't know who I'm related to.

He's not someone who's offering me a place to stay because my parents asked him to. Not someone who has any connections to Abby Nora. Not someone who will care one way or another what happens to me in the coming months.

Not someone who will be there every day for the next month. Month and a half, even. He said six weeks.

A house to myself—with a dog, no less—sounds pretty fucking awesome right now.

Provided it's nowhere near Belmont or Heartwood Valley.

So I take a leap and text him.

Me: *I'm not saying yes or no, but could I meet your dog and see your house?*

My parents can't pay my hotel bill if I'm not living in a hotel.

And they can't give me a guilt trip about moving out if I never move back in.

And Holt won't even be there. *He's leaving for a lacrosse camp in Europe.* Brydie said it a half dozen times last night while I was in earshot, most of those times to women who were asking if he was single.

And yes, I noticed that she didn't give a straight-up yes or no answer.

I took a leap when I accepted the job with Lusso Cruises.

I met locals in various ports and had meals in their homes and still get emails with family updates.

Sometimes you have to jump.

And meeting a dog isn't *jumping*.

It's dipping a toe in the water to see if it's the right temperature.

Holt replies almost immediately.

Holt: *Home the rest of the day.*

Me: *Great. Send me the address.*

5

Holt

ZIGGY CHANGED HER CLOTHES.

She's fancy again. But unlike last night's kind of fancy, when she was in black-and-white to match the serving crew during the event, today she's a splash of color.

Pale-green sleeveless blouse that looks soft as peach fuzz. Swishy skirt with a curvy pattern of blues and yellows and greens. Small, simple hoop earrings. Hair in a tidier bun that still shows her curls.

But her shoes—

She's wearing glittery pink Converse sneakers.

They don't match the rest of her.

Good thing I'm leaving town in four days. If I wasn't, I'd be asking a pregnant woman to move in to my house anyway.

So I could take care of her.

So I could see her every day.

So I could find out what other secrets and contradictions she's hiding, like her glittery pink Converse sneakers.

I haven't had a crush like this in what feels like decades.

"Is that a Viking oven?" she says as we enter the kitchen in the three-bedroom Craftsman that Caden bought ten years ago when he moved here to Copper Valley to take a job for an engineering firm. We're in an average neighborhood south of downtown. This room is among the half of the house that's been fully renovated. Still have my bedroom—not the primary suite, which I could move into, but don't want to—three bathrooms, and the basement to go. "And a subzero fridge? Am I in heaven?"

"Enough people have died in here that it might be," I mutter to myself.

She squints at me. "What?"

"Contractor suggested the appliances."

"Good taste. They look like they haven't been used."

"Not much of a chef."

"This kitchen says otherwise."

"Didn't really pick anything in here." Not the maple cabinets. Not the black granite countertops. Not the dark gray slate flooring.

She lifts her brows at me.

I don't know what changed since this morning—maybe getting out of the heat—but she's not as wary right now.

And I could drown in those wide blue eyes.

Get a fucking grip, Webster.

"Was my brother's house. He had plans. I just did what he would've."

I don't add *he died*.

Just let it linger in the air between us, watching as her expression goes from curious to a sympathetic sort of kind.

I brace myself for the inevitable *I'm sorry for your loss*, but it doesn't come. Instead, she runs a hand over the island countertop. "He had good taste."

I keep my expression neutral. "His designer had good taste."

"I see. Where's your dog?"

Probably plotting to take over the world with one of the neighbor's dogs. "Out back."

"In this heat?"

The hell-beast likes it. "She has odd preferences."

I walk over the new slate flooring to the thick back door that matches the cabinets, gesturing Ziggy out onto the covered porch first.

The sunroom is the one thing Caden finished before he got sick.

She pauses and looks up at the palm-leaf fan that looks like it belongs in a tourist trap in Florida, and then looks down at the bistro table and the 1980s-style wicker furniture with the old lady flower cushions.

"Well. This is...cozy," Ziggy says. "Did you pick the furniture?"

"My brother did."

She purses her lips.

Then purses them harder. "I see."

"It's the one room he finished before he got sick."

"He had interesting taste."

If he could hear her tone, he'd be equal parts amused and insulted. "He always said he was into men who loved their grandmas, so this was supposed to be his test room."

She puts her fingers to her mouth, and those bright blue eyes start dancing. "That's..."

"Special," I finish.

"I was going to say very strategic."

I gesture to the screen door. "Jessica's this way."

"Your dog's name is Jessica?"

"Didn't name her."

"Oh, you adopted her?"

"Inherited her."

"Your brother?"

"Neighbor. Asked me to dog-sit while she went on vacation. Had a heart attack in Florida. Died. Nobody wanted the dog."

"Oh my god."

The porch was a nice warm-up to the heat, but the porch has fans and shade. Walking down the steps and out into the backyard is like stepping into that oven Ziggy was so impressed with.

"You okay in the heat?" I ask as I head down the stairs to the yard.

"If I'm not, it won't be anything worse than what we've already dealt with."

True enough.

I reach the bottom of the steps and whistle. "Jessica, come meet a new friend."

A low growl from beneath the covered porch is my answer.

Dammit, dog.

She chewed through the lattice under the porch again. Don't have time to get that fixed—and reinforced—before I leave. "C'mon, Jessica. She's very nice, and she's probably the kind of pushover who'll bribe you with treats."

Ziggy watches me as I get down on all fours and peer under the porch.

A flat, dark gray face at the front of a tan barrel body stares back at me.

Fuckin' make me come out, that face says. *I fuckin' dare you.*

Yeah, yeah, I know. *Don't ask a pregnant woman to take care of a hell-beast.*

I wouldn't if I didn't know this dog's secret.

I'm the only one she has a problem with. Everyone else is great.

Until I ask if she wants a new home where she'd like her owners better.

Then she makes me feel like an asshole for suggesting it.

I lost my human and now you want to give me away instead of letting me grieve by being an asshole to you?

Swear on my favorite cleats, that's what it looks like she's thinking.

If I get picked up by a team overseas, figuring out what to do with Jessica will be the hardest part.

Yeah. Finding a house for a dog who hates me.

That'll be the hardest part.

Other than, you know, deciding what to do with my brother's house.

"You want a treat?" I ask her.

She replies by snorting dog snot all over my face.

I straighten and wipe my cheek, grateful she didn't hit my mouth too.

Jessica stalks out from under the porch, head high. She kicks dirt in my direction, turns and starts to sashay toward the steps, but suddenly stops.

I've had the dog for two months, and already, I know when the wheels are turning in her head.

They're turning now.

She looks back at me, then at Ziggy.

67

"You want a new friend?" I ask the dog.

She turns her back on me again, and I swear the little beast farts at me.

But she's turning on the charm for Ziggy. You can tell by the way Ziggy's face melts into a smile as she sinks to her knees in the grass seemingly without a care for grass stains on her skirt.

"Oh my god, you're adorable. What kind of a doggie are you?"

Jessica trots—*trots*—to Ziggy, flops on her back, and pants as she silently begs for belly pets.

She's an asshole.

That's what kind of dog she is.

"French bulldog," I supply. "She can be a handful."

Jessica snorts at me, which makes Ziggy laugh.

"Usually just for me," I mutter.

"Look at you!" Ziggy says to her. "You're the cutest thing. Yes, you are."

"You like dogs?"

"My parents have always had dogs. I made a few friends in various ports that had pets so I could get my fix while I was working for the cruise line. And sometimes I'd get to pet the dogs that guests would bring on."

"She might get mad when I leave. Jessica is the hardest part of house-sitting."

The hell-beast snorts at me again, which makes Ziggy laugh.

"My sister is a dog whisperer. If I have trouble, she'll help."

"You couldn't live with her?" *Fuck*. Now I sound like I don't want her here.

Problem is really that I want her here too much.

Boundaries, asshole.

I'm not hitting on a pregnant woman today.

Or ever.

Ziggy shakes her head, apparently not offended. "She's sharing an apartment with three friends. Also doesn't want to move back in with our parents. Even if she'd take those cushions on your porch furniture in a heartbeat."

Jessica is flopped out on her back in the *I'm never moving again* position while Ziggy scratches her belly, murmuring what I recognize as terms of endearment in Spanish.

So Ziggy loves the kitchen. And the sunroom. And the dog.

She fits here better than I do.

Hitting on her is a bad idea.

Fuck, even crushing on her is a bad idea.

But when I picture her sitting on the couch, playing a game on her phone or watching TV, rubbing her belly, bringing new life into this house after all of the sadness it's seen the past few years—

Yeah.

I want her to stay here.

I want to know something *good* is here.

"There's a spare car in the garage you can use," I tell her.

"Your brother's?"

I wince and look up at the sky, then jerk my thumb behind me. "Other neighbor's. That side. Had a stroke about four months ago. Didn't make it. Her kids didn't need an extra Buick, so they told me to keep it."

She lifts her head and looks straight at me. "Can I ask you a blunt and possibly awkward question?"

"Five."

"Five?"

"Five. My brother, the neighbor who was Jessica's owner, the Buick neighbor, the mailman—"

"*Your mailman?*"

"Three houses down. Heart attack while he was delivering mail. I was driving by when it happened. Did CPR. His family gave me a bunch of his paintings as a unique thank-you. They're in the basement."

"And the fifth?"

"Dude I knew on my team back in England."

She stares at me.

I'm not looking at her, but I can feel it.

"Did they give you—"

"You don't want to know."

Yes, they sent me something of his.

They sent me some of his ashes and asked me to scatter them on various rugby pitches across the US.

His dream was to play on every rugby pitch around the globe. Seemed fitting to scatter his ashes as far and wide as they could.

And because I'm me, of course I helped.

Quietly. It's apparently illegal or something. But dude had a dream, and we'll all be ash one day anyway, so why not? He had former teammates in at least six other countries who did the same.

"And how long since the first one...?" Ziggy prompts.

"About nine months. My brother."

"And the last?"

"Jessica's owner. Two months ago."

"Are you okay? Do you have enough friends right now?"

No, I'm not fucking okay. But I'm trying to be. "I'm looking forward to Europe."

She's still watching me.

Fuck. "If you don't want to live in a death house or a death neighborhood—"

"I'm not that kind of superstitious."

"The neighborhood is mostly older people who've been retired for a long time, so it's not like this is weird. Except for Caden. He was just—shitty genes. All around." Shut up. Shut up shut up shut up. "It's not cursed. Even if you're not superstitious, it can be a lot. And if you change your mind, I have a backup kennel for Jessica and it's not a big deal if the house is empty for a few weeks. I know most of the contractors pretty well. They can handle things."

"Jessica doesn't look like the type who'd enjoy the kennel."

"It's doggy daycare with friends during the day and fancy bedrooms at night." And Ziggy is absolutely correct that Jessica would hate it.

I left her there for our last two away matches and when I picked her up, she took a shit under my bed every night for a week.

Both times.

Back-to-back.

I took her to the vet to make sure she hadn't eaten anything wrong, and all the vet said was *sometimes dogs act out when their situation changes.*

"If you're still up for house-sitting and dog-sitting, I'm sure she'd be happy to have you," I add.

"I think we'll get along fabulously, don't you, Jessica?" Ziggy says to my dog.

Jessica pants happily in the sunshine.

Ziggy smiles at her.

There I go again, thinking of Ziggy inside the house. Hand on her lower back while she stirs something on the stove. Laughing at something on social media. Crawling into bed with me with a smile. Pretty wife growing a baby. Happy dog who doesn't snort in my face or fart at me at every opportunity. Laughter and smiles and hope and peace and happiness.

New life.

The aching, desperate *want* in my gut hits me like a sucker punch.

Not my life.

It's not in the cards.

Never know who'll get sick. Who'll get hurt. Who'll leave you next.

One of my teammates asked me the other day if I'm running away.

I lied and said no.

"My plane takes off on Friday," I tell Ziggy. "I'll get you a key so you can move in at your convenience after that."

She blinks at me. "Okay."

"So I'm not in your way. Before I leave." I'm fumbling over my words again, but this time, I know why.

I like her.

I shouldn't.

She's given me zero signs that she's into me.

Why would she be?

She's carrying some other guy's baby, and he's not in the picture.

Tells a story all on its own, doesn't it?

So I'll do the right thing and give her space.

"I'll leave enough dog food and treats for while I'm gone. And her schedule. You have my number if you have any questions." I pointedly gesture toward the front yard.

A not-so-subtle *now that we have that over with, get the hell out.*

So I can head out to the garage and beat the shit out of my punching bag.

She slowly rises, and when she sways on her feet, I go on high alert, shifting to the balls of my feet, ready to leap into action if she faints or gets sick or stumbles.

Ready to hold her like I did last night when the crow almost attacked her.

Smell her hair.

Feel her curves.

She notices.

The part where I'm trying to move to help her anyway.

You can tell by the way she holds out a hand to stop me. "I'm okay. Normal head rush after sitting on my legs. Thank you for the tour. And for a place to stay. I met my real estate agent at lunch today, and I'm sure I'll find a place of my own very soon."

I grunt like a complete dumbass who suddenly can't remember words.

She bends and gives Jessica one last belly rub. "See you soon, pup. Be good, okay?"

Jessica grins.

Jessica-speak for *not for this guy, but I'll smile like I'm agreeing.*

Ziggy pauses as she heads past me and waits until I look back at her.

"If you change your mind and don't want me to stay here, just let me know. I appreciate not having to move in with my parents, but it also wouldn't be the end of the world."

"House needs a sitter. You need a place to stay. It's a good arrangement."

She studies me while sweat drips down my back.

73

July heat or her seeing right through me to all of the fantasies I'm having about her that I need to stop having?

Hopefully the heat.

She nods and gives me a small smile that doesn't reach her eyes. "Okay. Thank you. I'll take good care of Jessica. And the house."

I nod.

She opens her mouth like she wants to say something else but shakes her head, gives me one last smile, and then heads for the gate to let herself out.

While I stand there like an awkward asshole.

Jessica trots to my side, then squats and pees beside me while she glares at me.

"She's coming back," I mutter. "And I'm leaving. Okay?"

She snorts on my leg.

Spain will be so, *so* good for me.

6

_____

From the text messages of Ziggy and Holt

Ziggy: Good morning. (Afternoon? Where are you in Europe? Which time zone? If you want to tell me. Which you don't have to. But I was texting with my roommate from the ship yesterday and she said the weather's been super hot over there too. I hope you're in a cooler area.) I got moved in quick and easy yesterday. Thank you for the note about which bedroom to use and for the contractor schedules. Jessica and I went on a walk today and one of the neighbors recognized her and asked if I was your girlfriend. Something happened with my mouth and I told her that I'm your kept woman. It won't happen again, but I thought you should know in case your neighbor texts you.

Holt: Which neighbor?

Ziggy: I'd say "the older one," but I realized you're right. The average age in this neighborhood has to be at least seventy-five. This one was watering a bed of white flowers three houses down.

Holt: Ok

Ziggy: Once on the ship, a colleague told a guest that he was dating me. That guest thought we were cute, and by the end of the cruise, neither of us could work a shift without at least four people congratulating us on our engagement. It was awkward. Especially when someone posted a congrats to us on their socials and his boyfriend saw. I know better than to spread relationship rumors and I'm sorry. It won't happen again.

Holt: Ok

Ziggy: Thanks for understanding. Glad we had this talk.

Ziggy, **two days later:** Does Jessica have any toy restrictions?

Holt: What does that mean?

Ziggy: I took her to a dog park this morning before my interview and she was trying to eat a toy that was half her size. I got a little worried that she'd hurt her neck.

Holt: No small toys. Big toys are fine.

Ziggy: Choking hazards are being avoided. Unrelated—I got a new job and once I get official documentation of steady income again for the loan company, I'll be making an offer on a house too, but I won't leave Jessica hanging if I move in to my new place before you get back.

Holt: Ok

Ziggy: Is this a bad time to text you?

Holt: No

Ziggy: Is this a good time to text you?

Holt: It's fine

Ziggy: Great. The plumber came by this afternoon to take some measurements and he said that the bathtub you picked for the hallway bathroom won't fit without moving a wall. Would you rather pick a new bathtub or move a wall?

Holt: Pick a new bathtub

Ziggy: I'll have him send you options.

Holt: Don't care. You pick

Ziggy: You want me to pick a new bathtub?

Holt: Yes

Ziggy: What if I have bad taste?

Holt: It's a bathtub

Ziggy: But is your style more clawfoot, tin bucket, or standard boring white porcelain?

Holt: Keep it in the budget

Ziggy: Great. Does the plumber have the budget? Or do I need to guess about it?

Holt: Plumber has it

Ziggy: You're not even going to ask what a tin bucket bathtub is?

Holt: Will it hold a person?

Ziggy: Yes. And I don't think it's actually called a tin bucket style. I'd have to look up the official name.

Holt: Then it's fine

Ziggy: I'd go clawfoot myself.

Holt: Great

Ziggy: But maybe not in your bathroom. The vanity wouldn't match, and you'd need a European-style shower curtain setup, which might not fly in the US.

Holt: I'll call the plumber tomorrow

Ziggy: Probably best.

Ziggy, another three days later: My sister met Jessica today and thinks she's amazing and wants to do a social media page for your dog. I told her no, but if you want Jessica to be a small-time internet star, let me know and I can make it happen.

Holt: No

Ziggy: Thanks for confirming! I'll pass along the definitive answer. Also, I unfortunately had to leave that last job (morning sickness is the absolute devil and I miss wine), and my offer on the house fell through, so it's no problem to stay with Jessica until you're back.

Ziggy, **three more days later:** I met Mrs. Massery today. She asked if you'll be back in time to buy a discount card from her grandson? I don't actually know what that means, but I got the feeling you would.

Holt: I'll send her cash. Feel free to use the card

Ziggy: Not to be obtuse, but discount for what?

Holt: Restaurants usually. Maybe an oil change

Ziggy: The last time I got my oil changed, I ended up pregnant.

Holt: Ok

Ziggy: That was a joke.

Holt: Yeah

Ziggy: A bad one.

Holt: Happens

Ziggy: I'll try to make better jokes in the future. Maybe I'll try limericks. There was a guest on one of my cruises who only spoke in limerick. It was funny at first, and then it got annoying. No one was sad when the cruise was over. Except maybe his wife. She had to listen to them all on her own after they left. Or so I assume.

Ziggy: *Speaking of limericks, I heard there used to be a player on the Thrusters who trash-talked in haiku. Do you lacrosse players ever do stuff with the hockey guys? Is that true?*

Holt: *Sometimes and yes*

Ziggy: *Do you have any habits when you're on the field?*

Holt: *The pitch*

Ziggy: *You pitch on the field?*

Holt: *Never mind*

Ziggy: *OH. It's a lacrosse PITCH. I get it now.*

Holt: **thumbs up emoji**

Ziggy, another four days later: *It just occurred to me that you're paying my electric and water and gas bills while I'm staying here. Can I help with those?*

Holt: *No*

Ziggy: *You're not here using them.*

Holt: *Don't care*

Ziggy: *Is this like the same thing where the plumber dropped off a*

80

pie that he said you bought from his kid's baseball team fundraiser? Am I another fundraiser?

Holt: *No*

Ziggy: *That's comforting. Thanks for the talk. Let me know if you change your mind about letting me pay for utilities.*

Ziggy, two days after that: *The plumber had an unexpected opening and can start tomorrow, but the new bathtub isn't arriving until next week. There's a possibility they could do rush shipping, but it would cost $$$. I told them both to stick to the original schedule unless they hear back from you otherwise in the next six hours.*

Holt: *Ok*

Ziggy: *Also, the white flower neighbor lady apparently told the Range Rover lady that I'm your cousin and that I make bad jokes. When I'm eighty-three, I want to drive a Range Rover too. She looks badass.*

Holt: *Ok*

Ziggy: **picture of Jessica wearing a necklace made of white flowers* And Jessica is doing well. She likes wearing sunglasses.*

Holt: *Ok*

Ziggy, one day later: *Someone named Red dropped off a lasagna last night. They apologized for taking ten months to bring it by and said the next time one of your family members dies, they'll try to* not be awkward about it and take too long. They also asked me to not tell you that part, but I remember when my grandma died (way different, I know, it's just the only experience I remember with death, since I was three when my dad died) and how I just wanted people to quit whispering about it without talking to me about it straight to my face. But also, death is really hard. And Red cares.

Holt: I don't know a Red

Ziggy: Seriously?

Holt: Seriously

Ziggy: I thought maybe he said Fred, but the card says Red. *picture of a sympathy card very clearly signed RED*

Holt: Huh

Ziggy: Maybe he knew your brother?

Holt: Must be

Ziggy: Or else he knew someone else with the same name as your brother and got confused and my sister is now eating someone else's grief lasagna. I gave it to her because it made my stomach revolt.

Holt: Ok

Ziggy: Am I annoying you? Ok is what you say to people when you want them to go away.

Holt: No

Ziggy: That's all you're gonna give me?

Holt: Yes

Ziggy: At least you have a very comfortable house. I'm breaking in the oven. Also, my mother insisted on sending her cleaning crew over. And her yard service.

Holt: I have a yard service

Ziggy: You haven't met my mother. I love her, and I have met her, and for your sake, I hope you never do.

Holt: Ok

Ziggy: How's your lacrosse camp?

Holt: Fine

Ziggy: Good. It would be terrible if it was less than fine.

*Ziggy, **four days later**: FYI, I was hearing noises from your bedroom, so I went in to investigate, and it turns out the hallway toilet is having some issues. Weird that the sound came from your room—at least, I assume that's your room?—but that's how I found it. The plumber turned off the water supply to that whole bathroom. He thinks you should move up the renovations so he can get in there and make sure there aren't bigger issues. Also, the tub has arrived, so he can.*

*Ziggy, **twelve hours later**: In case my last text didn't come through, the plumber needs to talk to you about the hallway bath-*

room. He's been trying to call, which I'm sure you've seen, but he asked me to reach out again too.

Ziggy, eight hours after that: *Not to be a pest, but you usually answer within an hour or two no matter what time I send you a message. Are you okay?*

Ziggy, four hours later: *I know I'm basically just your house sitter, but if you could let me know that you're okay, I'd be grateful. I'm getting worried about you. Oddly enough, I do know how to file a missing persons report in four European countries. But I don't actually know which country you're in or what part of that country, and when I googled lacrosse camps, I couldn't find any for adults. It turns out I worry about people when I'm living in their houses, which is the only reason I looked it up. And I could just have bad google skills. Or didn't actually know what I was looking for. Sorry to be a bother, I'd just really appreciate knowing you're okay.*

Ziggy: *Hello?*

Ziggy: *I really hope you're not dead. And I sincerely wish I could drink wine right now.*

7

Ziggy

Sleeping is impossible.

One, it's hot and the air conditioning is good, but it just can't keep up with the early August heat.

Two, I've been eating a mostly potato diet, and while I'm keeping more of my meals down, I'm having a bad morning sickness day.

Three, I finally broke and agreed to let my stepdad hire me to work in the office for the Pounders, his rugby team, until after the baby's born.

Four, I accidentally heard that Abby Nora was supposed to be induced today, and I can't stop wondering if she's had the baby yet and if I'll hear about it from my mom, who will *definitely* hear about it in the neighborhood, and when I'll finally have to tell her that Abby Nora and I aren't friends anymore.

And five, every time I close my eyes, I picture Holt with a

broken neck on a lacrosse field, or mangled in a car accident on the autobahn, or kidnapped by someone for some reason.

And that's the current life problem that my overactive brain is dedicating the most energy to.

None of my texts to Holt in the past day and a half show as read.

It's not like European cell towers are down. I've been texting with Francesca regularly.

Maybe he lost his phone and hasn't gotten a new one yet or he had to get an all-new number because he was replacing a phone in Europe and he didn't have my number saved and his cloud back-up glitched.

Been there myself, unfortunately.

Also, pregnancy hormones suck.

If I'm this worried about a man I barely know, how am I going to react when it's my own baby who doesn't answer me when I call for them in the house? Or text me back fast enough when they're on the bus home from school? Or when they get a driver's license and miss curfew? Or when they leave for college and don't call at all for weeks on end, then move to Europe?

Breathe, Ziggy. Breathe.

Is this level of anxiety normal in pregnancy?

Or is this level of anxiety normal when the man you're house- and dog-sitting for ghosts you?

I'm tossing and turning long after midnight when Jessica growls low and deep from her doggy bed on the floor beside me. I moved her into the bedroom with me after she wouldn't stop whining outside the door the first night.

"What's wrong?" I whisper to her.

She growls again.

I grab my phone and flip on the flashlight.

Her little ears are back flat, and she's glaring at my bedroom door.

Is it my bedroom door?

Or is it the crooked closet doors beside the bedroom door? I usually shut them. Forgot to close them tonight, apparently.

And that's when I hear it.

Noise.

Downstairs.

Someone's in the house.

Jessica leaps to her short little legs, barks like she's a German Shepherd, and takes off for the door, snarling all the way.

"*Jessica!*" I whisper-shriek. "Come back!"

Call someone.

I need to call someone.

Her ferocious bark echoes in the stairwell.

Phone.

Call.

I know how my phone works.

It's a thing where I push buttons.

But it won't turn on.

It won't turn on.

Why won't it—oh.

Upside down.

It doesn't turn on when it's upside down.

Bathroom. Closet. Hide.

Which one?

Jessica's still barking.

Oh my god.

What if they hurt the dog?

What if they hurt the dog?

"Get *off*, you mangy asshole," a voice says downstairs. "Christ on a karaoke machine, why aren't you in your goddamn crate?"

Jessica's still growling, but the voice makes me stop.

I can hear it saying *okay* in my head.

"*Holt?*" I shriek.

"Fuck me," he mutters back.

Maybe not *mutters*.

If he were muttering, I couldn't hear him.

But what in the holy hell is he doing here? He's not supposed to be here for another three weeks.

I fumble my phone upright and open it to the phone app, ready to call for help if this isn't Holt, if it's someone who sounds like him and knows Jessica was supposed to be sleeping in a crate, and I creep to the bedroom door. The bedroom that Holt told me to use—the primary suite—is at the top of the landing, so I can flip on the lights and peer out, then duck back into my room if I have to.

My heart is trying to outpace a cheetah racing after a gazelle. My hands are shaking. My stomach hurts like I'm going to hurl.

I flip the light switch, lean out just far enough to look down the steps, and my racing heart skids to a full and complete stop, which makes my stomach flip inside out too.

That's definitely Holt.

Same dark hair. Same broody, hooded eyes. Same chin dimple.

The thing that's different?

The crutches under his armpits and the boot on his lower right leg.

I gape for half a second, a whirlwind of emotions flooding me. "What happened?"

He boosts himself up a single stair. "Don't want to talk about it."

"You didn't call. Or text."

"Been busy."

"*Airplanes have basic text service.*" Deep breaths. *Deep breaths.*

He doesn't answer while he uses the crutches to get up one more stair while Jessica trails him, still growling.

My heart won't stop pounding. "I thought someone was breaking into the house in the middle of the night."

"Just me."

I swear in Italian and add, "*I didn't fucking know that.*"

He eyes me as he hits the fourth stair.

It's not a cautious enough look. It's more *why do I have to deal with the crazy-ass woman in the middle of the night?*

Why?

Because I spent the majority of the past seven years living, working, and breathing in a space where I was never alone. Even when there was someone unpleasant around, there would be someone else not unpleasant nearby.

Being alone is different, and my mind doesn't like the bumps in the night.

Unusual sounds don't mix well with pregnancy hormones either.

So my brain is overreacting to a lot of things.

"Good girl, Jessica," I say.

And my voice cracks.

My damn voice cracks.

I've cried a lot in the past three months. I sobbed when I hung up the phone after dialing in to watch Abby Nora's baby shower. I cried in the damn bar I went to.

I cried in the middle of the one-night stand with a

random Italian guy who got me pregnant behind a Greek bar.

I cried when I found out I was pregnant.

I cried when I got morning sickness too bad to finish out my last contract on the cruise ship.

I cried when I boarded the plane to come home. I cried when I told my parents why I was home. I cried after I lost my first job here.

But I'll be damned if I cry over someone who didn't have the freaking human decency to tell me he was coming back three weeks early—in the middle of the night—like he just forgot he had someone living in his house.

And *there's* the caution I was looking for.

Unfortunately, it's coming with a side of *yep, gonna have to deal with this.*

I suck in a breath and order the damn hormones to get a grip. *I am not crying over this man.* Not in fury that he scared me. Not in relief that he's okay. Not in aggravation that I'm drowning in every emotion known to humankind all at once.

"They say dogs are good judges of character. And you know what? I get it now. I get why she doesn't like you. Because you're an asshole. Welcome home, Holt. I hope your bed is lumpy and that your leg hurts like a bitch."

Well.

That wasn't like me.

But for two glorious seconds, it feels wonderful.

Right up until I realize I've slammed the door and left Jessica outside my room.

Which is quickly followed by the realization that if he's back, I need to find a new place to stay.

Again.

Fuck.

I jerk the door open.

He's made it almost to the top of the steps, which means he's almost at eye level. "You done?"

"No, I'm not done. For your information, I'm not moving out. We have a signed agreement that I'm staying here for another three weeks, so I'm fucking staying here for another three weeks. And I'm taking your dog with me when I leave because she deserves better. Jessica. Go to bed. Good girl. Who's a good girl? Yes, Jessica's a good girl. Good Jessica."

The dog lumbers into my room, and I shut the door again.

But it's not enough.

How *dare* he?

Is there anyone who wouldn't be terrified out of their minds at hearing someone breaking into their house in the middle of the night?

He should've told me he was coming.

And he didn't.

I fling the door open to find him right outside my bedroom.

Motherfucker. Does this door have a lock? It'd better have a lock.

"And one last thing." I glare up at him with every ounce of fury that I have inside me. "Don't touch my air fryer."

This time, I slam the door when I shut it.

Jessica snorts.

God*dammit*.

No lock.

Why doesn't this bedroom door have a lock?

I can't stay here.

There's no lock.

A heavy sigh drifts through the door.

Awesome.

It's not thick enough to block out the sound of a freaking *sigh*.

And I have to work tomorrow.

"I won't touch your fucking air fryer," he mutters.

The crutches clomp on the floor.

One clomp. Two clomps. Three clomps. Four clomps.

The hinges on his bedroom door creak.

There's a stifled *motherfucker* that I can only imagine is from finding half of the hallway bathroom supplies scattered over his bedroom floor, or possibly from the oversize boxes holding a new sink and a toilet and new tile for the bathroom floor, plus buckets with tools and grout and other stuff, since the plumber and I decided that if we didn't hear otherwise, he'd start on fixing and renovating the bathroom this weekend.

Apparently he has Holt's credit card number on file.

And also, he said he likes him well enough that he'd do this one for free if the credit card failed.

Guilt smacks me between the eyeballs.

Maybe Holt *did* lose his phone.

But if he did, *he could've fucking said so.*

Like a normal human being who can communicate with words when he scares the ever-loving shit out of the woman staying in his house—*at his invitation*—and his freaking dog too.

Jessica whimpers and pushes her body against my leg. I'm still standing at the door, ready to fight back if he tries to get in.

And there it is—

Clomp.

Clomp.

Clomp.

And a knock.

"Go away," I say. "I'm trying to sleep."

"I need to take a piss."

The right thing to do is to let him into my bedroom to use the bathroom. He gave me the best bedroom in the house. I've had a lovely three weeks here. He's injured.

But logic and being scared shitless aren't mixing well. "You should've thought of that before you were the kind of asshole who didn't tell your house sitter you were coming home in the middle of the damn night."

Jessica snorts in agreement.

"Use the bathroom downstairs," I add.

He doesn't answer.

And I do my damn best to not feel bad when I hear the clomps of his crutches on the stairs.

Nope.

I won't feel bad.

He did this to himself.

A decent person would've called or texted.

He did neither.

He can touch grass. Preferably grass that his dog has recently peed on.

Jessica makes a muffled snort that I've come to think of as her *it's okay, Ziggy, I'm here for you* snuffle.

The clomping stops, or at least drifts far enough away that I can't hear it anymore.

I do hear the downstairs bathroom door shut.

At least, I think that's the downstairs bathroom door. It's right under my bedroom. The sound came from the right place.

Guilt hits me again.

There's a bedroom downstairs. It's locked, so I shouldn't know it's a bedroom, but it's beneath the hall bathroom and the lock was easy enough to pop. I wanted to make sure there wasn't water leaking onto the ceiling down there.

It looked comfortable. Big bed. White bedding. Cozy blue chair in the corner. Pictures of Holt with a slightly smaller man who looked just like him, and who I assume was his brother. In one picture, they were on a fishing boat holding up matching fish. There was another with Holt in a team jersey, sweaty and hot with his arm wrapped around his brother with crowded stands in the background.

And there were no water stains on the ceiling, so I made myself leave and lock the door again behind me.

Like he left it.

I squeeze my eyes shut briefly.

This is a freaking disaster.

My legs tingle when I move away from the door to walk back to the bed.

My heart is still pounding. My stomach is trying to eat itself, so I pull out a sleeve of crackers that I keep in the nightstand, then sit at the edge of the bed eating them until I think I might be able to at least doze.

Definitely not sleep.

Not tonight.

Also—I have to find a new place to stay for another few weeks.

Dammit.

8

Holt

EVERYTHING HURTS.

My fucking foot hurts. My armpits hurt. My back hurts. My neck hurts. My head hurts. My fingers hurt. My ass hurts.

It all hurts.

But the thing that hurts worst?

Knowing I owe Ziggy an apology.

I don't have to. I could kick her out. Deny I did anything wrong. Never see her again.

Except she's right.

I should've let her know I was headed back early.

There's a pregnant woman in my house, watching my dog, keeping me updated on what's going on around here while I've been gone, and I scared the shit out of her in the middle of the night, coming back weeks before she expected me.

I can make all the excuses I want.

Hard to give her a heads-up when you lost your fucking cell phone somewhere between camp and the airport.

Hard to care when you're facing potentially missing part of the season playing ball in the US instead of signing with a team in Europe.

One goddamn accident in the weight room that ended with a broken foot and they're no longer interested.

I'm broken and they don't think I can get better enough to belong.

Not just my foot.

All of me. I'm not competitive in Europe anymore. There's a big crop of younger guys who've been training harder than I have. They're better than I am.

I can't compete overseas anymore.

Too old. Barely thirty, and I'm too fucking old.

And getting home—I can't even sleep in my own damn bedroom. Caden's bedroom is on the main floor, but I won't use it. Still not ready for that.

There's no water in the bathroom I use upstairs. Piles of renovation shit everywhere. Have to go up the damn stairs just to get to my bed.

So I lay down to sleep on my couch.

Not that I can sleep.

Feels like noon at six in the morning.

Fucking jet lag.

But I was wrong and I know it.

She'll probably never want to see me again.

And that's for the best.

After hours of tossing and turning and hitting my foot wrong and cussing to myself, I hoist myself off the couch, take a piss in the downstairs powder room—don't want to use Caden's bathroom either—and head to the kitchen.

Early morning sunlight streams through the side windows, but it's not enough light, so I switch on the overheads. Then I fumble around trying to figure out what to make for myself when I can't carry anything since it takes both hands on my crutches to keep weight off my foot.

There's Ziggy's air fryer on my countertop. The one I'm not supposed to touch.

Bananas on a banana hook that wasn't here before.

A ten-pound bag of potatoes front and center in the pantry. Six bags of tater tots in the freezer. Two leftover containers in the fridge—one with cubed potatoes, one with —I sniff it—mashed potatoes.

The vegetable drawer is full of peppers and green onions and carrots. There's a carton of eggs. A stick of butter. No milk. No cheese.

No chicken, I can hear Caden say.

Can see him smirking about it too.

I mentally flip him off.

I want a bowl of cinnamon cereal.

Which I also don't have in the cabinets.

Can't drive myself, which fucking sucks. No phone, so I don't have my app to order grocery delivery. Got a business card from the taxi driver who brought me home, but see again, I don't have my phone to call anyone for a ride to the store to get a new goddamn phone either.

I'm snarling as I tear open a banana like I have a personal vendetta against it.

And that's how Ziggy finds me.

Fuming over how all of the food in my house is easily

eaten by toddlers or old people who have lost all of their teeth and eating the banana in enormous bites out of spite.

I brace myself for more yelling, but when I slide a look at her, all I see is wariness. Wariness in her bloodshot blue eyes. Wariness in the way she's holding her shoulders. Wariness in the way her body is leaning away from me.

Fuuuuck.

I scared her last night, and I'm scaring her again this morning.

Look who's about to choose Naked Tuesdays over you.

Jessica growls.

"This way, pup," Ziggy says quietly.

Jessica takes the opportunity to full-on snarl at me before they both escape onto the porch.

And yes, I mean *escape.*

Ziggy's hugging her body, staying to the other side of the kitchen, as far from me as she can get.

Jessica's not making any attempts to be a vicious guard dog who wants me to believe she'd take out my good foot.

She's hovering at Ziggy's side as they slip out the door.

Dammit.

Dammit.

I haven't had enough sleep or pain meds to deal with this yet.

Did it to yourself, dude, I hear Caden say in my head. *Go tell her you're sorry.*

Great idea.

Right idea.

And I'm too damn pissed to muster up the *sorry* part of my personality.

Instead, I finish my banana, drop the peel on the counter, swing myself to the refrigerator, pull out the leftover mashed potatoes, set them on the counter too, and then push them around to the microwave.

Crutch-swing-push.

Crutch-swing-push.

Crutch-swing-push.

See?

I can cook for myself.

I shove the container into the microwave and hit the button for two minutes.

Do I want mashed potatoes?

No.

But they look like the easiest thing to reheat without using Princess Potato's beloved air fryer.

Yep.

Still in a mood.

I grunt to myself and head to the sink.

Thirsty.

Want water.

I'm bent over the sink, sucking water straight from the tap, balancing on one leg, when I hear the back door shut again.

And there's Ziggy.

Hovering just inside the kitchen.

Alone.

Eyeing me with that same wariness.

"What?" I growl.

And there it is.

The obvious answer to my *what?*

It's you, dummy, I hear Caden say. *You're being a shit.*

He's not wrong.

She's standing there looking at me like she's afraid I'm

going to turn into some kind of assassin who's only faking using crutches so that I can use them to murder her.

I need to—

A loud *pop!* in the microwave interrupts my thought.

Fucking mashed potatoes just exploded.

There's splattered white junk all over the inside of the door as the container inside keeps spinning.

Christ on a lollipop.

Did any of the mashed potatoes stay in the container?

That's a shit-ton of mashed potatoes.

If I believed in the supernatural, I'd say there's a ghost in the house making the appliances and the food agree with the sentiment

That's gonna be a bitch to clean up. "God*dammit.*"

"What happened to your leg?" Ziggy asks.

"Nothing."

"Yes, you obviously have one leg clearly in excellent health. What about the other leg? The one in a boot?"

I scowl at her.

Her eyes narrow.

Less wariness now.

That's good.

That's real good.

She's pretty when she finds her backbone.

There's another *pop!* in the microwave, and more mashed potato splatters the microwave walls and doors.

"Most people stop the microwave after the first explosion," she muses.

"I can't get to the fucking microwave."

"The mashed potatoes levitated themselves into it and turned it on?"

Get out.

It's all I have to say.

Get the fuck out of my house.

Then she'll leave, and I still won't have a goddamn phone and I still won't have food and I still won't have the ability to get around my house on my own.

Even if I take over her bedroom, I have to get up and down the steps.

And then I'll have put a pregnant woman in the awful position of having to find a new place to live if she doesn't want to move in with her parents.

I'm the asshole.

I am completely the asshole here.

I scowl less viciously at her.

"I was going to apologize for yelling at you last night," she says, "but I don't think either one of us is ready for that this morning."

Dammit.

She's extending an olive branch.

Or maybe just a leaf off the olive branch.

Where the fuck did that saying even come from? And why do I care that I don't like that she's being the bigger person? "Give me your phone."

The crankier I get, the less wary she gets.

Maybe she doesn't like to apologize any more than I do, and she's glad she doesn't have to because I don't deserve it.

"Men on crutches shouldn't make demands of women they've seen take down two-legged men with nothing but bodily fluids. Pro tip: you'll get a lot farther if you say things like *good morning, Ziggy. Sorry to startle you last night. Could I please borrow your phone?*"

There's a scratch at the back door.

Ziggy opens it, and Jessica trots back in.

The dog spots me and matches my energy, growling while she bares her teeth and paws the ground.

"I wouldn't do that if I were you," Ziggy says to her. "He seems like he's in the kind of mood where he'd smack you with one of his crutches. That *would* be a faster way of getting to go with me whenever I leave, but it would hurt, and that would make me sad."

"I'm not going to fucking beat her with my crutch."

The mashed potatoes explode one last time as the microwave beeps and turns off.

Ziggy looks at the microwave.

Then at me.

Then she heaves a sigh that I feel in the pit of my gut. "Do you have pain medication you're supposed to take?"

"Yes."

"Have you taken it?"

"No."

"Why not?"

"Food."

She's right. I shouldn't be an asshole. She's probably contemplating beating me with my own crutch.

I'd let her.

Everything's shit right now. Might as well make it shittier.

She points to the living room. "Go sit down and keep your mouth shut, and I'll make you breakfast so that maybe, just *maybe*, you'll be tolerable to talk to."

"Don't want to talk."

"That's obvious, Captain Okay."

I jerk my head at her.

Does she know I'm the Pounders' captain?

Was.

Was.

There's no fucking way they'll keep me when I go crutching into Coach's office later today to report my rugby camp accident to him.

Ziggy looks like she's three seconds from forgoing stealing my crutch in favor of strangling me with her bare hands instead. "Or don't go sit and don't get breakfast. I don't care. But I have to eat, so I'm making myself food, and you're in my way."

I take one last look at the microwave.

Ankle's aching like a bitch. Need to elevate it. Get my pain meds.

And I'm being an irrational jerk to the one person who's here and who can actually help me feel better.

Don't want to have to rely on other people.

I'm the guy they come to when they need things. Not the other way around.

Jessica growls at me.

"You're standing between my baby and food," Ziggy says to me. "Go. Away."

Fuck.

That does it.

That pushes me over the edge from *I'm hurting so I want to be an asshole* to *I'm being exactly the kind of asshole I tell the guys on the team not to be.*

I swing myself on the crutches right out of the kitchen and get the hell out of her way.

9

Ziggy

Is it a flex to serve a grumpy jerk a gourmet breakfast just to show him what he'll be missing out on if he doesn't fix his attitude?

If so, I have flexed the biggest flex to have ever flexed in the history of flexes.

But it's probably not.

It's probably stupid. He won't notice or care.

But *I'll* notice.

I care.

I drop silverware, a napkin, and the beautifully plated poached eggs atop breakfast potatoes drizzled with hollandaise sauce onto the end table next to where his head is, and I don't wait for him to acknowledge me.

I'm sure he's in pain.

I'm sure something happened to his phone.

I'm also sure I don't have to tolerate his bad attitude.

Have sympathy for his situation, yes.

Let him take it out on me, no.

I stalk back out of the room, grab my own plate, and take Jessica into the sunroom with me while I eat at the small bistro table beneath the ceiling fan.

No eggs for me.

Just potatoes. Breakfast potatoes with a side of tater tots.

Oh my god, do I love potatoes.

It's a new obsession. Before pregnancy, they were a nice side dish. After pregnancy, I'll likely never eat another potato in any form. Now, though, as I approach the end of my first trimester, they're the only food I eat that both tastes good and settles well.

Morning sickness is for—

Well.

I wish it could be for people who are unprovoked shit-heads to other people.

While I eat, I take a break from studying houses that went on the market overnight to look up the laws about how to take a man's dog from him without getting in trouble.

It doesn't look good.

I eyeball Jessica. "Are you worth going to jail for?"

She's splayed on the thin carpet beside me, back legs sticking out, head tilted up to gaze at me while she pants happily.

I nod. "Agreed. Definitely worth it. Want to go with me when I leave?"

She barks happily.

Just one little bark.

It's adorable.

This dog has my whole heart.

This dog and my baby. And hopefully soon a new house.

But not last week's house, because last week's chosen house failed the inspection badly enough that I had to withdraw my offer. I might've tackled it if I weren't pregnant, but I need a home that's ready for baby and me, not a fixer-upper with a leaky roof and a flood-prone basement.

I finish eating, trade a few texts with Francesca, catching up on what's going on with my friends from the ship. Then I clean up in the kitchen, including picking up a banana peel that Holt apparently left on the counter, then head for the stairs. He's lying on the couch with the boot propped up, one arm flung over his face.

But he's eaten the entire plate of food I took him.

Jessica scratches the floor with her back legs at him like he's her poop and she's covering him up.

I snort softly in amusement and head up the stairs.

She follows.

I should get packed. Start looking for a hotel that will allow dogs.

Or mentally prepare myself to move back in with my parents.

But I don't want to.

I like this house.

The bedroom isn't big by modern standards, but it's roomy compared to my cabin on the ship. The bathroom is on the renovations list because of the olive-green tub and toilet, but the water pressure's good. I'm not sure I've ever sat on a more comfortable couch than the one downstairs, and I've been catching up on so much TV that I missed while I was onboard.

Besides, the kitchen alone is worth putting up with a bad attitude.

I'm nearly done gathering what Jessica and I need to get

out of here for the day when I hear the *clomp...clomp...clomp* on the stairs.

My shoulders tighten. My cheek twitches. Jessica growls low in her throat from her position guarding the door.

Though *guarding* isn't quite right.

She's once again splooted out with her hind legs stretched behind her, and her head is resting on her front paws.

Still growling though.

I continue folding the laundry I did yesterday to finish the last few pieces.

And then he knocks on my bedroom door.

Jessica growls louder.

He sighs so heavily that I hear it through the bedroom door.

I square my shoulders and make myself walk the five steps to the door at a normal pace. I open it with the blankest of blank expressions on my face and channel the professional attitude I wore to work every day of my seven years on the cruise ship.

"Good morning again. Can I help you?"

Maybe not full professionalism.

But definitely as close as I can get.

His jaw works back and forth while his eye twitches. "I'm sorry," he says.

Grunts, really.

I give a short nod. "Thank you. I'll be out of your hair in approximately an hour."

His jaw tics. "Someone stole my phone."

"I'm sorry to hear that."

"At the airport. While I was waiting to check in. That's why I didn't text."

I bite my tongue to keep *was that so hard to say?* from coming out of my mouth.

"I can't drive," he adds.

Logical. It's his right foot in the boot. "I'm sorry to hear that too."

He lifts a hand and scrubs his face with it. There's at least three days' worth of dark stubble on his chin and cheeks. He smells like he hasn't showered in that long either. "Will you please drive me to get a new phone?"

Jessica growls.

"Knock it off," he says to her, but he's not nearly as grumpy as he's been with me. More resigned, if anything. "I didn't ask you to drive. I know better than to ask you for anything."

She sneezes.

At least, I think that's a sneeze.

It's not a sound she's made the past couple weeks while he's been gone, but it comes with snot firing out of her nose and landing on his bare leg and his boot.

Did she—did she do that on purpose?

She looks up at me and grins, doggy tongue hanging out happily, as if she's answering the silent question with *of course I did.*

"I'm happy to call a cab for you." I hope cabs still exist. Not too excited about paying for a rideshare for him. "But I need to finish packing, and the kitchen will take a while."

"You're leaving?"

My stomach twists.

I don't want to leave. I truly don't.

But I also won't stay here with a guy who thinks he can walk all over me.

"Seems like I should, doesn't it?"

Something shifts in his eyes. "You said last night you were staying. You were right. We have an agreement. You get three more weeks."

"I might not want those weeks anymore."

He's blocking the door of my room.

This hasn't escaped my notice.

While he might be on crutches, and while I'm not what you'd call a small woman, he's also over six feet tall and basically solid muscle.

Except for whatever's wrong with his right leg.

He growls softly to himself again.

Jessica growls right back.

I ignore both of them and head back to my day bag. It's still gruesomely hot, so I'll need to pack an extra water bottle.

Or three.

"Is your house ready?" he asks.

Somewhere it is, though I don't know yet *which* house it is or how long it'll take me to find it, make an offer, and close on it. "Not your concern."

"So it's not."

"My next living arrangement is my problem, not yours."

"You can stay here."

"Would you want to stay here with you?"

"I'm *sorry*."

"Me too."

"I can't—I can't do all of the things for myself."

My shoulders tighten so hard and fast that I feel it at the base of my neck.

I know that feeling. Getting sick on the ship, realizing my entire life would change if I decided to keep the baby, knowing I'd be dependent on other people to help me get settled after years of being out in the world, taking care of myself, when I was going back without my best friend—it was a lot.

But the Abby Nora situation taught me that I don't need to let other people take advantage of me either.

And that's what I'm slowly realizing the woman that I thought was my best friend has been doing for the past few years.

Letting me buy half the wine for her wedding since I could get excellent bottles at a good price in Europe. Hosting her bachelorette party on my ship. Taking her side every time she had a disagreement with someone, when I'm now wondering how much of those disagreements were her fault, but I was only getting her side of the story.

I force my shoulders to relax and look Holt directly in the eye. "While I'm sympathetic to your situation, I refuse to be a punching bag for your bad mood."

He winces. "I'm not trying—"

"You're not?"

The second wince gives him away.

Dammit.

I do want to stay.

But not with Mr. Anger Management Issues.

"I can pay you," he says. "For cooking. Light chores. Driving me a few places."

"It's not about money."

"*Please.*"

He's leaning in the doorway, and if I can read people at all, I'd say he needs his next dose of pain medication and is pretending he doesn't.

Is that a man thing or an athlete thing?

Doesn't matter.

"If you were me, would you want to stay here?" I ask him again.

His square jaw shifts back and forth while his cheek twitches and his bottom lip plumps out.

The man's pouting.

He knows there's one right answer, and he doesn't want to give it to me.

And my potatoes aren't settling as well as they usually do.

Likely not the potatoes.

It's likely the man standing between me and—*dammit*.

Between me and Naked Tuesdays and letting my parents have more control over my life than they're already getting with me taking a job at the Pounders.

Maybe Miranda knows someone who needs a temporary roommate.

"I can be..." He studies the ceiling, then pinches the bridge of his nose. "I can be more tolerable."

This would be funny if my ideal temporary living situation wasn't on the line. "That sounds really hard. I wouldn't want you to go to that trouble on my behalf."

He sags against the doorframe, head drooping while he rubs his eyes. "I'm a nice guy. I just—I don't like being like this either, okay? My life's been shit the past few years, and now—now just fucking look at me. I can't play. I can't sleep. I can't just be happy. There's nothing to be fucking happy about."

Dammit. I don't know him, but I know his type. Stubborn. Proud. Unable to handle being down.

"Are you taking your pain meds?" I ask him.

He grunts.

I'll take that as *I'm supposed to be but don't want to be*. Or *they're not working*. Or *I don't want to talk about it*.

"When are you supposed to take more?"

He mumbles something incoherent.

And do you know what's incredibly annoying?

I feel for the bastard.

Because I, too, am sometimes a little stubborn, proud, and unable to handle being down.

When morning sickness hit me on the ship, it hit hard. And I didn't want help. I wanted to handle it myself.

I didn't want to cause problems. Didn't want to be the person other people had to make accommodations for. Didn't want to be the person people gave special treatment to either. That's why I rarely mention who my stepdad is. The minute they find out you're related to one of the richest men in the city, they make all kinds of exceptions for you.

That's not how I want to live.

Honestly, when I get to the Pounders office on Monday, I don't *want* them to know I'm Roland Keating's stepdaughter. I want them to judge me on who I am and how I work.

Not that I get any say—Miranda says when she started for the team, Dad sent out an announcement threatening to end the career of any player who looked at her wrong, which means he'll probably do the same for me—but it would be nice if the pity job for health insurance came with anonymity too.

Holt's probably the same.

Doesn't want accommodations or special treatment.

I sigh. "Go take your medicine. I'll drop you off at the phone store when I leave."

Those deep brown eyes lift. They're bloodshot with blueish-purple bags beneath them.

That young man waters my garden for me in the summer when I can't do it myself.

You're staying at Holt's house? He helped me fix up my car and saved me over a grand since I didn't have to pay someone to do it.

He gave up his career to come home and nurse his brother, and not one of us on the block heard him complain once.

The freezer has four pies now from kids on the same baseball team. There are seven discount cards for various restaurants and local stores in a little basket in the kitchen, all fundraisers for marching bands or other sports teams.

Jessica has a home despite the two of them not getting along.

All evidence says this man is a good man who's not handling being hurt well.

His Adam's apple bobs and he looks down at the floor. "Are you leaving permanently?"

"Not yet."

"Thank you."

I've never heard a more defeated *thank you* in my life.

Baby first, I remind myself.

No, myself first.

Don't make friends with people who will betray you.

My phone dings.

I pull it out of my pocket and glance at it, and my stomach sinks to the floor.

Mom: *Ziggy!! Why didn't you tell us Abby Nora had her baby?!*

Mom hasn't just sent the question.

She's also sent a picture of Abby Nora in a hospital room, beaming as she holds a little bundle with a pink cap, with Josh, her handsome trophy husband, behind her.

They look exhausted.

And so, so happy.

While I'm the bitter former friend calling her husband her *trophy husband*.

I don't like breaking up with friends.

And I don't like the person I am when I'm mad at her either.

Tears sting my eyes.

I turn away so Holt won't see, mumble a quick, "You're welcome," and then head to the bathroom.

Because I'm going to be sick.

Again.

10

Holt

I SHOULDN'T WANT Ziggy to stay.

Bad idea, having a woman—a pregnant woman at that— in my house while I'm here.

Especially when I already spent the past three weeks being as brief as possible over text, lest I give away that I can't get her out of my head.

A camp buddy ordered a glass of wine at dinner—I thought of Ziggy.

I passed a pregnant woman in the offices—I thought of Ziggy.

I lay in my bed alone at night—I thought of Ziggy.

I should offer to put her up in a hotel. Find a short-term rental for her. Find a teammate who can move in with me and put her in his place instead.

But fuck me, if that's what she cooks for breakfast for

someone who doesn't deserve the honor of eating dog shit, what would she cook if I was nice to her?

And she was right—the pain meds have kicked in, and it's helping.

My mood anyway.

Not my panic.

I'm panicked that she'll leave. Panicked that she won't.

Panicked that I'll be alone. Panicked that I won't be alone.

I'm a goddamn mess.

And it's not because she's pretty.

It's because she made me breakfast.

She took care of me.

People don't take care of me. I take care of them.

But Ziggy—she looked through my attitude and my mood and she brought me exactly what I needed.

It's hitting me in places that I'm not supposed to get hit.

She meets me downstairs ten minutes after she disappeared into the bathroom to get sick again. "Okay. I'm ready. Let me put Jessica out and then we can go. I'll meet you at the car."

There's something different about her.

Subdued.

Like she's embarrassed she's sick or something.

I tell myself it's not my problem, but it's hard to exist in this house and not want to make a sick person more comfortable.

Did it for enough years.

It's instinctive now that I'm not in as much pain myself.

And I'm completely off-balance at being the one who needs help.

The one who can't offer her as much help as I'd like because of these damn crutches.

I head to the front door, manage to get myself out of it, and hobble down the steps. She catches up before I reach the driveway, where there's a new small Toyota SUV parked next to my Jeep.

"Could've used the Buick," I grunt. "Or my Jeep."

She doesn't reply as she unlocks the passenger door and opens it for me, then takes my crutches and puts them in the back.

She climbs in, starts the car, and shuts off the stereo before I can figure out the language of the podcast or talk show or whatever it is she'd be listening to if I weren't in the car with her.

And soon we're on our way as she backs us out of the driveway.

Her hair's up in a ponytail, and she's wearing short cotton shorts and a baggy T-shirt. All she needs to complete the *soccer mom running her kids to early morning practice* look is a coffee mug.

One day, that's what she'll be doing. Driving her baby to dance classes and soccer practice and piano lessons.

It's a life I'll never have—kids are out of the question with the genes I'd pass to them, and so dating to find forever hasn't been a priority either—but fuck if there isn't a howl of outraged yearning deep inside of me making my chest hurt at the idea of what she'll have that I won't.

I wonder if she knows the full health history of her baby daddy and his family.

Hell, I wonder if she knows her own.

I fiddle with the air conditioning vent to direct the right one toward me.

Hot as balls in here, and I'd say that even if I wasn't uncomfortable as hell.

Especially since the heat is making her scent of vanilla honey even stronger.

I aim my left vent in her direction as much as it'll go.

No chance the air conditioning will cool me off. She might as well have all of it.

She slides me a look.

She's been different since she got a text message earlier.

Quieter.

More subdued.

I want to ask why, but after my attitude since I got home, I doubt she'd tell me.

Doesn't stop me from wanting to know.

You could quit being a dumbass and be a human being who asks, Caden says in my head.

I ignore him and clear my throat. "Breakfast was good. Thank you."

"You're welcome."

"I feel better after my medicine."

She *hmm*s as she brakes for the stop sign at the end of my block.

It's an *I told you so* if ever there was one.

I'm getting a silent scolding from a librarian.

The kind of librarian who wears pencil skirts and glasses and keeps her hair tied up in a neat bun, but then dives into sweatpants and shakes her hair out as soon as—

Knock it off, asshole, I tell myself.

Last thing I need is to pop a boner over her.

Again.

This time in front of her.

That would be the end of this.

Caden once coached me through flirting with a girl in high school. *Tell her you like her backpack*, he said. *Ask if you can sit with her at lunch. Pay one of the bullies to run into her so you can save the day and help her pick up her books like in the movies.*

He was a fucking hilarious menace sometimes.

And I don't need to flirt with Ziggy. She's not interested.

"I'm not always an asshole," I tell Ziggy.

She doesn't look away from the road.

I'm still sweating. Not sure if it's the temperature inside the car or the effect of the fear that I'm afraid to be alone and injured in my house.

In Caden's house.

A house that's already seen too much sickness and injury and death.

Fucking honest truth?

I don't want to be alone in my own home.

I don't want bottles of pills with a medication schedule inside those walls again. I don't want to get set up to sleep on the first floor because it's too hard to get up to the second floor. I don't want to feel physically broken inside the same walls where my brother eventually couldn't get upstairs either. Or even go to the bathroom by himself.

Doesn't matter how much I renovate, paint, re-floor, whatever.

If I stay there by myself while I'm injured, I'll go fucking mad.

I might go mad anyway just having to be the patient inside the house.

Hell, I want Ziggy to stay almost more than I want to stay myself.

She's growing a new life.

That's something.

That's something good.

"Once I get a phone, I'll call a buddy. Crash at his place so you can have the house to yourself today."

"You don't have to do that."

"I can't—I can't get around well, but I don't want to be a constant burden."

She sucks in a breath through her nose, making her nostrils wobble, but she doesn't look at me again.

"Be a few weeks before I can take care of Jessica again."

"I'm taking your dog with me whenever I leave."

My heart dips.

She should, and I know it. Jessica likes her. Jessica hates me.

But it's one more failure.

And I need to accept it. "Okay."

She wrenches the wheel, jerking us to the side of the road at the very edge of the neighborhood, and slams on the brakes. "Are you fucking serious?"

Her eyes are blue flames heating the rest of her face until her cheeks are splotchy red.

I swallow and instinctively lean closer to the door. I'm six-two. Two-hundred-thirty pounds. At least six inches and fifty pounds bigger than she is. And at this moment, I'm absolutely shrinking away from her.

"She hates me. I try, but she hates me. You like her. You should have her."

"*You don't know me.* You don't know me at all, and you'll just give me your dog? *Who does that?*"

"You just told me you're taking her."

"But you're not even fighting for her."

"She doesn't like me. I took her because no one else would. But she likes you."

"You've seen *five minutes* of evidence of that. Maybe I'm a terrible person. Maybe I'm planning to ruin her life by making her internet famous and putting too much pressure on her. Maybe I won't let her have any other doggie friends."

What? "My neighbors texted me. They said she looked happy with you."

"What if they're lying? What if I'm terrible for Jessica?"

"Are you?"

"*No.* But how do you know that for sure? Why would you trust me?"

"She's still alive. House is still standing. You're driving me to the phone store."

She stares at me while I watch what seems to be my logic filtering through her brain. Her eyes start to water, and her entire expression tightens while she blinks and turns forward again and pulls back onto the street. She's breathing hard. The splotchy red stains are spreading down her neck, and her knuckles are white on the steering wheel. At the next three stop signs, she brakes so hard that we're both thrust forward against our seatbelts.

Tell her, I hear Caden say in the back of my head. *Just tell her you don't want to be alone.*

Great plan.

Everything about her says she wants to be alone.

Or at least not with me.

I keep my head forward as we leave the residential area and approach a major road lined with restaurants, markets, and strip malls. About a mile left to get to the right strip mall.

A dozen or so stoplights.

She hits the button on the display, then another button, and pop music comes out of the speakers. It's so drowned out by the sound of the air conditioning that I can't tell what song is playing.

Probably wouldn't know what it was even if I could hear it.

Ziggy's still breathing heavy. She's also blinking too much.

Fuck.

Is she having morning sickness?

Was it something with the text message she got?

Or is it me?

I open my mouth and get an instant side-eye glare.

So I keep my jaw shut until we pull up to the store.

She stops in the fire lane right at the door.

No messing around.

Just *get your fucking crutches and get out of my car.*

At least, that's what I presume she's thinking as she finally looks at me again.

Fuck it.

I look her straight in the eye. "House could use some life for once. Stay. Long as you need to. I don't—I don't want to be alone there, but I don't—I don't know where else to go. I don't—I'm the guy who takes care of other people. I'm not the guy who needs help, and I don't—I just *don't.*"

That wariness is back in her expression. "This—me—I guess we're both having a bad day."

Shiiiiiiit.

There's no mistaking the way the wheels instantly start turning in my brain.

An attractive woman in my orbit is having a bad day.

I need to fix it.

But *I don't.*

I can't.

Best thing I can do is to not be the person making her bad day worse.

I reach for the door handle to let myself out. "Relatable. Hope it gets better."

"Thank you. I hope—I hope you don't have to be on crutches long."

I grunt.

She sighs.

And if that doesn't say it all, I don't know what does.

11

Ziggy

I'D ASK the universe why today's the day that morning sickness has to make a resurgence, but I already know the answer to why.

I have to tell my parents about Abby Nora, and I don't want to.

But instead of sucking it up and going to see them, I'm hunched over the toilet while Jessica whimpers beside me. My stomach has had it, and I'm paying the price.

"How am I supposed to tell them I don't want to think about her ever again in my life?" I ask Jessica once I've given all I have to give to the porcelain gods.

I'm sweating and shaky and my stomach still hurts.

She grunt-snuffles and creeps closer, putting her big, broad head onto my leg.

"And do you know what's making it worse?"

She grunt-snuffles again like she's telling me to go on.

"I'm terrified to make more new friends because I'm afraid it'll end and I'll hurt all over again."

Swear the dog grunts in agreement.

I stroke her head. "Your owner died. They still wanted you, I promise. And you have a good home here."

She wags her cute little tail.

"That's right. You know it, even when you're drooling and throwing doggie snot on people."

She grins at me.

I'd laugh at her unashamed confession that she does it on purpose, but I still feel too crappy.

So instead, I sigh and let my head drop back against the wall.

I could see myself being friends with Holt if I trusted myself to have friends.

The world looks different once people you love have torn you to pieces.

When they leave you with a bottomless hole in your heart that your family and a new baby and a dog can't fill because they're not shaped the same.

I've never felt so unsure of new people in my life.

Dogs, though—the dog, I trust.

"I like this house," I tell Jessica. "But I think you're the biggest reason I was supposed to be here. What do you think? Should we go see my parents? Will you be my emotional support while I tell them?"

She growls softly.

"They have a big yard and other dogs you can play with."

That's a stink eye if I've ever seen one.

"You like other dogs. I've seen you at the dog park."

She barks and wags her tail.

My phone lights up with a message.

From Holt.

I don't like the way his name on my screen makes my heart beat faster.

Holt: *Stopping by to grab my meds.*

That's all it says. Normal housemate stuff. Like he was going to text me *new phone, who dis?*

He's not the type.

But he's apparently the type to make my pulse take off at a gallop because that's exactly what happens when I hear the door open downstairs.

Unfortunately, that's all it takes to make my stomach turn over the wrong way too.

I lunge for the toilet again.

Dammit.

Dammit dammit *dammit.*

And I don't have anything left to give, which means I'm stuck here until I get out of the cycle of angry stomach battling with empty stomach.

I'm hovering over the toilet, breathing hard, when I hear the *clomp...clomp...clomp* of crutches that suggests Holt's on his way up.

Jessica whines.

I squeeze my eyes shut and try to breathe through the roiling in my stomach that gets worse with every *clomp* of the crutches.

Who gave him a ride?

Why aren't they coming up to get his suitcase?

Wait.

How did his suitcase get upstairs?

It didn't.

The answer is that *it didn't.*

I can clearly picture it just inside the door downstairs in the living room.

Which means—

"Ziggy?"

"What?"

Nope.

Not going away.

He's *clomp-clomp-clomp*ing into the bedroom.

My stomach heaves. My arms and legs are shaky and I'm sweating and I hope this is just morning sickness.

It *is* just morning sickness, isn't it? "Please don't come in here."

He ignores me and angles himself and his crutches into the bathroom, then lifts a cloth grocery sack to set it on the counter. "Saltines and seltzer water."

I whimper.

Jessica whimpers.

She doesn't growl at him or fling imaginary poop at him either.

Not this time.

"Thank you," I force out.

He doesn't leave.

Instead, he props himself against the sink so he can pull a sleeve of crackers out of the bag. Then he bends, holding both of his crutches in one hand and not letting his booted foot touch the ground, and puts the crackers closer to me on the floor.

Same with a bottle of seltzer water from his magic cloth bag.

Tears blur my vision.

This is what friends do.

They take care of each other.

I grab the bottle, but I can't twist the cap.

I can't twist the fucking cap.

He bends over again, this time without his crutches but still only on one leg, takes it, opens it, and hands it back to me.

Doesn't say a word.

I don't know if he's looking at me, because I can't bring myself to look at him.

If I look at him, I might see kindness, and if I see kindness, I might start believing he's the good guy everyone insists he is, and if I believe he's that good guy, I might decide we can be friends.

I can be friends with a guy with a chiseled jaw and a five o'clock shadow and hooded brown eyes and dark hair that's still smushed funny from how he's slept—or not slept—on it. I can be friends with a guy who's injured and worried about his future.

I can keep it at *just friends* when he does things like bringing me saltines and seltzer water.

Stop it, Ziggy.

I take a sip, and my stomach starts to settle as soon as the first drop of seltzer water trickles down my throat.

"Thank you," I whisper again.

"Little bit of experience." His voice is gruff but soft. Like he doesn't want to talk about it any more than I want to open up about every choice I've made in the past few months and how those choices have led me to being sick here today.

I don't ask him more.

He doesn't offer more.

But he does linger, leaning on his crutches while I take slow sips.

Jessica wags her tail slowly and watches me. Occasionally she snorts in Holt's direction.

He rips open the cracker sleeve and hands that to me as well, which is when I realize I've been cradling my lower belly.

Subtly reminding myself that I want this. That I chose this. That the little pea-sized being wreaking havoc on my body is worth it. That I already love them with all of my heart.

I take another sip.

Holt's phone audibly vibrates. He glances at the screen, then thumbs over it.

"You don't have to stay here with me," I force out. "I'll be okay."

"Only thing worse than feeling like shit is feeling like shit alone."

"Jessica's here. And I can call my sister. She'll come over."

Yes. I should call Miranda.

She'll be a buffer when I tell my parents about Abby Nora.

"You sure?" Holt asks.

I nod.

Jessica tries to crawl into my lap.

He snorts softly. "Yeah, you're clearly a terrible person who's abusing her."

His crutches clomp as he turns to head out of the bathroom.

And when he's gone, the house feels emptier than it ever has.

12

Holt

FLETCHER HUXLEY WOULDN'T HAVE BEEN my first choice of teammate to call for a ride and a place to spend a day when we first met, but the guy's grown on me over the past two seasons. He's one of a few guys on the team who played seriously overseas long enough and well enough that he doesn't need an off-season job. He can also afford a penthouse with a guest room, where I intend to actually get some sleep at some point today.

Plus, his fiancée, Goldie, is one of my favorite people.

She's keeping me company in their living room while he grabs something he says I need to see.

"So what's the story on your foot? What happened?" she asks.

I readjust the pillows under my foot, then flop onto my back, facing her on the other wing of the sofa. "Weight room accident."

"How long are you on crutches?"

"Four weeks. Longer if it's not healing well enough."

I wait for her to wrinkle her nose or grimace or sip from her mug to hide her reaction at the idea of me potentially asking to be underfoot rather than home alone for the better part of a month, but instead, all I get is a sympathetic softening of her golden-brown eyes.

"I'm sorry, Holt. I know how frustrating that is."

She knows better than I do.

I got to play pro rugby.

She, meanwhile, saw her professional soccer dreams go up in smoke when she broke her hip in college.

I shouldn't be whining to her.

Sweet Pea, their miniature dachshund, barks. Goldie pulls her onto the couch too, and then Zinger, their other dog, a mutt, leaps up to join them.

These dogs like me.

It's just my own damn dog who hates me.

No, not *my* dog.

Ziggy's dog.

Jessica is Ziggy's dog. I need to think about her that way so it's less of an adjustment when they leave.

Maybe I'll get my own dog. Or a cat. I could get a cat. I like cats.

And I'll be here for the rest of my career—probably, if I still have a career—so I might as well get settled.

"Oh my god, *Fletcher,*" Goldie says on a sigh while Sweet Pea whines.

I glance up. My teammate strides to the center of the room in nothing but a black Speedo with a giant waffle printed over his dick.

"My new budgie smugglers came in," he says. "It's between these and the next pair. What do you think?"

He turns in a circle, showing off the word *POUNDERS* printed over the ass of the tight briefs he opts to wear under his kit shorts.

Most of the rest of us have gone to the longer compression shorts under our shorts, a basic requirement since it's not unusual for shorts to get pulled down during a match and we'd like rugby to make network TV in America eventually.

Nudity laws on the airwaves and all that.

But Fletcher will likely pick out special budgie smugglers to be buried in.

He's that type.

"What's with the waffle?" I ask.

"Don't you want to know?" He smirks, making his mustache twitch. Some guys can pull off a mustache. Fletcher isn't one of them, but when he grows it and posts to his socials, the Pounders sell more tickets.

I don't understand it, but I can't argue with more ticket sales.

"His favorite idea of a contender for a mascot," Goldie supplies.

I heard management was contemplating finally adding a mascot, but I hadn't paid much attention because I wasn't going to be here. "A waffle? What do waffles have to do with Pounders or pounding?"

Fletcher turns again, modeling. "If you can't see the connection, you don't deserve to know."

Goldie's laughing at him. "It was one of his ideas while we were hungover on Liege waffles in Belgium last month."

"And it's bloody brilliant," Fletcher says. "Waffles are

versatile. You can eat them plain. You can eat them with Nutella or ice cream or syrup. You can call someone a twat-waffle. Or a shitwaffle. Or a fuckwaffle. Or a wankwaffle. Bloody. Fucking. Brilliant."

Goldie's suppressing a smile while she shoos Fletcher. "Go put your clothes on and quit torturing Holt."

"Torturing Holt is my favorite hobby."

"Torturing Silas is your favorite hobby."

"Was. Got too easy. I'm moving on to bigger fish."

Silas, Goldie's little brother, is also on the team. He and Fletcher butted heads hardcore before Fletcher and Goldie hooked up. Even more in the weeks immediately after they hooked up, but the two of them came to some kind of under-standing and are mostly tolerable together. Still have their moments, but this past season was much easier than Fletch-er's first season with the team.

Fletcher says it's because Silas is growing up.

I think Goldie got to both of them and helped them both grow up. She's good like that.

"I see you naked almost every week," I remind Fletcher. "Try harder."

"Happily. Wait until you see the next pair. You need a picture to remember these?" He strikes another pose, this one like he's a bodybuilder, or like he's trying to show off all of the tattoos on his arms. "Goldie. Snap a pic."

She smiles at him. "Pretty sure I can remember these without a picture."

"Completely positive? This would help you when you're missing me the next time we're apart for an hour."

And *now* he's annoying me.

"I want a picture." I lift my phone, switch on the camera

app, and aim it at him while he poses again. "Also, I have your sister's number. She'll love these."

His face freezes, which is a massive fucking victory when it comes to Fletcher.

Goldie sees it too, judging by the way she laughs even harder. "So these *aren't* for your socials to wage a fan campaign for mascot. You're losing your touch, Fletcher."

As I'm hitting the shutter button for the seventh time, a new text comes in that startles me enough that I get three blurry pictures in a row.

Ziggy: *I called the plumber. He can have everything out of your bedroom today and the bathroom functional in two days.*

My heart leaps. I sit up—why, I don't know, to think better to reply to her?—but it's too fast and I pull a hamstring, which sends a lightning bolt of a cramp down my calf inside my boot.

I drop my phone and grab my leg as low as I can reach it while the pain flares so hard my shin bone aches too. *"Fuck."*

Fletcher's at my side in an instant, with his hairy chest and tattooed arms and the fucking tight briefs.

"Down," he says.

"I'm lying down," I grumble, once again flat on my back while I breathe through the cramp.

"When did you take your last meds?"

"Hour ago. I'm—fine."

Fuck, that hurts.

But it's fading.

He grabs my phone to hand it to me but pauses and tilts his head at my screen. "Who's *house sitter*? And where are they staying?"

I snatch my phone back from him, relieved that I hadn't got around to changing Ziggy's name in my phone. "Nobody."

"You have a house sitter while you're staying here?"

"Had one here while I was in Europe."

"So they're not the nursemaid type?"

I growl at him.

I don't want Ziggy meeting Fletcher.

He can be an asshole on a good day. Don't ask about bad days.

Plus, I don't want to share her with anyone. Even as friends. She's mine.

Fuck.

She's not mine. She's her own person, growing a baby all by herself, with zero interest in me.

Especially after last night and this morning.

The dogs circle Fletcher. Goldie squats next to him and presses his shoulder. "Go try on your other budgie smugglers. I've got this."

He doesn't listen. "If your house sitter was old and crotchety, you wouldn't be falling off the couch because they texted you."

I should've called a different teammate. Tatum or Crew wouldn't have been this annoying. "My house is getting renovated, and she's making it easier for me to get back in my room. End of story."

"You didn't say anything about renovations."

"I don't tell you everything." Far from it, in fact.

"You should. I'm a good listener."

I look at Goldie.

She suppresses another smile. "He listens more than you think he does."

"The guy who told everyone I was from Canada and didn't know my brother was sick until this time last year?" I say dryly.

"He listens better to more people now that he's less distracted with his world domination plans," she corrects.

She didn't know about Caden either, but she and Silas have a complicated relationship, so she wasn't around the team much before Fletcher arrived. Didn't really get in each other's business aside from Goldie making a regular effort to be involved in Silas's daughter's life.

"I've been to your house," Fletcher says. "Don't you have three or four bedrooms? Had to have at least two."

"I— It's complicated."

He stares at me.

"My house sitter doesn't have a good option of another place to live until her own house is ready. I fucked up her plans when I came back early, so I told her she could stay."

"In the only working bedroom in your house?"

"Yes." No. There's Caden's room. And I won't stay in it.

"One bedroom when you need a place to sleep and recover and heal."

"Everything will be normal again soon. My bedroom's getting fixed today. Mostly."

"If you need to stay here in our love nest—"

I groan and grab a pillow to shove over his mouth, but he's too quick and is out of reach in an instant.

"I'd say I'm sorry, but you know what you're getting into any time you see him," Goldie says while she rescues Sweet Pea before Fletcher trips on her.

"I can't get to my own bed easily yet, but she's working with a contractor to fix it. It's fine."

Fletcher starts to grin.

Goldie gives him a playful shove. "He can't even make his own food right now. Stop thinking what you're thinking."

He tosses her a grin before turning it on me. "Is she hot? Have you ever had nurse fantasies? Goldie was reading this book about a couple who hated each other but then they hooked up because they had to share a bed—"

"I'm calling Zander and getting out of here," I announce.

Calf's still cramping.

I feel like ass.

I smell like ass. Can't remember the last time I showered.

And I want to sleep.

And dream about vanilla honey and wide blue eyes.

Fuck.

Fletcher squints at me. "You're back. You don't need a live-in house sitter. So if she's still staying at the house—"

Goldie shoos Fletcher again. "If renovations aren't as fast as you think they'll be, I can talk to my friend Sheila. She has a spare bedroom, and she won't torture you about your house sitter. Or wear budgie smugglers in front of you."

I like Goldie's friends. They come to practices and matches and afterparties.

They're all at least sixty-five, and they all give fun aunt vibes.

So it's a relief that they won't have a budgie smugglers party.

"I can handle him," I tell her.

"That's why you're the captain."

I glance at my phone again.

Still the same message from Ziggy. No bubbles indicating she's texting more. No new messages about her staying.

My fingers hover over the keyboard, but I can't type *ok*.

She said something about me saying *ok* in text.

But what the fuck am I supposed to say? *Thanks* is the same as *ok*.

I should've called the plumber myself might make her think I don't appreciate what she did.

Breakfast was delicious and we're both going through shit and do you want to get married so I can give you health insurance for the baby? is unhinged.

Where did that even come from?

And why am I getting hot?

"Everything okay?" Goldie says.

Fletcher's gone. Probably trying on his other budgie smugglers.

Goldie works for herself as a life coach, and she's fucking good at it. Not unusual to see one or two of the guys corner her with questions when we're all hanging out.

She gives good advice.

"I scared the shit out of my house sitter when I got home last night, and then I was an asshole this morning because I didn't sleep and I was off my meds, and I can't take care of myself, but it doesn't feel right to ask her to take care of me when all she agreed to do was watch my house and my dog, and—"

"You have a dog?"

"Long story."

"How long have you had a dog?"

"Couple months."

"And you didn't tell us? *Us*. Fletcher. Fletcher who carries Sweet Pea everywhere in a pink baby sling. You didn't think to tell us you got a dog?"

"That's not the biggest issue here."

Sweet Pea gives me a look that clearly says I'm wrong. Her brother is sleeping and doesn't care at all.

Goldie seems to agree with Sweet Pea. "So you weren't your best when you came back early and now you're having trouble with your *dog sitter.*"

"I indirectly participated in getting her fired from a job, so I offered her my house to stay at while I was gone since her other options weren't ideal, and now I'm back early and I can't kick her out because she's pregnant."

Goldie blinks at me.

I've officially moved past the broad spectrum of situations in which she always has good advice.

After the longest pause I've ever seen her make when faced with a problem, she clears her throat. "I see."

"Do I get a point for stumping you?"

"I'm not stumped. I'm thinking."

"About what I should do?"

"About which questions I want to ask you next."

I shake my head. "Don't worry about it. I'll figure it out."

"Will you?"

Legit question. I'm asking myself the same thing. "I will. I'm just up in my head."

"So get out of your head and handle it like you'd handle a situation with Fletcher."

"I have zero intentions of telling this woman to quit being a fucknugget and then tackling her harder and harder until one of us gives."

She laughs.

Sweet Pea heaves the long-suffering sigh of a dog who loves her owner but knows he's not perfect and never will be.

Get out of my head.

I can get out of my head.

Maybe.

Ok is out as a response to her text.

But if she were one of the younger guys on the team—

Thanks. Let me know what I can do to be more helpful.

Yep.

That's good.

That's normal.

That's legitimate.

I hit send and watch as the status changes from *sending* to *delivered.*

But not *read.*

I hope she's not puking anymore. And that it's just morning sickness. Don't know much about pregnancy and babies, and I'm never having kids, so I don't need to know. But is she in the normal stage for morning sickness?

Or is this something wrong?

Did the house curse the baby?

Should I tell her to leave instead?

"Holt?" Goldie says.

Fuck. I'm breathing way too fast. "Shitty week. Still up in my head. I'm fine."

I'm not fine.

My phone dings.

Ziggy: *No worries. I've got this. But it turns out a baby pink tub was accidentally delivered, so that's what you're getting. You'll love it. It goes perfectly with the white marble sink and the fish shower curtain I just found online.*

For the first time in what feels like weeks, I take a full breath.

She's joking.

If she's joking with me and sending me long texts, we're normal.

Not okay—my foot is broken, and I'm going to have to pretend she's not the most attractive woman I've met in years—but normal.

That was a joke, in case it wasn't clear pops up on my screen.

I smile. I'm fucking exhausted, I smell like ass, and I hurt, but I'm smiling.

Me: *Damn. I've always wanted a pink tub with a fish shower curtain. Sorry again for being a shit. I'm not usually like this. Thanks for breakfast. It was delicious. I'll text before I head back so I don't scare you.*

The message almost instantly goes to *read*.

But no bubbles pop up suggesting she's texting back.

"I like the waffles better," Fletcher announces.

I look away from my phone.

Now he's in another pair of black budgie smugglers, but this time, there's a flaming meatball on his crotch.

"Are you fucking kidding me?" I mutter.

"Management says this was one of their real ideas. I think they're going for some play on the Thrusters having a hot dog—"

"Bratwurst," Goldie corrects.

"—and the Scorned having that weird mascot that looks like an angry chicken leg," he finishes.

"The Fireballs used that exact meatball when they did a contest to find a new mascot a few years ago," I tell him. "If management told you they're seriously considering it, they're either lying or they're doing some kind of joint promo with the baseball team."

We all look at his crotch again.

The meatball doesn't look any better on second glance. It's flaming and angry, shaking its fists.

"Maybe it's a pound of meat," he says.

"Why don't you use a hammerhead shark?" Goldie says.

Easy answer. "Too much like Miami."

"A jackhammer?"

Fletcher's still shaking his head at his junk. "They should do a hamburger named Quarter. The Quarter Pounder."

"Absolutely not," Goldie says. "A Quarter Pounder is never enough beef."

That does me in.

I laugh.

And I realize as I start to laugh just how long it's been since I laughed.

I might be a fucked-up disaster at the moment, but at least I have my friends.

13

Ziggy

I READ SOMEWHERE ONCE that you shouldn't delay the inevitable.

That the anxiety from pushing something off only makes it worse in the end.

And I'm completely ignoring that advice today.

I texted Mom back a quick *Sorry, got distracted, aren't they beautiful?* about Abby Nora and the baby after Miranda told me that our parents were headed up into the mountains today for a trip to a winery and to visit friends at their weekend house.

I can put off telling my parents that my best friend and I broke up.

Maybe they'll just subtly put the clues together. Or maybe Abby Nora's mother will say something to mine. Or maybe I'll randomly get a job offer in Napa for a job I haven't applied for, and I can run away and not deal with it at all.

Miranda shakes her head at me as we stand in the office that will be mine come Monday. "You should just tell them."

"I'm waiting for the best moment."

"Which is?"

"When I won't cry but when I'll also look so sad that they won't ask too many questions." I cross around the stately cherry desk to sit at the tall desk chair that has ten thousand levers and more cushions than any chair should have. Isn't one for your butt and one for your back standard? This has an individual cushion for each butt cheek and rows of cushions on the back that all seem to have their own controls.

"Is it just me, or is this chair too much?"

She rolls her eyes. "It's Dad's subtle clue that you're his daughter and everyone needs to be nice to you."

"So I should switch it out with the receptionist's desk and tell him I did it so that the team looks extra successful because looking successful is the first step in being successful."

"Only if you tell him first. If you do it without telling him, he'll think Quinoa stole it, and then Quinoa will get fired."

"Quinoa?"

"Our receptionist. His parents were very crunchy."

Ah. That makes sense. "But Dad wouldn't actually fire him."

"Oh, he would. Dad almost kicked one of the best guys off the team last year because he was new and didn't realize I was *the owner's daughter, ooooh.*"

"Dad almost fired him for not knowing who you were?"

"No, it was more that he was a little bit of a dick when I met him. But Fletcher's always a little bit of a dick. And there's something about him being a dick that sells tickets, so it's good that Dad didn't fire him."

"I'm going to have to learn everyone on the team, aren't I?"

"Yep. Want a rundown?"

"No, I want a twice-baked potato."

She laughs. "You're growing a twice-baked potato."

"Given the amount of potatoes I've eaten the past few weeks, I'm not sure you're wrong."

Jessica snuffles her agreement. She's sniffing the corners of my new office.

My new office.

I don't like those words.

I'd rather be working with a winery or at a restaurant or for a catering company.

Instead, Dad's created an *internal head of events* position for me.

I get to plan the meals for meetings, sales pitches, charity events, and banquets for the team. All while sitting in a gray-walled room with a window overlooking the little park behind the Pounders' administrative building.

It's not just the fancy desk chair.

I also got a window office. And not some window overlooking a parking lot either.

It's special treatment.

"Aw, don't make that face," Miranda says. "This really is a great place to work. Everyone's nice. The guys on the team are great."

"Are they?"

"They are. Even Fletcher. Once they found out who I was, they basically all adopted me as their little sister."

"That's not annoying?"

"Oh, it is, but it's much better than having all of them hitting on me."

"Because they're all unattractive?"

"No, because Dad would murder them, and I'd rather not be the cause of the fall of the Pounders."

I rub my belly. "So little one's going to have a lot of honorary uncles?"

Miranda grins at me. "Fuck Abby Nora and fancy lady baby showers. Wait until you see what these guys will do."

"I really didn't want to take a pity job," I whisper.

"It's better than moving in with them."

I blow out a heavy breath. "But what if I never find a job that's not a pity job?"

"You will definitely find the right job that's not a pity job."

"What if I can't afford daycare?"

"You'll be able to afford daycare."

"But what if I can't? What if keeping—"

I stop myself.

I can't say it out loud. I can't question my decision about the baby.

I want this baby. I want this baby so much it aches to think of something happening to them.

Not exactly how I envisioned motherhood happening for me, but the minute I saw those two pink lines on the pregnancy test, I knew.

I knew this was right.

That this was what I wanted.

That this baby is the start of the next phase of my life. The good to come from the bad.

"Ziggy. Stop." Miranda sits on the edge of the empty desk, facing me. "Do you remember the first time we met?"

"Vaguely. You were wearing a unicorn T-shirt. And my mom said I had to share my French fries with you. That's all I've got."

"My unicorn phase was legendary." She grins. "What I remember is you telling your mom that you didn't want her to marry my dad because you wouldn't make friends if you had to move."

I grimace. "Turns out I was right."

"*Stop.* You weren't right. You *did* make friends. Every weekend I spent with Dad, you had friends over or you were at friends' houses. And then when you left for culinary school, you said you didn't know if it was what you were really supposed to do, but you loved food, so you had to try it, and you crushed it. And then you were worried that Europe was too far away, but look what you did."

She's gesturing wildly with her hands, which means she's not done. "You spent how many years there? Living on a cruise ship, meeting fascinating people and having adventures and loving your life. Just because those things didn't last forever doesn't mean you didn't face your fears and conquer your challenges. You won't be pregnant forever. Your baby won't be in daycare forever. You won't work here forever. Life changes. You change with it. We hit rough patches and we get through them. You're not alone, and you'll be okay. You and the baby. I promise."

Dammit.

Dammit.

How is it that the little girl who used to make me share my French fries and spilled ketchup on her unicorn shirts is now a fount of life wisdom?

And why am I suddenly sobbing my brains out? "I hope—my baby—is—as smart—as you—one day."

She giggles as she hugs me. "I love you, you crazy beautiful hot mess."

"It's—the hormones," I wail.

"Mm-hmm."

"And fucking—Abby—Nora."

"I would wish very bad things on her, but I'm incapable of wishing bad things on a new mother."

"Don't—wish—bad things."

There's a clatter in the hallway, and both Miranda and I turn and look.

Three young men freeze in my doorway.

"We're not here," says the tallest of the bunch—a bulky Black man in a gray Pounders T-shirt.

"Yeah, we'll be here Monday, but we're not here right now," a slightly less-bulky but still larger-than-average white man with red hair and a thick red beard says.

The third man—just as built as the first two, with white skin and dark hair—doesn't say anything.

Instead, he doesn't look at us or at the potted plant that he's attempting to straighten.

It's like he's telegraphing *I'm not here either, and I didn't knock over this plant in the hallway, I have no idea what you're talking about.*

"Crew, Porter, Zander, meet my sister, Ziggy," Miranda says, pointing to each in turn. "She can cry on command to test how you'll all react."

"You have a sister?" Crew says.

"For real. I didn't know there were two of you," Porter says.

"I'm not here, and I didn't do anything," Zander says.

"Ziggy's starting Monday," Miranda tells them. "Be nice or I'll make you look terrible on our socials."

Porter snorts. "We're always nice."

"Until you have a rugby ball in your hand."

"She's got you there, bruh," Zander tells him.

148

"What are you doing here?" Miranda asks all of them.

"We were using the gym—" Porter starts.

"—Because it's our day off from working at the rock-climbing wall—" Crew continues.

"—And we saw your car in the parking lot—"

"—So we came to see why *you're* here on a Saturday."

She smiles at them, then looks at me. "These guys are the best. You'll like them. Promise."

Crew squints at me. "For real though—why didn't I know you have a sister?"

"Because we don't discuss personal matters at work?" Miranda says.

"And probably for the same reason we didn't even know Miranda existed until we got that email when she started here," Porter mutters to him.

All three of their phones go off simultaneously, though their ring tones don't really go together, and all three of them whip out their phones like they're glad to have a distraction.

"Oh, shit," Crew says.

"Fuck us," Porter adds.

Zander just stares at his screen.

"Everything okay?" Miranda asks.

All three of them look up at her, then trade glances, then look at me, then nod in unison.

"Yep."

"It's great."

"No problems. No problems at all."

Miranda and I share a look. "They're the best?" I say. "You mean the best liars?"

At least they're distracting.

"Captain's got a problem," Crew says.

"Small problem," Porter adds. "Inconsequential. Not life-altering or anything."

"We gotta go," Zander says. "Fletcher put out a love bomb call. Everything's fine. Just love bombs."

"Love bombs?" I repeat.

"Don't ask," Miranda whispers. "It'll make you cry again. I'll tell you in a year or two."

My eyes get hot. "Don't say the *cry* word or I'll do it," I whisper back.

"Good to meet you, Ziggy," Crew says.

"See you around," Porter says.

"Don't take a picture of that plant," Zander tells Miranda. "Unless you tell the world it fell over on its own. Maybe our mascot should be the ghosts. That was one powerful—right. Yeah. We're leaving. Captain needs us. Bye-ee!"

The three of them hustle out of the doorway, but we can still hear them as they make their way down the hall.

"Did you seriously just say *bye-ee*?"

"Shut up. Bad enough I broke a plant. But to do it in front of *both* of Keating's daughters? I'm fucked."

"He doesn't care about a plant, dude."

"He's gonna care if he knows Zander's flipping out 'cause Ziggy's pretty."

"*I am fucking not.* She's one more sister that we didn't know we had. Shut up."

Miranda looks at me. "It might not be perfect, but this job will totally be entertaining as hell."

"Can we go get a twice-baked potato now?"

She laughs.

Jessica barks.

And for five solid minutes, I let myself believe everything will be okay.

14

Holt

IT'S AMAZING the difference sleep can make.

I sleep so hard in Fletcher's guest room that it's Sunday morning when I wake up, and initially, I don't know where I am.

Why I'm here.

Which country *here* is.

What day it is.

My own name.

Once I'm fully aware of the world around me, I find a bottle of ibuprofen and a glass of water on the nightstand, along with a bunch of protein bars, and a banana and two apples arranged in a way that I'm positive was deliberate.

Whether Fletcher was calling me a dick or intentionally reminding me that he can often be one, I'm smiling while I grab one of the apples.

I manage a shower—fucking foot—and pull on clothes

that I find in the closet—a pair of plain gray cotton shorts and a bright red T-shirt that says *Goats are Spoons* with a smiley face and a sunflower on it.

Likely Fletcher's punishment for anyone who spends the night without bringing their own clothes.

The banana-apple dick was definitely about him, I decide.

No texts from Ziggy asking where I am, but I shoot her a quick message anyway, letting her know I'm booking a ride and will be back sometime this morning.

I realize I don't know where she's working right now.

If she's pulling weekend shifts.

If I should've added *hope you're feeling better* to my message.

No, I know that one. I definitely should've told her I hope she's feeling better.

And that she's pretty even when she's sick. And that I'll buy her whatever food she wants if she'll cook more for me. And that I want to know more about her.

Somebody has a crush...

I mentally flip off Caden's voice.

I'm well aware I have a crush. And I'm well aware it's going nowhere.

When I leave the bedroom and circle around to the living room, I almost fall off my crutches.

Bunch of guys from the team are here.

Crew's on the floor, using one of the dogs' beds for a pillow. Porter's next to him, curled on his side with his mouth hanging open, snoring. Tatum's on one end of the couch. Zander's on the other.

Crew cracks one eyelid. "Hey, Captain. Came to love bomb you but you were asleep. Nice boot."

No one else stirs.

Good thing. Not in much of a mood for them to see me getting wet in the eyeballs.

I'll never play overseas again. The days of playing in front of tens of thousands of screaming fans, being recognized in public, needing an agent to work endorsement deals are over.

This—the Pounders—this is where I'll be until I retire from rugby. And it's not a bad place to be.

It's been good the past few years. Even with fewer fans and less public recognition.

These guys are like family. Family with better genes than what runs in my bloodline. The team's nearly fully turned over from the team it was when I first came to Copper Valley to take care of Caden, but these guys were there for me the past year.

They're what I would've missed if I'd made a team in Europe.

I clear my throat and nod to Crew. "Thanks."

"Need anything?"

"Ride home."

He pulls himself up, glances around at everyone else, then nods. "You got it. Wanna wake these guys up before we go?"

I shake my head.

He doesn't question it. Just leaps to his feet, takes the bag with my dirty clothes from me, and leads me to the door.

Dogs don't even wake up.

In the elevator down to the parking garage, I text Fletcher and Goldie a quick thanks for taking care of me yesterday, then pull up my texts with Ziggy again.

Not read yet.

She's probably still sleeping.

Or puking, Caden's voice offers.

Shit.

Should I have offered to stop at the store and pick up more crackers and bubbly water?

"Captain?"

I jerk my head to look at Crew. "Yeah?"

"You okay?"

Am I okay?

Elevator door's open, and I'm standing here staring at my texts like a dumbass.

Clearly, I'm not fully okay. "Jet lag."

He grins. "Yeah, you look it."

He's chatty the whole way back to my place. Talking about mascot ideas for the team, some new guys he's heard we're getting, staff turnover in the office.

"Whoa, dude, you know Miranda?"

I snap out of the lazy *mm-hmm* mode I've been in and look at him.

First rule of playing for the Pounders is that you don't look at the owner's daughter, and I don't like his tone right now.

You don't look at the owner's daughter comes with caveats like *you don't gossip about the owner's daughter* too. "What about her?"

"She introduced me to her *sister* yesterday. I didn't know she had a sister. Did you know she has a sister?"

"Where'd you see Miranda?"

"At the office. Saw her car. We went to check it out. And she's all *this is my sister and she's starting on Monday*. Like, *what?* When did she get a sister?"

I stare at him blankly while something tickles the back of my brain.

This isn't entirely unfamiliar, but it's not right either. I don't know a lot about the Keating family.

Don't need to.

The times I see Roland Keating, it's for public appearances or charity events or postseason banquets. While the guy's in the office and we see him watching practices pretty regularly, for the most part, he stays out of our spaces and we stay out of his.

Unless you're Fletcher.

Fletcher's in there all the time because he thinks it's his second job to sell tickets for the team. So he's often butting in where the rest of us leave it to the office staff to do what they're best at.

Until Miranda joined the office staff with a position working social media, I hadn't actually seen her.

I only vaguely knew she existed—I overheard Keating talking to someone else once about going to visit his daughter at college—but that's about it.

Got the feeling he didn't want the younger knuckleheads on the team—some of them about her age—thinking of trying anything. And then he confirmed it when Coach sat us all down and told us Keating's daughter would be working with us for marketing and publicity and if any of us so much as looked at her wrong, we'd be welcome to go try playing rugby in Antarctica.

"Sorority sister?" I finally say.

"Dunno, man. Maybe. You want breakfast? Get to cheat since you're not playing for a while. There's this pancake place not far from your house. I can watch you eat and pretend I can taste it."

"Already had too many since the season ended?"

"*Yes*," he groans.

"At least you can still work out."

"You can do upper body. Bet we can get you one of those arm cycle machines too. Keep your ol' ticker in good shape."

Yeah.

Yeah, I'm gonna be okay playing for the Pounders.

And they do still want me. Coach said as much. I'm seeing the team doc tomorrow to get a plan for recovery. They think I can be ready before our season starts again early next year.

I'll do everything on my end to prove them right.

Crew pulls up in front of my house and insists on getting my door, then walking me to my own front door too. Plumber's van is here.

Good thing.

A second working bathroom upstairs will be helpful.

"You need anything else, Captain?" he asks. "Food? Something moved around? Someone to change the channel on your TV for you?"

"I got it. But thanks."

He gives me a one-armed hug. "Glad to have you back. I know it would've been awesome for you to go back to a bigger league, but we would've missed you bad, man. Fletcher wouldn't be the same as captain."

I grimace. "No."

"Heh. Gotcha. No way we'd pick Fletcher." He grins and points finger guns at me. "Call me if you need anything. Phone's on all day long for you."

I thank him again and head inside.

Smells like French fries.

Ziggy's been cooking.

I head upstairs—fucking stairs and crutches don't mix— and talk to the plumber. He's making good progress, and none of the pipes need to be replaced like he thought they might.

I leave him to it and debate if I want to take another nap, but I want to see Ziggy.

Make sure for myself she's okay.

Her car's here too, so when I glance in her room and find it empty, I assume she's out back with Jessica.

Stairs.

More damn stairs.

I sit on my ass and go down like a toddler because it's easier and faster, and as I reach the first floor, I hear voices.

No, just one voice.

Ziggy's voice.

I swing myself into the kitchen.

It's empty, but her voice is louder. "There's something I need to tell you."

The door to the porch is cracked. I angle closer, looking for her companion, and realize she doesn't have one. She's sitting in one of the chairs at the iron bistro table under the ceiling fan, talking on the phone.

Jessica's not on the porch.

Hell-beast is probably under it.

"Abby Nora and I broke up," Ziggy says.

And everything stops.

For me, anyway.

It's the tone of her voice.

The sadness. The regret.

The grief.

Shiiiiiiiitttt.

I'm not the only person in this house who's lost someone, it seems.

And fuck me if that doesn't make me want to help her even more.

15

Ziggy

I AM SUCH A CHICKEN.

I woke up to a text from Mom asking if I wanted to go with her to deliver a present to Abby Nora. That's when I should've asked her to meet me somewhere for breakfast so we could talk.

Instead, I've spent the past two hours making myself food, doing the dishes, letting the plumber in, scrubbing the kitchen, dusting and vacuuming the living room, taking care of Jessica, sketching out a menu plan for the next week, and starting a grocery list.

But I couldn't delay it anymore when Mom called as I was straightening the covered porch.

I could for a while.

I distracted her by asking how the dogs were, if she'd seen Miranda recently, if she and Dad went to this sports charity auction thing I read about, but now she's forcing my hand.

"Did you see my text?" she says. "I have a baby gift for Abby Nora and I thought you'd like to go with me when I take it over."

So now here I am, doing this the cowardly way.

Over the phone so I won't have to look at her and see the disappointment and confusion in her face while all of the best curse words I know in both Italian and Spanish roll through my head.

I will always support you no matter what, I silently tell my own little peanut. "Abby Nora and I broke up."

There's a beat of silence on the other end of the phone.

Then— "Ziggy. No. What does that even mean?"

"It means *we broke up*. Our relationship is over. She doesn't—" *Dammit.* Dammit, I didn't want to cry. I suck in a deep breath and force the lump back down out of my throat. "She doesn't like me anymore."

"She doesn't—did she say that?"

"She very much said that."

"To your face?"

"At her baby shower. She didn't get the memo that one of our other friends had me on video call so I could be there virtually."

"And you're sure—"

"Mom. There was *zero* mistaking what she said. It was very, *very* clear."

"What did she say?"

"I don't want to repeat it in front of the baby."

"Oh, honey. Maybe you two can patch things up."

I drop my head into one of my hands and squeeze my eyes shut. "I'll forgive a lot of things for the people I love, but that doesn't mean I need to stay in a relationship with them when they clearly don't want me."

"Sweetheart, Abby Nora wants you. She does. It was probably pregnancy hormones."

"She called me a stuck-up cunt who thinks she's better than everyone else."

Silence rings loudly in my ears.

Where's Jessica? Why doesn't she need something right now?

Would it be bad if I went into the kitchen and knocked something off the counter and blamed the dog and said I have to go?

"Maybe you misheard—" Mom starts.

"I didn't mishear anything."

"But you're best friends."

I had the flu once while I was recovering from a pulled back muscle after doing something stupid in gym class late in high school. It was like morning sickness, but with a fever and severe back pain every time I threw up.

This is worse.

And not only because Abby Nora won't be coming over after school to tell me what all I missed and make me smile while I'm recovering.

"Were, Mom. We *were*. And we're not anymore."

"But why would she say something like that about you?"

A familiar dull ache creeps up from the base of my skull, and my belly gives a warning groan as it starts to twist up again. "I don't know. She was my best friend for over half my life, and she's not anymore, and I can ask *why* all I want, but it won't change what *is*."

"Maybe if you reached out to her—"

"Or maybe when someone calls you a cunt in a roomful of people, it's on her to reach out if she wants to be friends."

"Does she even know you're home?"

"Yes."

"But she just had a baby. I'm sure she's been busy."

"She's known I'm home for weeks. Or at least, she knew I was home a few weeks ago. I ran into her at the club. In the bathroom. She pretended everything was fine, but I know she knows I overheard what she said. It's over, Mom."

"Ziggy. Oh, my sweet girl. Are you okay?"

And that's what does it. That's what finally makes my eyes hot and puts a lump in my throat. "No."

"Why didn't you tell me sooner?"

"Because it makes me want to puke and I'm tired of puking."

"I'm going to talk to her mother—"

"*No.* Please don't. Please. Don't. I don't want anyone to fix this. I just want to grieve and move on."

"Should I come over?"

"No. I'm okay. Ish. Okay-ish."

"Miranda and I can be there with *The Princess Bride* in thirty minutes."

I draw a deep breath and rub my still-twisted belly. "Rain check. I need to get groceries and get ready for my big day tomorrow. And I promised Jessica we'd go to a dog park."

"I worry about you."

"I'm okay." I'm not. Not yet. But I will be. "Promise. I just—"

"Need some new friends. You'll love the staff at Dad's office. They're so nice. And you'll get to see Miranda every day too. Before you know it, you'll have forgotten Abby Nora ever existed."

I blink quickly.

I don't want to forget.

Some of my best memories will always be with her.

But I could do with not feeling guilt and shame and embarrassment and stupidity and anger and pain every time I think about what we were and what we'll never be again.

"I'm looking forward to it," I lie.

I make up an excuse about Jessica needing something, and I get off the phone without crying.

Barely—it counts as not crying if the tears haven't actually fallen and you're trying to convince your eyeballs to suck them back in, right?

If so, then I make it without crying.

Feels like a miracle these days.

But then—

Clomp. Clomp. Clomp.

I jerk straight and turn around.

Holt's come back.

With a cloth bag hanging off one wrist while he uses his crutches to join me on the porch.

I swipe at my eyes because that's what it takes for getting rid of the reaction they're having to the pollen count.

Which is the story I'm giving him if he asks.

He sets the bag on the table in front of me, then takes a seat and pulls another chair over to prop his leg up.

I peek in the bag.

More crackers and seltzer water.

Then I do a double take at his shirt.

Goats are Spoons.

What...?

"My friends are the kind who give you weird-ass clothes when you pass out at their house and wake up and realize you haven't showered in three days," he says.

I clear my throat as I help myself to the crackers.

He twists the lid off of a seltzer water and sets it in front of me. Same as yesterday.

"Jet lag?" I ask.

"Jet lag, career-altering injury, pickpocket...yeah. Rough week. What's your excuse for looking like shit?"

There's zero heat in his words.

If anything, there's too much sympathy. "You heard that whole phone call, didn't you?"

"Enough of it."

He doesn't apologize for listening in.

And I don't care.

"Close friend, I gather?" he asks.

"Best friend. Since I was thirteen."

"But not anymore."

I shake my head.

He's staring out into the yard. I don't think he's looking for Jessica to make sure I'm taking good care of her. I don't think he's embarrassed to look at me either.

I think he's just *being*.

It's oddly comforting. Like I have permission to just *be* too.

I crunch on a cracker. Sip the fizzy water.

My stomach is settling down.

I slide another look at Holt.

He's good at this caretaker thing.

I shouldn't be surprised. This is the same guy who told me his job was to watch everyone and know where they all were at once so he could prevent what happened the one night we worked together. The same guy that the neighbors tell me waters their flowers and mows their lawns when he notices a need.

The same guy who offered a stranger a place to stay after she got fired from what would've been a really great job.

"Remember Vitamin Guy?" I say.

His dark brown eyes meet mine. "Who?"

"Vitamin Guy. That night we worked together. The one who trapped me by the bathrooms to try to convince me to buy his vitamins?"

He frowns. "No."

"For real? You don't remember the guy I threw up on at the aquarium?"

He stares at me for a long moment, and then it happens.

One corner of his mouth tips up in a sly grin.

"*Oh my god*, you—*argh*." I throw a cracker at him, call him a bastard in Italian, and then something even worse happens.

He grins at me.

Full-on smiles so broadly that his entire face lights up with mischief and amusement, and someone please protect me from myself.

He's *hot*.

Sexy hot.

Gorgeous hot.

Plus, *he* apologized for being a bear yesterday. Then came back and took care of me while I was sick.

And here he is, showing up again with exactly what I need to calm my stomach.

I need to move.

"What about Vitamin Guy?" he asks.

Vitamin Guy.

Who's Vitamin Guy?

What are we talking about?

"The guy you threw up on the night we met?" Holt prompts.

My brain is still riding the *holy shit, he's hot* train, but it finally pulls into *we can be normal* station. "He's my former best friend's brother-in-law. I danced with him at her wedding—which was *not* enjoyable, by the way—and he didn't remember who I was. When I puked on him, I mean. He didn't remember me from the wedding. Or any of the other times we met."

Holt straightens, the smile dropping off of his face.

The fuck?

Why is Mr. Growly-Face even hotter right now than Mr. Smile?

"Why wasn't it enjoyable?" he says. "Did he do something? Isn't he married? I swear to fuck, he was wearing a wedding ring."

This is pregnancy hormones. I've switched from first-trimester morning sickness to second-trimester horniness. This is the only explanation.

Focus, Ziggy.

I stuff a cracker in my mouth and nearly choke on it, then follow it with too big of a gulp of seltzer water and almost choke on that too.

All while Holt's watching me like I'm the whole room he has to guard.

Eli Harrison. Think about Eli Harrison.

I clear my throat. "Yes, he's married. Yes, he cheats on her. At least, that's the rumor. He told me he asked me to dance out of pity since no one else was asking, and he talked about his fantasy football leagues the whole time."

"Leagues?"

"He always has a side hustle. Fantasy football was that year's vitamins."

"And that's it? That's the only reason it sucked?"

Swoon. He wants to slay dragons for me. "He also smelled like burnt cheese."

"Like burnt cheddar? Or more like a burnt bleu cheese?"

Does he for real know the difference? "Like burnt ricotta in a lasagna."

"How do you burn ricotta?"

"That's a question I wish I didn't know the answer to. How do you burn bleu cheese?"

"Innate natural talent in the kitchen."

I'm smiling.

Am I smiling too big? Am I making a complete fool of myself? Does he suspect I suddenly think he's hot?

I grab another cracker, but I don't eat it, because I don't need to choke again. "Do you have any allergies?"

"Allergies?"

"To food. I started a menu for the week, but I can change it if you're allergic to anything. Or if you don't like anything. Or I don't have to cook. We can each feed ourselves if you want. Takeout or whatever. I'm flexible. I start a new nine-to-five tomorrow, so I can cook. Breakfasts. Dinners. Meals. Like we talked about."

"No allergies."

It's like getting an *ok* back in text.

I'm babbling. "Great. I'll text it to you."

"I don't like burnt cheese."

I smile again. Probably too big. "The smell of it would probably make me puke, so I promise not to make burnt cheese."

Gosh, Ziggy, why are you doing this solo parenting thing and not dating at all?

Well, Mom, it's because I'm an embarrassment to womankind when it comes to carrying on a normal conversation with a man.

But Holt doesn't seem turned off by my constant mention of bodily fluids.

Doesn't seem turned on by it either.

I desperately need to end this conversation and go somewhere else.

"Is it normal to be this sick for this long?" he asks. "With the baby?"

"Yes. And I'm mostly better. Except for when I'm stressed."

"Because some asshole scares the shit out of you in the middle of the night."

I shake my head, nod, then shake it again. "No. I mean, yes, but that was little. Honestly not as bad as finding out my former BFF had her baby when my mother texted me to ask why I didn't tell her first, and then realizing I can't put off telling my mom that we're not friends anymore."

He studies me like he doesn't believe me.

"I would've been throwing up yesterday morning regardless of what did or didn't happen the night before."

Jessica trots up the stairs and growls at Holt through the screen door.

"You'd think I didn't feed her and walk her and buy her seven different doggy beds," he mutters.

"Clearly, she needs eight. Plus a play set in the backyard." I get up and let her into the porch.

She trots to Holt, turns her back on him, and aims her butt like she's farting at him.

"*Jessica*," I chide.

She gives me the *what? He deserves it* look.

"He pays for your food," I point out.

She snorts.

"I must've murdered dogs in a former life," Holt mutters.

"It's not you—" I start, but the plumber interrupts me.

"Mr. Webster? I gotta run out and pick up a part. Should have everything installed by the end of the day though. You got a preference on grout color?"

Holt rises, giving me a clear view of his gray cotton shorts, and *fuck.*

Look away, Ziggy. Look. Away.

He's not wearing underwear.

I swear, he's not wearing underwear, and the movement under his shorts is—

Stop stop stop, Ziggy.

Jessica snarls at the plumber, and I barely grab her collar in time before she takes off running at him.

There's a solid reason the dog stays outside while the plumber's here.

"Doggie park?" I say to her.

She's still growling at the men.

"Your dog doesn't much like me," the plumber says to Holt, whose butt cheeks are perfectly displayed by the stretch of his shorts.

Good god.

The man's legs are thick as tree trunks and his ass—

STOP IT, ZIGGY.

It doesn't matter who sculpted his ass or how broad his shoulders are or that he's been incredibly kind about me puking nearly every time I see him.

It matters that he's giving me a place to stay for a few more weeks.

I don't want to mess that up.

We're in a good place today.

I won't let my hormones complicate this.

16

Holt

I'M UP EARLY MONDAY.

No specific reason for it—except possibly hearing the
water start in Ziggy's room, then the podcast she likes to
listen to in Spanish start right after, the voices too low for
me to make out any words.

My room.

She's in my room.

I told her to take it because I knew she'd be more
comfortable with the en-suite room, and I'm still not ready
to let anyone else move into Caden's room.

Unusual to have two en-suites, a third full bathroom, and
a powder room for guests in a house this old, but some
forward-thinker in the seventies gutted the interior to make
sure no one ever wanted for a place to piss or wash their
hands.

Caden said it was one of his favorite things about the house.

You're never more than a single room from a bathroom.

My brother was fascinatingly practical in unexpected ways.

I swing myself out of bed and crutch to the hall bath. Ziggy's door is cracked, and Jessica's staring at me when I leave the bathroom.

"You wanna go out?" I ask her.

She snorts on the door, turns, and points her ass at me. *You are mud, human, and I am too dignified to reply to you.*

"You're welcome for giving you a friend you like," I mutter back.

She scratches the floor like she's flinging poop in my direction.

I make my way downstairs and into the kitchen. Ziggy said she'd cook, but I don't need to be fully dependent on her for everything. I can do some things.

Like make coffee.

Probably.

Except the coffee maker is under the cabinet by the oven, and the coffee is stored in a lower cabinet on the other side of the fridge.

Because that's how Caden had it, and it was never a problem before.

Good for you to solve problems this early in the morning, I hear him say.

I flip him off in my head and hear him laugh.

Never mocking.

Always *life is fun, stop making mountains out of molehills. This won't matter in an hour, much less in ten years.*

He's right.

Won't matter if I hop on one leg across the kitchen and back so that I can carry the coffee over to the maker.

I open the streaming app on my phone and turn on my favorite rock station, then pause it.

Does Ziggy like rock?

Is she more of a Waverly Sweet or Levi Wilson fan?

Does she listen to French rock? Not only did I notice her foreign podcast in the car the other day, I also heard her doing a language app before bed last night. She could've picked up some favorite artists in Europe the past few years, but I couldn't begin to guess who she might like. I don't even know who exists.

Maybe classic something is better. Aren't babies supposed to listen to classical music in the womb to get smarter? Silas was babbling about that being why his daughter can already read small words before starting kindergarten this coming school year.

But does Ziggy's baby already have ears?

I'm bent over my phone, researching when babies can hear while in utero, when I hear Jessica's tags jingling on her collar and the normal *thump thump thump* of her thick little body navigating the stairs.

Fuck it.

I close my browser, switch back to the streaming app, and put on Waverly Sweet.

Then I turn it down nearly all the way and shove my phone out of reach so I can say it started playing on its own if she thinks it's odd or unusual.

Fuck me.

I'm being odd and unusual.

Jessica trots into the kitchen. I straighten and hop in a

circle on one foot so I'm leaning against the counter instead of hunching over it.

"Morning," I say to Ziggy.

Her hair's a slightly damp mass of curls hanging all over her shoulders, and she's in a patterned, colorful blouse and fancy pants that I honestly don't know the color of. They're not tan. Not gray. Is that mauve? Is that what mauve is?

And you're finishing my house. This is a disaster, I hear Caden say.

I know the basic rainbow.

He knew paint chips and could identify forty-three different shades of yellow. When I told Ziggy that Caden's designer picked stuff, I was lying.

He had a strong hand in it himself.

It's just easier to distance myself sometimes so it hurts less that he's gone.

She smiles at me, and my heart thumps hard.

"Morning," she says. "I didn't know if you'd be up. If you don't want to get up so early, I can just leave something to be reheated in the fridge. In a bag. I know that's easier to carry with the crutches. Yes, Jessica, I'm coming. I know. *I know.* Here."

She disappears onto the porch, then returns a moment later without the dog.

And I suddenly have no idea what to say to this woman.

I had a list before I went to sleep last night.

First day, huh?

When did you know you wanted to be a chef?

You don't have to go to the store. I'll order through the app.

I don't want to say any of that.

"You a morning person?" I finally blurt.

"Absolutely not," she replies far more cheerfully than any not-morning person should.

I don't know if I'm supposed to smile at that or call her on the contradiction.

Not that she's strange.

She's anything but strange.

She's fucking gorgeous. And nice. And in a tough spot.

"I'm faking it until I make it," she says.

"Oh. Coffee?"

Her face screws up into a tight ball of wrinkled angst. "I wish."

"Should be some in that cabinet. Saw it yesterday. Unless Jessica ate all of it overnight."

"No, it's there. It's just—I'm supposed to limit how much caffeine I have, and I am definitely having a cup at the office this morning. They have an espresso machine. It's ridiculously over-the-top. But also, if it's there, I should use it, right? So I can't have coffee here too. I'd spend the morning talking too fast and making too many trips to the bathroom and being paranoid that I'm getting the baby addicted."

Ah, shit.

First day jitters.

"We can get decaf."

The way she looks at me like I've just solved the world's biggest problem—it makes my dick twitch.

Knock it off, asshole, I tell myself. *She's out of our league.*

And also freaking gorgeous. And barefoot with rainbow toenails. Each one a different color.

"Food," she blurts. "I need to make you breakfast. How do you like your eggs? Do eggs sound okay? I'm having potatoes —they settle and they're delicious, okay?—and I can make you coffee. I'll move the beans closer to the machine before I go. If I have time. Oh my god, I want a glass of wine. Why am I nervous? It's a freaking favor job. It's not a real job. Maybe that's why I'm nervous. Everyone knows it's a favor job. Can't get fired when—never mind. I'll do a good job. At least it's with food. I—"

"Ziggy."

She blinks at me. Her cheeks go splotchy pink.

Swear to fuck, if I wasn't on crutches, I'd be pulling this woman into a hug and telling her she'll do great.

While I sniff her hair.

Is that why she always smells like honey? Is it her hair?

I think it's her hair.

The whole kitchen is starting to smell like honey.

Subtle vanilla honey.

"Food," she says again. This time, she turns and squats to grab the coffee beans from the cabinet by the fridge. "Go sit. No reason to be on your leg right now. Do you want coffee? You have coffee. So I assume—"

This time, she cuts herself off with a sigh. "I'm done babbling. Would you like coffee?"

"I can get it later."

"It's no problem. I know how to make coffee."

"You want to smell it?"

"*Yes.*"

The way I want to hear her say that while she's naked and riding—

Knock. It. Off. Pervert.

I swallow hard, then crutch around the island and get out of her way, partially so she doesn't see my dick lifting my sleep shorts. "Okay. Then yeah. Coffee. Sounds good. Thanks."

Caden got me hooked on fresh-ground beans. Ziggy

pours beans into the grinder and hits the button, and the motor drowns out every other sound while she grabs a bright red tea kettle off the stovetop and fills it with water.

I blink.

I don't have a teakettle.

Didn't notice that when I got home.

I should've.

Stovetop's on the island. Middle of the kitchen. Can't walk in here without seeing it.

But it *was* there.

The grinder halts, and all that's left is the sound of Waverly Sweet crooning out a love song.

One of those *I didn't know it was you until you were gone* ballads.

Ziggy sets the kettle on the stove and lights the burner beneath it. "How do you—*oh my god*, are you a Waverly Sweet fan too? You know she lives here part of the year now? Married a local baseball player? That guy on the Fireballs who was really good when the team sucked before they got new owners and turned everything around? *My parents met her.* They were at this thing where she was, and *they met her*, and I basically will never forgive them now for not calling me when it happened. Anyway. How do you like your eggs again? Or did you want something else?"

"I know her husband," I say.

Ziggy's eyes go comically round. "Shut up."

I shrug. "Athletes network. Good dude. Supports the smaller teams around the city."

He came out to celebrate when we won the championship last year. Commiserated with us when we got knocked out of the playoffs this year.

Ziggy eyes me, and I find myself smiling broadly at the silent question radiating off her body.

I shake my head. "I don't know him well enough to ask him to come over with his wife."

"Well, just tell me you're useless up front next time."

I like her, I hear Caden say.

She claps a hand over her mouth. "Sorry. That was rude."

"That was fucking hilarious."

"It was rude," she insists.

"It was like having my brother back giving me shit. You're good."

That gets me a look.

"Not that you look anything like him. Very different. He had curly hair, but he kept it short. Wore fancy clothes too. Worked an office job. Liked wine. Hooked up with random men and regretted it later. Wait. Are you my brother?"

Fuuuuck.

Should not have said that about regretting random hookups.

But also, good job, me.

Pursuing a crush on my temporary housemate is a bad idea.

She has enough going on.

Making her actively dislike me without being an outright dick is the best way forward.

But when she finally stops gaping at me and doubles over laughing—legit, she's holding on to the edge of the island as she bends over, wheezing—something loosens in my chest.

Something that feels like all of the grief that's been holding my heart back from fully beating lets go, and I feel a solid *thump thump thump* against my breastbone that hasn't been the same since Caden passed away.

House needs laughter, dummy, he whispers in my head. *Welcome back to living here.*

The teakettle whistles. Ziggy straightens, still giggling, her cheeks completely and fully red now, her blue eyes dancing as she carries the kettle to the other counter.

She's not using the coffee machine.

Instead, she's doing that pour-over thing Caden always did too.

I didn't do it for myself because it was too much effort. I did it for him anytime he wanted coffee but wasn't up for making it himself, especially in those last months, but I don't do it for myself.

Reminded me too much of him.

But now—it's nice.

Weird to be on this side of it, having someone else do it for me.

But the memory doesn't tighten my chest again.

It just lives there, existing, next to my still-beating heart.

Right next to the gratitude that someone's here taking care of me the way I always try to take care of everyone else.

Making me feel far less alone than I've been since Caden died.

"My sister is a lot younger than I am," Ziggy says. "We weren't really close while she was growing up. But you were tight with your brother?"

"Best friends," I confirm.

"I'd give you my best friend as a substitute, but it turns out she's a dick."

She flashes me the tiniest hint of a villain smile, and it makes my balls tighten.

"You don't know what happened?" I ask. "Why you're not friends anymore?"

178

If you looked up *exasperation* in the dictionary, you'd find the face she's making now. "Best I can tell, I just wasn't around enough, and when I was, I talked too much about enjoying my life? I shipped wine from Italy for her wedding. I saved up all of my credits that the cruise line gave us so that she could have a week-long bachelorette party with a dozen of her friends at sea in the Med. I thought I was sharing my life with her, but I suppose...it looked like I was showing off? I don't know. Best guess? I probably insulted her mother-in-law or didn't call often enough or something. Can you *please* tell me how you like your eggs?"

That's shitty. All of it. "Cooked."

Hello, stern librarian look.

Hello, painful hard-on.

"Scrambled," I finally say. "I liked how you made them Saturday too, but that seems like a lot of work for a Monday morning."

She delivers coffee to me, then moves around the kitchen, pulling things out of the fridge and prepping breakfast.

"Do you have other friends around town still?" I ask her as she cracks eggs one-handed into a bowl.

"I could call a few people, but I don't know who knows what happened with Abby Nora and who doesn't and who'd take sides and it's all just—it's too much work. Too many mind games. None of the people who would've been at the baby shower have reached out since then, and it's not like I kept in touch with other people from high school who wouldn't think it was odd that I randomly wanted to catch up after not talking for over ten years."

"Huh."

"What about you? Where did you grow up? Do you keep in touch with them?"

I shake my head.

"You didn't grow up?"

"Nebraska," I tell her. "Shitty parents. Not interested in ever going back."

I get the normal sharp glance, but she doesn't ask the question that usually goes with it. *They're still alive?*

Beats the fuck out of me if they are or they aren't.

Don't really care.

Just glad I'm not there anymore.

I finally sip my coffee, and holy hell.

Did she sprinkle magic in this?

"Oh, I forgot to ask if you want anything in it," she says.

I shake my head and sip it again.

Fuck me. "We could get married if you need insurance for the baby. That thing that happens in TV shows. We could do that."

I get one long, slow blink, and then she cracks up again. "Stop being funny before I've had *my* coffee," she says.

"You've never had someone propose to you for your culinary prowess before?"

"No."

"Why not?"

"Because I'm a workaholic wine connoisseur who doesn't have time to date and never cooks for people."

"Never?"

"No reason to. We had fantastic chefs on the ship, and I loved my job, which was pairing the wines with the food, not making the food, and my job was also my life. So no, I never cook for people."

Except me.

She's cooking for me.

And making me coffee.

And marrying her would be a terrible idea.

I could fall for this woman. I could fall so hard for this woman.

What do they call them on that show Caden liked?

Marriage of convenience.

There would be nothing convenient about the boner situation if I was serious about marrying her to give her health insurance and then keeping her here to cook for me.

But it's the first time in a couple years that anything remotely romantic has crossed my mind.

It's like Ziggy Barnes is good for me.

She's helping me remember that the world exists beyond rugby and grief.

"Don't smirk like that," she says. "I'm only cooking for you because you're saving me from Naked Tuesdays."

Yep.

My cock is officially dead from a case of over-bonering.

That's what thinking about Ziggy naked all day on any given Tuesday is doing for me.

"Happy to be of service," I say.

I think.

There's a definite lack of blood flow to my thinking brain happening right now. And that's before she slides a pat of butter into a hot skillet, making the entire kitchen smell like buttery heaven now too.

She eyes me, then cracks up again. "You're more trouble than I thought you'd be."

If I'm half as good for her recovery from her friend breakup as she's been for me feeling somewhat normal in my own house again…

"You're welcome."

17

Ziggy

By WEDNESDAY NIGHT, I'm so flipping tired I could fall asleep on a bed of rocks.

You wouldn't think a desk job was so demanding, but being *on* around new people all day has me drained.

I used to do this all day, often using language skills where I have proficiency but still had to concentrate to get it right, and yet now, simply smiling for strangers wears me out.

Maybe it's because I was never considering that any one of those strangers could be my new best friend. I could be my professional best without wondering if I was saying something that would mark me off the list of consideration for being worthy of a lunch date.

That isn't the case in the Pounders' home office, where I have to overcome both being the owner's daughter and also not knowing anything about rugby or the team.

Maybe this is why Abby Nora doesn't consider me a

friend anymore. Maybe I didn't pay enough attention to the things that mattered to her, even when I thought I was.

Dad bought the team five years ago, and I know basically nothing about it. I can defend myself all I want with excuses about Dad having interests in various businesses all over Copper Valley and it being hard to keep up sometimes, but I didn't make an effort either.

It's a sports team.

This is theoretically fun.

Though walking around painters and other contractors who are putting a shiny new finish on the office isn't the greatest.

The paint fumes are annoying me and the baby.

And now I'm the persnickety spoiled pity hire who's moaning to herself about the working conditions.

I sigh and drop my head to my steering wheel as soon as I put my little SUV in park in the driveway next to Holt's Jeep.

Time to get inside.

Let Jessica out if Holt hasn't.

Make dinner.

I whimper.

I'm so freaking tired that I don't even have the energy to reply to a quick text from Francesca. Maybe I can get a thirty-minute nap in before dinner.

Maybe—

A knock at my window makes me shriek in surprise.

I look up, expecting to see Holt, imagining him frowning at me like he's caught me eating another rotisserie chicken in another car, but it's Mrs. Massery from across the street.

I kill the engine and pop open the door. "Afternoon, Mrs. Massery. How are you today?"

"Is Holt home?" the older white woman asks. She's in the cutest flowery housedress, and her white hair is in curlers.

But it's the cake dish in her hands that truly catches my attention.

Swear it's crystal, and the cake inside is covered in white frosting and coated in coconut.

I feel like I'm in another era anytime I see her, but even more so when she shows up with a crystal cake dish.

"If he's not, he likely will be soon," I tell her. "I'm not sure what his schedule was today."

The neighbors all know he's home. They've commented to me about it when I've taken Jessica out on her nightly walks.

I don't know how the hell I'll find the energy for it tonight, but somehow, I will.

Maybe food will help.

Food and a nap.

"It was his birthday last week. I made him a cake. Can you make sure he gets this?"

I step the rest of the way out of my car, grab my bag, and fling it over my shoulder. It was his birthday?

And he didn't tell me?

Right. Of course he didn't tell me. We were barely texting then. And he celebrated his birthday by breaking his foot.

Who'd want to talk about that?

And why does it make me feel like an even shittier friend, even though I couldn't have possibly known it was his birthday?

"I'll make sure he gets this," I tell Mrs. Massery.

"Don't go eating it before he gets a piece."

"I would never."

"It's for his birthday. You know this is his first birthday since his brother passed. That's a hard birthday."

"I promise I'll tell him you made it with extra love, and I won't take a single piece unless he insists."

"Don't let Jessica have any either."

"Pretty sure cake's not good for dogs."

"This is my world-famous coconut cream cake. You make sure he knows that, okay? You tell him it won a gold ribbon at the Iowa State Fair in 1996. And you tell him I don't make one for just anyone. Not with my arthritis the way it is."

"I will tell him all of that."

"There's no rush on getting the dish back to me. But I do need it by the first of September. Bernie's birthday is in September, and if he lives long enough to have that birthday, I'll make him one too. People deserve a good cake on what might be their last birthday. Even if I've made him a last birthday cake for five years straight now."

The neighbors here are endlessly entertaining on top of being kind.

I like it.

And liking it here is making looking for a house of my own even harder. If a house went up for sale in this neighborhood, and it was solid and didn't need too much work, I'd jump on it in a heartbeat.

The issue is that most of the houses around here are in need of renovation, and the paint fumes at work this week have taught me that I cannot consider living like that for the rest of my pregnancy. A day or two here and there for the bathroom renovations in Holt's house have been fine—small rooms, good ventilation, little smell.

A whole house wouldn't be the same.

Plus, my parents would insist on paying for it, and I'm

struggling enough with how much help I'm taking from them right now.

I take the cake from Mrs. Massery and head inside after promising her once again to take good care of her crystal dish and to let only Holt eat the cake unless he insists on sharing.

I don't tell her coconut sounds like it would make me puke right now.

But also, if Holt's birthday was last week, I should make something extra nice for dinner.

Something next-level. I'd planned chicken Alfredo, but don't birthdays call for steak?

Except I'm so damn tired, and we don't have steak. I'd have to go to the store.

I might be whimpering to myself as I push past the front door, balancing the cake and my bag and my own whininess.

Holt's home.

He's passed out on the couch, his booted leg propped up and his head tipped back in a pile of throw pillows. He's wearing black athletic shorts that show off his muscular legs and a Copper Valley University T-shirt that seems to be stretched as far as the fabric will go over his broad chest as it rises and falls. Mouth ajar, he's snoring the slightest bit.

It's freaking adorable.

I get three steps in before the floor creaks, and he jolts awake, flinging himself upright with wild, confused eyes scanning the room until they land on me.

The softest smile curves his lips, and his eyes take on a glow.

And for one long heartbeat, I feel appreciated.

Welcome.

Loved.

Get a grip, Ziggy.

He swipes a hand over his face, and when he pulls it away, all I see is a weary man. "Hey. You're back. What's with the cake?"

"Mrs. Massery says happy birthday. Hope you like coconut cream."

The grimace he grimaces says he does not, in fact, like coconut cream. "Yeah," he lies. "My favorite."

I'm too tired to do anything but stare blankly at him.

"That shitty parent thing?" he says. "It was my father's favorite. I don't—"

"I'll take it to work tomorrow. The savages will eat it."

His shoulders sag. "Thank you. Wait. You work with savages?"

"Have you ever worked in an office?"

He shakes his head.

"Honestly, me neither. But I have never seen a dash to the breakroom for free donuts like I witnessed this morning. You'd think they'd never seen fried dough before."

He tilts his head. "You okay? You look tired."

"Says the man who was snoring a minute ago..."

"Sorry. I know. Don't tell a woman she looks tired."

"No, you're right." I set the cake on an end table and collapse into the easy chair next to the sofa, then indulge in lifting the footrest.

Just for a minute. "Why is sitting on your ass for eight hours a day so exhausting?"

"Because office jobs suck."

I want to laugh at that, but my eyes are sliding closed.

So.

Freaking.

Tired.

I'm grateful to have a job. I'm grateful that Dad managed to assign me something that makes me feel partially useful. I'm getting to plan an awards banquet for the team. That's better than deciding where to order takeout when the business development and marketing guy's hosting potential sponsors, which I've also been put in charge of.

And next week, I'm supposed to cater a lunch that will include at least one of the players.

Apparently Dad scored a coup getting some huge star from the UK who wants to build American rugby up enough to outsell American soccer tickets. The Fletcher guy that Miranda mentioned last weekend. She says we're allowed to talk to him now because he's in a very serious relationship with a woman that the entire office staff loves so much that he'd get fired if he ever broke up with her.

No matter what it means for the team.

Sort of like Dad almost fired him for being a dick to Miranda once last year.

As much as I'd rather not be taking a pity job so that I can have a baby, I'm glad that Dad makes such an effort to take care of the women in his circles.

Me included.

"Where's Jessica?" I mutter to Holt.

"Afternoon nap on the porch, I think. I'll go check on her."

"I can get up."

"I can open a door. I've been off my feet all day."

I should argue, but I don't want to. "'Kay," I murmur. "I'll make dinner. Just a minute."

"Uh-huh," he says.

Uh-huh.

That's a funny word.

Who made that a word? Is it a leftover from caveman times? It feels so primitive. Just grunts that tell you so much.

Especially when it's a sarcastic uh-huh.

Holt's sarcastic. But not in a mean way. He's funny.

He told me about his neighbors having bubble races yesterday.

Wait.

That's not right.

Why are his neighbors floating on bubbles and speaking Spanish and riding into the ship's wine cellar?

Oh.

Right.

Because I'm dreaming.

This chair is damn comfortable.

I make the executive decision to let myself dream for just five minutes.

And at the end of those five minutes, I open my eyes and realize it's dark outside.

It shouldn't be this dark this early. Not halfway through summer.

Holt's at the door.

I stretch, and I realize I've slept harder than I thought. There's a light blanket covering me, and the noise at my feet is Jessica.

She's breathing heavy like she sometimes does. But she's not snorting at Holt, who's closing the front door now, plastic takeout bags dangling from his fingers as he uses his crutches to pivot and face me.

"You awake, or are your eyes just open?" he asks.

"I didn't make dinner," I blurt. "It's your birthday."

"Had a birthday dinner in Spain last week," he replies. "And fried chicken sounded good. Got mashed potatoes and

fries and potato casserole and tater tots and rosemary potatoes too. Wasn't sure which potato you'd be in the mood for."

He covered me with a blanket.

He took care of the dog.

He ordered us dinner.

And he ordered me potatoes.

Every kind of potato.

My eyes get hot.

I haven't even asked him what position he plays on his
lacrosse team, and he's ordering me potatoes.

"Who has that many potatoes?"

"Strip mall not far from here. Deli and a diner next to
each other. One has the best sweet tea. The other has the best
fried chicken. I'm not telling which. You hungry? I can put it
in the fridge if not."

My belly grumbles.

But not like it has been.

This is true, legitimate, actual hunger pangs.

Just like it's true, legitimate, actual warmth flooding my
heart at the simple kindness of having someone else order
me potatoes for dinner while I napped.

"I'm hungry." I stretch, reaching as far as I can with my
fingers and my toes, arching my back too. "What time is it?
How long was I asleep?"

His lips twitch like he's trying to hold back a smile. "It's
almost nine."

"*Oh my god.*"

"I need to know about Bernie and Mrs. Massery and the
bubble races, by the way."

So I was out cold.

I only talk in my sleep when I'm sleeping *hard*.

"Food's getting cold. Can't talk while I'm hungry," I say.

He grins at me and heads to the kitchen, bags swinging with his crutches.

I swipe at my eyes.

I can blame sleep. Say it's a yawn.

But really, it's just a kind gesture from a guy who looks good in athletic shorts and who's nicer and nicer by the day.

I legit don't know how it's possible he doesn't have a girlfriend.

Unless he doesn't want one.

That would make sense.

And he doesn't want a pregnant one, idiot, I remind myself.

He's just being nice.

He's one of the nice guys in the world.

But he's not my guy.

No matter how much I'm starting to enjoy everything about him.

18

Holt

WE'RE ONLY A WEEK IN, but this thing with Ziggy is working out well so far.

I pay for groceries. She cooks. I eat what she cooks. She makes herself potatoes.

She goes to work.

Fletcher picks me up to go see the team doc and physical therapy staff and sometimes some of our other teammates.

I nap.

Monday, Ziggy took Jessica to her parents' house to play with their dogs before going to work.

The rest of the days, Jessica tolerates me being the person who takes care of her until Ziggy comes home and cooks, then falls asleep on the couch while watching some period piece with fancy costumes and British accents and a snarky narrator.

Most nights.

Apparently on Wednesdays, she falls asleep *before* dinner. We'll have to see if she does the same next Wednesday.

Fine by me. She didn't think I was a creep for watching her sleep, and she was more grateful than she should've been that I could do something as simple as ordering dinner for us.

My bathroom gets finished.

And then I crutch into the kitchen Friday morning and find her eating mashed potatoes while looking at apartments on her phone.

Apartments.

"No house?" I ask.

She gets up from the table and pulls eggs, cheese and butter from the fridge. "If I like it, it needs too much work. If my mother likes it, it's too expensive. If we both like it, the owner decides last minute to pull it off the market instead of taking my offer. So looking for something I can get month-to-month makes sense."

"You can stay longer." The words leave my mouth before I realize I've opened it.

She pauses with her arms full of ingredients, hope flashing over her face so briefly that I think I'm imagining it.

Wanting it.

"You're nice. I'm nice. You're gone most of the day. I still can't get around easily for another few weeks. You don't need to waste money on rent when this is working out. Unless you want a place of your own. I get it. Been there."

She sets everything on the counter. "No, I don't mind not being alone. I just—I don't need to be in your hair if you'd rather be alone."

"Can't cook for myself," I remind her. "Stick around. Save

193

the rent money. You'll find the right house for you and Tater Tot soon."

She blinks at me.

Shit.

Fuck.

I just said that out loud.

"Tater Tot?"

My face gets hot. "What else do you call a baby fed exclusively by potatoes?"

Her lips part, and then she smiles.

She's so goddamn pretty when she smiles.

She glows. Her eyes light up. Her cheeks take on a rosy hue. And those lips—fucking gorgeous.

Which is irrelevant.

She's here until she finds a house of her own. I'm just helping out a fellow human being going through a rough patch.

"Tater Tot," she repeats. She looks down at her belly and rubs it. "What do you think? Is that your name?"

She's barely showing. The average person walking by her would have no idea she's pregnant.

But I know.

I know, and she's smiling as she moves about the kitchen again. "Well, I didn't throw up, so that's a good sign baby likes it."

Baby likes it.

Jesus.

She's really growing a whole-ass human inside of her. And she's doing this on her own. No partner. Abandoned by her best friend too.

She's amazing.

"You getting sick at work?" I ask.

"No, I think the worst of morning sickness has passed."

"But not the potato cravings."

"Potatoes are delicious and I won't stand for potato slander, so be careful what you say next."

It's impossible to not smile back at her.

Even when Jessica trots in and scratches the floor like she's flinging poop at me, I'm still smiling.

Ziggy tosses me an apple.

I sit at the kitchen table and tell her about the time Caden got a dog who chewed up all of his stuff.

She tells me about her former best friend helping her get over her fear of dogs and about a story one of her ship friends told her about something that happened onboard this week.

She also tells me turkey bacon is an abomination and it goes against everything she's ever believed in to serve it to me, but she dishes me up a plate heaped with fluffy scrambled eggs, whole wheat toast, fresh berries, and turkey bacon.

This morning routine has me completely certain that I don't want her to go.

I like talking to her. I like eating what she cooks. I like watching her take care of my—her—our?—dog.

I like that she feels safe enough around me to talk about her former best friend.

Important to the grieving process.

Ask me how I know.

"You ever watch superhero movies?" I ask her while I eat.

"All of them," she replies. "Usually late, which is when the ship would get them, but I caught up since I've been back home."

"New one out this weekend. We should go."

Ziggy jerks a look at me.

A delicate pink creeps up her cheeks, and I'm instantly hard as a rock.

Fuck?

Or *thank fuck?*

I can't decide.

That's definitely going to depend on her answer.

I think the blush is a good sign.

Isn't it?

Wait.

Is it bad to date your roommate?

Would it be a date?

Dumbass, of course it would be a date, Caden chides me in my head.

Unless she doesn't want it to be a date.

I can go to the movies with a friend.

How's that any different from sitting in the living room and watching TV with her?

"That sounds fun," she finally says.

Do not push dinner too. Do not push dinner too. Do not— "My favorite burger place is right by the IMAX."

The pink is spreading in her cheeks. It's splotchy, like it was the morning I met her at her hotel parking lot. "Does your favorite burger place serve good fries?"

"Define *good fries.*"

"Shoestring. Golden-brown. Not burnt at any edges. *Maybe* with ranch dressing. Maybe."

"Walking on the wild side there."

"I haven't reliably kept anything but potatoes down in the last month."

"You haven't eaten anything but potatoes and a single rotisserie chicken in the last month."

She grimaces. "The rotisserie chicken is why I don't trust

the new ranch dressing craving."

I shouldn't smile at that, but it's difficult not to.

"You haven't clarified if these French fries are shoestring or not," she says.

"What's the size between shoestring and wedges?"

"Steak fries or standard cut?"

"What's the normal size fries that's one size up from shoestring?"

"Standard cut. Steak fries are one size bigger, then wedges are the biggest."

"They're standard fries then."

"Battered?"

"Battered?" I repeat. "What's *battered fries?*"

"The kind with the extra delicious outside because they've been tossed in batter."

"I have no idea what you're talking about."

She gasps.

She actually gasps.

"Is this like when you pretended you didn't know who Vitamin Man was?" she asks.

This?

This feels good. Ziggy and I are developing a history. We have inside jokes. We have stories. We're friends.

She needs new friends.

"No, I don't know what battered fries are. But if you don't like the fries, I'll stop at Cod Pieces just for you. Actually, I'll call a buddy. He has zero shame. He'll just bring Cod Pieces fries for you. And his fiancée. She's nice. You'll like her."

Two slow blinks are my answer.

Nice, inviting her on a double date with people she's never met, Caden says. *Smooth move. She KNOWS it's a date now.*

I blink back.

She purses her lips together, but I see the wobble in the corner.

She's holding in a smile.

"You know Cod Pieces?" I ask her.

"Fast-food fish."

"Shoestring fries."

"They do make good shoestring fries."

"Good. It's a date. I'll text Fletcher."

Her brows knit together. "Fletcher?"

"My buddy. He'll bring the fries. I'd do it myself, but I can't carry them." I tap my crutches. "Not as fast anyway. Also, I don't care if he gets banned for life from my favorite burger joint for bringing in contraband fries. Better to let him take the risk."

She's still frowning at me. "That's…an interesting friend."

"Teammate. I didn't pick him. But his fiancée is top-notch. You'll like her." I'm pushing too hard.

And I don't even know what I want.

To take Ziggy on a date?

Yes.

But to what end?

Where would this even go?

I think she likes me.

I definitely like her.

And she's having a baby and making a life for herself. Looking for places to live that aren't here with me.

As she should.

We've only really gotten to know each other for under a week.

"Everybody needs friends," I say in the awkward silence.

She shakes her head, then smiles at me. "Yes. Yes. That sounds lovely. Thank you. Ignore me. I just—still feel cautious about friends. Worried. Paranoid. It's me. I'm working on it. But that's very thoughtful. I do need to meet more people. Make new friends. Thank you. Very sweet. Kind. Fun. Is it okay with you if I take Jessica to my parents' house again today? My mom loves her and gets so distracted that she forgets to try to buy too many things for the baby."

"Yeah. She farts at me less on the days she goes with you."

Ziggy straightens. "*Oh*. Oh. I forgot to tell you. It's not you. Jessica. Her problem. It's not you. She hates men in general."

I stare at her.

Then at the dog, who scowls at me.

"For real?" I ask.

"I'm nearly positive. I started noticing a pattern a little bit ago. In any case, you're definitely not the only person she doesn't like. Remember how she reacted to the plumber?"

I stare at the dog again. "Did some fucker hurt you?"

She stares back in *as if I'd tell you, you punk*.

"Very likely," Ziggy says. "She likes you more than most men. For whatever that's worth."

"Huh."

She rises. "Time to go if you're going to Grandma's house, Jessica. Otherwise, I'll be late for work."

The dog stretches out her barrel body, yawns like she doesn't care, snorts in my direction, then trots to the front door.

I rub my breastbone.

It's not me.

The dog's problem isn't *me*.

Didn't realize I needed to know that.

I snag Ziggy's wrist as she walks past, and electricity shoots up my arm.

Her eyes flare as they meet mine.

I drop her hand. "Sorry. I—thank you. The dog— I felt like an asshole."

She smiles at me. "You're not an asshole. Most of the time."

I'm in so much trouble.

This woman is making me feel alive in ways I haven't even *wanted* to be for months. "I'll get tickets."

She blushes. Again. "Can't wait."

Me either.

Me fucking either.

19

Ziggy

Oнннн, this is bad.

Every time I start to think maybe it's not *that* bad, I hear Miranda in my head again. *The guys all know Dad would murder them if they look at me wrong. Or at least trade them to a less desirable team.*

And here I am, literally *living with the team captain.*

Lacrosse, my ass.

Holt's the freaking captain of the Pounders.

I've picked up my phone to text him a half-dozen times in the hour since I gave in to what I thought was over-paranoid paranoia to look up the Pounders' roster, and every time, I've put it back down.

He asked me on a date.

And I want to go.

And I think it's a date.

But maybe it's not a date. Maybe it's just him setting me up to make a friend.

With *Fletcher's fiancée*.

It was the *Fletcher's fiancée* that got me. I don't know many Fletchers. But I looked up the roster anyway because there was this little voice whispering in the back of my head that this last week with Holt was too good to be true after the absolute roller coaster that my life has been since Abby Nora's baby shower.

And there it is in full color.

A picture of Holt—*my* Holt—at the very top of the team roster. All of that dark hair. The chin dimple. The hooded brown eyes. The broad shoulders and thick chest.

Holding a rugby ball under one arm.

Miranda walks past my door, camera in hand, and gives me a wave.

I wave back.

Frantically.

Like, a *get in here and shut the door* wave.

She grins as she joins me. "That's a face. What's up? Did you take out a billboard calling Abby Nora a twatmuffin and now you're having second thoughts or need someone to blame it on? I would totally take the blame if you did. Our parents would blame my prefrontal cortex still not being fully developed. You don't get that pass."

"What? No. Shut the door. I—did you get a billboard?"

"No, but now I sort of want to."

"*Do not get a billboard.* Please, *please* shut the door."

She gives me a *what the hell is wrong with you?* look as she shuts the door. "The billboard's getting more appealing by the minute…"

I wave away the teasing. "I have to ask you something and

you have to not laugh and also not tell anyone I asked because I'm asking for *absolutely no reason at all*. Also, I'm so pissed that you picked French instead of Spanish or Italian in school, because I don't want to say this in English."

Her hazel eyes spark with mischief as she props a hip at the edge of my desk. "Riiiiiiight. Idle curiosity about something you can't ask me in our native tongue with the door open. I'm sure it's completely innocent."

I'm screwed.

Whether or not I go to the movies with Holt and his friend tomorrow, I'm so screwed. "Why aren't there pictures of the team players all over this building?"

"Usually are. They took them down for the renovations. Supposed to be done soon." She grins at me. "Why? Did someone meet a player and not know it?"

I drop my head into my hands. "How serious is Dad about the players not looking at his daughters and how much of it is all talk?"

"*Oh my god*, is one of the players your baby daddy?"

"*Sshhhhhh!* Keep your voice down. What the hell is wrong with you? And *no*. He's—"

I freeze.

Oh my god.

Oh my god.

What if he is? What if one of the players was on vacation in Greece and I—

No.

I pull up the roster of players again and scroll through.

None look familiar.

Except Holt.

And my god, he's handsome. He's not smiling in his official team photo, but his eyes are. And it's not just any eye-smile.

It's an eye-smile that says he's a beast on the pitch—not the field, as I've been told numerous times at work this week —and a gentleman in the streets and still-to-be-determined in the sheets.

"No, it was definitely not one of the players," I tell my sister. "And even if it was, we could only communicate because we both spoke Italian, so he definitely wouldn't be playing for the Pounders. I think. Right? Do any of the guys on the team not speak English?"

"They all speak English. Well enough to communicate *I want to hook up with you* anyway. But didn't you get pregnant in May? The season was still going on. None of our guys would've been overseas." She angles a look at my computer.

I hit the lock button on my keyboard so she can only see the log-in screen and not what I was researching.

She looks at me.

My entire body goes hot.

Not just my face. My entire *body*.

Miranda gives me the *spill it all now* look.

"You *cannot* tell a soul," I whisper and wish once again that we could have this discussion in a way that couldn't be overheard.

She crosses her heart, then holds out a pinky. "Secret to the grave."

"I'm living in Holt Webster's house," I whisper. "He's the guy I was—*am*—house-sitting for. But more like cooking for now. Since he's on crutches."

She blinks at me once.

Then twice.

She starts to gasp but finishes the gasp doubled over in laughter.

I sag back in my chair. "So it's not as bad as I think it is? If you're laughing this hard, it can't be as bad as I think it is."

"Oh no," she says between chortles. "You're fucked. Or he is. More likely he is. Dad's gonna lose his effing mind. Holt's fired. He is so fired. And it's not funny. It's really not. But if I stop laughing, I'll start crying. Tell me you're lying. *Please* tell me you're making this up."

"*I didn't know who he was.* One of the catering staff told me he played lacrosse. The night we met. He was doing security at the event where I puked on Abby Nora's brother-in-law."

"Ziggy. Copper Valley doesn't have a lacrosse team. At least, not on a professional level."

"I was a little distracted trying to get a new life together to care to look that up. My options were continuing to bleed money staying in a hotel, continue to let Mom and Dad cover the hotel, move in with Mom and Dad and Naked Tuesdays, or house-sit for a guy who was going to *lacrosse camp* for six weeks."

"Does he know who you are?"

"I don't know. I don't think—"

A bark in the hallway interrupts me.

I stare at my door.

Miranda does too. "Was that Jessica?"

I bolt to my feet, stifling my favorite Italian curse word. My stomach swishes, but I don't feel like I have to run to the bathroom.

This is progress.

Definitely progress.

But only on the morning sickness front.

Definitely not progress on the part where I'm living with

—and have a crazy stupid crush on—the captain of the Pounders and my stepfather might kill him.

"Tell me Dad will be reasonable about this," I whisper to Miranda as I fling my door open.

"Zero chance." She trails me down the short hallway to the entrance of the Pounders' admin building, where Mom's holding Jessica, who's growling at Quinoa because the Pounders have a male receptionist and Jessica needs therapy.

But Mom bringing Jessica to a building with a fair number of men isn't the biggest problem.

The biggest problem is the large *rugby* player on crutches swinging into the waiting area from the other side of the building—the side of the building where the players come to work out and *see the physical therapist*—sputtering, "*Jessica?*"

"What the fuck did you just say?" the slightly taller, slightly bigger, mustachioed guy behind him says while the dark-haired woman with both of them gapes at Holt.

Jessica snorts at Holt.

"*Mom.* You can't have the dog here," I say.

Holt's eyes whip to me and go comically round. I shake my head at him. *Don't talk to me. Don't talk to me. Don't talk to me.*

Have we known each other long enough for subliminal communication to work?

He blinks like he's clearing his vision, then squints harder at me, and I wonder briefly if he knows enough Spanish for me to tell him he doesn't know me.

He *did* say he was in Spain.

But I don't want to risk it, so I subliminally communicate harder.

Miranda makes a noise. "Oh, I see it," she whispers.

"Who the fuck are you calling *Jessica?*" the other guy—

rugby player too, I assume, based on the build and the mustache that half of them seemed to have in their team pictures—says to Holt, which jerks him out of gaping at me.

"Fletcher, my goodness, your language," my mom says. "Jessica is my daughter's dog."

The woman makes a noise.

I don't know if it's a laugh or a whimper or something entirely different, but she clears her throat, then makes it again.

Do I know her?

She seems familiar.

Roughly my age—*fuck*.

Was she at Abby Nora's baby shower?

How does this keep getting worse? *How?*

"Apologies, Mrs. Keating," Fletcher says.

"He has a longstanding, difficult history with Jessicas," the woman says.

Holt's staring at me again, and it's not hard to see that he's putting the pieces together and realizing that this is very, very, very bad.

His cheeks are going pink over the dark scruff he's been growing, and there's no easy comfort between us like there was at breakfast this morning.

I want to go back to breakfast.

I want to go back to breakfast and skip work and go see a movie with him today.

Dammit dammit dammit.

"How did you know Jessica's name, dear?" Mom says to him.

He jerks his attention to her awkwardly enough that his companions look at him funny too.

"We ran into each other in the parking lot a couple

days ago," I blurt, "and she growled at him and I told him she doesn't like men so he knows she's not supposed to be here since there are so many men in this building."

And now everyone's staring at me.

"*Nice,*" Miranda whispers.

No, not *nice*.

Nice would be if this wasn't happening.

How the *hell* is this happening?

Well, your dad got you the job with the catering company, and he likes to help people out, so it makes logical sense that at some point, he also set Holt up to work security for the company since the players need extra jobs in the off-season to supplement their income, which means—

Which means it doesn't matter.

This is happening.

I'll just have to go talk to Dad and explain it to him and make him be rational about it.

"Ziggy, that's nonsense," Mom says. "Of course Jessica likes men."

"She does not like men," I repeat.

"She likes your father."

"Does she?"

Mom opens her mouth, then closes it.

"Huxley." Holt looks at Fletcher. "Pet the dog."

"Dogs love him," the woman with them tells me.

"They really do," Miranda agrees. "He almost didn't make it out alive the day the whole team volunteered at that dog shelter because they were killing him with how much they love him."

Fletcher's eyeing Jessica.

The woman—I assume his fiancée at this point, who is

definitely familiar—squats down at Jessica's level. "Do you hate men, sweet thing?"

Jessica snuffles at her.

Fletcher squats too, and Jessica instantly growls, her little ears going back.

"Fuck me," he mutters, then glances at my mom, but doesn't apologize for his language.

She sighs and shakes her head. "I suppose I can give that one a pass."

"It could be the mustache," his fiancée says to him, which makes Miranda snort.

Holt looks at me again.

I shake my head again too.

It's clear the questions are coming. But we have to make it through today without him blowing it so I can make a plan and fix this.

I have to make sure my dad doesn't kill him.

The woman scoots closer to Jessica and scratches her head. "Mrs. Keating, Fletcher didn't tell me your other daughter had started working for the team too."

"Dad hasn't made the announcement yet," Miranda says. "This is Ziggy. She hates favoritism and wouldn't be here except he begged her since she's so good with food and wine and he wants to show Copper Valley's other team owners that we're the best."

"Lovely to meet you, Ziggy." The woman flicks another glance at me, her eyes narrowing slightly like she recognizes me too. "I'm Goldie. I don't play. But this is Fletcher and Holt. They do."

Goldie.

Has Abby Nora mentioned a Goldie?

"I play," Fletcher says. "Captain, not so much."

"You're not a Keating," Holt says to me.

I freeze.

Mom straightens.

Fletcher and Goldie both look at me, and Fletcher says a long, *"Oooooooh,"* that earns him a look from Goldie that I interpret to mean Holt's already told them we're going to see a movie together, and Goldie put together much faster that this situation is bad.

I know her.

How do I know her?

"Nice eyes spotting Ziggy's new nameplate on her office, Captain," Miranda says. "She never changed her name after her mom married my dad, but we don't really do the step-thing because family's family, you know?"

He stares at her for a minute, then looks at Fletcher. "Lunch time."

Like that's not the most awkward answer to Miranda's family explanation.

Oh god.

Oh god oh god oh god.

I told him my parents have Naked Tuesdays.

He knows my parents have Naked Tuesdays.

I almost choke on my own horror. They'd be mortified if they found out one of their players knew. And what if he casually mentioned it to the rest of the team?

I have a house sitter because I took pity on this pregnant woman who would've been stuck living through Naked Tuesdays at her parents' house if I hadn't.

Am I whimpering out loud or is that just in my head?

Goldie rises. "Definitely lunchtime. Can't heal if we don't feed you well."

"How's your foot doing, Holt?" Mom asks.

"Getting there."

"Roland told me you should be able to play again next season."

"That's the goal, ma'am."

"He's such a good captain," Mom tells me. "The players just adore him."

"Some of us just tolerate him," Fletcher says.

"They say the same about you and your mustache, dear," Mom replies.

He grins. "I know. I like it that way."

Jessica sneezes toward him, which isn't something she did at home at all the two weeks Holt was gone but has done to Holt every day since he's been back.

Apparently Jessica's decided she doesn't like Fletcher specifically enough to snot on him too.

Fletcher looks down at her, and she spins around to aim her butt—

I leap forward and grab her leash from Mom. "*Jessica, we do not fart at people. Especially in offices.*"

Goldie chokes on a laugh. Miranda lets hers roll free.

Fletcher mutters something that sounds like, "Yeah, Jessica," which makes Goldie cough again.

And Holt rubs his brow with a sigh. "I'll wait in your car," he says to Fletcher.

"It's eleventy billion bloody degrees outside," Fletcher says.

"So hurry your ass up. Mrs. Keating, nice to see you. Miranda, stay out of trouble." He pauses and stares at me for an awkward pause. "Nice to meet you."

"Nice to meet you too," I choke out. "All of you."

Goldie squints at me the same way I've probably squinted at her a half dozen times already.

Like she knows me too.

It had to be Abby Nora's baby shower. Which means Holt's teammate's fiancée knows that her friend Abby Nora thinks I'm a horrible person.

Awesome.

My brain hurts.

My stomach is starting to as well.

"They're good people, but don't get too close," Mom says after Goldie and Fletcher have left to catch up with Holt in the parking lot. "There are lines when it comes to fraternizing with the players and their significant others."

"Goldie's good people. Fletcher's questionable. Holt's nice though," Miranda says.

"And still a player," Mom says.

Fuck. "Right. Of course. What are you doing here? Why'd you bring Jessica?"

She smiles at me. "I thought you'd like it if we brought you lunch to celebrate the end of your first week on the job."

"Just me? Did you bring enough for Miranda too?"

"I'm calling in an order to that Greek place you loved so much the last time you were home."

I might've hooked up with a guy in Greece that ended with me pregnant, but Tater Tot isn't having anything to do with the idea of gyros and tzatziki and grape leaves just yet.

"Can we do pasta instead?"

Plain noodles.

I can do plain noodles.

And then I can figure out how to move into a new apartment immediately.

20

Holt

THERE ARE NOT enough fucks in the world to adequately express my feelings right now, and I wish I knew some of Ziggy's favorite curses in other languages to add to the string in my head.

"So your house sitter is Roland Keating's stepdaughter," Fletcher says as he steers his stupid fancy Bentley out of the parking lot of the Pounders' admin/gym building across the street from the stadium. "Nicely done fucking up your entire life again. Wow. Didn't see that coming."

"The only reason I'm not making you shut your face is because you're driving."

"And you're on crutches."

"I can still shut your face when I'm on crutches."

Goldie leans forward. She and I fought over the back seat. I lost, so I'm in front.

"I didn't even know he had two daughters," she says.

I stare out the window. "I did. Vaguely."

It's a distant memory of something Roland or his wife, Deedee, said once.

Distant, *distant* memory from one of my first years on the team. It's more of a feeling than a specific *this is what happened* kind of memory. I think I knew he had a stepdaughter. And I think I got the impression she had a fancy job somewhere relatively far away and wasn't interested in the Pounders at all.

Completely lines up with the Ziggy I know.

Sommelier for a luxury cruise line in the Med. Asks more about how I'm healing than about my sports career.

"She should've told you," Fletcher says.

"I let her think I played lacrosse," I mutter. Gonna get yelled at for that one. Deserve it. But it shouldn't have mattered.

Hell, I *liked* that she wasn't into sports. Felt like she cared more about me as a person than the possibility that I could be a rich athlete. They all assume if you play professionally, you're loaded.

Joke's on me.

Her family's loaded, and she's completely off-limits.

"You don't have Pounders shit all over your house?" Fletcher asks.

"Never put up a lot of it when I moved in with Caden since it was supposed to be temporary until he was better. Took down the little bit I had when I started renovations. It's packed up in the garage."

"You said she said she couldn't live with her parents," Goldie says.

"I wouldn't want to live with them," Fletcher mutters.

Naked Tuesdays.

Fuck me.

I squeeze my eyes shut and rub my fists into them, but now it's there, and I can't make it go away.

Roland has Naked Tuesdays with Deedee.

Think about potatoes.

Shit.

Potatoes.

Ziggy.

Roland's daughter. Naked Tuesdays.

I pull up my phone and switch to pictures of Fletcher in his budgie smugglers.

Better.

That's better.

"What are you doing?" Goldie asks me.

"I know things and I don't want to know things now that I know I know things."

My phone buzzes in my hand, and a message pops up from Ziggy.

Ziggy: *Can't talk now, but we need to talk when I get off work. OMG. HOW DID THIS HAPPEN?*

Yep.

I'm in trouble.

"So your dog's name is Jessica," Goldie says. "That's an interesting choice."

"I didn't name her."

"I didn't even know you had a dog," Fletcher says. "Why didn't you tell me you had a dog?"

"It was a pity adoption when someone in my neighborhood died. Also, the dog hates me."

"Does she fart in your general direction often?" Goldie asks.

"Every fucking day."

"I like her. I think she's living up to everything a Jessica should be."

Fletcher slides her a scowl in the rearview mirror.

She grins.

Every time I wonder why someone as awesome as Goldie would hook up with someone as annoying and obnoxious as Fletcher, she shows a new side of herself that makes me think he's getting some of what he deserves.

"Tell the inside joke or quit making it," I say.

"I'll stop." Goldie's grin says she's still making it in her head.

Fletcher's grunt says he can hear it.

Sort of like I could hear Ziggy saying *do not recognize me, you don't know me, fuck, this is bad* when we locked eyes in the reception area.

"So the movie's off tomorrow," Fletcher says.

"The movie is on," Goldie corrects. "I don't care if you two go, but I am. There's something familiar about her, but I can't place it. I need to work this out."

I want to go.

I want to fucking take a woman I like to the movies and introduce her to my friends like she's never met them and watch the two women bond over being betrayed by their former best friends.

Happened to Goldie too, which our whole team knows since Fletcher and Silas ordered us all to be nice to her, as if we wouldn't be. I've been working on the right way to figure out how to introduce the two of them all week.

Ziggy needs friends.

Goldie's ninety percent angel with a decent grip on the ten percent chaos part of her personality. She's a good friend.

She'll be good for Ziggy too.

Fletcher slides a look at me, then back at Goldie. "Huh."

"What does *huh* mean?" I ask him.

"Means I might have to decide if you're worth putting my career on the line."

"You *are* old," Goldie says.

He grins. "Always wanted to go out in a blaze of glory."

"Are you fucking retiring?" I ask him.

"No. I'm gonna play until I'm dead. Unless I put my neck on the line for you and get fired or traded, which is the same as getting fired. Goldie's friends would murder me if I asked her to move away for me."

"I can never decide if you're the best kind of wingman or the worst."

"If he's not both, he's not doing it right," Goldie says.

Fletcher nods. "Accurate."

"How'd your waffle mascot presentation go?" she asks him.

"They're putting Waffy on the ballot to shut me up."

Goldie's right.

He's somehow always the best and the worst at the same time.

"Speaking of Goldie's friends," Fletcher says, "we're having lunch with them. Want me to drop you at your house, or do you want three seasoned ladies fussing over you for the next three hours?"

"Don't you work anymore?" I ask Goldie. She's a life coach with a couple books out.

"Not on days when we have lunch with the girls."

"You know what else?" Fletcher says. "You can ask any

one of Goldie's friends to the movies without worrying it'll cost you your spot on the team."

I flip him off.

Goldie pats me on the shoulder. "Don't worry, Holt. This is all going to work out. How can it not when you have us on your side?"

I've seen her work miracles. She got Fletcher and her brother to get along, after all.

But this feels like a mountain too high even for her.

And her friends.

But her friends have far more life experience than the rest of us, so I opt to tag along for lunch.

Six brains are better than three.

Usually.

21

Ziggy

IT'S STILL hot as hell outside, but the dread I'm feeling as I walk up the steps to Holt's house is far more oppressive than the weather.

Miranda ran interference and dominated the conversation with Mom at lunch, then convinced her to leave Jessica with me so I wouldn't have to pick her up after work, and that Jessica and I had to be barricaded in my office all afternoon so the dog wouldn't scare the men. I spent half the time texting Francesca, filling her in on what I've fucked up at home now.

She tells me the only answer is for me to come back to work on the ship now that I'm not sick anymore.

Which I can't do, and she knows it.

And now my work week is over.

I'm exhausted.

Jessica is taking her sweet time getting from the car to the front door in the heat.

And the house I left happily this morning is now a place of doom.

I have to move out.

I have to find a new place to live and move out quickly.

And I don't want to. I like this house. Jessica likes this house. Having Holt as a housemate is nice, and not just because I can't help getting a little turned on every time I see him.

I like not being alone. I like having someone to talk to first thing in the morning. I like the way he smirks at me when I wake up on the couch and realize I've fallen asleep watching a TV show. I like the way he tells me something completely ridiculous happened in the show while I was sleeping, and I have that moment of believing him before I realize he's teasing me.

I like that he says good night through my door when he passes by on his crutches to get to his room.

Fine.

Fine.

I like him.

I shouldn't. He's probably just being a nice guy to the pregnant lady who was only supposed to be in his house while he was gone.

His neighbors say he's nice.

Miranda says he's nice.

Brydie at the catering company said he was nice, even if she didn't know what sport he plays.

He's just a nice guy doing a nice thing and when he asked me to the movies, it was because he was being a nice guy who wanted to introduce me to someone who might be my friend, but in actuality is probably one of Abby Nora's friends because the universe is a dick sometimes.

He's taking me in the same way he took Jessica in.

That's it.

I finally shove through the door with my hair sticking to the back of my neck and sweat lining my bra. Jessica snorts, snuffles, and then sneezes toward the couch, where, sure enough, Holt is swinging himself up from a sprawled-out position to sitting like he's been waiting for us.

His hair is a mess. It's not hard to imagine him running his fingers through it all day. His lips are turned down in the barest pout. And his eyes—*god*, his eyes. They're sad and worried and alert as he scans me from top to bottom like he's making sure I'm in one piece.

My heart skips a beat and my nipples tighten and the rest of me lets out a silent howl of *whhhhyyyyyy?*

Why does he have to be a *rugby* player?

Why can't he just be a guy who works security? Just a normal, muscular, scruffy-faced security guy with a chiseled jaw?

Dammit.

Realizing he's off-limits has made it clear just how bad I have it.

I unclip Jessica to distract myself. "Who wants a treat?"

She spins in three circles and barks happily.

"Have to go in the backyard."

She grins.

I have no idea how a dog that stout loves the heat so much, but she does.

And that's when I look up and spot the sign hanging over the entrance to the kitchen.

It's homemade—three poster boards taped together, with

SORRY I DIDN'T TELL YOU I PLAY RUGBY written in large black, purple, and blue letters.

There's also a messy ball in one corner—round, not oblong like the balls the guys were holding in their team pictures—and a square with hash marks in another corner.

"Fletcher helped Goldie and me make it. He did the sloppy letters. And the mascots." Holt shoves up from the couch and onto his crutches. "We didn't have time to get a professional one made, and even if we had, that might've gotten back to the office and prompted questions."

He made a sign.

This is—hilarious and sweet and very forward-thinking of him.

Why didn't you tell me Brydie was confused and you play rugby? was definitely going to be my first question.

This is like coming home from a long trip and being greeted by your family at the airport with signs that say things like "Sorry I broke your blender while you were gone" and "Your boyfriend ran away to the Caribbean but you can do better."

Neither of which has happened to me but did happen to friends and crewmates on various ships that I worked on over the years.

I think I won this game.

Not that it's a contest, but *he made me a sign.*

With a big SORRY on it and everything, even though he's definitely not the only one who needs to be sorry here.

Yep.

I'm deceased. Completely dead with how much harder I'm crushing on him right now.

"I really didn't think it mattered," he adds. "If the sign was professional or...this. And that's a waffle. In the corner. Fletcher wants the team mascot to be waffles."

Jessica slides him a look and makes a noise like she wants to throw up.

I eyeball her. "Be nice." He's rambly. And it's freaking adorable.

Jessica stares back at me like she *is* being nice, he is *never* adorable, and she would like her treat now.

No manners from this dog today.

That's probably my mother's fault.

"Sit," I tell Holt. "I'll put Jessica out."

We haven't texted all day since my message to him that we have to talk.

It's been so much more fun to sit in the panic and anxiety mixed with the howling outrage that a guy I like is completely and totally off-limits.

Someday I need to learn to immediately deal with my problems head-on. That's apparently not today though.

He watches me warily. "Because you don't want witnesses, or because you don't want to scare the dog?"

"I'm not mad."

Jessica barks.

"I'm not," I tell her. "I'd like a glass of wine and I'm irritated that I can't have one, but I'm not mad."

She rolls her eyes like she's disappointed in me.

As if I'm missing my chance to take out all of my feelings on a man.

"You need therapy," I tell her.

She grins.

I hustle her through the kitchen and onto the porch, then toss three doggy treats into the yard for her. After I make sure she has enough water in her outside bowl, I prop the door open so that she can come in if she gets too hot, and I head back inside.

And yes, I'm taking entirely too long.

I don't want to have this conversation. I want to go back to this morning, to when he asked me on a date and I felt like someone who had a beautiful new life ahead of me instead of someone who's actually been living in a situation that could fuck everything up for a lot of people.

Holt's waiting for me in the living room, still standing, when I get back.

"Would you *please* sit down?"

"I'm gonna move in with Fletcher and Goldie for a while."

"That's ridiculous. This is your house. I'll leave."

"You can't leave. You know what's worse than having Keating's daughter—"

"Stepdaughter, technically."

He's not amused. "What's worse than having *you* living in my house? It looking like I kicked you out. That's worse. You stay. The dog likes you. The house likes you. You stay. As long as you want."

Funny thing—I wasn't mad before.

Surprised.

Mildly horrified as I realized how my dad would take this.

Worried about how fast I could—or couldn't—fix it.

Angry that *I freaking like him* and I can't do anything about it.

But now?

Now I'm mad.

I'm mad because the man should want to live in his own house and he's just rolling over and giving it to me because he's afraid of what my dad will do to him.

"Why aren't you asking me why I never told you I'm related to Roland Keating?"

"Past the point where it matters." He winces.

"You're thinking about Naked Tuesdays, aren't you?"

"I'm seeing a hypnotist next week to get that knowledge permanently removed from my brain."

"Good. You shouldn't know that about the owner of your team."

"Are you threatening me or baiting me?"

"Baiting. Is it working?"

"No."

"Why not?"

"Because half the guys on the team don't want to talk about where they came from, and you already told me you weren't happy about taking a pity job from family, and I know how people treat Miranda at the office, and sometimes at big events too, just because of who your dad is, and I get why you wouldn't want that."

Yep.

I'm madder now.

Furious, actually.

Here's a nice, attractive, thoughtful guy who spent the time working on a reason to give me the benefit of the doubt in a way that my own former best friend probably wouldn't have, and because he's a rugby player on the team that my stepfather owns, we can't be friends.

Much less anything more.

It's not fucking fair.

It's not fucking fair, and I hate that I can't have him as a friend.

"Shit, don't cry." He finally sits on the couch, but it's more to grab the box of tissues sitting on an end table and hold them out to me than it is because he wanted to sit.

Or so I assume since he's refused to sit until now.

I take the offered tissues and drop into the easy chair next to the couch while I fail to swallow the lump in my throat and blink back the hot moisture in my eyes.

"There's nothing wrong with crying. This is hard. Crying is normal. Crying is natural. Don't tell me not to cry."

"I don't mean you can't cry. I just mean I don't want to be the reason you cry."

It's in my sinuses now too. The crying has hit my sinuses. *I don't want special treatment.*

"I should've moved in with friends anyway. Their place doesn't have stairs. Unless the elevator breaks, and then I'd be stuck, but it's a good building. The elevator shouldn't break. Unless there's a fire, and then it's just my time to go."

"Stop talking."

"I can't stop talking unless you stop crying."

"I can't stop crying while you're talking!"

He drops his head in his hands.

I blow my nose again while I sniffle.

This is probably partially pregnancy hormones, but that's not all it is.

"I liked you," I whisper.

Not what I need to say to make this situation better.

But it's the truth.

I'm crying because I'm mourning what I can't have.

Friends. Home. A crush on a nice guy who might or might not want me back—I'm well aware that I'm a lot right now and I shouldn't read into a nice guy asking me to go to the movies with him and some friends that he thinks I'll like.

But I can't even have a date.

"I was excited about going to the movies."

Yep. I say that too.

Those fathomless brown eyes lift to study me, more serious than I've seen him since the night we met when he thought I was an intruder looking for a good place to devour a chicken in my car.

"Me too," he says. "And that's why I need to leave."

My battered heart whimpers in frustration. *He likes me too.* "That's so *stupid*. I didn't move in here because you play rugby. You didn't ask me to house-sit because of who my dad is." I pause. "Did you?"

"I like my job."

I blow my nose again and stare at him. "What does that mean?"

"I absolutely wouldn't have offered to let you stay at my house if I knew who you were. I would've talked Brydie into helping you instead so it wouldn't have looked like I had anything to do with it at all."

"But you were leaving the Pounders to play overseas. You weren't going to be one of my dad's players anymore. What did it matter?"

"Coming back was always the contingency plan."

"We didn't do anything wrong. So why can't everything stay the same?"

"Because your dad would fire my ass or trade me, and the only thing worse than an injury killing my chances of ever playing in Europe again is the idea of not having the family I've made here to come back to."

My heart squeezes as tightly as I want to hug him.

I came home to be with family when my world flipped upside down.

Apparently, so did he.

And now, months after his brother died, he's injured. If Dad traded him, he'd be injured and alone without knowing who on his new team were the people he could trust and who would be the people who'd help him because they were obligated to and who'd stab him in the back at the first opportunity.

How stupid.

"I won't let him fire you or trade you."

"Ziggy—"

"I'm not living in your house because we're trying to sneak around behind his back. You did me a favor. Now I'm doing you a favor. Home is the best place to heal. I'm already here. You need a good diet to get better too. Knowing your dog is taken care of. Feeling as normal as possible. We didn't do anything wrong. We're not doing anything wrong. And if he doesn't like it, I'll—I'll—*dammit.*"

I don't know what I'll do.

Threaten to move to Napa and never let them see the baby is extreme.

But it *is* top on my list of ideas.

My bad ideas.

Doing that would make me exactly what Abby Nora accused me of being.

A completely selfish jerk who only cares about herself.

"How's it going to look to my dad if his captain doesn't recover well because I kicked him out of his own house?" I add.

"Shit." Holt slouches back on the couch. "Your mom's been here. She hired a yard crew. You said so."

"It was only once. She's not in this part of the city very often."

Say we can both stay. Say we can be friends. Say we can work this out.

"Does Miranda know?"

"She's a vault. She won't tell."

He eyes me.

"She won't," I insist. "She's had her own problems with friends and secrets. If it doesn't hurt anyone, it stays locked up. She knew about Abby Nora the day I got home, but I didn't tell my mom until—well, until you heard me telling my mom. I put it off for weeks, and Miranda didn't breathe a word. Mom still doesn't know she knew first."

"Is there a price to her silence?"

"Yes. It's called cherry hand pies and Italian wine."

"Cherry hand pies?"

It's always the stomach. It is *always* the stomach. I latch onto that, and I run. Because I want to stay. And I want him to stay. And I will play dirty for it. "With an airy, buttery crust that you can't find anywhere else. And fresh cherries too."

His pupils dilate.

"And when I add homemade ice cream, they cannot be beat."

"You can make ice cream?"

"Yes."

"How's that work?"

"You've never had homemade ice cream?"

He shakes his head. His Adam's apple bobs.

"Happiness is vital to healing." My voice keeps dropping softer and softer, and he keeps leaning closer and closer. "I'll run to the store in the morning. I needed to get more potatoes anyway. But I'm feeling better. I can make hand pies and ice cream too. I can probably even eat some with you."

"This is a bad idea." His voice is husky.

It resonates through me, setting my skin on fire.

"We're already screwed," I whisper. "Let's just make the most of it for as long as we can."

The dark scruff on his face, the way he's staring at me—he's a pirate who's decided I'm the treasure he wants.

And I like it.

Even knowing I shouldn't, I like it.

"My dad isn't completely unreasonable. Maybe he'll understand this was all an accident." I rub my lower belly. "Having a few of those these days. No regrets though."

"Just roommates. *Housemates*. We are just housemates." He's gone completely hoarse.

He's also not looking at me anymore, so I don't think he sees me nod my agreement. "Housemates. Totally normal. Accidental housemates."

He lifts his gaze to me. "I can't take you to the movies tomorrow."

That shouldn't hurt as bad as it does. The way I would kill for a glass of wine right now to drown this day in… "But we can still be friends."

"Hard not to be."

"Agreed." I rise before this gets worse or before he changes his mind. "I'll go start on dinner. And a menu for next week."

"Ziggy?"

"Hmm?"

"This team is the only family I have left."

How is it possible that I've never hugged this man?

And now that I can't, it's all I want to do.

Well, not *all*.

But definitely my highest priority at the moment. "I won't let him take that from you. Promise."

He studies me like he's looking for the cracks in my statement, then nods. "Thank you."

Talk about the weight of the world.

The trade-off for getting to stay here, to pretend everything's normal here, is that I'm now carrying the weight of *his* world.

Funny thing though—I don't mind.

Not a bit.

22

Holt

ZIGGY DIDN'T YELL.

I was positive she'd yell, but she didn't.

Instead, she melted in front of my eyes, all because of the goofball sign that I said I needed to make but didn't think my friends would take me seriously about.

How the fuck am I going to live with a woman in my house who gets more irresistible by the minute when she's completely and irrevocably off-limits?

Especially when I know she feels this thing between us too?

I liked you.

She said it like she doesn't anymore, as if she could just turn off liking someone because she found out it was a bad idea, but if she didn't like me anymore, she wouldn't have been so upset.

Fuck, this is hard.

Dinner is awkward. She takes hers onto the porch and turns on one of her language podcasts while I sit in the kitchen.

I skip sitting with her to watch TV because I say I need to get a little extra rest.

Not that I want to be in my room.

Anything has to be better than stripping down to my boxers, flopping down into my bed, not tired enough to sleep, ordering myself not to rub one out to fantasies about my team's owner's daughter.

Again.

Anymore.

Fuck knows I've done it enough already. Mostly in Spain, when I'd get a text from her, picture those pretty blue eyes and the way she made friends with Jessica, and then let my mind wander to far more explicit situations that never happened.

And will never happen.

And that was before she told me about her cherry hand pies.

Cherry.

Hand.

Pies.

There's not a word in that pastry's name that doesn't make me hard as granite.

You're so fucked, Caden says cheerfully in my head.

He would've laughed his ass off.

And then he would've helped me come up with a plan to fix this.

My door is ajar, so I hear her moving around downstairs, letting Jessica outside.

She sings along to a Waverly Sweet album while she does

the dishes, turning the kitchen faucet on and off, clinking plates and silverware into the dishwasher, and then I hear her practicing her language app again.

Spanish and Italian. She speaks both. Better Spanish, but her Italian greatly improved while she was working on the cruise ship, she told me when I asked what she was listening to one morning this week.

And it made me feel, once again, like she was out of my league, except then she made me buckwheat pancakes in the shape of smiley faces that were also phallic if you looked at them wrong, and we both laughed until she was crying.

Fuck, I miss that Ziggy.

The Ziggy who wasn't Roland Keating's daughter.

The Ziggy I was going to take on a date tomorrow.

The Ziggy I get to see cradling her small baby bump when she doesn't realize I'm watching.

I stare at the cracks in the ceiling as the sun sets, wondering if she'll watch TV or if she'll come up to get ready for bed.

Long day.

Hard day.

For both of us.

"C'mon, Jessica. Bedtime."

My pulse ticks higher.

She's coming.

She's coming up the stairs with the dog to get ready for bed.

She'll be stripping down and changing into pajamas in mere minutes.

Naked across the hall.

Is my air conditioner broken?

Christ on a radiator, it's hot in here.

Jessica's nails click-clack on the steps. Need to get those trimmed.

"Somebody's a good girl who needs her claws trimmed," Ziggy murmurs softly.

If I said that to the dog, she'd blow snot all over me. But when Ziggy says it, all I hear is panting.

And the sound of my heart beating faster.

We're thinking the same things.

We have a vibe.

She's special.

And I can't fucking have her.

I want to flop on my side, but I can't flop and also keep my foot elevated, so instead, I shove a pillow over my head.

But I can still hear her.

I hear the door across the hall creak as she enters the room.

I hear Jessica snuffling a happy noise, and it's easy to picture Ziggy petting her.

I hear a drawer open.

My balls tighten harder.

She's probably taking her clothes off.

Quit being a creeper. Stop it.

Nope.

Still imagining Ziggy unbuttoning the bright pink and yellow shirt she wore to work today.

I wonder if her bra is plain or if she's hiding lace under her shirt. If it's pink too, or beige, or if she's secretly got lacy black or red lingerie under her clothes.

If her belly swelling with the baby is more noticeable in ways you can only see when she's undressed.

If she has any birthmarks.

Stop stop STOP.

I can't do this.

She's my boss's daughter, and I already feel like the world's biggest fuck-up for coming back to the Pounders injured.

I can't live with an obsession with the big boss's daughter while she's sleeping across the hall from me every night too.

I have to go.

I have to find a different place to live.

Say it was my preference.

The stair thing. There was a good reason about stairs.

I forget what it was, but I had it.

Her door is ajar too.

It has to be.

How else am I hearing the water turn on in the bathroom this loudly?

Oh, fuck.

Is she showering?

Is she completely naked?

Am I fucking fifteen years old again? What the fuck is wrong with me?

I squash the pillow harder over my face, trying to suffocate myself.

Or stop the noises.

I liked you.

I like you too, Ziggy Barnes.

Entirely too much.

Cherry hand pies.

I. Have. To. Move.

Tomorrow.

First thing.

I'm getting up, I'm packing, and I'm—
"*Aaahhhhh!*"
Ziggy.
Something's wrong with Ziggy.
I don't pause. Don't think. I just leap.
Ziggy needs me.

23

Ziggy

This has been a night.

A whole damn day actually.

I'm not paying attention to the faucet as I crank it on to get warm water flowing to the shower so I can wash today off of me. I'm barely paying attention to my clothes as I peel them off too.

The only things I'm aware of are my irritation with my stepfather for his rules and the hopeless desperation that comes with facing the end of another friendship.

Not that Holt and I are *anywhere* close to what Abby Nora and I were.

But I was finally risking getting close to someone as a friend, a *new* friend—an attractive friend, let's be honest here —and I can't have him either.

He won't stay. He won't be my friend.

Because Roland doesn't want him to be.

In the immortal words of every teenager to ever live, it's not fair.

That's what I'm thinking as I pull the shower curtain back, step inside, and come face-to-face with a big, ugly, too-many-legged spider dangling in the air.

"*Aaahhhhh!*"

It swings from the ceiling, swaying in the mist coming off of the faucet, getting closer to my face as I scramble to get back out of the tub and away from its creepy round body and weird-ass bitey mouth and the sticky web.

I hate spiders.

Hate spiders.

Know what I loved about the ship?

No spiders.

"Ziggy."

"*Aaahh!*" I screech again.

I'm naked.

Completely, totally buck naked in front of a spider and now in front of Holt.

I yank blindly for anything to cover myself with, find the shower curtain, and spin inside of it.

There's brief tension, then a *clink!* as the curtain rod gives way and clatters into the tub.

The spider.

Where is the spider?

Is it still in the tub? Is it on the shower curtain? Did it crawl up to its little secret lair in the ceiling?

Why does my body itch?

Is it on me?

Holt's scanning my body, then the bathroom. "What? What's wrong? Is it a mouse? Fucking mice. I took care of the mice last year."

"Spider," I gasp.

I'm turning in circles without enough room to turn in circles, looking for the spider, pulling the curtain and the rod with me.

It's not hanging from the ceiling anymore.

Where the fuck did it go?

Is it in my hair?

Oh my god, is it in my hair?

"Ziggy," Holt says again. "Hey. *Hey.* I'll get the spider."

"Is it on me?" I gasp.

"No."

It is. He's trying to make me feel better by telling me it's not, but I itch.

I itch everywhere.

The spider's on me.

I start to spin again, but warm hands grip me by the shoulders. "It's not on you. I can see it. Hold still. I'll get it."

I finally blink up at him.

He's staring at something behind me.

The spider.

He can see the spider.

I gulp for air.

He angles past me, limping.

Oh no.

Oh no no no no.

"Don't hurt yourself," I choke out.

"I can handle this one."

"Your foot—"

"It'll be okay."

"But—"

"It will be okay."

I look down.

But I don't see his foot.

I see black boxers, half-tented with a thick hard-on, and my gaze freezes.

Not so much that I don't also take in hard, flat abs and massive thighs, but enough that I momentarily forget I'm worried about his foot.

You're an asshole friend, Ziggy.

His foot.

I need to worry about his foot, and instead, I'm staring at the outline of his penis.

"Got it," he says. "Flush it or let it go free?"

"*Flush it!*"

His dick's only so distracting when it comes to spiders.

But his chuckle—that sends a delicious shiver down my spine.

"Okay. He's gone."

He leans over, flicks something, and flushes the toilet.

"All safe now."

I lift my gaze, but it snags on his chest.

My god, he's built.

His slim waist with the man-V leads up to a broad chest and broader shoulders. Dark hair covers his pecs. His arms are a sculpted masterpiece, and I have the most intense desire to bite his biceps.

I have it bad.

I have it *so* bad.

"Thank you," I whisper.

Do not touch the man-god standing in your bathroom, Ziggy. Do not touch. Not yours. Don't—

"Better?" His voice is soft and gravelly.

And there's more movement in his boxers.

Upward movement.

Why?

Why can't we have this?

"Your foot—"

"Boot's got it."

He doesn't move to show me.

I keep gaping at him.

His body.

I want to touch.

I want to touch and lick and taste.

"You gonna be able to get out of that mess okay?"

That husky timbre to his voice sends a shiver down my spine. "I broke your bathroom."

"You dislodged a flimsy curtain rod. I can fix it tomorrow."

The water's still running. Steam's beginning to circle us. "I should turn that off."

Don't say it, Ziggy. Do it. Turn around. Turn the water off.

Don't want to though.

I want to stay here, soaking up every inch of Holt's body.

He has a scar on one shoulder. Not a surgical scar—it's too uneven. Another on his neck.

I skim a finger over his shoulder scar.

He sucks in a breath but doesn't move away.

"What did you do?"

"Don't remember."

The shower.

I need to turn the shower off.

But I'm obsessed with the way his Adam's apple bobs when he swallows. "Ziggy—"

"Thank you for saving me." My fingers trail down from his scar to trace the edge of muscle in his upper arm.

Goosebumps break out all over his skin. "My pleasure."

He hasn't tried to touch me since he steadied me when I was worried about the spider.

But his fingers are twitching like he wants to.

"If this were yesterday," I whisper, "I'd tell you I don't have any expectations. I come with a lot of baggage. But not today. Today, I'm just here. Being me."

"Tater Tot isn't baggage."

My heart swells.

I know this isn't going anywhere.

I know we shouldn't.

But I finally lift my head to study his face and find him watching me with the kind of intensity that makes my nipples tight and my vagina wet.

His pupils are dilated, lips parted, breath coming quickly.

His hair is even messier than it was when I got home tonight.

And I want to kiss him.

I want to go up on my tiptoes, wrap my arms around his thick neck, and kiss him until I can't breathe.

Instead, I'm still drifting my fingers down his arm. "If I was someone else, would you kiss me?"

"No."

A shudder rips through me.

No.

No.

I step back and almost fall into the tub, but Holt catches me.

Both arms wrapped around me.

His face inches from mine.

"Sorry," I stammer. "I—"

"I want to kiss you. You. Exactly as you are. Not if you

were someone else. You wouldn't be you if you were someone else."

Oh.

I lift my face to his again.

"I shouldn't want to." His voice is hoarse and delicious. "But I do. I've wanted to kiss you since the first night we met."

My heart squeezes.

So do a few other regions in my body. "I was a mess."

"You were fucking adorable. The memory of you and that chicken lives rent-free in my head. In the good way."

Embarrassment would be the proper reaction to remembering the way I was hoovering a whole rotisserie chicken in my car, but he's so sincere that I get a little hot in the eyeballs.

It's special to feel appreciated even in your not-best moments.

"As far as I'm concerned, you still play lacrosse," I tell the man who hasn't let go of me since he saved me from tripping over the bathtub.

A hint of a smile teases his lips, and that's it.

I'm done.

I can't take this anymore.

If I don't kiss him, I might die.

So I do.

I cup his cheeks in my hands and go up on my toes and press my lips to his.

His whole body shudders against mine, and then he's kissing me back. Lips teasing and suckling. Arms wrapping tighter around me. His breath warm on my face, his nose touching mine.

The stubble on his face is just long enough to be the

softest sandpaper, and when he parts his lips and touches his tongue to mine, I whimper in relief and deepen the kiss.

Finally.

Finally.

It feels like I've waited my entire life for this moment. Waited my entire life for this kiss.

Waited my entire life for *him.*

He strokes my shoulders, his fingers brushing my bare back, and it's my turn for goosebumps.

I thread my hands into his hair.

He lowers one hand to my ass.

I kiss him harder.

He makes a rough noise at the back of his throat, and then I'm against the wall, straddling one thick, powerful leg, the shower curtain slipping down, exposing my breasts to steamy air while his tongue strokes mine, hot and wet and demanding.

My breasts are heavy. My nipples are tight. My clit pulses as I press my sex against his hard muscle, shamelessly rubbing myself against his leg.

I don't know if he'll ever kiss me again after tonight.

If one of us will suddenly remember we're not supposed to do this and actually care to stop.

I don't want to stop.

I want to stay here, his body pressing against mine while he devours my mouth and presses a leg between my thighs and slides his hands up to the sides of my breasts, his thumbs sneaking between us to rub my hard nipples, his erection pressing into my belly.

He breaks the kiss with a gasp. "Fuck, Ziggy."

"No no no," I whisper. "No thinking. Just—kiss me again. Please."

He's panting as he looks down between us to where his hands are now cradling my breasts. "So fucking gorgeous."

I press a kiss to his scruffy cheek, then another, and another, angling to his square jawline while I stroke his neck.

He shudders again. "Don't stop."

Don't stop. I want you. I need you.

He doesn't say it.

Of course he doesn't.

But I can feel it. I feel it in the rise and fall of his chest between us. I see it in the hooded desire in his eyes. I hear it in the yearning in his voice.

You think a man can carry the weight of the world with all of his strength, but he's not meant to be alone either.

"Come to bed with me," I whisper between kisses.

"Ziggy—"

"I want you." He smells like salty ocean and raw earth and summer kisses in a lake, and I can't get enough. I kiss his neck and breathe him in. "Please. Just once. I know you're leaving tomorrow. Don't—don't go before you give me one night. Just one night. Please."

He pulls back until he can look down at me, pulling his leg back from between my thighs too.

I do.

I know he's leaving.

He doesn't have to tell me. It was so damn awkward at dinner and afterward—there was no question.

He's leaving.

This is my last chance.

My only chance.

His eyes are nearly black now, and I swear I know what he's thinking.

One night will never be enough.

He's not wrong.

But tomorrow Ziggy doesn't care.

We'll deal with tomorrow when it gets here.

What if tomorrow doesn't come?

What if tonight is all we have?

"Lose the shower curtain," he says hoarsely.

I wiggle out of it, letting it drop to the floor.

He looks down, his hands stroking from my breasts down to my hips as his erection bobs inside his boxers.

I bite my lip. I'm still stroking his neck, but I'd like to be stroking his penis.

Licking it.

Sucking on it.

His thumbs brush my lower belly where the barest hint of swelling is finally showing off my pregnancy. I bought new pants to be more comfortable weeks ago, but I haven't started showing at all until this past week.

"So fucking gorgeous."

Steam curls around us. I shift, rubbing my calf against his as I step out of the twisted curtain at my feet, and I let my hands drift down his chest, to his stomach, and lower, tracing the line of hair to where it disappears into his boxers.

"Come to bed," I say.

Once more, he lifts that serious gaze to me.

He doesn't say a word, but again, I swear I hear what he's thinking.

This will change everything.

Maybe it will.

Maybe it won't.

But something that feels this good, this *right*, can't be bad for us.

And if it is, I don't want good anymore.

I just want him.

He lowers his mouth to mine, and this time the kiss is slow and long and deep, with his hips rolling against mine, pressing his erection into my belly while I let my hands glide around his trim waist until I'm squeezing his ass.

So much muscle.

So much power.

He growls low in his throat, and then he shifts, pulling out of the kiss to drift lower, licking and suckling at my jaw, my throat, my collarbones, and lower.

I gasp when he swirls his tongue around one nipple, then the other. His hands hold my hips while he kisses me lower, down my breastbone, over my stomach to my belly button. My clit is aching to be touched, and I'm so turned on that I'm wet between my thighs.

"Holt—"

"You smell fucking fantastic." His face drifts down, peppering kisses over my lower abdomen, making me tingle with anticipation, with desire, with desperate, heavy need.

And then he's parting my legs as he kneels, pushing my trembling thighs apart.

His tongue touches my clit while his whiskers tickle my most sensitive skin, and I almost come unglued. "Oh god," I gasp.

"Wider, kitten. Spread these legs wider so I can eat all of you."

I grip his hair while I open myself wider, braced against the wall.

"Ah, good girl," he murmurs. He lifts one of my legs to rest on his shoulder and then his face is between my thighs, his breath in the dark curls covering my mound, licking my pussy, his rough scruff rubbing against my inner thighs, and *oh my god.*

"You're so wet." He flicks my clit with his tongue.

I gasp in sheer pleasure at the electric sensation building deep inside me. "You—make me—wet."

"Good." He licks me again.

My legs fall open more, offering all of me to him. I can't think. Can't fully catch my breath.

Don't want to do either.

I just want to ride the sensations of Holt licking and sucking and teasing my pussy while desperate heat coils deep, deep inside me, revel in his approving hums while he eats me.

He swirls his tongue around my clit, and my hips buck into his face.

"That's a good girl," he murmurs. "Give me more of this delicious pussy."

"Holt—"

"So good." He licks me again. "Touch your breasts, Ziggy. Squeeze your nipples."

I don't know how I have enough control of my own body to obey his orders, but I do.

I rub my breasts, so much fuller today than they were before I got pregnant.

So much more sensitive too.

I squeeze my nipples while he sucks on my clit, and when he slides two fingers into my vagina, a high cry leaves my throat.

Oh my holy Chianti in heaven.

I'm coming so hard and fast I don't even realize it's happening until I'm throwing my head back against the wall, dropping my hands to grip his hair and hold him between my legs, my toes curling while one foot presses hard into the floor and my other leg goes straight.

The world is glittery rainbows flashing in my vision. I feel the orgasm in my breasts, in my belly, in my heart.

Everything releasing.

Everything letting go on endless waves of hot, thick, wet ecstasy.

All courtesy of this utterly irresistible man who's holding my hips while he licks and suckles at my pussy, eating me through my orgasm.

I don't want it to end. I don't want the world outside to exist.

I want to just be here, free to explore this thing between us.

No pressure one way or another.

Dammit.

Dammit.

My eyeballs are getting leaky.

The best orgasm of my life, and my eyeballs are getting leaky.

My body releases its last shudder, and I slump lower against the wall. "Oh my god," I whisper.

My voice cracks.

Holt angles a look at me.

"Good," I whisper as I stroke my hand through his hair. "Just so good."

God, he's beautiful.

Those observant brown eyes. Strong nose. Scruff just long enough to almost be a full beard, glistening with the moisture from between my legs. Thick neck. Broad shoulders.

And a boot on the leg he's kneeling on as he reaches behind us to shut off the shower.

"We're not done," he tells me.

I smile. "Good. Let me get your crutches, and—*ahh!*"

And apparently not.

Because this deity of a man is scooping me into his arms.

Being the hero I didn't even know I needed.

For now.

For tonight.

Tomorrow doesn't matter.

Even if it should.

24

Holt

THERE WAS one right answer after I disposed of the spider.

It's *good night, Ziggy, I'll see you in the morning.*

That was the right answer.

But the wrong answer, kissing her, touching her, was the *only* answer.

I'm fired.

I am so fired when her stepfather finds out.

And I don't fucking care.

Not when those wide blue eyes and that smile are telling me I hold the key to her happiness. Not when she's using every bit of her being to communicate that she trusts me. When she's showing me with the way she kisses me and touches me that she likes me.

When she's fucking delicious and so responsive and so vulnerable all at the same time.

Fuck tomorrow. Fuck being fired.

I want this woman.

End of story.

That's all I'm thinking about as I lift her up to carry her out of the bathroom.

After she shrieks, she wraps her arms around my neck and presses her lips to my neck again. "Holt, your foot—"

Hurts like a bitch as I put weight on it for the first time in weeks, and I'm limping as I carry her out of the bathroom, but ask me if I care. I have Ziggy in my arms and a raging erection. The foot will be fine. "What foot? I don't have feet."

Ziggy snort-giggles. "If you hurt yourself—"

"Can't hear you over the beauty of your naked body."

Jessica snorts at me—some guard dog, letting us battle a spider on our own—but she doesn't get up out of her doggie bed and she doesn't try to stop me from manhandling her favorite person.

Smart dog.

She'd find out what a doghouse is if she tried.

Ziggy's fingers brush the back of my neck, and she nestles closer in my arms.

My dick aches. My balls are so tight they're on fire. I can still taste her on my tongue, and I fucking love it.

She licks my jawline. Considering how hard and ready and desperate I am after tasting her pussy, the feel of her tongue on my face makes me nearly cross-eyed.

I want this woman.

I want her in my bed. I want her in my house. I want her in my life.

Her and her baby.

The dog. With another dog who likes me.

Family.

She doesn't ask where we're going as I carry her across

the hall to my room. Doesn't object when I settle her in the center of my bed amongst the twisted sheets.

Not Ziggy.

No, she's cradling my face again and kissing me before I can get into bed myself.

I crawl onto the mattress, the fucking boot catching on the edge.

"Your foot—okay?" she says between kisses.

I grunt in response and capture her mouth so she can't ask any more questions.

I love kissing this woman. Her eager tongue, her possessive hands, the little noises she makes when I stroke her ass —there's no chance in hell this is the last time I'll ever kiss her.

She feels too good.

Too *right*.

But my fucking foot is stuck on the edge of the bed and I can't get closer.

I try lifting the boot, and it takes the crumpled sheets with it.

"Holt?" Ziggy whispers.

"It's fine."

She blinks at me, lit only by the moonlight coming in the window and the light from her room filtering across the hall. I can't tell if her gaze is addled with lust or fully aware of something not being right.

"What's not fine?" she asks.

I sigh.

"Your foot?" She twists beneath me, looking down my body. "Here. Let me help."

No.

No.

She's naked. Completely bare. I can touch her anywhere. Kiss her anywhere. Lick her anywhere. Again.

And I'm ruining the fucking moment by being unable to get around in my own damn bed.

"I got it. It's just—stuck."

She slips out from beneath me like a freaking magician, tugs once on the sheets, and then I'm free.

"How do you usually sleep?" she asks.

I roll to my side. "I don't want to *sleep*."

A grin flashes at me as she walks on her knees back onto the bed. She pushes my shoulder until I'm on my back. "Okay, grumpy pants."

Shit. "Ziggy—"

"Shh." She slides one hand down my chest, leaning in to press a kiss to my jaw. "You're allowed to be frustrated."

"Some parts more than others," I mutter.

Her hand drifts lower. "Like this part?"

She grips my cock through my boxers, and I hiss out a tortured breath. "*Yes.*"

"I might have something for that."

My dick twitches in her hand. I squeeze my eyes shut and concentrate on the sensation of someone else touching me, even through my boxers. "Feels—so—good."

"Feels very large," she whispers.

My frustration melts away, replaced with raging-hot desire for this glorious creature praising my cock.

My booted foot is hanging off the edge of my bed. I can't flip her over without banging it around, which means I can't make her scream.

But it doesn't matter, because she's slipping her hands under my boxers, letting my hard-on spring free into the cool air.

Relief mingles with the desperate need to stroke my cock, but before I can grip myself, she leans over, tucks her hair behind her back, wraps both hands around me, and licks me, her tongue swirling around the tip of my penis.

My hips jerk off the bed.

She giggles. "So that's all it takes…"

I might not be able to roll around, but I can sit up, and I do. "Do you have any idea just how close I am already after eating you?" I growl as I grip her under the arms and pull her onto me.

"No. How close?" She leans over me, kissing my neck, her hair slipping down to tickle my chest. Her belly brushes my dick, and my eyes cross again.

"So—close," I grit out.

Breathe.

Breathe.

Think about Fletcher in his waffle budgie smugglers.

"That's good," she whispers, "because I'd hate for you to not feel as good as I do."

"You feel better than winning a cup after being written off as the worst team in the league."

She strokes my chest while she presses soft kisses to my jaw, hovering over my dick like she's giving me a minute. "That's very specific."

"Best day of my life."

"I haven't had the best day of my life yet."

"Challenge accepted. Get on my cock."

She laughs.

Fuck, I do too.

It's been months since I've been with a woman, but probably years since I laughed in bed with one.

And it feels so damn good.

I hook a hand behind her neck and shift so I can kiss her. She tastes like paradise. All of her. Her skin. Her mouth. Her pussy.

And while she kisses me back, she centers herself over my hard-on.

"Condom?" I ask against her mouth, barely getting the word out.

She half-laughs. "Can't get more pregnant. And I've had all of the STI tests done the past couple months. I'm clear."

"Same."

"Good."

I kiss her again, and she slowly takes me into her body, making me nearly whimper at her hot, slick core squeezing me.

"You *are* big," she murmurs.

For the amount of extra blood surging to my cock, it's a wonder I can think. "You're welcome."

She giggles again, and fuck me if she doesn't squeeze me tighter.

Bliss.

Pure bliss.

She sinks all the way down with a shudder that makes her breasts jiggle.

Fucking perfection.

I shift my pelvis to press up into her, then freeze. "The baby?" I whisper hoarsely.

Shit.

Is this okay for the baby?

She smiles at me as she lifts her hips, then settles on me again. "Baby's fine."

"This won't—"

"No. This won't hurt Tater Tot."

My damn heart swells up eight sizes.

She's using my nickname for her baby.

She presses another kiss to my jaw, then shifts to lift her hips again, finding a rhythm as she rides me.

Her hands rest on my chest, fingers digging into me. When she dips her head, her hair brushes my shoulders. I thrust to meet her as she pumps my dick.

I can still taste her on my tongue, mingling with the scent of her vanilla honey shampoo. I roam her body with my hands, squeezing her ass, teasing her nipples, stroking down her spine from nape to crack, until we're both panting and my cock is so hard and ready.

"Ziggy—" I gasp.

"Oh god, almost there," she whimpers. "Feel—so—good. You—so—good."

I can do this.

I can hold on for one more minute.

I grit my teeth and thrust harder into her, gripping her thighs, shifting my hands until I can brush my thumb over that sweet little nub at the top of her sex.

She gasps and throws her head back, squeezing me tighter, and then the spasms come around my cock.

Thank *fuck*.

I let go with a groan of relief as I hit my climax too, cock pulsing, squeezing her thighs tighter while she grinds hard on my hips.

Dots dance in my vision.

One foot curls.

The other's fucking stuck in place.

But Ziggy's gasping breath as she comes all over my cock is music.

Her grip on my shoulders makes me feel like her anchor.

The thing holding her life together.

I want to hold this woman's life together.

I want her to know she matters. That I care.

I want new life in this house.

I want *her*.

For as long as I can have her.

Ziggy will cost me my rugby career. Maybe not tomorrow. Maybe not next week.

But eventually.

And as the last of her orgasm leaves her and she collapses on top of me in time with my own body relaxing, panting and blowing her soft breath across my chest, her fingers gently drifting over my shoulder as she releases her grip, I don't care.

For this moment?

Worth it.

"Can I—stay?" she gasps.

I slide my tired arms around her back and squeeze.

Let her stay in bed with me tonight?

That's the least I'll do for her.

The very, very least.

25

Ziggy

I wake up to a growl.

Is that my stomach?

Wait. I'm not alone.

Holt.

Oh god.

Holt.

I'm in bed with Holt.

I pry my eyes open, registering bright sunlight and soft gray sheets and dark blue walls and a warm body beside me.

A warm body whose arm I'm drooling on.

I suck the drool back into my mouth and hear the growl again.

Is that his stomach?

He jerks in bed. "*Ow*. Stop it, asshole," he mutters.

I lift a sleepy head.

He swings himself up to sitting and swats at something at the edge of the bed.

The growl—*Jessica.*

Jessica's growling at both of us.

I leap to my feet, trip on a bag next to the bed, catch myself, realize I'm completely and totally naked, and start to laugh.

Jessica's jumping at the end of the bed, trying to bite Holt's boot, which is hanging off the edge. Holt's staring at me like he doesn't know who I am or where I came from.

And I'm naked.

Just naked.

"Stop," I tell the dog.

She grunts, but she also plops her stout body down to sit beside the bed, scowling at me.

"Do you need to go outside?"

I don't know what time it is, but it has to be past her breakfast time.

"I'll go take care of her." I look at Holt, and then I freeze.

The man's rubbing the dark whiskers around his jaw, hooded eyes dark as midnight as they look me up and down.

And I like it.

Heat builds between my thighs, and I realize they're sore.

Muscle and skin.

I have whisker burn between my thighs.

He gave that to me last night.

And now it's tomorrow.

When we have to face what we did last night.

"And then I can make breakfast. I'm feeling like omelets. Weird, right? Potatoes on the side, but I want eggs today. Are you hungry? Does anything sound good? We're a little low on groceries. I was going to make a menu for next week and hit the store later today. My mom—we're going to look at a few more houses this afternoon. In case one's right. Early. Early afternoon. Not later. When it's dinnertime. And would've been movie time. If we were—"

As I'm babbling, he's scooting down to the edge of the bed.

Naked.

Long, thick cock straining out from a bed of dark curls.

Stalking me.

I'm equal parts thrilled at the idea he wants me still and terrified that this is the only way off the bed and he just needs to get up to pee or something.

Or rub out his morning wood without me.

I like his morning wood. I want to stroke it. Silky skin. Thick veins wrapped around it. Deep pink. Thick, broad head.

That is theoretically no longer mine to touch.

He didn't confirm or deny that he's leaving today, but I could sense it last night.

It's what's best for both of us.

For his career. For his life.

For my peace with my family.

But that penis—

His is my favorite penis.

He reaches the end of the bed, snags me by the hips, pulls me flush to his body, then slides his hands up, over my breasts, up my neck, to hook one hand behind my head and pull my face down to his.

"I'm hungry," he says.

And then he's kissing me.

Hard.

Deep.

It's a once-in-a-lifetime, bone-melting, heart-pounding, *I own you now* kiss.

My belly flips.

My tender thighs quiver.

My breasts ache, and my nipples tighten so hard I feel it all the way in my vagina.

I rest my hands on his chest, hot skin and wiry hair beneath my fingers as his tongue strokes mine.

So this isn't just me.

There's something here.

He still wants it.

He still wants *me*.

A loud bark startles me out of the kiss.

Jessica's glaring at us as she does the potty dance.

Dammit.

"Ohright," I stammer. "Alkay. *Okay. All right.* I'm coming."

Holt snorts softly.

I look at him, and he's poker-faced.

"Robe by the door. Use it."

More warmth floods my entire body.

Don't get all the way dressed, but wear my clothes so you don't horrify the neighbors.

Right.

I'm naked.

I snag the robe from the hook by the door and, as I'm wrapping the copious amount of fabric around my body, glance back at him.

He's staring at my ass and stroking his cock.

Our eyes meet.

"You would too if you could see what I see," he says.

"Save some for me," I reply.

"Fuck, Ziggy."

I slowly lick my lips. "Good plan. I like it."

Those eyes bore into me. *We're fucked.*

In trouble.

Dancing with danger.

Until three months ago, my entire life was spent being the good girl.

I'm over it.

"I'll convince him," I whisper. "Just—give me time."

He nods as Jessica barks at me.

Crap.

We're in dangerous territory.

I finish tying Holt's thick terry cloth robe around me, then hustle myself and the dog down the stairs and out back.

It's humid already, but the air is only lukewarm. Not yet fires-of-hell hot.

Not nearly as hot as Holt's bedroom last night. Or my bathroom.

I smile to myself as I wait at the porch door for the dog to come back in for breakfast.

He *did* want to take me on a date.

I rub my lower belly.

He wanted to take *us* on a date.

Didn't he?

He doesn't strike me as the type who'd put his career on the line for a fling.

But what do I really know about him?

I can ask.

That would be fun.

Hi, Holt, about your hard-on, we'll get there, but first, can I ask how you feel about being a father? I know you offered to marry me, but haha, that was just a joke and we both know it. Wasn't it? Or was it?

I need to get a grip.

One day at a time.

That's what this is.

One day at a time.

And we have six months until Tater Tot arrives.

Is six months long enough to know if it's forever?

Get out of your head, Ziggy.

I blow out a breath as Jessica bounces back up the stairs. She gives me the stink eye.

"I realize you don't like men, but he's one of the good guys," I tell her.

She snorts at me, getting doggy snot all over Holt's robe.

"Are you for real right now?" I ask her. "Was that because it's his clothes, or because you think I've gone to the dark side?"

She lifts her head in the air and doesn't answer me as she trots past me and demands entrance to the kitchen.

When we step inside, Holt's there.

Disappointment slithers through me.

He's only wearing shorts, balancing on his crutches again, and there's evidence that he's still semi-hard dancing under the fabric as he pulls food out of the fridge and sets it on the counter.

He glances over at me. "Baby's not going hungry on my watch."

How the hell could my dad object to this?

I blink hard and fast against the joy threatening to leak out of my eyes. "Thank you."

Jessica grumbles to herself.

I get her breakfast and fresh water, then shoo Holt away from the food. "Go put your foot up. I've got this."

"Are you sure it's okay for you to eat eggs?" he asks as he backs away. "I'm wary of you and chicken products."

It takes me a hot minute to process what he means, but when I do, I crack up. "Understandable. I'll try to keep it down."

"We're out of saltines."

I blink at him while he settles onto a stool across the island, then I start chopping vegetables for our omelets. "We are, aren't we? I took the last sleeve to work. I'll grab more at the store after I'm done with Mom. You can text me if you need anything else."

"What if someone sees your phone?"

"I changed your contact info. You're now *Cole Webber*."

"Boring. You're *Hellbeast Dogsitter* in my phone."

"That's more letters than your average text response to people."

He cracks a short laugh. "I text long."

"Do you, now?"

"I do, but not to women I have crushes on when I know it can't go anywhere."

There's that warm glow again. And I think I'm blushing.

The man had his face between my thighs last night. I drooled on him in my sleep.

And I'm blushing at the confirmation that he has a crush on me.

"You make the list. I'll order it for delivery," he says. "So we can still go see the movie. If you're up for it. And have time."

Yes. "I'll make sure I'm done in time."

We stare at each other.

We're doing this.

We're going to date under my dad's nose.

See if this is real.

"I really do have a lot of baggage," I whisper.

"Everyone does."

"A baby's a bit more work than a dog."

He chuckles to himself, shaking his head. "About like taking care of a guy dying of cancer, but with a better payoff in the end."

I pause with my knife and study him.

"Sorry. Dark. Dark humor helps."

"No, I know. I do it too sometimes. We all do."

"I just meant—I take care of people, Ziggy. It's what I do. What I've always done. My brother. My teammates. My neighbors. If I'd made it in Spain, I would've made a whole new family of new teammates to take care of there. Commitment doesn't scare me. People don't scare me. A baby's just a little person. More family. More *good* family."

I don't know who put this man in my path to be the one to find me gnawing on a grocery-store rotisserie chicken in a parking lot a month ago, but for the first time since I found out my best friend hated me, I feel like I've found a place I belong.

If I can get my dad on board.

"How are you single?" I ask him.

"Grief's a bitch. How are *you* single?"

"Subliminal messages in my teenage years about no boy being good enough for me coupled with lingering childhood money fears making me a workaholic and a career environment where coworkers leave every week because their contracts have ended or they're reassigned."

That gets me a slow blink. "Your dad bought a fucking rugby team on a whim because the cost of the team was a good tax write-off. I read the articles. What we cost him every year in not being fully profitable is in the noise."

"Stepdad." I focus on the vegetables again.

"You call him Dad."

"Doesn't mean I want or should get any of his money. Not like I helped him make it. If he dies, Miranda gets everything but the house, which will go to my mom, and a trust fund for Mom now that they've made it past their ten-year anniversary. It was in the prenup."

He scratches his jaw and watches me.

"Honestly? I think that's part of why he's so insistent that she not date any of the players. She could own the team one day. Messy dynamics."

"But you won't."

"I will not. Every time he's said he's changing his will to include me, I tell him no. He'll probably leave me something anyway, because I can't stop him, but I don't want to live off of what he built. I don't want to depend on it. I want to be able to take care of myself. To build and live my own life. Get back to working in the wine industry. Directly. Not doing a made-up-for-me job running catering for the team. I *miss* wine. Having a glass with dinner. Trying a new vintage of an old favorite. Watching people find one they like… It's a fun job. I miss it. And I have no idea if I'll ever work in the industry again once the baby's born, but I hope I do."

"If it makes you happy, then I do too."

I put a sauté pan on the stove to heat while I crack eggs. "That's what I hope Dad says too. *If it makes you happy.*"

He lifts his brows. "Think he will?"

"No. I mean, not immediately. But maybe eventually? Even if I moved in with my parents or you moved in with a teammate, you've been my friend. Those are in short supply in my life right now. If anyone in my family wants to tell me we can't be friends, they can fuck right off."

He lifts his brows.

I grin. "Or so I'd tell them if I didn't know how that would end. Diplomacy is going to get us much further than *fuck off*."

"You like him?"

Isn't that the question. "I didn't at first. I thought he was trying to buy my approval with phones and video games and money for shopping trips. I might've whined a time or two to Abby Nora that I wished my biological dad hadn't died in a car accident before I was old enough to remember him. But Roland took me to school—himself, no driver—and he picked me up from my after-school activities, and he helped me with my homework. Miranda didn't live with us, not full-time, so I could've been a major inconvenience, but he did the dad things without complaining. He likes taking care of people too. He just takes it too far sometimes."

"He's not wrong. Your sister shouldn't date any of the guys on the team."

"Are they all that awful?"

"Yes."

His grin says he's lying. "But you're not."

"I'm fucking perfect."

I smile instead of agreeing with him out loud.

Because from where I'm standing, he *is* pretty damn perfect.

I *do* want to spend more time with him. Get to know him better. Sleep with him every night.

And figure out how to convince my stepdad that me

dating one of his players isn't the worst thing that could ever happen.

"I think Dad can be reasonable," I say as Holt's phone dings.

He glances at it, then at me, then back at the phone.

"What?" I ask.

"Coach emailed." He thumbs over the screen. "New addition in the office... Owner's daughter... You know the rules... Only time I'll say it..."

My heart sinks. "No."

His smile is grim. "Yep."

His phone dings again.

He reads the screen and sighs.

"What now?"

He holds out the phone.

I wipe my hands and lean across the island to see.

It's a text from Fletcher.

Fletcher: *You're fucked, man. Been nice knowing you. Extra bummer that I can't take your dog when Roland kills you. But can I have your weight set? Good grips.*

It's not funny.

It's not.

But I laugh anyway.

Yeah, dark humor absolutely gets you through sometimes.

"If I'm a dead man, I'm going out happy," Holt says. "We still on for the movies? Please?"

Go on a date with this handsome, kind, generous man?

And then come home with him afterward?

How could I say no?

"Only if I get fries at Cod Pieces first."

"Deal."

We're likely in trouble. And right now, I don't care.

26

Ziggy

THERE'S nothing like seeing your mom after a night of panty-melting sex to make you feel like a teenager again.

"Ziggy! Look at you. You're glowing." She hugs me tight as she meets me at her doorstep, where I'm early since she was making noises about coming to pick me up. I do *not* want to risk her realizing the house I'm staying at is Holt's house. What if she recognizes his Jeep? Or she sees him through the window? Or one of the neighbors sees her and mentions him? "Pregnancy looks so good on you, sweetheart."

It's not the pregnancy.

It's the serotonin. It's the sex.

It's Holt.

If he were any other man, I'd tell her, and then she'd fuss about me dating while my hormones are out of whack and tell me to be extra careful with my heart right now.

Too late, Mom, and by the way, he's one of Dad's players.

I stifle a sigh and force a smile. "Second-trimester glow."

"We're finding the right house for you today. I can feel it."

"Hope so." Maybe.

Maybe not.

Holt's house is comfortable. I like living there.

Before I left, I finished the grocery list and he ordered everything for delivery. Tomorrow, I'm making hand pies for Miranda with extras to keep at home for us.

Now, though, I'm getting into Mom's Mercedes as she drives us to the first house of the day, a two-story colonial at the edge of Heartwood Valley.

Two weeks ago, I would've simply thought to myself that it won't be this one. I can tell by the large, pristine lawn and the size of the neighbors' houses that this one's outside of my price range.

Today, I have a completely different reason I'm not interested.

It's because I love the house I'm living in now.

The dog who just fits there.

The man who owns the house and is sneaking into my heart.

And it's not the mind-blowing orgasms. It's the thoughtful little things like ordering dinner when I'm tired or handling grocery delivery since I'm supposed to be looking at houses, even though that's weird when we've basically agreed that we want to explore a relationship and we're already living together. The admirable things like the way he keeps trying to win Jessica over. The easy things like telling him more about Abby Nora and working on the cruise ships, and listening to his stories of living overseas and things he misses about his brother.

Niki pulls into the driveway behind us, and Mom stops gushing over how pretty the lawn is to wave at her.

Moms are hilarious.

Of course Niki can see us.

But it's polite to wave.

"Good morning, ladies," Niki calls as she climbs out of her car. "We're going to find something amazing today, I can feel it."

I eyeball the house we're supposed to tour first again.

"Now, I know it looks bigger than what you were thinking, but it's very cozy inside," Niki says. "Just wait. You'll love it."

My mom loves it before we even walk in the door. It's pretty obvious with the way her gaze goes soft and she seems to reach out to pet it from afar.

Not that I can blame her.

I'd be within walking distance of her house, which would mean more Grandma time for the baby, and more baby time for Grandma.

But when Niki hands us the promotional packet, the first thing I look at is the listing price.

Definitely not cozy, even if it's less than I'd expect for a house in this neighborhood.

"Divorce fire sale," she whispers. "Don't say anything about it inside. I don't know if they have their cameras turned on."

Awesome.

As expected, Mom loves it, and I have waking nightmares about how much it would cost to furnish the four bedrooms, two living rooms, den, office, basement, and sitting room.

I've saved a good bit over the past seven years, but saving *that* much wasn't actually physically—or fiscally—possible.

The next three houses aren't right either.

The family home in the Belmont District truly is cozy. It's in the right price range and it doesn't seem to need any major upgrades or renovations to be livable, but it's also on the main road into the neighborhood, and we see a dog almost get hit by a car as we're leaving.

I picture Jessica, and the possibility tips into the *absolutely not* column.

Even if I could logic my way into believing Jessica wouldn't run into the street, I imagine the baby toddling out there, and the hormones take over and I break down bawling.

Not the house's fault.

As Niki says, location matters.

There's a bungalow in a neighborhood of smaller homes closer to downtown that has uneven air conditioning. It's quaint in that you can tell it's been expanded a few times, but we smell mold in the basement.

Not hard to tell that Mom's glad to have a solid reason to issue a veto. It was already clear she didn't want me to like it —*Oh, Ziggy, it's so far from the garage to the kitchen. You don't want to spend the next twenty years hauling groceries that far*— but it's even more clear she's glad to have a health reason to stand on.

This house is perfect for someone. That someone isn't me though.

And then there's the last house.

It's about six blocks from Holt's house in a part of the neighborhood that I haven't explored on walks with Jessica yet.

Light blue siding. Simple landscaping. We can see from

the front that the backyard has a fence. It's old, but from the outside, it looks like it's been well cared for.

Like Holt's house.

My heart picks up.

This.

This could be it.

I slide a look at Niki as she climbs out of her car behind us and she winks at me.

Oh my god.

The last house was a setup.

She knew Mom would hate it.

My pulse is on fire as we walk to the front door.

I'd be within walking distance of Holt.

My friend.

My lover.

My maybe-more.

We'd have time to explore and work out what we are without the pressure of living together.

Niki unlocks the door, and we enter through the foyer and into—*uh-oh.*

"Oh no," she murmurs.

"Absolutely not," Mom declares.

I stare in horror at the, ah, *furniture* in the living room. "This wouldn't stay with the house," I say. "Surely they'd take it with them."

It's a sex den.

The living room is a sex den.

There's a bed in the living room, but it's not a *normal* bed. There's a cage under the mattress.

A cage.

And next to it is a chair with cutouts and attachments for wrist and ankle ties.

A full wall of items that I am actively refusing to acknowledge that I'm seeing.

With a—what *is* that hanging from the ceiling?

It looks like a chandelier, but it also looks like an octopus. A sparkly purple octopus. With—*oh my god.*

With penises at the ends of each of its tentacles.

Mom eyes me.

She knows as well as I do what this is.

I know why I know what it is. I had a roommate who watched documentaries, and I saw one with her about sex rooms.

Hopefully Mom saw it too and that's the only reason she also knows what we're staring at.

"This isn't the furniture in the listing," Niki sputters. "Here. Look. Isn't this quaint with the way the staging photos are set? You could put a chair in front of the window. And the fireplace could be opened back up to work again. Some new curtains, a new rug, and *voilà.* Cozy living room. Let's check the kitchen, shall we? The listing says the owners are happy to offer a credit toward kitchen upgrades."

We head toward what we assume is the kitchen, but instead, we find ourselves in a pink-flower wallpapered room lined with shelves and shelves of dolls.

Mom gasps and grabs my hand.

I squeeze it back. "They'd...surely...take those too."

All three of us hustle into the next room, which is the kitchen.

When Holt told me he'd renovated his kitchen, I assumed it had likely had yellowing Formica countertops and peeling brown vinyl flooring and a chipped porcelain sink and small cabinets that had possibly been painted white or green or blue in an attempt to do a quick makeover.

Something similar to the kitchen that Mom and I lived with before she married Dad.

And that's what I expect to find here too.

But that's not what we find.

That's not what we find at all.

There's only one row of cabinets, and they look more like industrial cabinets than kitchen cabinets. Instead of a full-size fridge—even a small full-size fridge—there are two dorm fridges stacked on top of each other. Countless clocks hang on the walls that would otherwise be covered by cabinets. The sink has a hose for a faucet. The flooring is dirt.

Dirt.

And— "Where is the oven?" Mom asks.

We all stare at an open space between two windows that looks oven-sized, but which has a fire pit sitting inside it instead.

A wood firepit.

With ash and blackened sticks and something that looks like cotton inside of it.

"This was *not* in the listing photo," Niki says.

"Are you sure we're in the right house?" Mom murmurs back.

We don't even look at the bedrooms.

We definitely don't go into the basement.

And my heart is sinking to my toes as we head back to our cars.

Rush, honestly.

I'm no longer glad this house is only six blocks from Holt's house.

"That first house isn't looking so bad now, is it?" Mom says quietly to me while Niki re-locks the door. "You know we'd help you—"

She's not wrong. It doesn't look so bad now. But still—
"Mom. It's not a good long-term plan for me."

"But what if you meet someone and fall in love and want more kids? You wouldn't have to uproot our little bean like I had to uproot you."

Does she know?

Does she know my glow is more than just pregnancy hormones?

I try to picture Holt in the colonial house, and I can't do it.

It's too...*posh* for him.

And I don't mean he's not smart or classy or white-collar enough.

I just mean it doesn't feel right. I try to picture him here, and instead I see him mowing the neighbor's postage stamp yard and helping change someone's oil and fixing the air pressure in a kid's bike tire.

Not living in a neighborhood where there are yard services and everyone's cars are picked up by the dealer when it's time for an oil change.

There wouldn't be a Mrs. Massery dropping by with a coconut cream cake. Or a Bernie asking me if I'm having trouble with the postal worker who delivers mail in the neighborhood too.

And honestly?

I like it.

It's not just about where a guy I slept with last night would fit.

It's about how much I like the community of his neighborhood.

It's like being on the ship, always surrounded by people that you know and help out as you can, but with a little more space between fancier, bigger cabins.

Mom sighs. "We'll talk more at lunch."

At her suggestion, we head to Noble V, a wine bar downtown.

I can't have the wine, but they have a non-alcoholic ginger cocktail that sounds delicious.

And the best roasted potatoes in all of downtown.

I shouldn't have lunch.

I'm meeting Holt in two hours to have fried fish and French fries.

But my appetite is coming back, and honestly, I think I could eat two meals back-to-back today.

Making up for all of the food I didn't have while I was morning sick.

Or possibly I worked up an appetite last night.

And this morning while thanking Holt for ordering groceries.

We park in a nearby garage and walk the block to the restaurant while Niki tells us about some lofts she's shown in this area.

Not practical long-term with a baby, but it could be a short-term solution.

If I want to have space from Holt while we figure out if this is real or not.

Except I don't want space.

That's what I'm thinking—that I don't want space from Holt—when we step into Noble V. I've been here a few times before on various trips home between contracts, so the exposed brick walls and the slick classic wood bar and the metal dome lights over black tablecloths are all familiar.

Unfortunately, so is the blond head of the woman bouncing a newborn baby in front of us at the hostess stand.

I suck in an audible breath, and that little noise is enough to attract her attention, and she turns fully around to look back at us.

I drop my gaze while Abby Nora stares at me. My heart starts pounding.

"Ziggy. What a…surprise," she says. "I didn't know you were still here."

I make myself square my shoulders and look back at her despite the sudden grief and anger and touch of fear raging in my veins, but Mom's replying before I can.

"Oh, you didn't know Ziggy moved home? We're so lucky to get to see her every day."

"Ship life got too hard, hmm?"

The door swooshes open behind us, and Abby Nora lifts her chin to whoever's there. "They're getting our table ready."

"Fantastic. Thanks, babe." Josh, her husband, steps around us to plant a kiss on her head.

And then Eli Harrison steps around her too.

Shit.

Shit.

"Mom—" I whisper, turning away.

"Oh. Ziggy," Josh says. "You're…here."

I don't need to look to know he and Abby Nora are trading a look. Probably grimaces. Maybe overly polite smiles to mask the *we hate you* vibes.

Relax, Ziggy. They'll be polite in public. This is paranoia. They're not hoping someone spills something on you or that you get hit by the light-rail when you leave. They won't cause a scene.

"She's home for good," Mom says. "I'm surprised you didn't know. Everyone in our circles is so excited. We've missed her terribly. And she's giving us a grandbaby too."

I flinch. *"Mom,"* I start to hiss—*we are not telling people yet* —but Abby Nora interrupts me.

"She—what? Wow. Original."

I flinch again at Abby Nora's sarcasm.

Take it back, my brain yells at my mother. *Take it back and don't tell her.*

Why are you being such an asshole to me? it yells at Abby Nora too. *Just leave me alone.*

But that's not what comes out of my mouth. "Mom, I left something in the car."

"Original?" Mom repeats. "What, exactly, does that mean?"

"It's just so funny that I got married and had a baby, and now all of my friends are doing it too," Abby Nora says. "Well...some of us got married first. But isn't it nice that we don't have to if we don't want to? Or if we can't find someone?"

"Who's that?" I hear Eli say to Josh.

My toes are tingling and my stomach rolls over in a way that I would've sworn I was over just this morning. "My phone," I tell Mom. "I have to go get my phone out of my car."

"Abby Nora's old friend Ziggy," Josh says to Eli. "She was at the wedding."

"She sent half the wine for your wedding, didn't she?" Mom says.

"No, I know her from somewhere else," Eli says to Josh.

He's going to remember because of a repeat performance of what happened when I saw him at the aquarium if I don't get out of here *now*. I look at Niki. "I'm going to my car. I lost my phone. Forgot it. In the car."

She nods and shakes her head and looks between me and Abby Nora like she knows there's a problem but doesn't know what. Everyone in Mom's circles knows Abby Nora and I have always been besties.

Except now they're going to know that I'm pregnant and Abby Nora and I are fighting and Abby Nora's probably already prepared for this and will get her version out first and—

"You're the fucker who puked on me!" Eli shrieks.

Sound shouldn't bounce off exposed brick, but it does.

And silence follows.

The kind of silence that says every single person in the crowded wine bar has turned to stare at us.

At me.

My face was already hot, but it gets hotter. My hands too. My legs shake. My stomach twists and gurgles and my heart tries to pound out of my chest.

How much longer will she still affect me like this?

Why can't we just be *done*?

"My goodness, young man, do you kiss your mother with that mouth?" Mom says dryly. "What an absurd thing to yell in a crowded restaurant. I hope you're seeing someone to discuss your issues. Your baby is beautiful, Abby Nora. I hope she has a good appetite. I seem to have lost mine. Ziggy, Niki, we're leaving."

Mom grips my arm and squeezes as she tugs me into motion.

I make it to the sidewalk and almost to the corner before the first tear rolls down my cheek.

"What an awful person." Niki clucks.

"Accusing my daughter of puking on him in public." Mom sniffs.

"I meant Abby Nora. Who in their right mind would accuse someone of getting pregnant just to copy them?"

That would mean something if I didn't know Niki was likely to be hitting a text chain to spill the beans to all of their friends as soon as she's alone.

Did you hear? Deedee's daughter left her job on the cruise ship because she was fired because she got pregnant. I wonder who the father is. If she even knows.

"You realize your commission depends on your discretion?" Mom murmurs.

Niki makes an offended noise. "Deedee. I would *never*."

"I certainly hope not. Ziggy's had enough of an ordeal with having her entire friend group turn their backs on her out of jealousy of her life. It would be a shame if that carried over to our generation."

I hate this.

Hate it.

I'm gulping for air as we make our way down the sidewalk.

"We should have lunch at that hockey bar," Mom says. "It's been ages since I've been to a sports bar, and we're just a block or two away."

"I'm not hungry," I force out between my attempts to control my emotions. "I think I want a nap."

I want to go home.

I want to pet Jessica and cry on Holt's shoulder and be safe.

Be somewhere that might not ultimately prove to be my home, but somewhere that I at least won't have to brace myself for the next slap in the face.

"Of course, sweetheart. Pregnancy is hard on the body. You need extra sleep. You can rest at my house. You shouldn't drive yourself while you're tired. I'll make you soup. The kind I used to make when you were sick."

I don't want soup.

I want my heart to not hurt over a friend who clearly doesn't want me anymore. I want to only have the happiness of what's blossoming with Holt and with the joy of knowing I'm growing my own little wee one in my belly.

I want to be over the hurt.

That's what I truly want.

But I have this feeling it's going to take a while.

A very long while.

Dammit.

27

Holt

ZIGGY'S LATE.

I'm at the right Cod Pieces. I have her fries. Fish too—she texted that she was in the mood for something greasy after living on crackers and soda water for a month—but there's no Ziggy.

"Do you think her mom found out?" Goldie murmurs as we huddle at a booth with as little view of the outside windows as you can get at a fast-food fish restaurant shaped like a fishbowl in a strip mall parking lot.

"Given my luck, probably," I mutter.

"Why do people always say that?" Fletcher says. "My dude, you don't have bad luck. None of us have persistent bad luck."

Says the guy who arrived on the team furious and taking it out on the whole world when he was unceremoniously fired by one of the best teams in the most prestigious league in the UK and lied to about why.

Sounds like bad luck to me.

I frown at him. "When you find a dog, it loves you. When I find a dog, it's the one dog in the entire city who hates men. Your sister saves people's lives. My brother's dead. You're engaged to an absolute saint. The last woman I hooked up with" —before last night— "snuck out of my house with all my spatulas and sent me the Instagram page she set up to show their adventures. *My spatulas* have a spite spatula travels Instagram page. *Plus* she kept leaving cheeses of all varieties in my mailbox. You got fired from the club you'd played with for years, and now you're shoving your success in their faces. I tried to make another team overseas, and I broke my foot. Don't fucking talk to me about luck."

Fletcher opens his mouth, but Goldie touches him lightly on the shoulder. "I think we need to let him have this one for now, yeah? Good. Glad we agree. Will you please go get me more tartar sauce?"

"Anything for you." He leaps out of the booth like he wasn't grunting and swearing and moaning *I won't be able to move tomorrow* during weight training while I was having PT yesterday and heads for the condiments.

Knew it.

I knew he was whining for my benefit.

Or possibly to mock Silas. Goldie's brother also whines a lot on leg days.

Goldie leans across the table and grabs my arm. "The hardest things in life are worth fighting for. If she's worth it, she'll be here, or she'll let you know a real reason why she can't. There's probably traffic."

"A car accident."

"Holt. Stop."

"I fucking like her, and Coach sent that email, and we already knew it was dicey, and *I like her*. How the *fuck* did I find the one woman in the entire city who'd be off-limits to house-sit for me?"

Goldie smiles. "You're down bad, aren't you?"

"If I don't hear from her in the next five minutes, I'll—"

I stop myself.

Because there she is, walking through the door.

Her hair's tied up in another messy bun, and her cheeks are red like she had to park too far away in the heat.

I should've told her to pull up front and made Fletcher park her car for her.

Wary eyes scan the room, and her smile isn't bright enough when she spots me.

My heart starts a slow barrel roll of doom.

She told her mom.

She told her mom, and now she's coming to tell me she can't be seen with me and she's moving in with them until she finds a house and we're going to never see each other again.

I'm bracing myself when she slides into the seat next to me. "Sorry I'm late." Her gaze flicks to me, and the next thing I notice is the way her eyes are rimmed in red. "We ran into Abby Nora and Vitamin Guy, and I needed a minute. Okay, an hour. I needed an hour. And to convince my mom I was okay to drive after that hour."

It takes everything I have to not wrap her in a hug and tell her *fuck Abby Nora* and offer to plant my fist in Vitamin Guy's face. Or offer to have Fletcher egg their houses. I settle for squeezing her thigh under the table.

"You okay?"

She shakes her head. Nods. Shakes her head again.

And Goldie squeaks. "*Oh my god*, that's where I know you from!"

We both look at her.

"You were besties with Abby Nora Ewing. In high school. We went to high school together. Heartwood Valley High? Same year, weren't we?"

The color drains from Ziggy's face. "Oh *no*," she whispers.

"What?" I slip my arm around her.

"You were on student council." Goldie pauses, her smile fading. "What's wrong? Oh, crap, was I a complete wanker? Please don't judge me based on high school Goldie. Adult Goldie is a lot nicer, I promise."

"You were a wanker in high school and never told me?" Fletcher says as he retakes his seat and dumps a fistful of tartar sauce packets on the table. "I call foul. That would've evened the wanker tables in our relationship."

"Everyone's a wanker in high school. Most of us grow out of it." She winces. "But not all of us."

Fletcher coughs out a *your brother*.

She elbows him while I toss a tartar sauce packet at him, hitting him square in the chest despite using my left hand. "I can still tell Coach to make you run extra laps."

"Some of us don't mind hard work." He smirks.

Still taking digs at Goldie's brother.

When he landed on the team, that annoyed me.

Now, I'd be amused—I was yesterday, when I was positive Fletcher was whining for show—except Ziggy's still shrinking in her seat next to me.

My heart starts that slow slide toward panic.

Did Ziggy and Goldie hate each other in high school?

Is this a bad idea?

"Ziggy?" I murmur.

"Abby Nora dumped me," she blurts to Goldie. "We're not friends anymore."

Goldie makes like a goldfish and goes bug-eyed and slack-jawed. "Wait, wait, wait. You and Abby Nora—you were still friends? Holt said you had a friend breakup, but I wouldn't have thought—never mind. Not important what I thought. Ziggy. Girl. I know it hurts right now, but trust me, this is for the better."

"What kind of name is *Abby Nora?*" Fletcher mutters to me.

"Both of her grandmothers," Ziggy and Goldie say together, Goldie with an eye roll.

Pretty unusual if she's not rolling her eyes at Fletcher or Silas.

Goldie doesn't roll her eyes at anyone. She's too *rah-rah, you can do it.*

So this is interesting.

"You weren't at her baby shower, were you?" Ziggy asks Goldie.

"I don't hang out with anyone from high school anymore."

"No one?"

"The good ones moved away, and the Abby Noras stayed."

"You don't like her."

Goldie winces. "How do I put this delicately…"

"Don't be delicate," Fletcher says. "Call her a fuckwanker."

Goldie covers his mouth. "When people would rather hire a private chef to recreate a Cod Pieces meal so that no one can see that they like to eat fast-food fish and fries, they generally also have other life philosophies and habits that make me not want to be around them."

"Did she just use a hundred words to call your former BFF a snob?" I ask Ziggy.

She blinks quickly. "Yes."

"Not too many hits to the head yet, Captain. You still got it. Way to go." Fletcher holds up a high five to me, and I reluctantly smack his hand.

Ziggy reaches for a fry. "Was I stuck up too?"

Goldie shakes her head. "I don't think so. And I could be wrong. I shouldn't judge people. We *were* all at an exclusive private high school. I just get a vibe."

Ziggy's still frowning as she chews and takes three more fries. "Mom and I were pretty normal until she married Roland."

"I was never normal."

"Who needs normal when you're perfect?" Fletcher says.

We all ignore him.

"You were overseas?" Goldie says to Ziggy, who nods.

"And home now permanently for the first time since high school?"

Ziggy nods again.

"It's hard to keep up when you're not home a lot. And I don't know her well now, but she married into the Harrison family, didn't she? The real estate family?"

If Ziggy nods much more, she'll look like a bobblehead.

It's freaking adorable.

"They were friends with my father, and they're the absolute worst. It's all about appearances. The façade. Don't get me started on the sons. Eli was such a dick."

"I puked on him," Ziggy says. "About a month ago. That's when Holt and I met."

Goldie laughs. "Seriously?"

Ziggy nods.

291

And Goldie cackles.

Goldie.

Cackling over something bad happening to someone.

I squeeze Ziggy's thigh again, and she covers my hand and squeezes back.

"Good," Goldie says. "Guys like that deserve some discomfort."

Fletcher grins at me. "Best date ever. Goldie never shit-talks people."

"Hush," she says to him while she takes a discreet glance around the room.

She's a life coach. Semi-famous on socials. I'm not kidding about her *you can do it, I believe in you* attitude. She grew an entire business off of inspirational posts.

Really shouldn't get caught shit-talking people in public.

But Ziggy's leaning forward as she digs into her fish too. "I knew you were familiar yesterday, but I thought it was because you were friends with Abby Nora. I can't even tell you how relieved I am right now that you don't hate me like she does."

"I don't take social guidance from Abby Nora."

"You played soccer, right? You were aiming to go pro. Did you make it?"

Goldie shakes her head. "Broke my hip my senior year of college. Ended my dreams."

"Oh my god. I'm so sorry."

"Life worked out." She looks at me. "Even when it feels like it won't, it always works out if you look for the good you can still find in the world."

"Bad luck, my ass," Fletcher mutters.

I take the opportunity to throw another sauce packet at him and get the reward of having a Ziggy smile aimed at me.

Goldie ignores us both and leans closer to Ziggy. "So here's what we're gonna do. You and I were high school friends, and I can't imagine your family would be upset at you reconnecting with a *good* old friend instead of an Abby Nora. So we're going to hang out, and that means you'll be around Fletcher some. And probably Silas too. My brother."

"You have a brother?"

"Four years younger. He wasn't in high school the same time we were. I don't think you would've known him."

"Lucky you," Fletcher adds.

"They don't get along," I murmur to Ziggy.

"I can clearly see how it must be completely her brother's fault," she murmurs back, which makes me snicker.

"I've quit telling them both to behave because I think they do it just to annoy me now," Goldie says. "But this is good. This is *really* good. You and I can hang out. There will inevitably be interactions with other guys on the team since they're at our place regularly. And no one at Pounders head-quarters can possibly object because you deserve good friends and I have this reputation for being a pretty decent one."

"Don't listen to her," Fletcher says. "She's not *decent*. She's the best."

"Has Coach wrapped around her little finger," I add.

"Because she gave the whole team therapy," Fletcher continues.

I nod. "Helped us get along better when an asswanker invaded, thinking he was better than all of us."

"Helped our captain see that the asswanker knew what was best."

"The asswanker was always the problem."

"The asswanker took the team all the way to the championship match one year and would've done it a second year if the asswanker's girlfriend's brother hadn't pulled a fucking hamstring."

"The asswanker forgets the *team* part sometimes."

"The captain's a dick sometimes who doesn't appreciate having the stands full at home matches."

"That's because the captain gets tired of the asswanker's bad mustache."

Goldie's cracking up.

Ziggy's watching us both with a fascination that's much better than the wounded wariness she walked in with a few minutes ago.

Smiling too.

It's an *I'm not sure I'm supposed to smile at this* smile, but it's still a smile.

I rub my hand over her thigh. "Fish settling okay?"

She leans closer to me, all soft curves and honey vanilla scent. "I want seconds."

"On it." Fletcher leaps to his feet. "Because asswankers have to make points that they're not always asswankers sometimes."

"Is he really your favorite teammate?" Ziggy asks me.

"Not even close, but he comes with Goldie, and he doesn't need a second job to get by in the off-season, so it's a default thing."

"He's obnoxious, but he's very self-aware about it," Goldie says. "But might I point out, Silas also doesn't work in the off-season. You could be hanging with my brother instead."

I grimace.

She grins, then turns to Ziggy again. "You worked cruise ships? That sounds exciting."

Ziggy takes the opening and starts telling stories about

her life before she came back to Copper Valley. It's fun to realize I know some of these stories.

Most of them involve her friend Francesca.

No one asks about the baby.

No one asks if we slept together last night.

Ziggy asks Goldie about what she's been up to since high school too, and by the time we leave for the movie, my girl's bright-eyed and happy.

Yes.

My girl.

I licked her. She's mine.

For as long as the world lets me have her.

The subtle cramping in my gut is warning me it won't be long enough. That I should keep her at arm's length. That I should acknowledge this is for fun, not for forever.

Eventually, I'll consider admitting this could be just infatuation.

It might fade.

Probably for her first.

But today?

Today, I get to be with her. And that's all that matters.

"Feel better?" I ask as I limp along with my crutches out to her car.

The smile she gives me makes me believe this could last forever.

That there's still good in the world. That maybe my bad luck streak is over.

If we can prove to ourselves that this is worth fighting her dad over.

"You're very good at knowing what people need," she says to me.

"Tell that to Jessica."

"Not to brag, but I think Jessica's pretty happy with the dog sitter you got her."

"Accident. Good accident, but still an accident."

"Was it though? Or do you have magic powers you don't even know you're using sometimes?"

Shit.

I think I'm blushing.

"Glad you liked Goldie."

"I want to hold your hand right now so I can squeeze it to say thank you for introducing us."

"We'll be in a dark movie theater in a few minutes here."

Her smile grows.

My dick twitches.

Dark movie theater with a pretty date—this was an excellent idea.

28

Ziggy

WHAT'S the word for when you like someone so much that your heart beats a little faster every time you see them, you find yourself smiling for no reason in the middle of the day, and you catch yourself picking up the heart-shaped pasta instead of the regular spaghetti noodles when you make an impromptu menu plan change merely because you want to use heart-shaped pasta?

It's not love.

I haven't known Holt long enough for this to be love.

It's more than like though.

Enchantment?

The *puppy* love stage?

Obsession?

Whatever it is, it's what I have after a couple weeks of lying to my family about who my landlord is and why he's letting me stay after he's back, all while spending every night in his bed.

The people around me are starting to notice my glow.

Thankfully, they still attribute it to pregnancy.

Mostly.

Miranda isn't fooled though, though she was absolutely bought off with the cherry hand pies.

The same cherry hand pies that got me—let's call it *rewarded for good kitchen behavior.*

I might have made them again this past weekend too.

And I saved a few for Miranda again. I think she knows what I got out of them at home, though she didn't do anything beyond smirk at me when I said I had a craving.

She swings into my office shortly after I get in for the day about two weeks after the incident with Jessica in the lobby. I'm late today, but with good reason.

I had my first appointment with my new doctor.

"Heads up—Dad's in today," she murmurs.

He's not in every day. Holt wasn't wrong when he pointed out that the cost of the rugby team is in the noise for Roland Keating. He sits on the board of at least three big engineering firms around the city, plus he's built and sold at least four other businesses himself. He's not fully self-made —his parents were comfortable enough to give him seed money for his first business—but he's worked hard to grow what he started with.

He keeps busy with his hands in a lot of different inter-ests and has for as long as I've known him. Mom occasion-ally drops the retirement word, but it's more wishful thinking than a true possibility.

Dad wouldn't know what to do with himself if he had too much free time on his hands. He's not built for sitting still.

"So I should work harder and prove my value?" I murmur back. We're a couple weeks out from my first big event for the team—a postseason awards banquet celebrating their finals run. Holt says they basically finished third. Fletcher says not winning it all is the same as finishing last.

They're hilarious. It's been fantastic getting to watch Holt interact with his friends and making friends with Goldie too.

"Half the team's in too," Miranda adds. "Something about planning a surprise for the coach. Just—watch the way you light up when someone walks past your office, okay?"

"Fletcher makes me happy."

She cracks up.

We both know Holt's only in the office if he's in with Fletcher, who's pretending he doesn't know he's a decoy, and it's safer to like Fletcher since he can't go three sentences without talking about Goldie.

And Fletcher's in the office all the time.

Apparently his life mission is growing US rugby to be as big as US football is, and you can't tell him he's fighting an impossible battle.

That just makes him more determined. Or so Goldie tells me.

When Miranda finally gets her snickers under control, she looks at me and doubles over again. "Fletcher—makes you—happy," she gasps through gales of laughter.

"Is this like saying that guy who does that annoying local TV commercial for his furniture store is my favorite?" I ask her.

"Worse," she chortles.

"Well, I think of Goldie every time I see Fletcher. Did you know she told me she saw Abby Nora at a Pounders match late last year and Abby Nora completely snubbed her? *Who does that?* And to *Goldie?* And don't tell me Abby Nora doesn't know who Goldie is. Goldie's basically famous around here. How did I not see how insecure Abby Nora always was? And how she judged people based on what they could do for her?"

I've gotten through the biggest part of my sadness over my friendship breakup, and I'm on to the petty phase where I'm mad that I didn't realize she wasn't the person I thought she was. I'm also hoping that she's not getting a lot of sleep these days, which I shouldn't wish on someone given my own circumstances, but I'm only human.

I'm a little embarrassed that I didn't realize how much emphasis Abby Nora put on people's perceived class in life too, how I feel like I was a charity case in high school now, her way of making herself feel good for doing something for someone so far beneath her, but I'm working through that.

When you only see what someone wants you to see over text and socials, and then don't see them in person regularly, it's apparently not uncommon to miss the red flags.

"She's sad people," Miranda says. "Sad people that you shouldn't waste—what's that?"

She points to a black-and-white image on my desk.

I touch it gingerly at the edges. "This?"

"*Ziggy!*"

Deep voices drift down the hallway as she lunges for the ultrasound picture. "Oh my god, is this the baby?"

My eyes get hot. "That's the baby."

"Look at her. Him. Them. What are we calling the baby?"

"Tater Tot."

She squeals. "Is that their little elbow?"

I grin as I lean over the picture too. "It's like they're chilling in a hammock."

"They think Mommy should've worked the tropics instead of the Med."

"They wouldn't be happening if Mommy worked the tropics instead of the Med."

The voices outside get closer, and a full-body shiver works its way from my neck to my toes as I recognize Holt's in the mix.

"Hey, Ziggy," Crew calls. "Oh, Miranda. You too. Hey."

Silas Collins stops in the doorway and stares at Miranda. "Is that an ultrasound picture?"

Right.

He has a daughter.

Goldie talks about her a lot.

He'd recognize baby stuff.

Miranda waves the image at the growing group of rugby players gathering in my doorway. "It's Ziggy's baby."

Crew's eyes go wide. Porter's mouth forms an O.

Silas stares for one more beat, then shrugs. "Cool."

For all of the gossip I know Mom's keeping from me about what people in her circles are saying as news of my pregnancy—and my puking on Eli Harrison—spreads, the office and the team have had no idea.

"*Cool?*" Tatum says. "Dude. We're gonna be *uncles*, and all you can say is *cool?*"

Fletcher rubs the younger guy's head. "He sucks. What did you expect?"

Only Holt is staying silent, his gaze flickering between me and the picture Miranda is carrying to the doorway to show off.

He knew I was going to the doctor.

I hadn't had a chance to sit down and email him pictures yet.

I smile at him, trying to make it look normal and natural and no more intense than I'd smile at anyone else.

His gaze softens, and he almost smiles back.

My heart flips.

And then I squeak and cover it with a cough.

He's not on his crutches.

He's walking.

I can't see his legs though. Is he still in the boot? Or is he *good*-good?

Can I ask?

Would it be obvious I pay attention if I ask?

Or would it be rude not to when I've seen him in the office several times over the past couple weeks?

It's polite to say something.

Right?

One corner of his mouth hitches up.

It does that anytime I start rambling. *Overthinking again, Zig. You're good.*

"Look at the baby!" Miranda says, interrupting my internal panic as she shows off my picture to the guys on the team. "Doesn't he—she—they look like a total beach bum? I'm in love. We're calling them *Tater Tot*. How cute is that?"

Most of the guys murmur the appropriate *awws*.

Fletcher coughs.

Holt purses his lips together like he's trying not to beam with pride about his nickname for the baby.

"When are you due?" Silas asks me.

"Early February."

"Nice. Baby with a new season."

"My goodness, gentlemen, what is going on here?" Mom says over the crowd.

"Ziggy got her ultrasound," Miranda says.

"What? Where?"

The men part, and Mom bustles in. *"Ziggy.* Oh my word, is that my grandbaby?"

"It is," I confirm.

Mom takes one look at the picture and bursts into tears.

"Mom—" I start.

"Deedee—" Miranda adds, getting to her first for a hug.

"My baby's having a *baby,*" Mom wails.

"Happens to a lot of women," I say as I reach her and wrap my arms around both of them, turning this into a group hug.

"Whoa, whoa, what's going on here?" I hear Dad say out in the hallway.

"We're celebrating that we're gonna be uncles, sir," Crew says.

Holt and Fletcher share a look.

Holt limps back further against the opposite wall.

Still in the boot if he's limping.

I think.

Dammit.

Poor guy. The boot sucks.

Fletcher angles in front of him.

"Better be all that's going on," Dad says, making my shoulders tighten. "Why's my wife crying?"

"She's happy," I report.

"Are we gonna have to throw a baby shower?" Tatum says to Porter. "I don't know how to throw a baby shower."

"I'm planning the baby shower," Miranda says.

"Brittany had three baby showers for Hallie," Silas says.

Miranda smiles at him. "Three's better than one when it comes to showing a baby and their mama how much they're loved."

He stares back at her, then steps back to join Fletcher and Holt.

Dad angles into the doorway too. He's a big guy, tall and broad all around, with sixty-five years' worth of cheese, wine, and desserts lending itself to his waistline. His dark hair is dotted with silver, and his face is clean-shaven, as always.

Miranda hands him the picture.

He smiles, and then blinks quickly like he, too, might want to cry. "Looks like a rugby player," he declares.

"Lady rugby players are badasses," Miranda says. "But sorry, Dad, this one's gonna be a beach bum."

"Can we just let the baby be whoever the baby wants to be?" I ask.

"They're going to be perfect," Mom wails.

"Move, Porter," Fletcher says. "Surprise for Coach won't surprise itself. We have work to do. And they have to do all that mushy family shit."

I meet Holt's eyes one more time.

He doesn't react at all, but that doesn't mean he doesn't want to.

I can feel it in the way my belly's fluttering.

The rest of the day crawls by. Mom and Dad want to take Miranda and me out to dinner to celebrate the ultrasound pictures. I plead exhaustion, and they let me off, but only if I promise them brunch tomorrow.

Brunch and looking at more houses.

Am I stalling on finding a house because I don't want to leave Holt's place?

Yes.

Is this going to bite me in the ass?

One way or another.

But we've made it two weeks without my parents having any clue, and I've started mentioning hanging out with Goldie. Mom and Dad both love her, and I've made sure to point out that we went to high school together so that it's not suspicious.

So this plan to warm them up to the idea of me being friends with the guys on the team is almost coming along.

Almost.

I'll work on it more tomorrow.

After this interminable day ends, which it finally, eventually does.

It's time to go home.

And honestly?

I *am* tired.

Tired from the baby zapping my energy. Tired of hiding that I like Holt. Tired of going over the same particulars about the awards banquet with the same people both in and out of the office who *want to make sure we get every detail perfect.*

Holt and Fletcher have both told me that so long as the food is edible, the team will think it's a success.

The mics could fail and the slide show could get replaced with a pornographic cartoon and the awards could be giant dicks and we'd be happy, Holt keeps saying. *You can't screw this up. We're an easy bunch. Especially if no one's facial hair gets burned off.*

Having just seen more of the team in the office here and there, I believe him, though I have questions about why there would have to be burning facial hair disclaimers.

Also, I miss being a sommelier.

Even if I'm overall happy in Copper Valley, and excited about the baby, I still miss what I had before.

Goldie tells me it's okay to feel all of those things, because humans are complicated and we're allowed to be conflicted.

I pull into the driveway and smile at the sight of the house.

I like this house.

It's cozy and comfortable.

The bedroom I'd been staying in has been completely redone in the past two weeks, with proper ventilation so that the paint fumes don't bother me, and we're moving into it so that Holt's bedroom can get finished.

Then the third bedroom on the main floor—the one that no one uses because it was Caden's room—will get some sprucing up, and the basement, and then the house is complete, though Holt doesn't have immediate plans for either.

I stride up the front steps in the waning heat of the day, and when I push into the living room, there's no sign waiting like there was just about two weeks ago, but there's something better.

Holt moving around the kitchen without his crutches.

"You ditched the sticks?" I say as I wrap my arms around him and go up on tiptoes to kiss his chin.

"I'm two-legged again." He pulls me tight and kisses me, and my heart does a full Olympic vault routine, leaping and twisting and flying, but it doesn't land.

It's too busy soaring.

I still have so much work to do to convince my parents that Holt and I are two grown adults who can date without it interfering with the rest of our lives.

But right now, it doesn't matter.

Not when I feel like I'm *home*.

29

Holt

THIS HAS BEEN the longest day of my life.

I tried distracting myself with my physical therapy.

I tried distracting myself by playing pinball at Fletcher's place.

I tried distracting myself by dreaming up new ways to convince my dog to like me.

I finally gave up and decided the best way to distract myself would be to step out of my comfort zone and make Ziggy dinner for once, and even that hasn't fully occupied my brain.

But she's finally here.

She's home.

Smiling at me as she pulls out of kissing me. "Where's Jessica?"

"I got her a doggy pool. She's outside living the life of her dreams."

"No."

"Yep. Got her an umbrella too. She's in heaven." Just checked on her a few minutes ago.

With the temperatures finally dropping and only an inch of water in the pool, she's fine.

"You're too good to all of us." She pecks my cheek. "I smell food."

"Twice-baked potatoes, bean salad, and fake wine."

Plus candles.

Two place settings at the kitchen table with Caden's fancy dishes.

Soft jazz.

Her lips part. "Fake wine?"

"It's a substitute. I found a thing with tea and juice and bitters online. It probably sucks, but—"

She cuts me off with another kiss. "You are the absolute best," she whispers against my lips as she strokes my cheeks.

"Tell me about your doctor appointment," I say.

"You first."

"I ditched the crutches. Two more weeks in the boot. Then the hard PT starts, and I can't fucking wait. Your turn."

"I have a dozen pictures of the baby."

And *that* has been the worst part of my day.

Waiting for her to get home to see the images of Tater Tot.

A bunch of guys on the team have already seen the baby, but I barely got a glance.

Didn't want to see.

Not if I couldn't see it with Ziggy.

While I'm touching her. Smelling her. Listening to her describe every photo in detail.

The oven buzzer goes off, and I reluctantly let her go so I can pull out the potatoes.

No idea if my lumpy offering will meet her standards, but she's the type who'll give me credit for trying.

And if they're awful, I have a food delivery app on my phone.

Anything she wants, it's hers.

"Those look amazing," she says.

"Go sit. My turn to serve you."

The table's against the window overlooking the side yard and the neighbor's house, angled just right for one of us to keep an eye on Jessica.

Table's also small.

Just the right size for two.

We can fit a high chair though.

And the fact that I'm thinking about high chairs tells you how far I'm gone.

This isn't Ziggy's baby.

This is *our* baby.

I will go to the ends of the earth to protect this baby.

The guys might've seen the ultrasound images first, but I'm the guy who falls asleep with my hand on her subtle baby bump every night. I'm the one watching her belly swell and grow and measuring it by how much of my hand covers the baby. I'm the one who caught her looking at a baby name website last night.

And I'm the one she's smiling at as she sniffs the red wine substitute, swirls the glass, holding it up to the light, and then sniffs it again.

I brace myself.

I'm not a wine guy. I have no idea if it's awful. I don't

know if it's doing the thing it's supposed to do when it gets swirled.

I don't even know why people swirl wine. Something to do with air. That's all I've got.

She takes a sip and her brows furrow.

"Is it awful?"

"No." She frowns at it, swirls it again, and sips once more. "It's surprisingly good, actually. Not that I doubted you. I don't mean that. I mean—"

"I doubted me."

That smile lights up her eyes. "Thank you. It's perfect."

I'm limping slightly in the boot as I carry our plates across the kitchen to the table.

She leans over, peering out the window. "Tell me you have a picture of the dog."

"I have many, many pictures of the dog."

"In the pool?"

"Endless pictures of the dog in the pool, because I knew you'd want to see them."

"You are the best."

"Not even close."

She smiles at me as I take my seat. "Agree to disagree. Want to see the baby?"

"It's all I've wanted all day."

She pulls out her phone and opens an album, and soon I'm flipping through black-and-white images as she digs into her potato.

"Oh my god, this is so good," she says.

I lift my gaze from a blurry black-and-white image to eye her.

"It *is*," she says.

"Okay, chef."

Her foot slides along my calf. "It's far easier for you to make a good meal than it would be for me to be impressive on the rugby pitch."

"You're not allowed anywhere near a rugby pitch."

She grins. "What about in the stands?"

"Only if I get to pick your seats. Ball sometimes goes up there. Don't want you or Tater Tot getting hurt." I look down at the image again. "Is that a leg?"

She leans across the table and points out various parts of the baby's body in a dozen different pictures.

"Healthy?" I ask.

"All looks good. Strong heartbeat. Right on target for development in all of the areas that matter."

I didn't realize how badly I needed to hear that until my eyes get hot. "Good."

Ziggy squeezes my hand.

She doesn't say anything, but she doesn't have to.

I haven't explicitly told her Caden's cancer was genetic, but I've told her I have shitty genes. I haven't explicitly told her it's a little terrifying to me that she has no idea if her baby will have any genetic disadvantages either, but who says that to a pregnant woman?

She has enough on her plate without adding my anxieties to it.

And no matter what this baby needs, I'll be here for them.

Just like I'll be here for her.

"I ordered Tater Tot something," I confess.

"*Holt.* You didn't have to do that."

"It's a teething ring in the shape of a wine glass. Should be here Monday."

"I stand corrected. You did, in fact, have to do that."

I grin at her, then flip through the images again before I dive into my food.

And she's not wrong. It's edible. Even decently good.

Cooking isn't something I learned to do when I was younger, and it's always been more of a necessity than a joy.

So making something with flavor that's not just an energy delivery mechanism is new.

You could say having a professional chef cooking for me the past couple weeks has inspired me.

We catch up on everything—her banquet plans, my physical therapy orders, her still dealing with the gut-instinct feelings of wanting to text her former best friend ultrasound pictures before the reminder that they're not friends anymore sets in, Jessica getting up and shaking off and resettling herself in the pool, Fletcher being annoying, Goldie inviting her to lunch with her besties soon.

That has me grinning. "You're gonna love them."

"Why does everyone keep saying that with that exact shit-eating grin?"

Because Goldie's besties are a trio of seasoned citizens who speak their minds and have given their last fucks.

They're awesome. And I'm absolutely not ruining the surprise. "It's impossible to explain Goldie's friends. You just have to meet them for yourself."

"Has Miranda met them?"

"No idea. They come to matches sometimes. But to the best of my knowledge, you're the only office staff Goldie hangs out with."

When we're finished, Ziggy rises to wash the dishes.

I join her at the sink.

Feels fucking good to have the use of both of my legs again. And my arms.

"You made dinner. Go sit," she says.

"You make dinner and do the dishes every night. You go sit."

"Holt."

"Ziggy."

"I like doing dishes."

"No one likes doing dishes."

"I like doing dishes *for you*."

That one hits right in the center of my chest.

It's nice to be taken care of.

No, it's fucking amazing to be taken care of.

My parents didn't do it. I was older, so Caden didn't do it. I've had coaches and teammates try, but never like this.

Ziggy had no obligations to me when she made me breakfast that first morning I was home.

Teammates, coaches, teachers—caring is their job.

It's not hers.

But she's done it for me anyway.

I slide behind her and dip my face to her neck, kissing her soft skin. "Maybe we should leave them for tomorrow and see who's up first to take care of them."

"You'd cheat and set an alarm."

"I don't have to set an alarm to wake up before you do. I can just tell my brain to wake me up and it will."

She cracks up, and truly, there's nothing better than holding a laughing woman in my arms while I kiss her neck again.

Her happy sigh as she leans back into me gives me life.

I like this woman.

I like her entirely too much.

She turns the water off and rotates in my arms until she's facing me, sliding wet hands over my shirt.

"I'm your towel now?" I tease her.

"Seems fair, considering you're the biggest reason I get wet these days."

I get hard so fast it's like a gut punch. "Tell me more."

Her eyes are sparkling even as her pupils dilate. "When I see you walk past my office, my breasts ache because I want you to touch them."

Fantasies of sneaking beneath her desk to eat her pussy while she's working fill my head.

She slides her hands up my neck. "And when I see you doing everything in your power to win over the dog, I want to kiss you until I can't breathe."

"You can always kiss me. Always."

"And when your hard-on presses against my belly, I get wet between my thighs with how badly I want you."

My cock pulses harder. "Are you wet now?"

"I've been wet since the first bite of dinner."

I angle my hand between us and stroke between her legs and fuck me.

She's soaked through her linen pants.

Her head falls back and she purrs, spreading her legs wider as I stroke her again.

"These pants have to go." I can barely get the words out. I'm hoarse. My mouth is dry. My balls ache.

I need this woman.

I need her *now*.

"*Your* pants need to go." She shoves my shorts down, then grips my cock in both hands and strokes me from root to tip and back again.

Fuck me, it feels so good when she's gripping me.

"Ziggy," I gasp.

That's all I get out before she's on her knees, licking the

pre-cum off the tip of my dick, swirling her tongue around my head, and then sucking me into her mouth while she cradles my balls.

She glides over my cock with her mouth, sucking on me and teasing the underside with her tongue. My fingers curl into her hair while I make unintelligible sounds, letting the world outside disappear while I melt into nothing but the thick, electric sensations radiating from my cock while she takes me deep, then pulls off and sucks me into her hot, wet mouth again.

My hips jerk and my grip tightens.

Hold on, I tell myself.

"Ziggy—" I rasp out.

She rolls my balls in her hand and sucks harder, those wide blue eyes watching me while she puts her other hand between her thighs, touching herself.

My legs shake. My hips thrust on their own.

She knows.

She knows she's driving me wild, that I'm close.

"Kitten, I can't—"

I cut myself off as she takes me so deep that I can't think anymore.

Can't think.

Can't catch my breath.

Can't control myself.

Can't stop the hard, fast, sudden release that comes as she sucks even harder once more.

I strain into my orgasm as she holds me in her mouth, vaguely aware that she's jerking one hand between her own thighs too while she squeezes my balls with the other.

I come so hard that I'm not sure my eyes will ever uncross. And as the last of the shudders leave my body, my dick spent, Ziggy slides off my cock, presses a kiss to the very tip of my wet, drooping hard-on, and smiles at me.

"Thank you for dessert," she whispers.

Her shoulders shudder, and she slides her eyes closed, and I get to watch as she brings herself to orgasm too.

It's the hottest fucking thing I've ever seen in my life, and by the time she slumps back against the cabinet beneath the sink, I'm hard again.

Fully hard.

No questions.

I need to get this woman into my bed.

Now.

And then figure out how to keep her.

Because this thing with Ziggy?

It's not temporary. It's not a distraction. It's not subconsciously self-sabotaging my career.

It's real.

It's heavy.

It's everything.

And I won't let her go.

30

Ziggy

NOT THE DAMN CLUB AGAIN.

But yes, the damn club again.

It's where everyone brunches on a Saturday morning, so here we are.

Brunching before house-hunting.

We're at a window table overlooking the lake and the golf course, which is, naturally, one of the best seats in the dining room.

It's also where everyone else sees you.

And this is the first time everyone has seen us—me— since Mom told Abby Nora and Niki that I'm pregnant.

Since Eli Harrison connected the dots on the somm who puked on him outside the bathroom.

I don't see Abby Nora. I don't see her parents. I don't see her in-laws.

Have to wonder if Mom called ahead to verify they wouldn't be here. I wouldn't put it past her.

She's learned to navigate Dad's world pretty well since we moved to this part of the city.

But I'm still acutely aware of every glance and every lowered voice around us.

Francesca was right. I should've shoved Holt in a suitcase and taken him with me back to Europe when I realized he was one of Dad's players.

"Why can't anyone tell me if this baby's a boy or a girl?" Dad asks as he studies the ultrasound picture after we've ordered.

"Can't see yet," I reply. "And I don't want to know. I want to be surprised."

"I love that," Miranda says. "This is the one time in Tater Tot's life that they won't be put in a box. They should get to enjoy it."

"I hardly think the baby's aware that it's enjoying a time of not having expectations put on it," Mom murmurs.

"But *we* know, and that matters."

"I'm also getting worried we won't find a permanent place for Ziggy and the baby before Baby's born," Mom says. "Honey, I know your landlord is being flexible now, but we really need to get you settled. Maybe we should consider some apartments if you won't move in with us. Something temporary until the house of your dreams comes on the market."

This?

This is called progress.

And it's time for me to make some of my own. "Goldie offered to show me the building she used to live in," I say. "Fletcher likes it too."

As expected, Dad's focus narrows in on me like a lightning bolt. "Fletcher? Huxley? My player? You were talking to him?"

"Dad, he's engaged to Goldie," Miranda says. "You want Ziggy to have friends but not acknowledge the existence of their significant others?"

"He was fired from his last team for being inappropriate with the coach's daughter."

"He was fired from his last team because the coach's daughter had a crush on him and he didn't know it," Miranda retorts. "He didn't do anything wrong, and there's ample evidence to support the fact that he was completely blindsided. And *he's engaged to Goldie.* Ziggy's high school friend. He's not gonna be trying to hit this ass on the side."

"Miranda," Mom murmurs. "Language."

"Well, he's not," she says, quieter, and I realize the people at the next table are watching us.

Awesome.

Just love being that single pregnant failure who had to run home to Mom and Dad, got fired for assaulting Eli Harrison with body fluids, and now wants to get involved in a threesome with one of Dad's players.

Not that they know it would be a threesome, but I'm sure they're enjoying thinking their version of the worst of me.

I sip my ginger soda. "Did I ever tell you about the time on the ship that a guy's best friend—who was a woman—was traveling with him and his girlfriend and they almost broke up because the girlfriend was jealous of the platonic friend, who was helping plan the most epic proposal I've ever seen? It involved a hot air balloon and a flash mob that had half of a symphony orchestra participating."

"Aww, how sweet," Miranda says. "Did they get married?"

"The wedding happened at an Italian castle. I saw it on their socials about a year later."

She sighs dreamily. "I want to get married at an Italian castle. But then I'd have to date someone. And *ew*. Half the guys I've met in the last year are either unhinged in the bad way somehow or they want to move way too fast to the *I love you* stuff."

I'm moving fast.

I'm probably moving too fast.

But it's so easy to be with Holt right now. Natural. Like he's the real reason I came home.

So that I could meet him.

His lonely, grieving soul complements my lonely, grieving soul.

And we're both on a mission to find the joy in life again.

To find the trust in life again. To be willing to take risks again.

On new friends. New family.

Believing in *hope* again.

"You have all the time in the world, sweetheart," Dad says to her. "Unlike Ziggy. Who needs to find a place to settle, and soon."

It's so hard not to squirm, especially knowing the people around us are listening in. "I'm getting there."

"What if we asked your landlord to sell us his house since you seem to like it so much?" Mom says. "Surely someone who'd leave for a month at a time could find a better place to live. What does he do? I don't recall you mentioning his job."

"High school track coach," I blurt.

Miranda makes a strangled noise.

Shit.

Shit.

Does Dad know every high school track coach? There are like ten public high schools in Copper Valley. At least. Surely he doesn't know all of them.

Does he?

And when is track season?

Oh my god.

Did I just make up a lie that's so very obviously a lie because a high school track coach actually works summers?

"Which high school?" he asks.

Crap. Is my face turning red? "I don't know. I didn't ask."

"He a rugby fan?" Dad asks. "I could sweeten the deal. Season tickets. Concession stand coupons. Let him meet the team."

"I don't really talk about the team with him." *Lie lie lie.* "I mean, we each do our own things."

Like, he does things with his penis.

I do things with my vagina.

Way, totally different.

Also, I do most of the cooking, and he does most of the entertaining me while I cook.

I give him blow jobs when he does dishes.

He fingers me while I do the dishes.

Completely different.

Mom and Dad are both frowning at me.

"I'm in bed almost the whole time I'm home," I babble.

Miranda chokes on her mimosa.

I am drowning in absolute mortification. This isn't going well.

Not at all.

"Because I'm tired all the time," I add.

"My goodness, my dear, are you okay?" Mom pats Miranda on the back.

"Wrong pipe," she gasps.

Divert. Divert! "That happened to me once when I was doing a wine presentation on my first cruise, except it wasn't a mimosa, it was a fly that flew into my throat."

"I should talk to your landlord," Dad says. "I'm sure we can come to an arrangement."

"It was his dead grandmother's house." The lies are coming out of my mouth in direct proportion to the sweat sliding down my back. "She was his favorite person on the planet. She baked him chocolate chip cookies in that kitchen and she read him good night stories in his bedroom and she mortgaged her house to pay for his college. You can't ask a man to leave a house that means so much to him."

My mom stares at me over her mimosa.

Dad's mouth does that thing where he doesn't like that he can't get something, and he subtly cracks a single knuckle.

Miranda is still coughing, but quieter and less frequently.

"It's a nice house because it has a nice homey story to it," I say. "I lived in cabins on a ship for seven years. I can find an equally nice two-bedroom condo and the baby and I can use community gardens and parks and we'll be fine."

I don't want a condo. I don't want an apartment. I don't want a house.

I just want everything to stay as it is with Holt right now, except I want to not be spewing lies to my parents about who he is.

"Goldie said her friends can help me find an apartment," I add. "I'm probably seeing her again tomorrow."

Dad eyes me. "Be very, very careful if you're around Huxley."

Huxley. Fletcher. Same guy. Last name, first name. Right. "He's the one who's always in the home office?"

"The social media team love-hates him," Miranda says. "His socials are fire. He sells a *lot* of tickets. But sometimes he wants us to do really crazy things."

"Still can't believe Collins's daughter is dating him. Wouldn't be my first choice," Dad mutters. "He's a good player, but he's not good enough for her."

"But they're so happy together," Miranda says. "Isn't happy better than not happy?"

Dad grunts.

"*And* his *son* plays rugby. So his son is good enough to play a sport but his daughter is too good to date men who also play the same sport?" she presses.

"Yes," Dad says.

Miranda cocks her head and watches him.

He grunts again and keeps eating.

Yay, double-standard land is alive and well. It's truly no wonder I haven't dated much. There's always this voice of my stepdad sitting on my shoulder grunting, *this one's not good enough for you.*

"So I heard one of the players twisted an ankle or something a few weeks ago?" I say in the continued silence. "Is that...bad for the team next year?"

"Webster," Dad says. "Team captain. Broke his foot. He'll be back. Good guy. He wouldn't have made a pass at Goldie, and he knows not to look at my daughters."

Fuck.

Just *fuck.*

Mom pats his hand. "None of your players are looking at our girls. Now, Ziggy. Show me those baby pictures again. What names are you thinking of? It's so nice that you don't have to compromise with anyone about your favorite names. Unless you're thinking Robert for a boy. I've known too many Roberts and Bobs and Robs and Bobbys who were just absolute terrors, and I don't want to put that kind of bad energy around my grandbaby."

"I doubt Ziggy's thinking of Robert for her baby," Miranda says. "But I kinda like the name Fletcher."

"Over my dead body," Dad declares.

Miranda smirks. "Crew? Silas? Zander? Tatum?"

"Oh, stop tormenting him," Mom chides. "We know Ziggy's not naming her baby after any of the players either."

"Out of curiosity, if I randomly met the CEO of one of your companies and we hit it off, and he didn't care that I was pregnant, and he made me feel loved and cherished and worshipped me like a goddess, would that also be a bad thing?" I ask.

"Yes."

At least he's consistent.

"You own half the city."

"And that means I get to vet the men my daughters date, and none of them are good enough for you."

"Canada," Miranda whispers. "We can both run away to Canada."

"Roland, you're being slightly ridiculous. It's not fair to the girls. If they want to date an accomplished man who has a good job and doesn't have any skeletons in his closet and who makes them happy, then they should have *some* flexibility here."

"That's a very low bar," Dad replies.

"Is it? I don't see either one of the girls settling for someone who doesn't make them happy. It was the critical element when *I* fell in love."

He grunts.

"Glad you agree," she says, "because I actually wanted to

introduce Ziggy to that nice young man from the Environmental Engineering Club that we had lunch with earlier this week."

"*Mom.* No." I shake my head. "If I meet someone, and it's natural and we click and he can handle dating a single mom, then I meet someone. But I don't want to get set up on dates. I don't want that obligation. I'd rather meet him by accident."

Dad eyes me. "So long as he can take care of you and isn't traveling all the time and doesn't put you second behind anything. And I do mean *anything.*"

That should be a good statement.

But it's not.

I know it's not.

Miranda knows it's not.

And I suddenly understand better what Dad's issue is with either of us dating one of his rugby players.

It's their life, Goldie said to me the other day while she and I had lunch and Holt and Fletcher were at the gym.

Not because Holt was working out, but because he wanted to soak in the atmosphere until he *can* get back to working out.

When you're dating an athlete, you accept that they possibly love their sport more than they love you. But they love you with everything they have available to love you, and given the extra-big size of their hearts, it's more than enough.

I told her she was crazy, that Fletcher seemed like he'd sacrifice the world for her, to include rugby, and she agreed.

She said he's special. And that he *did* try to quit rugby for her once.

But Dad might not know that.

All he knows is that he asks his players for everything they have.

Which doesn't leave anything for the rest of their lives.

And what will happen when Holt can get back to the gym?

What if I *am* just a distraction to pass the time while he's injured?

Dammit.

Dammit.

A plate of breakfast potatoes and a side of biscuits appear in front of me, and I do what's expected.

I pick up my fork and chat with my family about the baby and about the banquet I'm planning and about what Miranda has been up to and about Mom's shifting social life now that she's cut out Abby Nora's family too.

But inside, I'm having a minor freak-out.

I like Holt.

I know he likes me.

But what if it's not enough?

What happens then?

And now that Holt's off the crutches, how soon is *then* coming?

I sneak a subtle peek at my phone under the table, wanting a quick message, or even to read our last messages, just to reassure myself, but my phone doesn't turn on.

Dammit.

Because the battery died because I forgot to charge it last night after doing the dishes with Holt.

But this is okay.

It's all okay.

I'll be home soon, and I'll see him soon, and everything will be okay.

31

Holt

WHAT'S that feeling when the woman you're falling hard for is due back any minute, but your teammates have invaded your house for an impromptu party to celebrate you being off crutches, and if they see your team's owner's daughter walk through your front door, you're fucked?

Right.

Panic.

That's what I'm feeling right now.

Ziggy hasn't answered any of my texts, to the point that I went and hid in the bathroom to make sure I wasn't accidentally texting someone else.

It's too early in our relationship to use a location app so we always know where the other is.

And that's stalkerish. Right?

But in a bad way?

It would be good to know when she's done with brunch.

And what happened at brunch.

Sounded like she was in danger of running into Abby Nora.

I hope she's not upset somewhere.

"What the fuck?" Porter crows in my living room. "That wasn't offside! Are you shitting me?"

"Was too, my dude," Tatum says to him.

A half dozen guys are crowded in my living room, all of us watching the local women's soccer team. Nice that they're broadcast. Sucks that the guys didn't think—or couldn't afford—to get tickets *at* the match for us to celebrate me being off crutches.

Why the fuck isn't Ziggy answering my texts?

Is she hurt?

Was there an accident?

Did she tell her dad about us and he took her phone away and she's locked in a Heartwood Valley mansion, needing me to come rescue her?

Fuck.

I'm getting worried and I need to breathe and not panic and trust that everything will be fine.

She's okay.

She's okay.

There's a legit explanation for her not texting me back.

And I will find out.

Soon.

"Better not cost us the match," Crew mutters.

They're passing around brown paper bags with Cadbury chocolate inside. Fletcher says it's the real stuff from the UK, not the imitation stuff they make here in the US.

He says he got it from a senior citizen smuggling ring.

I tell him to shut up because I don't want to know.

Haven't touched a single bar. Not when I'm still on activity restrictions. Eating chocolate means working off chocolate. I haven't even let myself ask for more cherry hand pies, and I actively asked Ziggy not to make more so I wouldn't have to work them off, which was freaking hard.

But if I don't hear from her soon, I might have two chocolate bars.

Or more.

I hope she's okay.

I will fucking kill something if she's not okay.

"What's with all of the potatoes in your kitchen?" Zander asks me.

Focus. "What are you doing in my cabinets?"

"Looking for peanut butter."

"We bring our own peanut butter when we invade someone's house," Silas tells him.

"How was I supposed to know there'd be chocolate that would need peanut butter?"

"There's always chocolate," Fletcher answers.

Silas hooks a thumb at him. "What the shitbasket said."

Fletcher smirks. "Thank you, fuckwanker, for acknowledging that I'm always right and always do what's best."

Silas flips him off.

Fletcher rises and stretches like he's about to moon Silas and doesn't care who's in the blast zone of having to see his ass when the door opens and Ziggy walks in.

Relief that she's okay floods my body.

She's okay.

She's in one piece.

One beautiful, glorious, curly-haired, wide-blue-eyed, full-breasted, baby-carrying piece.

And all of that relief almost instantly headbutts against

the *shit, we're caught* panic taking over the *did something happen to her* panic, and I leap to my feet and almost trip over my boot.

"*Oh my god*, the way everyone kept staaaaarr—oh, fuuuuuuuck."

Crew drops his chocolate bar on my couch.

Porter makes a choking noise.

Zander stares at her, mostly in horror, which is a mirror of how she's now staring at me.

"Heh. Called it," Silas mutters.

Fletcher shoves him. "Shut up."

"Called what?" Tatum asks.

Everyone else just keeps staring while Ziggy's face breaks out in that blotchy blush.

I curl my hands into fists to keep myself from leaping across the room to wrap her in a hug and hustle her out of here, which would give us away.

But what won't?

What the fuck *won't*?

"Thanks for coming, food lady," Fletcher says. "We need to talk about the banquet menu and there's no fucking way we're talking about it when there are cameras in the office. I don't want witnesses to my opinions."

Ziggy blinks at him while I freeze halfway across the room, blocking the TV as the announcer shouts about a goal.

"There are cameras in the office?" she says to Fletcher.

My wingman.

It's impossible to not love and hate him at the same time.

He shakes his head as he replies, "Yeah, they're everywhere. In case anyone does anything that'll go viral on the internet and sell more tickets."

"There aren't fucking cameras," I mutter.

My heart is about to beat out of my chest.

Only about a quarter of the team is here, but all of them have phones with cameras, and all of them know that Ziggy Barnes should not be in my house.

Crew's staring at me. So is Porter.

"Fuck yeah, we scored," Tatum says. "But wait. What's wrong with the catering menu for the banquet?"

"It's tofu," Fletcher says.

"With a side of lima beans," Silas adds.

Freaking both of them.

Working together.

I will never understand their relationship.

I look at Ziggy again, trying to silently ask her what she wants to do without putting it all on her. And I'm coming to a realization I don't like.

"Hey, don't hate on limas." Porter shoves Silas from the other side, but he's still half eyeing me. "And don't talk shit about Ziggy's food choices. She promised me we're getting steak. And not bad catering steak either. *Good* steak. Like, she's hiring a rancher to come in and fix it for us."

"How do you know about the rancher?" Ziggy asks him. She's clutching her handbag so tightly that her knuckles are white.

He grins. "I was with the social media team for a volunteer thing this week and I told them I'd show my tattoo for the camera if they told me how you could keep a promise about good steak."

Ziggy squeezes her eyes shut. "I didn't hear that. I don't want to know who you're showing your tattoo to."

"It's on my arm. See?" He lifts his sleeve, and there's the tattoo that all of us in the locker room are familiar with but the rest of the world doesn't see often.

He has the cartoon lion mascot of his favorite breakfast cereal on his shoulder.

Ziggy blinks at him, glances at me, then swiftly looks away.

Like anyone's gonna believe she doesn't know me when this is my fucking house and it's pretty clear no one believes the catering story.

"You still gonna be playing for us next year, Cap'n?" Zander says quietly.

"Yes," I grit out.

He looks at Ziggy, then at me.

Then at Jessica, who runs as fast as her little barrel body will go as she dashes in from the porch.

I've been leaving the doors open so she can go in and out as she pleases, and as she pleases is right to Ziggy.

Even if it means being in the same room with a half dozen men.

"How'd this happen?" Crew asks me.

"How did what happen?"

He looks pointedly at Ziggy, who's squatting down and whispering things in Italian to Jessica, who's soaking in the love, then back at me.

I get the eyebrow cock of *don't fucking lie to us.*

"Oh, shit, are you the father?" Tatum says.

Ziggy jerks her head up so fast she almost falls over. "*No.*"

I swallow a muttered *thanks* because it wouldn't come out as nice as it should.

I know what she means.

He didn't get me pregnant.

But fuck yes that baby is mine.

All of those eyeballs shift between us.

My house isn't big enough for this mountain of scrutiny,

and all I want to do is pick Ziggy up and carry her somewhere away from the prying eyes and ask if she's okay.

What happened at brunch.

If something happened to her phone.

What I can do.

"So what's going on then?" Porter says.

"What's going on is nobody's fucking business until someone makes it everybody's fucking business," Fletcher says. "Maybe something's going on. Maybe nothing's going on. You want to sit here and speculate on some shit that could get Holt fired? Even if it's not true?"

If they're really family, they'll be on your side, I hear Caden say. *I'd be on your side.*

Shit.

Fuck.

I look at Ziggy again.

Pretty sure she wants to crawl through the floor and live in the floorboards for the next few months.

And I have to tell my teammates what's going on.

Trust them.

This is a fuckton easier when it's someone else's problem. Someone else's secret.

"It was an accident," I say on a sigh.

"You *are* the dad!" Tatum says.

"Christ on a cinnamon roll," I mutter to the ceiling.

"I was pregnant before I came back to the States," Ziggy tells him, her attention still half on me.

I nod. *Tell them.*

She's not getting fired.

Roland will take good care of her.

It's me. I'm the one with the most to lose. With everything to lose.

We both know it.

So I have to do this. Not her.

"Ziggy and I met by accident," I say, louder. More specific. "I asked her to house-sit for me while I was in Spain."

"Like you met in a car accident?" Tatum asks.

"At my night job," I tell him.

"Where the other staff told me he played lacrosse," Ziggy fills in.

Groans go up around the room.

She stifles a smile by pinching her lips together, and that little smile—knowing she mentioned lacrosse on purpose to get a reaction and unite them—it helps me breathe again.

Jessica snorts happily.

She can apparently handle being in a room of men so long as Ziggy's rubbing her belly.

Relatable.

"Why didn't you tell him who you are?" Zander asks her.

"Wasn't relevant," I say. "She needed a place to stay. Jessica needed a keeper."

"And people treat you differently when they find out Roland Keating is your stepfather," Ziggy says. "I don't tell anyone if I don't have to."

"So you two are..." Porter says, letting the rest of the sentence hang in the air.

"Trying to not get me fired," I finish.

Ziggy winces.

"So that's how brunch went?" I ask her.

"My mom might come around." She looks down at Jessica and adds, "In another year or two."

My teammates all share a look.

They don't need more context.

Even the slower ones.

"Fuck this," Crew says. "You treating her right?"

"It's the captain, you dipshit," Porter says. "He treats everyone right. Of course he's treating her right. Probably better than right. You think a single woman choosing to have a baby on her own's gonna tolerate being treated like anything less than a queen? Not a fucking chance."

"She treating you right?" Silas asks me.

Fletcher hits him in the face with a pillow. "Don't talk about your sister's friends like that."

Silas pushes the pillow away. "Since when are they friends?"

"Since high school."

"Goldie doesn't see anyone from high school anymore."

"That's because Ziggy lived overseas after she graduated culinary school. Who knows your sister better? I know your sister better."

"Why do we invite both of them to stuff like this?" Tatum says to Zander.

"Because when we say things like *knock it off and focus, you assholes*, they're the ones with the time and resources to make shit happen," Zander replies.

"Dammit."

"Agreed."

Tatum looks at me. "How can we help?"

"Help what?" Ziggy says.

"Help convince Roland that you two should get to date."

She blinks at him.

See? Told you, Caden whispers while another knot deep in my stomach loosens.

Might be one in my heart area relaxing too.

"Captain's been through shit the past couple years," Crew tells Ziggy.

"Haven't seen him happy in a while," Porter adds.

"It's like he came back to life even though he's been walking around on crutches," Zander says. "I'd be a shit show if I was on crutches. But he's been happy. Guessing it's not the broken foot effect. So that means it's you."

Crew nods. "And that means we're your guys for whatever it takes to win your family over and not have our captain get fired when your stepdad finds out."

I swallow the lump at the base of my throat. "Just don't tell anybody while we figure this out."

"Lame," Silas says.

Fletcher nods. "Fuckwanker's right. We can do a lot better than not tell anybody."

"You two have a very strange relationship," Ziggy says.

"He's a whiny-ass baby," Fletcher says, jerking a head at Silas.

"He's a stuck-up bossy shithead," Silas replies.

"But I make his sister happy."

"The day he cheats on her, he's a dead man, and I'll enjoy every minute of torturing him before I murder him."

"We're on a truce until one of us dies because I'm never doing another thing in my life to make Goldie anything less than ecstatically happy."

"Can we focus on the captain and his lady?" Zander says to them.

Silas hooks a thumb at Fletcher. "He started it."

"You must truly be a superhero if you convince these guys to play nicely together on the field," Ziggy says to me.

"*Pitch*," everyone replies at once.

Ziggy stifles another smile, and once again, I'm positive she used the wrong word on purpose.

Glorious woman.

She gets them all back on the same page so easily.

"Pitch," she says. "Apologies. Your pitchinesses."

"We wouldn't get along for another captain," Fletcher says. "I'll make sure everyone knows if Captain goes, this team's never making the playoffs again because I'm quitting."

"You're old," Silas fires back. "They'd just retire your ass if you said that."

"And then I'd be your boss from the office."

"Unless you go work for league headquarters," Porter says. He looks at me. "So those two are out, but don't worry, Cap'n. The rest of us will still help."

"Lots of talking about how much we like playing under your leadership," Crew says.

Zander nods. "And we'll get you back out on the volunteer circuit for some community recognition. Make it so you're selling more tickets than Fletcher does."

Fletcher snorts. "Not likely. But I'll give you credit for half the tickets I sell."

"How do you even track that?" Ziggy asks.

Fletcher whips out his phone. "Selfie," he commands, and half the guys lean in, showing off their Copper Valley Scorned soccer jerseys or flashing peace signs.

Including Silas.

"It's ridiculous," I tell Ziggy.

I'm too far away from her.

It's maybe six feet between where I'm standing and where she's squatting and rubbing Jessica's belly, but it's too far.

I want to hold her hand. I want to hug her. I want to kiss her.

I want to promise her this will work out.

I want her to promise me she wants it to.

The guys pull away, and Fletcher bends over his phone.

"Grabbing a promo shot from last season too…and posting both together on socials…"

"He'll text the ticket office that he posted, and they'll tell him how many more tickets move this weekend than did before," Porter says.

"Are you an influencer?" Ziggy asks.

"I don't do titles," Fletcher says. "I just *am*."

"That was the captain's inspiration," Porter says. "The *just am* thing."

Fletcher snorts. "Was not. It was Goldie."

"Is now. That's what I'm telling everyone I see at headquarters. Captain made you a better person."

I look at Ziggy and shrug. "I can't fully explain them, but they're mine."

Her slow-growing smile makes my heart beat faster. "Like a real family. Complete with the annoying siblings."

Exactly.

I might lose my job.

But for the first time in a long time, I'm finally not worried that I'll lose my family.

32

Ziggy

HOLT ORDERS DINNER in from a local Middle Eastern restaurant, plus mashed potatoes and rosemary potatoes for me from the deli. I end up eating half of his food on top of most of my potatoes while we snuggle on the couch with my favorite TV show playing, which he says was his brother's favorite too.

It's been quite the day.

I thought for sure everything was doomed when I didn't pay attention to the extra cars on the street when I got home.

And my phone had died, so I missed all of Holt's texts telling me not to come home.

But— "Are your teammates always so nice?"

He grins down at me. "Not on the pitch."

"*Off* the pitch."

"Unless it's Fletcher and Silas, yes."

"Do you think they can be subtle enough? With their plans?"

They left after the soccer game was over, all of them declaring they would take every opportunity to sing Holt's praises anytime they're in the headquarters office.

And they took all of my gratitude with them.

Even if they fail, they care. They're cheering for us.

I didn't realize how much that would mean to me. But after everything with Abby Nora, I haven't had a lot of faith in people.

If you can't trust your best friend, who can you trust?

Apparently a ragtag team of rugby players.

Holt sets his plate aside and stretches out, pulling me closer. "Guess we'll find out."

I lean my head on his chest, listening to his beating heart. "Mom wants to introduce me to some business guy Dad has other dealings with."

His pulse kicks up under my ear. "Ew."

"That's what Miranda said too. But also, I figured out one of Dad's biggest issues."

He kisses my hair. "Is it overcome-able?"

"Maybe. I got the impression he's worried that we'd come second after the sport. That he thinks all of you would put rugby over relationships and family and everything else."

He rubs his pec. "Great to hear our club's owner thinks so much of us. Or maybe expects that much of us."

For real. "You literally gave up your career in Europe to take care of your brother. I don't understand why he can't see that. And if you're gone for games—"

"Matches."

"—if you're gone for matches, how's that any different

340

from a businessperson going on a business trip? You come home—"

"Usually only one night away."

"—and you cannot possibly work your bodies and have practices fourteen hours a day and still play games—*matches* on the weekends."

He chuckles. "You're half right."

"Where am I half wrong?"

"It's not all about practice time. We also watch a lot of match video to study our opponents. Spend a lot of time doing community service and volunteer work for visibility. Help sell tickets. Do photo ops. Help the social media team. It's a full-time job during the season. Sometimes more."

And the season starts in February.

Right after the baby's born.

"But when Crew's down with a cold, Porter and Tatum step in and cover for him. If Fletcher twists an ankle, believe it or not, Silas steps in to do the public appearances that he doesn't want to limp around at. And when Silas's girlfriend had a baby five years ago, the coaches sent him home with match video so he could be around to help Brittany with Hallie and watch when he had time."

I snuggle closer to him. "Because you're a family."

"Because we're a family," he agrees.

It makes something flutter low in my belly.

I freeze.

Wait.

Wait.

"Ziggy?" he murmurs.

There it is.

There it is again.

A flutter.

341

Low in my belly.

Right about where Tater Tot is sitting.

"I think I just felt the baby move," I whisper.

No.

No way.

It's too early. I'm a first-time mom. I shouldn't—but I can.

"Where?" His hand shifts to my stomach.

"I don't think you can feel it yet, but *oh my god.*" I move his hand right over where I'm feeling the tiniest of bubbles popping inside me. "It's right there. *That's the baby.*"

It could be gas, but I don't think it is.

I think it's actually the baby.

I wait, but there aren't more.

Still, my eyes are wet and I can't stop smiling.

This.

A kind, gentle man cradling my belly while my baby kicks inside and our dog snoozes on the floor in front of us.

Family.

Home.

This is what I've been searching for.

"I should call my mom," I whisper, grateful for once that *I should call Abby Nora* isn't an immediate next gut reaction.

He kisses my hair again, inhaling deeply against me. "I'll be quiet."

"I'll tell her I heard you saved an old lady from a burning building."

He chuckles, the reverberations of his chest against me almost as joy-inducing as feeling my baby kick for the first time.

I don't want to move.

Not when I'm wrapped in love.

And I swear that's what this is.

He wouldn't put his career on the line for anything less. Would he?

"We're going to make this work," I whisper.

He rubs his hand over my belly. "One way or another."

I lift my head to look at him, and I lose my breath.

Has anyone *ever* gazed back at me with that much adoration?

If they have, it hasn't registered.

But when Holt looks at me, I feel like I'm not just the center of his world, but like I *am* his world.

And it's scary and beautiful and nerve-racking and soothing all at the same time. "What did I do? What did I do to make you like me?"

He cradles my head with one hand while he continues gently rubbing my belly with his other. "You stayed."

"Anyone would've stayed."

He shakes his head. "Not the way you did."

He's wrong.

Other people would've stayed with him.

Wouldn't they?

"All my life, I've been the guy who takes care of everyone else. But you—when you made me breakfast that first day I was back—when you didn't have to and shouldn't have, when you stayed—that wasn't a little thing. That was an *everything*."

"It was a spite breakfast," I whisper.

He grins. "Everything I didn't know I needed. But exactly what I needed. Besides, I was already long gone after watching you with that chicken."

I laugh. "Stop."

"It's true. I watched you with that bird, and I wanted to know how I could get you to want to keep reaching for me even when I was filthy and on the ground and better left for the crows the same way you kept trying to get to that chicken. That's dedication. That's commitment. It's admirable as hell."

He's not mocking me.

He's serious.

The baby flutters again, and I squeal and put my hand over his.

"Again?" he asks.

"Again," I whisper. "I felt it again."

He leans in and kisses my neck. "I love watching you be happy."

Happy.

I am.

I'm happy.

And it's such a stark difference from when I wasn't happy just a few hours ago.

When I wasn't happy after I discovered my best friend wasn't so best after all.

When I've been scared at how fast my life has changed, even knowing I actively chose to keep the baby when I could've instead decided now wasn't the right time to be pregnant, and stayed on the ship, and kept living the same life I'd mostly enjoyed for years.

"Everyone was staring at me at brunch today," I tell Holt. "Me and my family, but I know it was mostly me. They know I came home pregnant and alone. They know what Abby Nora thinks of me. They know what happened with her brother-in-law. It was like being the whale shark in the aquarium. I was the beast spotted in the wild who blew up her whole life and came home to take a pity job from her parents. You could practically hear them thinking that I got pregnant on purpose so I could have what Abby Nora has. Or that it was only a matter of time before I fucked up my life."

"You don't think you fucked up your life, do you?"

"It's hard to not feel like a complete loser when I'm at my parents' club. But here? No. Here, I'm safe. Here, I'm okay."

"Good. Also, I think I know a few guys who would be happy to solve the club problem for you. They're super subtle."

I giggle at the image of the Pounders all invading the Heartwood Valley Owners Club to try to make me feel better. "Do you know why I decided to stay pregnant and keep the baby?"

"Felt right?"

"Because I always thought I'd find someone and settle down and have a family, but I realized I hadn't dated anyone seriously *ever*. When I was in high school, Dad was—well, he was exactly what you'd expect. No boy was ever good enough. There was a guy in culinary school, and I thought we might have had a future, but he called it off not long after I told him I loved him for the first time, and I just—I didn't date again."

"At all?"

I shake my head. "Not really. I started to think I had unrealistic expectations, or that I was too picky, or that I was too difficult, but ironically enough, not that my stepdad had trained me to think no man would ever be good enough for me. And I worked all the time, and so when I realized I was pregnant, I knew this was my last opportunity. My only opportunity to have kids of my own unless I waited and went the sperm donor route. I shouldn't be pregnant. We used a condom. I had an IUD. But I *am*. It's like this was supposed to happen."

His hand stills on my belly and I feel him swallow.

"I decided I was never having kids after I had genetic testing when Caden got sick," he says quietly. "Didn't want to pass that down. So I—I had a vasectomy. I *won't* have kids. Not genetic kids."

I look up at him again.

"You're not a substitute," he adds quickly. "You're not a shortcut to something I didn't think I'd ever have. It scares the ever-loving fuck out of me that you don't have any idea what kind of genetic diseases or disorders the baby might have. But being afraid of losing something isn't a reason to deny yourself the chance to be happy while you have it."

I brush his hair off his forehead. "Loving people is scary."

"Terrifying."

"They leave you for all kinds of different reasons."

"But sometimes, they stay and remind you what matters. Why they're worth fighting for even when it might mean sacrificing something else."

"I'll fight for you," I whisper. "You make me feel loved."

"You are loved."

My eyes are hot and wet. "So are you."

He kisses me, and the rest of the world fades away.

I love kissing this man. I love touching him. I love when he pulls me onto his lap and tugs my shirt off and strokes my back and unhooks my bra.

I love when he cradles my breasts and plays with my nipples.

I love running my hands all over his broad chest and shoulders, up his thick neck, to hold his face while I kiss him back.

I love the feel of his thick, heavy erection between my thighs.

And I love knowing that when we wake up together tomorrow morning, the world outside might not be fully right yet, but inside, here, in this house, *we* will be right.

We'll convince my dad that this is okay.

We will.

Because love shouldn't ever be wrong. It's rare and it's beautiful and maybe it won't last, but why shouldn't we have it while it does?

That's all I want.

I want Holt for as long as we make each other happy.

And I'm planning on that being forever.

33

Holt

THE BEST PART of the team knowing my and Ziggy's secret is that they've been going above and beyond to support us.

Random baby presents show up on my doorstep.

Someone—probably Fletcher—had a potato feast delivered to the main office for all of the headquarters staff one day, which resulted in leftovers at my house for three days.

Tatum flat-out asked Roland if the team could throw Ziggy a baby shower.

Since we're all the baby's uncles and all.

Miranda's been working overtime getting me visible community service opportunities and more interviews, and the guys on the team are taking turns driving me everywhere since I'm still in the damn boot.

But that can't beat what I find when Silas drops me off from a rugby clinic for kids that we volunteered at a week after the team found out.

It's Ziggy.

On the couch.

Eating fried mozzarella sticks.

In a silver Pounders jersey.

Watching the championship match from a year ago. The one that we took that made us league champions.

I pause in the doorway, and that's when I realize she's not the only one in a jersey.

Jessica's wearing my name and number on her back.

Wait.

Wait.

"Turn around," I say to Ziggy.

She grins at me, then shifts so I can verify that it is, in fact, *my* name and number on her back.

My dick twitches. "Somebody's been in my closet."

"It looked comfortable. Come sit. I need you to explain the rules to me. Right now, all I know is that you look seriously hot when you tackle someone, and I might've played a clip of you spraying water on your face about thirty-four times. And then grabbed my vibrator."

I am no longer twitching.

I am now full-mast.

"While you were wearing my jersey?" Fuck. My voice is hoarse.

"Yes." She shifts again, parting her legs slightly, and fuck me sideways.

All she's wearing is my jersey.

I thought maybe she was in short shorts, but nope.

No shorts.

No underwear.

No bra.

Just Ziggy skin against my jersey.

The jersey I'm never washing again.

I strip out of my own Pounders polo and drop my shorts and boxer briefs, which get stuck on the fucking boot.

While I lean over and tug the damn fabric around the boot, Jessica grumbles to herself, rises, shakes, and heads to the kitchen, which makes Ziggy laugh.

Her breasts bounce under my jersey as she shifts on the couch to make room for me. "Should I take this off?" she asks, toying with the hem and lifting it enough for me to see her pussy.

"Absolutely not."

"It's a little tight in the boob area."

And I thought I couldn't get any harder.

I finally free myself from the damn boot, kick my other shoe off, and stalk to the couch, gripping my bobbing cock.

She bites her lower lip as she looks down at my hard-on. "Is that all for me?"

"Tell me how you touched yourself while you were watching me on the pitch."

"Well…" She spreads her legs and dips her fingers into her curls. "It went something like this…"

I growl as I push her legs wider and settle my shoulders between them, getting a better view of the pink skin hiding between her curls and her fingers stroking her seam.

She's wet.

It's fucking beautiful.

She touches her clit and tilts her head back with a sigh, and I'm done.

Just done.

Don't want to watch anymore.

Now, I want to taste. Lick. Suck.

Devour.

And I do.

I bury my head between her thighs and feast on her pussy until she's crying my name and bucking her hips into my face, coming all over my tongue.

This.

This is what I want to come home to every night.

Ziggy.

Naked or wearing my kit or fully dressed.

Trusting me.

Being my best friend.

My lover.

My world.

I don't care if she wants a dozen dogs who hate me. I don't care if Tater Tot has colic and doesn't sleep. I don't care if Ziggy quits cooking.

I just want to *be*.

I want to be with her.

The woman who's brought me out of the fog I'd been living in, looking for a way to run away from the pain instead of working through it, the way she's been working through losing her best friend.

Her body sags beneath me. "Holt?" she whispers.

"Yes, kitten?"

"That was—the best—ever—and I want—you—inside me —now. Please."

I lift my head and watch her chest rising and falling rapidly under my jersey as she pants and tugs on my ears. "Already?"

"*Now,*" she repeats.

Still a pain in the ass to move in the boot, but I pull myself up her body, pushing my jersey out of the way so that I can kiss that swelling belly that I love so much, her belly button, her breastbone, sucking on one nipple, then the other as she wraps her legs around my hips and tilts them up to brush the tip of my cock.

I slide into her swollen, hot, wet center, and my eyes cross.

"Oh god, yes," she gasps.

I can't imagine going a second round immediately after the first the way she is, but I stroke in and out of her, my balls getting hot and heavy and tight with every moan and whimper out of her mouth.

She arches her head back and tightens her legs around me while I slam into her, harder and faster, following the cues from her cries and *yes*es and *there*s until her pussy clenches around my rock-hard cock, and she's gasping my name again, straining into me while her inner walls pulse around me, gripping me tightly as I let my own release go.

I'm wrapped in Ziggy, the fabric of my jersey bunched up over her breasts, her breath hot on my shoulder as she pants while her body sags under me.

She's everything.

Every fucking thing.

"I love you," she whispers. "My god, I love you so much."

I kiss her neck and she shivers.

"I love you too," I whisper back.

I do.

I love her with everything inside me. I love her with everything outside of me.

I love her with the whole universe.

"When...baby comes...harder...do this," she pants.

"Ziggy. I love you for so much more than how good the sex is."

The woman hugs me even tighter.

With her arms. With her legs. With her face pressed to my shoulder, kissing me between gulps of air.

"You gonna make it?" I tease.

"I need to work out more."

"You just did, kitten."

She laughs a breathy, relaxed laugh. "Why kitten?"

Why kitten? Why indeed. "It was the way you ate that chicken. Like a kitten would."

She laughs harder, but my dick's still inside her, and the squeeze of her inner muscles is too much, and now I'm the one gasping for breath as my oversensitive cock tries to go into hiding.

"Thank you for being my friend," she whispers.

"Thank you for being my everything."

34

Ziggy

I'M A NERVOUS WRECK.

I shouldn't be. The caterers are here. The bar is set up. The room is perfectly decorated. Dad's beaming as he welcomes the team to the postseason banquet, delayed because a few players were traveling over the summer and weren't supposed to be back until now.

And this is the first time I'll be in a room with two dozen men who know that I'm dating their captain.

And my stepdad.

Their team's owner.

Dad insists that the whole family greet the team, so I'm standing next to Mom, who's next to Miranda, who's next to Dad.

All four of us in a row.

"Hey, Ziggy," Crew says to me after he shakes my mom's hand. He's first in line. "Looks great in here. Did you hear we have a player on the team who saved a puppy from a fire last week?"

"*No,*" Mom gasps.

I glare at Crew as much as I can without giving away that I'm glaring at him. "I hope we hear all about it later. That's something to celebrate."

"My goodness, is he okay?" Mom asks.

"Barely even singed his arm hairs," Crew says.

Holt's not here yet. He's coming with Fletcher and Goldie and Silas.

And they're intentionally arriving almost last.

They might even be in the parking garage right now, waiting for most of the other guys to arrive.

Wouldn't surprise me.

I wonder if he's as nervous as I am.

I hope not. Only one of us should feel like this.

"Ziggy? Are you okay?" Mom whispers.

Another player's here, talking to Dad and taking a minute.

"Yes! Yes. Why? Do I have something between my teeth? Is my lipstick smeared? Oh god, did I lose an earring?"

"Sweetheart, you look perfect." She puts a hand to my forehead, like anxiety can present itself with a fever or something. "What's going on?"

"I just want to do a good job," I blurt.

"You've done a fabulous job. Look at this place. No one else could've pulled this together like you did."

I can think of a dozen people I personally know who could've pulled this together, but I don't say that.

Instead, I smile politely at Holt's teammate, who gives me a kind smile in return before shaking Mom's hand and telling her thanks for hosting tonight.

Two. Dozen. Men.

Including several I'm meeting for the first time tonight because not all of the guys come into the office regularly. Two were retiring at the end of the year. A couple more have been traded but came back for the banquet.

And all of them know my secret.

Mine and Holt's.

I manage to shove the worries far enough into a mental box that Mom quits fussing.

Doesn't hurt that the players and the sponsors Dad invited are showing up in thicker crowds now, and I'm saying polite *nice to meet you*s and *good to see you again*s and *thank you for coming*s to suited man after suited man and occasionally their dates too.

We're telling my parents tomorrow.

After the banquet.

To give the team one more night of semi-normalcy to celebrate what they certainly deserve to celebrate.

And then Holt and I will handle the aftermath of our announcement without taking away from anyone's joy.

Because the team really did do amazingly well this season.

If it weren't for a few injuries to some key players, they would've gone all the way again this past season.

More businessmen and their wives come through the line.

I keep alternating between looking at the rancher I hired to come and grill steaks on the patio outside the banquet hall and watching for Holt to show up in the line.

And that's why I almost miss it.

The introduction.

The introduction.

"Ziggy," Mom says with that tone of voice that says she's said my name at least three times now.

I snap to attention and force a smile at her, consciously *not* asking if my dress is stuck in my panties. "Yes?"

"This is Kyle Vince. The nice young man I told you about who works with your father at the Environmental Engineering Club?"

It takes seven heartbeats—fast heartbeats, but still—for me to catch on.

The nice young man I told you about.

Shit.

Dammit.

I keep my forced smile in place and hold out a hand, blocking him from going in for a cheek kiss.

Not on purpose, though it would've been if I'd realized he was going to try to do the cheek kiss.

What in the hell has my mother been telling him about me? "Hello, thank you for coming. What's your connection to the team?"

"*Ziggy,*" Mom hisses.

Kyle smiles at me. He's a few inches taller than me, slender, in a suit that smells both expensive and new. "Big fan."

"Like season ticket holder?"

"I, ah, no. Just a game or two every season. But I subscribe to the rugby channel. Watch a lot at home."

He's so lying.

I slide a look at Mom, who's beaming at him. "Kyle was just promoted to senior lead manager engineer for one of the biggest environmental firms in Copper Valley."

"That's...not actually a title," he tells her with a bashful smile.

Bashful.

It's fake.

It has to be fake.

But even if it isn't, I don't care.

"Congratulations on whatever your title is," I manage to say without any snark at all. Thank you, seven years of hardcore hospitality training on cruise ships. "We need more people in the world who care about the environment."

I look to the guest waiting to say hi to Mom, and I almost squeak.

It's Fletcher.

Followed by Goldie.

Followed by Holt, who's shaking Dad's hand with what I would've called a relaxed smile a month ago, but now, I can see the tension in his shoulders and the strain in his neck and the way his mouth is too tight at the corners.

He's nervous.

And Fletcher's glaring at Kyle while Goldie leans around him and gives me a finger wave.

Miranda looks like she's torn between wanting a tub of popcorn to watch the show and wanting to leap in and save me.

I appreciate both of those things about her.

"Kyle will be sitting with us," Mom tells me. "I can't wait to hear more about his job. How about you, Ziggy? Aren't you fascinated?"

"It's not quite as exciting as a rugby game," Kyle says.

Match, I hear the entire Pounders team yell in my head.

"I'm pregnant," I tell Kyle.

His brows lift, but only slightly. "Yes, your mother told me. That's exciting. I personally hope to have several kids whenever I meet the right woman and settle down."

"He wants to be a *dad*," Mom whispers.

Loudly.

"Mrs. Keating, so good to see you," Goldie says, slipping around Fletcher, who's still glaring at Kyle.

"So we'll talk more at dinner?" Kyle says to me.

"It seems so. Enjoy the bar. It's free. Thank you for coming and supporting the Pounders."

He winks.

I momentarily wish for morning sickness to come back.

There's nothing innately wrong with him, aside from the fact that my mother invited him here to attempt to make him my date.

And he's not Holt, who just said something to Miranda to make her snort-laugh so loudly that all of us are looking at her now.

"Oh shit, I blew snot on your coat," she says to Holt.

"Not the first woman to do that to me today," he replies, which makes me choke on a laugh too.

Jessica did get him spectacularly well this morning.

"Oh, are you dating someone, my dear?" Mom says to him.

"I have a—" He freezes, his gaze darting swiftly from me to Fletcher to Mom to Miranda to Dad to me and back to Fletcher.

He can't say a dog who hates him.

He can't say a dog who hates men.

He probably shouldn't say dog at all.

"Friend with a kid with a cold," Goldie interjects smoothly. "He was telling us all about it on the way over. Though why we had to drive a man with two good feet is such a great question, isn't it?"

Thank the wine gods for Goldie.

"You're out of the cast!" Mom shrieks. She tackles Holt

with a mom hug. "Oh, what a wonderful day! Roland. Did you see this? Holt's out of his cast."

"It was a boot, Deedee," Miranda murmurs.

"Yes, great day for the Pounders," Dad says before going back to talking to Silas.

Goldie slips to my side and hugs me. "Thank you *so much* for talking your dad out of inviting mine again this year," she whispers.

"Of course," I whisper back.

I don't know all of the details, but I know Dad likes Goldie's dad because he created a rugby league for kids so Silas would have a league to train in, but Goldie and Silas aren't big fans of the man themselves. Our families weren't really tight growing up because it was before Dad cared to buy a rugby team.

And now I wonder if they weren't tight for other reasons, despite having kids in the same schools at roughly the same times.

Honestly, watching Goldie and Silas both thrive—and watching Holt thrive as well—without their parents makes me hope mine can see how happy Holt makes me, and that they'll be supportive.

Guess we'll see tomorrow.

Also, I want a glass of wine.

I very much want a glass of wine.

"You look beautiful tonight," she adds as she pulls back. "Look at you showing off your baby bump."

I run a hand over the smooth fabric of my dress that is, indeed, showing off the small but unmistakable baby bump that is Tater Tot. "Thank you. You look like a million bucks."

She's in a skin-tight red dress that reaches mid-calf, with

360

her dark hair twisted up in a fancy knot. "Fletcher calls this my *fuck you* dress. It's his favorite."

"Only when we're home alone," he grumbles as he turns to us after kissing Mom on the cheek and thanking her for having them.

"That might be too much information," I say.

Goldie's golden-hazel eyes sparkle with mischief. "That's what my brother said too."

"We really getting steak?" Fletcher asks me.

I point toward the double glass doors to the patio, where plumes of grill smoke are billowing around the patio and an older gentleman in a cowboy hat is flipping steaks at the grill. "I've been in catering and hospitality too long to disappoint. The wine is fabulous too. Which I won't be having. But I still know it's great."

"The decorations are beautiful," Goldie says, gesturing to the glinting silver streamers and the balloon arch at the photo station.

"Miranda told me what to do there. I just put it in motion."

"You both did a fantastic job." She squeezes my hand. "So now you get to enjoy the evening, yeah?"

"Yes," I say out loud while my brain says *I'm going to try.*

Fletcher pats me on the shoulder. "Good job. See you later."

Holt's getting another hug from my mom, who pulls out of it and smiles at me. "Ziggy, do you remember Holt? He sent flowers when we lost our sweet Oreo last year, and he's always the first to hold a door for any of us when he has both feet. Which he does. Finally. He was going to leave us to play in Europe but decided to come back to the Pounders after all, and we couldn't be more thrilled."

The whisper campaign is clearly working.

I hold out a hand when I want to leap into his arms and ask him to please take me somewhere to hide from an arranged dinner date. "Nice to see you again."

He takes my hand in his large, warm one, and he squeezes. "Likewise."

Swear that's a *likewise* to my internal thoughts rather than my boring greeting. "If my mom is happy you're still on the team, then I'm happy too."

"One of the best teams I've ever played for."

We're still shaking hands. I need to let him go.

But this is the only time I'll get to touch him at all tonight.

"Oh, you," Mom says, playfully batting his arm. She shakes her head at me. "He's the kind who would say that about any team he played for. Always looking for the bright side."

And he struggles to find it.

I know that much after getting to know him the past couple months.

But he's here, and I'm glad.

I give his hand one last squeeze, then drop it. "I hope you have a lovely time tonight. The food should be good."

"Hope so," Silas says behind him.

"Oh, Silas, so good to see you too." Mom hugs him as well. "I was sorry to hear your dad couldn't make it this year."

Holt snorts.

Silas grimaces too, behind Mom's back. "Yeah. Really sad."

He extricates himself from Mom's grip and holds out a hand to me. "So you're Ziggy. Goldie keeps talking about you."

"Who are you, and how do you know Goldie?" I ask.

I hear Holt snort again, and I let myself smile as Silas rolls his eyes. "She might not say good things about me, but I know she talks about me."

"She does. Is your daughter with you tonight?"

He shakes his head.

"That's too bad. She's adorable. And so smart." Hallie was tagging along with Goldie for one of our lunches last week.

He smiles. "Kids are great. You'll love yours."

"Already do, even if they keep kicking me."

Another businessman is lined up with Mom, waiting to say hi, so Silas joins Holt, Fletcher, and Goldie, who are waiting for him, and then the four of them head for the picture station.

Holt doesn't look back.

And I should quit looking at him.

But what would it be like if we could openly be here together?

If I could go take pictures with them?

If we could sit at the same table where I could hear more stories from his teammates and friends about their season together?

"Ziggy?" Mom says, again in that *I've said your name three times now* tone.

My fake smile reappears, and I turn to the next man in line and hold out my hand, shaking as Mom introduces me to another sponsor and his wife.

"You seem very close with Silas," she murmurs between guests.

Silas.

Close with *Silas*.

She'll find out otherwise tomorrow. "He's Goldie's brother. I met his daughter last week. What was I supposed to say? I'd hope someone would tell me if they think Tater Tot is an absolute delight."

She puts her hand to my forehead again. "Are you sure you're feeling okay? Are you getting enough sleep? Is this job too much right now? You know, we can—"

"Deedee, say hi to Zander," Miranda interrupts. "You can fuss over Ziggy later. She's doing great. Who wouldn't be stressed worrying about making sure a hundred people are happy with a gourmet steak dinner?"

Zander looks between all of us, then makes quick work of shaking hands and thanking us for having a party for the team, then departs.

Thanks for having us. Thanks for having me.

Such a strange expression.

We're literally here because the guys played an amazing season. *We* should be thanking *them* for giving us a reason to have a big, festive dinner where my mom has brought a date for me and where I can't be seen privately talking to the man who has my heart.

Finally—*finally*—the line is over, and it's time for us to get drinks and mingle for a few minutes before dinner's called.

I slip to the bathroom, Miranda on my heels. "You okay?" she whispers.

"We're telling them tomorrow," I whisper back.

"Your mom brought you a date."

"*I know.*"

"This is gonna be awkward. Want me to sit between you?"

"Yes."

"On it. Give me a signal if I need to accidentally spill my wine on you to get you out of anything else too. Cough twice. That's a good signal."

All good plans.

But the best-laid plans are no match for my mother, and I end up seated right next to Kyle.

While Miranda is seated next to another businessman's son.

With his parents between us on one side, and our parents between us on another.

And with Holt four tables away.

Yep.

Gonna be a long night.

35

Holt

THIS IS the worst banquet in the history of banquets.

Even though I know my foot is solid, I feel like I'm going to break it again every time I step on it.

Fletcher and Silas are both at my table, and they're being Fletcher and Silas, which is clearly amusing Goldie but annoying me.

And I can't see Ziggy.

Not only is Zander's big head in the way, I have to turn around to even look at her table.

But I know she's there.

Seated next to a guy Fletcher's already called Fuckwank Two-Point-Oh.

Occasionally her voice drifts my way as we eat thick, juicy ribeyes and loaded baked potatoes that taste like shit without her next to me.

They're fine.

Likely excellent, in fact, based on the way everyone at my table is moaning over their food.

Porter even grins at me and says it's too bad we can't give me credit for the menu because no man in their right mind would object to his daughter dating a man with good food taste like this.

Roland gets up and makes a speech about how proud he is to have such a great team and how all of us players are like sons to him, which makes me want to howl in outrage.

If I were like a son, he wouldn't be making proclamations that none of us are allowed to look at his daughters.

I hear a couple soft grunts and snorts behind me, which tells me there are other people not buying it.

I've at least turned around to watch the speech, which means I can glance toward Ziggy's table and look for her curly hair.

She wore it all down tonight.

Down, over a black cocktail dress that highlights her baby bump and was driving me mad while we were getting ready.

She's a bundle of nerves tonight, and I can't solve it.

Check that: I could solve it, but she doesn't like my solution.

I catch a glimpse of the fuckwank leaning in to say something to her.

Another glimpse of her nodding.

Politely? Or does she like him?

She doesn't like him, idiot, Caden whispers to me. *She likes you. She LOVES you. If she's fickle enough to toss you for a business twatwaffle, she doesn't deserve you.*

I'm hearing him less these days.

Not because I don't still miss him. More because missing him isn't the biggest part of my personality anymore.

I've found a new life to live for. A reminder that I *am* alive.

And it's killing me to be this far away from her right now.

I wonder if the baby's kicking her right now. If Tater Tot knows she's nervous tonight.

After her dad talks for an eternity, he announces a short break, and then the awards will start.

I try to stay subtle as I watch Ziggy get up and say something to Miranda, then head toward the patio.

Checking on the catering, no doubt. Making sure they don't need anything else.

But when the fuckwank rises after a minute and heads that direction too, I bolt out of my seat.

Fletcher's next to me before I can process that I've even moved. "Going somewhere, Captain?"

Shit.

"Need to take a piss," I lie.

He's following her.

The fuckwank is following her.

I didn't act fast enough the last time someone followed her, and it cost her a job.

While her job might not be in danger tonight, I'm not risking her sense of safety either.

Fletcher eyes me, then nods. "Cool. Need a piss buddy?"

"No."

"Women do it. We should try it."

"Sit down. You're annoying me."

And there the fuckwank goes.

Outside.

Same door that Ziggy went through thirty seconds ago.

Miranda's watching me as I stride around the tables toward the patio too.

Deedee is not, thank fuck. Roland's distracted because my teammates are top-notch friends who are *on it*.

I don't see the guy who was grilling out here before as I approach the patio doors. Grills are still open, but otherwise, there's no evidence he was here.

And at first, I don't see Ziggy.

But then—

"Yeah, it's a start-up. We're recycling stickers. *Stickers*. Do you know how many stickers there are in the world? And like, you can't recycle cardboard if it has shipping labels on it. And what are shipping labels? *Stickers*."

The fuck?

I can hear them, but I can't see them.

I can see bushes though.

Christ on a kumquat. Is this one of those hedge mazes?

Why would Ziggy go into a hedge maze with him?

"It was my sister's idea, but she doesn't have the vision to execute it. You have a sister. You know how it is. So I was thinking, if you don't want to work for your dad anymore, I could hire you. Can't really pay anything, but the couple that works together, *works* together. Heh. Get it?"

I'm crashing through the bushes, tracking his voice, when I hear Ziggy too. "Very...jokey. But as I told you at dinner, I'm quite happy with my current job."

Good.

Good.

She's okay.

"Come on, Ziggy, you and I both know you had to say that because your dad was watching. It's just us now."

"And I'd prefer to get back inside."

The fuckwank snorts. "Neither one of us wants to get back inside, and we both know it."

There.

There.

I feel like I've gone in six circles, but there they are, at the edge of this row I've just turned down.

She's stiff as a board, half-pressed against a corner of the maze, and she spots me a second after I spot her.

"Problem?" I say.

Her shoulders drop from around her ears, her eyes soften, and the slightest smile turns her lips up. "Not enough bodily fluid tonight."

The fuckwank squints at her before boxing her into a corner while he turns to face me. "No problem. None of your business."

"Excuse me, I'd like to leave," Ziggy says behind him.

"You're bothering my girlfriend," the fuckwank tells me.

"*You're* bothering *my* girlfriend," I growl back.

He pulls himself up to his full height, but he's still three inches and forty pounds smaller than I am. I get the satisfaction of seeing a flicker of fear in his eyes to accompany his sputtered, "She's not your girlfriend."

"You're three seconds from finding out what I do to guys who don't move their scrawny little worthless asses out of the way so that I can make sure you didn't hurt a single hair on her head, and if you did, you don't get warning before I destroy you."

His jaw works up and down.

"Three," I count. "Two."

The chickenshit dashes down the hedgerow. "You're gonna regret this."

The fuck I am.

Not when I have Ziggy in my arms, sagging against me.

I bury my face in her hair. "Are you fucking kidding

me?" I mutter to her. "Is there a single dude in this city who doesn't want to corner you with a business proposition?"

She starts giggling.

"You okay?" I add.

She squeezes me tight. "I am now."

"A fucking *maze?*"

"I thought *you* would come find me. Not him."

"No more mazes. No more events. No more anything unless I'm right by your side. Understand?"

"I knew you'd be here."

Her cheek rests on my shoulder, and I give in to the moment of privacy to slip my fingers through her hair. "You smell amazing."

"You feel amazing."

"I want to go home and peel this dress off you and inspect every inch of you to make sure you're really okay."

She shivers. "I've wanted to hold your hand and lean against you and smell you all night."

"Fuck, Ziggy, we're only halfway done with tonight."

"But we're alone now," she whispers. "We have a few minutes."

This woman. "Only if we're quiet," I whisper back. "Sound carries through the maze."

"Good. We'll hear if anyone's coming."

She lifts her head and brushes her lips against mine.

I groan in relief at kissing her after barely being able to even see her most of the night.

She's okay.

I'm okay.

She doesn't want the fuckwank.

She wants me.

Me, the guy whose ass she's gripping as she touches her tongue to mine.

Me, the guy who's slipping my fingers under her dress while I hold her tight, feeling the silky skin of her leg, the muscle tone, the hair between her thighs.

She whimpers and spreads her legs as I realize—

She's not wearing underwear.

She's completely bare under this dress.

"Fuck, Ziggy," I whisper again.

"Surprise," she whispers back against my lips. "I was going to save this for the drive home, but we're here *now*, and *ohh, yes, there, right there, oh my god.*"

The barest flick of her clit is all it takes to get her moaning.

And she's so slick. So wet.

I'm hard as a rock, and I'm going to stay that way. But slipping two fingers into her vagina while I thumb her clit—this is heaven.

Listening to her soft pants and stifled moans while I finger-fuck her in the bushes—worth it.

Worth the ache in my balls and the strain in my cock and the knowledge that it'll still be another two hours before we're alone again.

Her gasps intensify as I jerk my fingers in and out of her channel.

"You're so fucking gorgeous," I whisper. "So fucking gorgeous when I'm fucking you."

She stares back at me, glassy-eyed, pink all over her cheeks, lips parted as she pants. "You—Holt—love—*oh my god.*"

Her inner walls clench around my fingers while her head falls back, eyes drifting shut, mouth clamping shut to stifle her moans, that long, beautiful neck bared for me to suck on as she rides her orgasm.

How did I ever live before I had this woman in my life?

What was even the meaning of life before I first laid eyes on her?

The way I love this woman—

"*Get your goddamn filthy hands off my daughter,*" someone roars.

Someone close.

Someone in my ear, actually.

The world tilts, and I'm being flung backward while Ziggy gasps. "*No.*"

"I told you," someone else says.

Bushes catch me, and I come to my senses a split second before a meaty fist connects with my jaw and sends stars through my vision.

"*Stop!*" Ziggy shrieks.

There's a flash of black and a whiff of vanilla, and my blurry double vision focuses on one point.

Ziggy.

Arms spread, back to me, standing between me and her stepfather.

"Do not," she says, "*ever* lay a hand on him *again*. Do you understand me?"

"He knows the goddamn rules, and *you do too.* What the fuck are you doing?" Roland snarls at her.

"Making up my own mind about what I want." She's panting.

She's panting and she's crying.

It's the crying that splinters my heart.

"Roland? Ziggy? What's going on?"

"That rugby player is fucking her," the fuckwank who wanted her to go into business with him says.

I eye him.

He steps backward and trips over Deedee, who's rushing out here with Miranda and three of my teammates behind her.

"He had Ziggy trapped out here," I say to Fletcher. "Murder him."

"On it, Captain," Fletcher replies.

"Can't wait," Silas adds.

"Oh, wow, that's bad," Tatum says.

"You don't issue orders here anymore," Roland says to me, but Fletcher and Silas have each grabbed one of the fuck-wank's arms, and they're dragging him out of the maze, muttering things to him that I can't hear while Tatum tags along.

"*Stop it*," Ziggy says.

"I will *not* stop it," Roland roars at her. "*There are goddamn rules for a reason.*"

"*Roland*," Deedee snaps while Ziggy tumbles backward into me.

"It's okay," I murmur to her. I squeeze her waist. "It'll be okay."

"Get your filthy hands *off my daughter*," Roland repeats.

So this is Ziggy's stepdad when he's mad.

I know a thing or two about angry fathers.

"She doesn't belong to you," I tell him. "You gonna make her pick? I'm not gonna make her pick. My world, she gets all of us. She gets an even bigger family to love her and the baby. But you wanna make her pick? Go ahead. Tell her she has to pick. Tell me I'm fired. Tell me I'm traded. See how well that works out for you. Everywhere. Your family. The team. Your standing in the community. Go on. Tell her she has to pick."

He glares at me.

"Holt," Ziggy whispers.

I squeeze her waist again. "I love you," I whisper in her ear.

She whimpers and looks up at me, and my heart cracks in two.

I have to choose.

That's what she's thinking.

The thing is—her stepdad's mad. He's having a full-blown temper tantrum.

But he's been good for her.

He's not the shit my father was. He loves her in his own way. He loves her the best he can.

Whose relationship with their parents isn't dysfunctional? Hers is at least salvageable.

It will be okay.

That's what I'm trying to telegraph back to her.

I love you and this will be okay.

But I don't know if it will.

If I'm fired—he'll make the team pick between me and him. A couple guys will stay with me, maybe, but not for long. They all have their own lives. Their own dreams.

If I'm traded, she'll have to pick between staying here and going with me.

If I'm traded, what the fuck does it even matter?

"I'm getting Ziggy out of here," Deedee's saying to Roland. "Go back inside. Pretend everything's fine. You still have an awards banquet."

"I'm not awarding this fucker a *single damn thing*," Roland replies.

375

I squeeze Ziggy's waist one last time, then straighten. Jaw's starting to hurt like a bitch.

It's minor compared to the ache in my heart. "I'm leaving. But only because you need to get a fucking grip on your temper and your attitude." I jerk my head toward the maze entrance, where Crew and Zander are waiting. "They're gonna make sure you let Ziggy leave on her own too. To go wherever she wants to go."

Deedee glares at me. "*I* will make sure my daughter is okay."

"And they're gonna make sure you agree with her definition of *okay* because she gets to choose for herself what she wants."

Dropping my hand from her is like tearing off a bandage, except it hurts worse in far more places than just my skin.

She does have to decide.

She has to decide what she wants.

Will I fight for her?

Fucking right I will.

But it won't matter if she decides she doesn't want to fight for me now that we've seen firsthand what we're truly fighting against.

"Holt," Ziggy says.

I look at her one more time. She's no longer between me and her stepfather. He could attack again without hurting her or the baby.

"I'll be home," she says.

I start to nod, but Deedee's hugging her so tight, I don't think she sees.

"I know, baby," Deedee croons. "It's time. It's time to come home."

My breath freezes.

Is that what she meant?

That she'd be at her parents' home?

Or that she'd be at ours?

Roland growls again, and I turn my back on him and stride out of the maze.

Fucking thing.

I circled the whole fucking thing to end up almost back at the beginning again.

"This is bullshit," Zander mutters to me.

"Life usually is," I reply.

"We got Ziggy," Crew tells me.

I nod my thanks.

I pass Silas and Fletcher, who've trapped the fuckwank against the building and are asking how he likes being trapped by someone bigger than he is.

They won't hurt him.

Just gonna teach him a lesson.

Especially since Goldie's watching from the door.

She makes eye contact with me. "You okay?"

I look back at the maze, where no one else is leaving yet. "Guess we'll see."

36

Ziggy

YEP.

That went as poorly as I expected it to.

"Ziggy, I just don't understand." Mom's wringing her hands. She's literally wringing her hands. Who does that? "You knew you weren't supposed to fraternize with the players."

We're in the parking lot.

Holt's car is gone.

Everyone else's is still here because the banquet must go on.

Without the team captain.

With most of the guys on the team completely grim-faced.

And I'd expect the sponsors and distinguished guests inside aren't entirely sure what's happening either.

I don't bother telling Mom the whole story.

What's the point?

"Why not?" I say instead. "Why can't I? He's an adult. I'm an adult. We made an adult decision to see each other. And that should be the end of the discussion."

"Sweetheart, you're in a delicate position, and your hormones—"

"Do *not* tell me that I'm in no position to decide that I want to date just because I'm pregnant. You didn't have any problem with the idea of me dropping thousands and thousands of dollars on a house while I'm hormonal, but spending time with someone who likes and respects me is too far? Would you like to lock me in a room and make sure that I don't see anything sad on TV or hear any shocking news and watch over my delicate constitution too? Or maybe, Ms. *It's Fine To Set My Pregnant Daughter Up With Kyle*, you're being an ass about me making my own decisions."

I feel like a brat. Like I'm back in puberty, unable to control my mouth.

But I didn't do anything wrong.

We didn't do anything wrong.

Mom blows out a sigh.

I'm very, very familiar with that sigh.

It's a sigh I heard many times when I was in puberty.

Hormonal. Moody. Unpredictable.

Why do I feel like a teenage asshole?

"I'm going home," I tell Mom. "We can talk later, but I'm not doing this tonight."

"I already texted the housekeeper to get your bedroom ready—"

"*My* home, Mom. My home."

She eyes me. "Will...he...be there?"

I don't answer, but I do glare at her.

Ziggy's such a cunt. She thinks she's better than everyone else. And did you hear? Now, she cut her mother out of her life. Her MOTHER. The woman offered to buy her a house, and that wasn't good enough. She offered to pay for furniture, and that wasn't good enough. Nothing's ever good enough for Ziggy. She's such a stuck-up cunt.

Tears burn my eyes as the ghost of Abby Nora's voice haunts me. "Is it really that wrong for me to want to make it on my own two feet, and to make my own decisions and mistakes and choices?"

Mom blinks too.

She shakes her head. "No. It's not wrong. It's what I taught you to do."

"I love him," I whisper. "If you make me choose—"

I cut myself off as she sucks in a breath.

"Okay. Okay." She pats my shoulder, then squeezes my arm. "You...go home. We'll talk tomorrow. After we've all calmed down."

I have to pull over two blocks from the banquet hall because my vision is too blurry to drive. I pull up my phone and text Holt.

Me: *I'm coming home.*

Reply bubbles pop up instantly, and then—

Holt: *I'm here. And I'm sorry.*

I finally get myself together enough to drive the rest of the way home, but I don't make it inside before I'm crying again.

Holt opens the door for me like he's been watching

for me.

I stumble inside to an alarmed bark from Jessica, and then he's wrapping me in his arms while the dog dances around us, panting and snuffling, and it should make me feel better, but I can't stop crying.

"He hit you," I sob.

"Taken a lot worse," he murmurs. "I'm okay."

"He shouldn't—*hic!*—have hit—*hic!*—you."

Dammit.

Dammit.

Not the hiccups.

Jessica howls.

"Come. Sit."

When I don't move from clinging to him, Holt shifts, and then I'm in his arms, feet off the floor.

"Your—*hic!*—foot," I gasp.

He sits on the couch with me in his lap, and then Jessica's crawling all over both of us too, grunting in my face.

"She'll be okay." Holt rubs the dog's head. "Settle down. Don't step on the baby or you'll have to get off."

She snorts at him with a fraction of her normal heat.

"I shouldn't—*hic!*—have gone—*hic!*—outside," I say. "I shouldn't—*hic!*—have taken—*hic!*—the job."

"I should've sent Fletcher and Silas to find you."

He's so calm.

So calm.

"Why—*hic!*—aren't you—*hic!*—freaking out?"

He threads his fingers through my hair and presses a kiss to my forehead. "Because you're here. This sucks, Zig. It fucking sucks. But we'll get through it. You're here. I'm here. Jessica's here. We've got this."

I wish I had even the smallest bit of his confidence.

I wish I didn't think he was putting on a brave face for me.

"He was so mad," I whisper.

I've honestly never seen my stepfather that angry.

Holt strokes my neck. "For the rest of the night, that's a him problem. Not an us problem."

But it's a tomorrow problem.

My hiccups gradually slow. Jessica splays across my legs, panting while I pet her. And Holt holds me.

Is he calm because he's accepted this is over?

Or is he calm because he knows we can make this work?

Is he quitting rugby?

Will he get traded?

Will I have to decide if I want to follow him?

And what about the house?

What will happen to Caden's house?

My handbag buzzes.

Someone's calling or texting me.

I squeeze my eyes shut and snuggle closer to Holt, but when the buzzing doesn't stop, I ask him to hand me my phone, then hold it so we can both see the wall of texts from Miranda.

Miranda: *I love you.*

Miranda: *I'm so sorry my dad is being an asshole. I tried to talk to him and now I'm on his shit list too.*

Miranda: *This is the most awkward awards banquet I've ever been at. Everyone's eating cheesecake like it's funeral cheesecake. Not a single player has smiled while taking an award. They're all looking at Dad like he's a monster.*

Miranda: He'll calm down. He has to. I've never seen him mad like this, but it can't be the first time. Which means he'll calm down. There's not really another option.

Miranda: The dude your mom brought for me just asked me if there's a gas leak in the building and I think I'm going to stand up and yell FIRE just to break the tension and get everyone out of here.

Miranda: Goldie says to tell you that you can call her anytime. Holt can too. Are you there with him? I hope so. He's a good guy. Waaaaay better than Fletcher, and if someone as amazing as Goldie Collins can fall in love with Fletcher Huxley and actively believe that he's worthy of forever with her, then there's zero reason for Dad to have any objections about Holt.

Miranda: Fletcher just got an award for team commitment and he accepted it with a fart joke and then called his future brother-in-law a fuckwanker. RIGHT THERE. ON STAGE. Gotta hand it to the guy—he knows how to break tension and cause a scene.

Miranda: Are you okay? Are you home? Please tell me you're okay. I just need to know you made it home safely, or that you're safe somewhere. This is going to be okay, I promise. I hope. Just please— please let me know you're okay.

Miranda: I love you.

I text her back that I'm home, I'm safe, I love her too, and that I'll be okay.

The little bubbles in my belly tell me that Tater Tot's happy and safe and sound.

That's good.

That's reason enough for me to be okay.

Jessica lays her head down, over the edge of my leg, and lets out a long, happy sigh.

Holt kisses my forehead again. His chest rises and falls against me as he holds me.

I am.

I'm *home*.

I'm *safe*.

And everything I want and need to feel at home and safe is everything that my parents object to.

"I just don't understand why," I whisper to Holt. "Who can object to you? Why is he being such a stubborn ass about this?"

He clears his throat. "It's possible…if he'd found out while we were both…fully clothed with our hands to ourselves… that he would've taken it better."

I contemplate that for a second.

Then I shake my head. "Honestly? I don't think he would've."

Holt tightens his arms around me. "Maybe a little."

"There might've been less yelling, but the sentiment would've been the same."

"Everything will look better in the morning."

I hope he's right.

I don't think he is, but if he can hope, then so can I.

37

Holt

ZIGGY'S CRYING AGAIN.

It's early, early morning. Pitch black. And she's huddled on the other side of the bed, crying quietly.

I scoot over behind her and wrap her in a hug, ignoring the ache in the growing bruise on my face.

"Go back to sleep," she chokes out. "I'll be okay."

I'll be okay.

We didn't hear from either of her parents again after the banquet last night.

I heard from several teammates over text.

Total shit show and *we've got your back* were the basics.

Ziggy's not going to be okay.

Not until we work this out with her family.

Her family isn't like my family.

Her family loves her. I believe they want her to be happy. They just have a few hang-ups getting in the way.

"I'm going to talk to your parents as soon as the sun's up," I tell her.

"*No.*"

"Ziggy—"

"They hurt *you.* They hurt *me.* They owe *you* an apology. You don't owe them anything. You don't have to be the bigger person here."

She's not the only person who thinks so.

As soon as the sun rises, there's a knock on my door.

It's Silas.

He holds up a brown paper bag. "Ziggy like chocolate?"

"Is it chocolate-covered potatoes?"

He stares at me for half a second before he's on his phone, texting Porter to grab chocolate-covered potatoes on his way.

"Don't want company," I tell him.

"Tough shit. You're the kind who's gonna try to say sorry for something you don't need to be sorry for, so we're all taking turns babysitting you."

Ziggy's so in support of the plan that the next thing I know, my pregnant girlfriend is cooking breakfast for half my team.

If they're still my team.

If I'm not fired.

"Holy shit, no wonder you fell in love," Tatum says after his first bite of eggs Benedict. "Can she date all of us?"

Crew smacks him in the head. "Don't be an asshole at the captain's house. He's had a rough summer."

Ziggy smiles down at her belly and rubs it gently.

Tater Tot must be kicking.

The guys are in and out all day.

Ziggy tears up approximately every fifteen minutes.

I hug her approximately every five minutes.

Kiss her in front of my teammates.

Claim her.

Help her cook. Do the dishes.

Wait for a phone call from headquarters.

Realize that all of these guys who are here today are putting their necks on the line for me.

It's enough that I have to step out of the room so they won't see me getting choked up.

But I don't want to be the reason any of them get fired. I don't want to be the reason any of them get traded.

I don't want them to choose me over themselves.

And when we still haven't heard from Ziggy's parents by late Sunday night, I'm getting worried that that's exactly what's going to happen.

"Do *not* cave first," she whispers to me as we snuggle in bed together. "Please. *Please*. Give them three more days."

"What difference will three days make?"

"I'm not going to work tomorrow."

"Ziggy—"

"I don't work for people who try to control me."

"Zig, I get that, but are you sure this is the best way to do it?"

"No." She cuddles closer. "But I'm still so mad that I can't think about them without crying. I'm tired of crying. *I* need three more days. And they need to realize if they're going to make me choose, they won't like the outcome."

I stifle a frustrated sigh.

There's a problem.

I want to fix it. I know how to fix it.

I go see Roland, I apologize, I tell him I quit, and I tell him he can come to grips with me dating his daughter and letting her be an adult, or he's going to lose her.

Not a threat.

Just the actuality.

She's leaving her job, isn't she?

She's here, isn't she?

But no one else in my life wants me to fix it my way.

Not immediately anyway.

"Goldie's introducing me to the people who run Sarcasm Cellars," Ziggy says. "It's a little winery up in the mountains. Fletcher did an ad for them last year. They're looking for a new regional sales rep. I'd be interested even if I wasn't furious with my dad right now. It gets me back into the wine industry, and Goldie says she wouldn't recommend them if she wasn't sure they'd be good about me needing maternity leave."

I kiss her hair again. "If I told you I'd take care of you and you didn't have to work—"

"I'd tell you I *want* to work."

"Thought so."

"And I'm also grateful that you'd offer." Her hands slide down my back.

I offered before to marry her for her cooking and to give her benefits for the baby.

If I did it again now, I don't know what she'd say.

I know I love her. She's put color and laughter and life back into my world. I'd go to the ends of the earth to make her happy.

But proposing to someone who's being thrown back into family turmoil just as she's getting through the grief of losing her best friend isn't going to make her life better.

Even if I'd feel better knowing she truly has chosen me.

Not to spite anyone else, but because she wants me.

"Thank you for being you," she whispers against my chest. "And thank you for wanting me back."

A shudder ripples through me. "I can't resist you."

She kisses my pec, then my neck, then tilts her head up to kiss my lips.

Making love to her is so easy.

So right.

The rest of the world doesn't exist when I'm inside her and she's panting my name and raking her nails down my back.

But the rest of the world exists Monday morning when she finally gets a text from her mom.

Why aren't you at work today? Why aren't you talking to us? Are you honestly choosing a man over your family?

She tears up, but she doesn't cry.

And she texts back *I'm not the one making me choose.*

Fletcher and Silas show up.

The rest of the team are at their off-season jobs.

Ziggy's mom doesn't text back.

And I'm about to crawl out of my skin.

I can fix this.

I can fucking fix this.

Unless I can't.

Ziggy catches me at the sink, doing dishes after lunch, and hugs me hard from behind. "Thank you for giving me two more days."

And that?

That's why it's worth it.

She knows this is hard.

She knows she's asking a lot.

And she's showing up to support me in my own struggles too.

Because that's what someone who deserves you does, Caden whispers in my head.

I didn't even know her four months ago, and today, she's my everything.

Today, I'm putting my entire career on the line for her.

Regrets? Caden whispers.

It'll depend.

It'll depend on if I cost her having her family.

38

Ziggy

I SHOULDN'T BE madder with every passing day but I am.

And that's what Goldie's friends are meeting late Tuesday morning.

Angry Ziggy.

Have I ever been this mad in my life?

I don't think I have.

"How did the interview go?" Goldie asks me as I slide into a round corner booth at Give Two Sips, her favorite wine bar in the Warehouse District. It's a cool two-story bar with plants hanging from the ceiling and plush velvet seating. We're a couple blocks from her and Fletcher's place, and she has a ginger ale waiting for me.

Another time, another place, I'd be enchanted and looking forward to coming back when I can drink. A quick scan of the wine list tells me this place is excellent.

Right now, I'm too mad to care.

"It went well," I tell her. "Thank you. Sincerely. I'm looking forward to getting back into the wine industry, and the owners are lovely people."

She lifts her brows.

I snort and flop back in the booth. "My family hasn't reached out *at all* aside from a single guilt trip asking why I'd pick a player over them, and if I wasn't working in the main office for the team, they probably wouldn't have reached out at all."

"Even Miranda?"

I've been in constant contact with my sister. She's amazing. "Miranda's not family. She's *family*. There's a difference."

Goldie smiles at me as an older white lady in a bright pink shirt slides into the round booth on the other side. She has shoulder-length white hair and a bright smile that shows off the depth of her crow's feet, and I do a double take when I realize the logo on her T-shirt says *Outlive Our Ex-Boyfriends Club*. I'd guess she's a few years older than my mom, maybe a full decade.

"The sidewalks are so busy today. Did I miss a festival announcement? In the middle of the week?" she says.

"Rain's coming tomorrow and bringing a cold front," Goldie replies. "It's everyone getting one last bit of late summer sunshine."

"I'll go out in the rain. We need the rain. How's your hip? Weather bothering it?"

"Barely achy. I'm good."

"Good. You stay inside and make sure Fletcher spoils you." She breaks out into a grin. "You know who won't go out in the rain?"

"The Old Man Bikers Club," Goldie says in unison with her.

The woman beams. "Exactly."

"Ziggy, meet Sheila," Goldie says to me. "She's one of my three favorite BFFs."

I gape at her for a moment before gathering myself and reaching across the table to shake hands with Sheila. "Nice to meet you."

Sheila grins. "They didn't tell you Goldie hangs out with us seasoned ladies, did they?"

I shake my head, picture Holt's grin as he mentioned Goldie's friends, and now I get it.

Another white woman, this one with light-brown hair cut in a bob, but the same crow's feet, slides in next to her. "Are we meeting Goldie's friend? Finally? Good. We need more young blood in this club. Hello, you gorgeous thing. I'm Evelyn."

I shake her hand too. "Hi. I'm Ziggy."

"I'm gonna get a hug as soon as we stand up, but I know better than to ask a pregnant lady to stand before she wants to. I actually got divorced once because my husband didn't respect my need to sit while I was carrying."

The enchantment is starting to win over the rage inside me, but it's not the bar. It's the friends. "I'm barely five months. I'm good."

"Still. We'll hug at the end. I'm so excited you're here. Do you have any ex-boyfriends you'd like to outlive? Or any who have died and need alternative obituaries to those awful stuffy pieces they print in the papers?"

"These are your best friends?" I whisper to Goldie.

"My favorite people on the planet," she confirms with a smile as she sips a wine spritzer.

"Even more than Fletcher is," a Black lady in a matching

shirt to the other two older women says as she, too, joins the group. "That boy…"

"That boy," Sheila and Evelyn echo.

Goldie's smiling so widely, I don't question if I'm being pranked. She's too happy. "Ziggy, this is Odette. She's president of the Outlive Our Ex-Boyfriends Club."

I shake Odette's hand too. "How many more of you are there?"

"It's just us three," Sheila says.

"Goldie couldn't handle us if there were more," Odette adds.

"The *world* couldn't handle us if there were more," Sheila corrects.

"They adopted me after I found my ex-boyfriend cheating on me with one of my best friends," Goldie tells me.

"Did you get to write his obituary yet?" I ask.

The three older women cackle.

Goldie's grin glows even brighter. "No, but I did recently get the satisfaction of hearing they broke up when she was traded to a team on the West Coast and he refused to follow her since he likes to think of himself as the most successful one in any given relationship."

"Traded?"

"Women's soccer."

"Goldie has more friends her own age now, but she still makes time for us," Evelyn says.

"Because she knows who good people are," Odette adds.

Sheila beams at all of us. "She likes our wisdom, and we like that she thinks we're wise."

"And hilarious and kind and generous," Goldie adds.

This is the kind of relationship I would've loved to have had with my grandma.

Crap.

Dammit.

My eyes are getting wet.

Will my baby get this kind of relationship with my mom?

Or is there zero chance at all now that we'll ever be the same?

Goldie slips an arm around me and squeezes. "Everything will be okay," she whispers.

"We can pre-write obituaries for people who've pissed you off," Evelyn says.

"Done it before," Odette agrees.

Sheila shakes her head. "I don't like to manifest that. Manifest that we live a long time, yes. Manifest that others intentionally die...that's not my cup of tea."

"We know, hon, and that's why we love you." Evelyn smiles at her, then turns the smile to me. "So what can three old ladies who know a little bit about this rugby team do to help you today? We have a *lot* of pull in certain places in the office, if you know what I mean."

I somehow doubt they have more pull with my dad than I do. "Tell me I'm not making a mistake fighting to date a guy my parents are opposed to?"

It's remarkable how three women can spring into action while sitting still.

"Your parents don't like the captain?"

"What's wrong with them?"

"He's the nicest man. Do you know he once walked me to my car, holding an umbrella over my head while he was getting soaking wet, when I went to see training all by my lonesome because I was having a day and I needed to see some strong men beating on each other to feel better? And he even gave me a hug and told me I was going to be okay.

And *shew*. Do you know what that man smells like? Like all the best things and all the best things that are bad for you, if you know what I mean."

All of us stare at Sheila.

I do, in fact, know what Holt smells like.

Intimately.

And I like it, and I'm suddenly a little unsure what to think of Sheila liking it too.

"What?" she says. "I might be the sweet one, but clearly, I'm not dead yet. Let an old lady have a thrill once in a while. I didn't make a pass at him. I just enjoyed that there are still polite young men out there in the world."

Evelyn and Odette both grin at her.

Goldie hides her own smile behind another sip of spritzer.

"What's your plan, hon?" Odette asks me.

"Wait them out."

All three of the older women cluck their tongues.

"Bad idea."

"You wait them out, they'll wait you out longer."

"Next thing you know, you haven't talked to your parents in four years."

And there go the wet eyeballs again.

I love my mom. I'm so grateful she found a man for herself who—until this weekend—was exactly who I would've hoped for her to find. Miranda's stuck in the middle, and that's not fair to her, even if she keeps telling me she's not in the middle, she's on my side.

And this isn't how it's supposed to be with them.

I'm supposed to be mildly frustrated that they want to do too much for me when I want to be more independent, and that's it.

We're not supposed to be fighting over me being capable of deciding for myself who I want to date and working with my partner to mitigate the potential consequences for the team.

"I'm thirty. Why don't they trust me to decide for myself who I should and shouldn't date? Why don't they trust *him* to not let it interfere with the team? Players date all the time. How is this any different? He was already the team captain. He was already proving himself. I'm not dating him because he's a rugby player. I'm dating him because he's a good man who makes me feel safe and loved at a time when everything else in my life is falling apart."

"I think it's complete bullshit that they're mad at you," Goldie says. "It's not like you're dating Silas."

The three older ladies murmur their agreement.

Tater Tot bubbles around in my belly like they, too, have an opinion.

I freaking love feeling my baby move.

It's magic.

And all of the people in my life that I previously thought I'd call and squeal with about feeling my baby move aren't in the circle of trust right now.

Abby Nora never will be again.

My mom could be, but— "I feel like a teenage brat throwing a tantrum over a boy."

"You are *not* a teenage brat," Sheila says. "You're an intelligent, independent, worldly woman who knows what she wants. I knew my Sinclair was the love of my life five days after I met him when I was twenty-one, and we had twenty-eight beautiful years together. The people who are there for you when life is hardest are the ones who'll be your favorites when life is easy."

"Exactly right," Odette says.

"And god knows that man's had a tough go of it too," Evelyn says. "I'm sure he's grateful for you every bit as much as you're grateful for him."

I swipe my eyes. I didn't used to cry this much.

"We take care of each other."

My mom wants to buy me a house, and Holt buys me potatoes.

Dad wants to give me a job, and Holt opened his house and heart to me and gave me a home and a dog.

My parents want what's best, but they don't ask me how I define what's best.

Goldie's phone audibly dings while mine vibrates inside the wristlet on my lap.

We look at each other, then both go digging.

She gets hers out first. "Oh, *fuck.*"

"Fletcher's been a good influence on her," Sheila whispers.

"It's nice that she doesn't censor herself anymore," Odette agrees.

And then I have my phone in hand, opening it, to look at the text from Miranda.

Miranda: *Dad just put out a call for candidates to be the new Pounders captain.*

I make a noise. Possibly a squeak. Possibly a howl. I'm not sure which.

And then I'm moving.

"Ziggy. Wait. I'll drive." Goldie's on my heels as I rise from the booth and head toward the door.

"We'll get the check," Evelyn calls.

"Text us the goss," Sheila adds.

"Tell us if we need to suit up and ride," Odette says.

"How—fucking—*dare*—he," I gasp as I push out onto the street. Where's the parking garage? Where's my car?

Shit.

I can't drive.

I'm too angry.

Where's Goldie's car?

"This way," she says quietly behind me. "Three blocks. Call Holt."

Call Holt.

Call Holt.

Oh god.

Does he know?

I trail her while I dial his number and wait for him to pick up.

He doesn't.

My call goes to voicemail.

It goes to voicemail three times in a row.

"Oh my god," I whisper to Goldie while we load up in a red sports car in her building's underground parking garage. "He quit. *He quit.*"

"Did he tell you that?"

"No, but he's not answering."

"There's approximately zero chance Holt would quit. Fletcher's text didn't say he quit, and Fletcher knows everything before it happens. Swear he does. Did Miranda tell you he quit?"

I shake my head as she starts the engine.

"Then he didn't quit until he tells you he quit." She eyes me before she puts the car in gear. "Even if he quit...that's not going to fix things with your parents, will it?"

Dammit. "No."

"So we're going?"

I nod. "We're going. My parents' house. I'll talk to Mom first."

I barely notice the city passing and the strip malls taking over and then the entrance to Heartwood Valley Estates.

I'm too busy staring at my phone after texting Holt to call me.

He hasn't.

Goldie pulls the sports car into my parents' circle drive in front of their three-story mansion, and I don't wait for her to kill the engine before I'm out and racing for the door.

I burst inside the foyer and head for the living room, but no one's there.

I check Mom's office.

Empty.

The dogs aren't even barking.

And then I hear it.

Voices.

Dad's office down the hall.

I don't pause.

I don't think.

I don't check a calendar, because why the fuck would I?

And that's my fatal mistake.

That's absolutely my fatal mistake.

Because it's Tuesday.

And when I burst into my dad's office, ready to go off like a banshee...

I find the two of them cuddling on his office couch.

Buck naked.

39

Holt

THERE'S a red sports car outside Roland Keating's house. A familiar red sports car with its owner's girlfriend leaning against the driver's side door.

Goldie doesn't look surprised to see me as I hop out of my Jeep. "Ziggy's been trying to call you."

Shit.

My phone doesn't ring through when I'm driving. Some setting I haven't fixed yet since the last operating system update. "She inside?"

"Yeah. We got here about thirty seconds ago."

A scream emanates from inside the house, and that's all it takes.

I'm in motion, busting through the front door, following the raised voices through a maze of hallways because the house is freaking ridiculous.

I don't process the words—just the voices—until too late.

Too late being when I'm diving through an open door, following the sound of Ziggy's high-pitched shrieks, to find—

Fuck me.

Fuck me fuck me fuck me fuck me.

"Naked Tuesday," I gasp, looking up at the ceiling.

"*Holt?*"

"Don't look. Shield the baby's eyes. Where are you? I'll cover your eyes."

"What the fuck are you doing here?" Roland snarls.

"My god, Roland, put some pants on before you chew him out," Deedee says.

"It's my goddamn house, and these two both need to *leave.*"

"Then maybe I'm leaving too," Deedee shouts back.

"*Stop it,*" Ziggy cries. "Just *stop.*"

I feel her hair and pull her into me. "Don't look. Don't look anymore."

"What the ever-loving fuck are you doing here?" Roland hollers again.

"What the ever-loving fuck do you *think*?" Ziggy replies, mostly into my chest now.

Eyes shielded.

Thank god.

I've seen too much, and I only saw a glimpse.

A man has limits.

I've reached mine.

"You fired Holt." She's shaking. "You fired Holt and you didn't think I'd show up here and fight you on this?"

Ever been both the problem and the most grateful man on the planet?

That's me right now.

But more than feeling like I'm the issue, I'm overwhelmed that Ziggy's here to fight for me.

I fight for me.

I fight for everyone around me.

But I'm not used to people fighting for me. Yet, since she came into my life, I've discovered they do.

She fights for me.

My team fights for me.

My neighbors fight for me.

The couch croaks like Roland or Deedee is shifting on it.

Bare skin on leather.

I am never walking through this door again.

"You're not in charge," Roland says. "I am. He knew the rules."

"Then congratulations. Your stupid, inane, pointless rule is going to cost you your entire rugby team. They're quitting. All of them. You fire Holt, they quit. You trade Holt, they quit. And when they quit, Fletcher's not selling tickets anymore. Crew and Porter and Tatum and the rest of them— they're not either. The city won't have any familiar players they want to root for, and all the work you've done for the past five years will be for nothing. *For nothing.* You lose. Game over. *Match* over."

Silence settles in the room.

She's not wrong.

We don't have fan loyalty yet. We have people who show up because Fletcher's socials are the kind of train wreck that draws you in and makes you want to see more. We have people who show up because they're starting to see that Crew has the potential to be a superstar. Because they're finding out that Silas's family started a rugby league that another family took over when his parents divorced, but that he's still involved with. Because the guys on this team are willing to put in the extra time and effort during the season to get out and talk to the fans and make them feel like they're part of something.

It's not something you get with a less cohesive group.

Deedee breaks the silence. "That sounds bad, Roland."

"I can afford the loss."

Ziggy snorts. "Dick thing to do to the whole city. To the whole league."

"Language, young lady," he growls at her.

She switches to a different language with words I haven't heard her use before.

Italian, I think. Has to be, because it's not Spanish.

And I think she just called him worse than a dick.

Maybe.

The only thing I know how to say in Italian is *gelato* despite how much I've listened to her listening to her podcasts and newscasts to stay current with her language skills.

"*Sigourney Jane Barnes*," Deedee says, confirming for me that it was bad. Also confirming for me that I had no idea Ziggy was a nickname.

Huh.

Look at that.

Still so much to learn about this woman that I love.

"Sell the team," Ziggy says. "If you don't want me dating one of your players, sell the team."

My eyes fly open and I accidentally gape at Roland.

He's at least covered his crotch with a throw pillow.

A throw pillow that looks like something you'd get at a museum, with artwork of stick figures on it that are probably supposed to be groundbreaking in some way.

"I'm not selling the team," he says.

Deedee's covered most of her bits too with a strategically placed pillow and the urn that she's holding in front of her chest.

Big urn.

Very big urn.

I hope it doesn't have someone's ashes in it.

"Then we're done here," Ziggy says. "If you don't want me dating one of your players, who's been my very best friend since I got home, who loves me, who takes care of me, who accepts me for who I am, and you won't sell the team so he can keep reaching for his dreams, then we'll find a new team for him to play for, and I'm going with him when we do."

My heart swells.

Swells and cracks at the same time.

I didn't want this.

I didn't want her to have to choose between us.

But she's choosing me.

Over and over and over again.

She hugs me tightly, then releases me. "Let's go."

Roland eyes me.

Deedee leaps to her feet, and I remember to look up at the ceiling before I get another show as Ziggy and I turn toward the door.

"Wait," Deedee says.

"Holt gets his job back and Dad sells the team, or we're gone," Ziggy says.

"Wait." There's no mistaking the desperation in Deedee's voice.

It's the same desperation I'd feel if Ziggy told me I couldn't be part of her life anymore. That she and the baby don't want me anymore. That she's taking Jessica too.

Jessica, who's finally starting to warm up to me.

She hasn't snorted snot on me in three full days now.

Almost three full days.

Not since Saturday night when Ziggy got home.

I glance at Ziggy, and I don't miss the pain that she's trying to hide as she squeezes her eyes shut. "Dad sells the team. Holt keeps his job," she repeats.

"He'll sell it," Deedee says. "He'll sell it."

Roland makes a rough noise. "The hell I—"

"You'd pick the goddamn team over our daughter?" Deedee says. Squawks, really. "I won't. I *don't.* Sell the team. Quit with this—this—this stupid *rule.* She's an adult, and he's one of the finest young men I've had the privilege of meeting."

Ziggy sags against me and I hear a telltale sniffle.

Fucking fearless.

But she was still willing to give up her family for me.

"I love you," I whisper to her.

"You are my everything," she whispers back.

"Her father—" Roland starts, and both of us turn.

Both of us regret it and look back at the door.

Throw pillows and the urn are gone.

"What about my father?" Ziggy asks.

Can you hear someone wince?

Because I'm not looking, but I swear Deedee's wincing.

"He played football," she says quietly.

"My father played football," Ziggy repeats. "My biological father. The college professor who died in a car accident when I was three. He played football."

"He wasn't a college professor," Deedee says. "He was a football player. And football came first. He didn't want me to have you. He didn't want anything disrupting his career. And I—I want better for you than what I had."

I look my girlfriend's naked mother straight in the eye. "I *am* fucking better than what you had."

She flinches.

I'm not done, and this time, I'm talking to both of them. "I'm not standing here asking her to choose between us. *You're* doing that. *You're* putting her in an impossible situation. She's smart. She's strong. She's kind. And all she's asking is for you to accept who she is and what she wants. I don't give two shits what you do to me. But don't make her life harder because you want to lump me into the same bucket as some ass-nugget who could've had her in his life."

Deedee flinches again, but I keep going. "I know what I have. I know what an amazing person she is. I cannot wait to be the kind of father to her baby that apparently neither of us had, but both of us deserved. And I'm doing everything I fucking can to not be the reason she hurts. If you're not willing to do the same, then you don't deserve her."

Ziggy squeezes my hand.

"Roland, sell the team," Deedee says. "So help me, if you don't sell the team, you'll lose your daughter *and* your wife."

He grunts at all of us, but there's no heat to it.

"Love you, Mom," Ziggy whispers, "but there's no fucking way I'm hugging you right now."

Deedee's head bobs, and she discreetly covers herself as best she can. "I'll hug you later. I'll—I'll come see you later. At your house. *Your* house. With clothes."

"Tomorrow's fine." Ziggy sniffles.

Deedee sniffles too. "No, I can get dressed and come over today."

Roland's still eyeing me, but I'm not worried he'll try to hit me.

Be a dumb thing to do with his balls hanging out.

Especially considering he fired me.

Ziggy squeezes my hand again.

I squeeze back, and we duck out of the office together.

Neither of us says a word as we walk through the house.

When we get outside, Goldie straightens.

She's still alone, but I suspect she won't be for long. And it won't just be Fletcher.

It'll be the whole team.

Fuck me. I haven't wanted to cry this much since Caden died, but this is different.

This isn't grief.

This is *family*.

"All okay?" she asks.

"Don't go in there," Ziggy says.

I cough.

She whimpers.

"Did someone have a digestive issue?" Goldie asks.

"Naked Tuesdays," Ziggy whispers back.

Goldie stares at her. Blinks once. Once more. "Well, that's some extortion material that I wish I didn't know and will definitely *not* be sharing with Fletcher. Actually, I heard you wrong. I am a thousand percent positive I heard you wrong."

I look at Ziggy.

She looks back at me.

"I don't want you to give up your—" I start but don't finish.

Because she's throwing herself into my arms and kissing me, gripping my head and holding me while her lips caress mine, pausing only to whisper quick *I love you*s and *least I can do for you*s.

We startle apart when the Maserati's engine roars to life beside us.

Goldie rolls down the window and waves. "You two might want to take it home," she calls with a grin.

And then she's gone.

"Home," Ziggy says.

I look back at the front door of her parents' house. "You're good?"

"Mom's on our side. She'll either convince Dad, or she won't, and I believe her when she says she'll pick me. She has before."

I wrap her in a hug, then swing her up into my arms to carry her to the Jeep. "Anyone would be a fool to not pick you."

"They'd be a fool to not pick *you*," she replies.

For the first time in days, she's smiling.

We're not all the way there with her parents, but we will be.

And that's what matters.

40

Ziggy

IT FEELS good to breathe again.

Breathe. Laugh. Kiss. Snuggle. Make love. Kiss more. Laugh more. Snuggle more.

That's how I spend the rest of my Naked Tuesday.

We're dressed again as night falls, watching my favorite show over ice cream, when someone knocks hard and fast on the door.

Holt's still moving slow on his foot, but he beats me to check it out.

Then gives me a *what's this about?* look as he pulls the door open and lets Miranda in.

Her cheeks are flushed. Her hazel eyes are wide. And she's gasping for air like she ran the six miles here from her apartment.

I rise.

Jessica jumps to her paws and barks in alarm.

"What?" My brain goes to the dark place.

Dad had a heart attack.

The fight we had this morning wasn't the first step in making up, it was the end.

We killed him.

"Dad's giving me the team," she squeaks.

I drop back onto the couch like the world shoved me. "*What?*"

"Dad's giving me the team. He says he can't sell it because it operates at a loss, but he's setting up a trust and giving me the team."

I look at Holt.

He's gaping at my sister with the door as wide open still as his mouth is now.

Miranda squats and pets Jessica. "Did you hear that, Jessica? *I own a rugby team.* Or I will. When the paperwork goes through. How nuts is this? It's completely nuts, isn't it? *Completely nuts.*"

"So Holt can have his job back?" I ask.

She straightens and flings herself at him, hugging him hard. "*Please* come back and play for the Pounders. You're my favorite. Don't tell Fletcher. Or do. I'd love to see how he tries to win the title himself."

She spins away from Holt, who finally shuts the front door, to dance across the living room and plop down next to me, then hug me too. "Ziggy, I am *freaking out*," she whisper-shrieks. "I don't know anything about owning a rugby team."

I hug her back. "Do you want this?"

"*Yes.* I mean, I didn't know I wanted it, but—but I do. I so don't deserve this. I haven't earned it. I don't know enough about rugby. I don't know enough about *business.* And that's what it is. It's a business. Oh my god. I'm going to destroy it.

411

I'm going to completely and totally *wreck* the club. What am I doing? *I can't own a rugby team.* I barely know how to change a lightbulb and there are like seventy million of them at the stadium. *Oh my god.*"

"Breathe." I know. I know. Not helpful.

But she clearly needs the reminder.

"Dad said he's fucked up too much and the guys need new leadership, and he thinks it's me," she says. "He says I'm ready, but am I? I'm not. I am absolutely not."

"Breathe," Holt echoes.

"What is *breathe?*" Miranda says. "I don't know that word."

He sits on the couch on her other side.

Jessica prances at all of our feet.

"Happen to know a guy who knows more than he should about how to run a rugby team," Holt says.

Miranda wrinkles her nose. "But then I have to talk to him and his ego."

Holt looks at her, then he cracks up.

I do too.

But not for long.

Miranda's still freaking out. "What if they don't respect me? Who *would* respect me? I haven't earned this."

"You will," Holt says.

I love his quiet authority. His belief in the people around him. His support.

How *did* a man this perfect land in my world?

No idea, but I do know I'll do everything in my power to deserve him every day.

Just like I know Miranda is up to the challenge of proving she has what it takes to run the Pounders.

"And you're not alone," I add. "You have a whole team who already adore you. The office staff too."

"They think I'm that cute kid."

"They know you work hard and that you're smart and that you care about them."

"Half the key to leadership," Holt says. "People will do almost anything for people who care about them."

Truer words...

I smile at him over her head. *I'll do anything for you.*

He smiles back. *Counting on it. Very soon.*

And there go my nipples, getting hard while I'm supposed to be helping my sister process this unexpected news.

"What if—" she starts, but I cut her off.

"What if we realize the world has given you an advantage, and now you get to choose what to do with what you've been given? What if we find a way to make this the best possible thing that's ever happened for the Pounders, from the staff to the players to the fans?"

She gapes at me. "Oh my god, *pressure.*"

"That's the job," Holt says.

"He said I can sell it if I want, but I don't want." She blows out a heavy breath. "I can do this. *I can do this.* Can't I?"

"You can," Holt says. "But can you maybe not carry on the tradition of Naked Tuesdays?"

She looks at him, then turns to me, and then she bursts out laughing.

"It wasn't funny," I say.

"It was a little funny," Holt says.

"You forgot it was Tuesday?" Miranda gasps.

I sigh. "Been a little preoccupied with thinking we were never going to be a real family again."

"Dad feels awful," she tells us. "He's not ready to admit it out loud yet, but he does. I could tell because Deedee did

413

most of the talking. I'd expect some very nice baby presents coming your way soon."

"I've got the baby covered," Holt says.

"You and the whole team. They're totally throwing Ziggy a surprise baby shower next month. I already got my invitation."

"Most loved baby ever." He smiles.

Miranda smiles.

And I burst into tears.

Naturally.

It's what I do these days.

But these are the good tears, and they come with me being wrapped in tight hugs from my sister and the man I love, the man who wants me, who wants my baby, who's claimed us both as his own.

Miranda stays long enough to pick Holt's entire brain about what she should look for in support staff who can teach her what she needs to know, who he knows in the league, what he's learned from his time overseas, and how she can ask for Fletcher's help without him being insufferable.

She leaves far less worked up than she arrived, but I have a text message waiting for me that has me in happy tears all over again.

"Mom says she and Dad want to have us over for lunch on Saturday to fully apologize for how they treated you," I tell Holt through sniffles.

He smiles softly at me as he pulls my hand to his mouth and kisses it. "They love you."

"They're going to love you too."

"Very likely. I'm irresistible."

He is, even if he says it like he's joking.

"Your ice cream melted. Want more?" he asks.

I shake my head. "I want *you*."

"Huh. I happen to want you too."

He hefts me into his arms and carries me upstairs and shows me once more just how much he loves me.

But it's not just the kissing. The touching. The sex.

It's the way he holds me. The way he cradles my belly.

The way he whispers, "I'm ready to renovate Caden's room. We can move into it and turn this room into a nursery and the other room into a play room. If you want to stay here."

"Holt—"

"We can find a different house if you'd rather. We don't— I love the idea of new life in this house, but we don't have to stay here."

"I love this house."

His gaze flickers over my body, lit by a lone lamp on his nightstand, and when his eyes reach mine again, he studies me closely. "You do?"

"It's *you*."

"I didn't pick anything. Caden picked everything."

"You don't think he picked it for you? Because everything I know about you—I think he did."

He blinks at me.

His eyes go shiny, and then I'm on my back, trapped beneath this massive man with a big heart and a bigger family than he realizes. "Fuck me," he mutters. "You're right. He did."

"He loved you as much as you loved him."

He buries his head in my neck while his breath shudders through him. "Thank you."

I kiss his hair.

Stroke his back.

Bask in the feel of him while Tater Tot does flips that bubble in my belly.

"It's home," I whisper.

"It's home," he agrees. "Fuck, Ziggy...I'm so glad I broke my foot."

A surprised laugh catches in my throat.

I'm not glad he got hurt.

But I will forever be grateful that he's mine.

41

Ziggy

I HAVE TO PEE AGAIN.

I *always* have to pee again.

We're barely inside Give Two Sips, where we're meeting Goldie and Fletcher and Goldie's friends and half the team for a holiday dinner, and I'm not going for the banquet room.

I'm going for the bathroom.

This is what it's like being seven months pregnant.

I burst through the restroom door, and Odette and Sheila look up from the sinks, surveying me in the mirrors. Odette's touching up her lipstick and Sheila's washing her hands.

"It'll get better, hon," Sheila says.

"After the baby's born," Odette adds. "And I'm gonna get you the name of my physical therapist. That'll help even more."

"You're the best," I call as I dash into the stall.

"Is physical therapy why you don't have to pee as much as the rest of us?" Sheila asks.

"I keep telling you, and you all don't want to listen. That's on you."

I love these ladies.

And Goldie.

And Miranda.

And Tater Tot.

And Holt.

Oh my god, I love Holt so much.

He's waiting for all three of us near the dark cherrywood bar when we leave the bathroom together a few minutes later.

But he's not alone.

He's—no.

My heart sinks and then races.

He's smiling and chatting with Abby Nora and her husband, Josh.

"What's wrong, sweetie?" Odette asks.

Abby Nora's gaze flies to me, and she flinches.

"He's talking to my former BFF and I don't think he knows it," I whisper to Odette and Sheila.

He doesn't.

Does he?

I've refused to go back to the Heartwood Valley Owners Club for anything, because fuck them.

I like going where I belong and where I'm appreciated, not where I'm the center of gossip.

And Miranda tells me that Mom and Dad haven't gone as much lately either.

So does Abby Nora know?

Does she know she's talking to my boyfriend?

Is this one more stupid game?

Odette clucks her tongue.

Sheila snorts. "We'll see about that."

And that's when Holt glances over his shoulder, spots me, and winks.

Winks.

The man doesn't wink at me.

Sneak behind me and cradle my belly and kiss my neck while I'm cooking when I won't let him help? Yes.

Turn my alarm off before it can ring on Saturday mornings so I get extra sleep when he knows I'm tired? Yes.

Rub my feet and spoil me and pamper me and make me laugh and fall in love a little more every day? Yes.

But he has never, *ever* winked at me.

He beckons me over. "Zig, this is Josh Harrison. You know him? He's a big Pounders fan. And his wife, Abby Nora. Really unusual name. Is this the same Abby Nora who used to be your best friend?"

Odette chokes.

Sheila does too.

And me?

I don't know what I do.

I just know I'm suddenly frozen on the spot.

He is *not* calling her out, is he?

"You know," he continues, his eyes sparkling more with every word, "the one whose wedding you got half the wine for with special bottles that you collected all over Europe while you were thinking about her? The one whose bachelorette party you hosted with all of the bridesmaids getting free cruises? The one who called you a cunt during her baby shower? Is this her?"

Abby Nora's going a shade of purple I've never seen.

"Hey, you listen up—" Josh starts, but Holt turns to him, pulls himself up to his full height, broadens his shoulders, and while I can't see his face, I know what face he's making based on his posture alone.

It's the *I will fucking tear you limb from limb if you want to take this onto a rugby pitch* face.

"Yes," I squeak.

"Thought so," Holt says without looking back at me. "Josh, dude, you might want to pick a different team. The Pounders don't like you or your wife. Not when you're absolute cunts to my girlfriend."

"Oh my word, I think I'm a little turned on," Odette whispers.

Sheila's fanning herself. "I hope you and Holt both live a long, long time and never have need of our little club."

I'm still gaping as Holt turns away from Abby Nora and Josh.

He slips an arm around my waist, kisses me square and solid until I'm a little wet in the panties, and then pulls back with a self-satisfied grin. "Well. That felt good. Where's the party room?"

Abby Nora's dashing toward the bathroom.

Josh is angling away from the bar and in the direction of the door.

"We're upstairs, you sexy beast," Sheila says.

"*Sheila,*" Goldie says from the stairs beyond the bar. She's in a holiday dress, and *oh my god*, is she going to die laughing when I recover from what just happened and tell her everything. "*Why* do I have to keep telling them you're the nice one and not the horny one?"

"No, no," I manage, finally finding my voice. "He earned

that. Everyone in the building should be calling him a sexy beast right now."

The man's smile just keeps growing. "That felt fucking amazing. You good?"

"What *was* that?" I whisper as my feet finally engage and we head toward the stairs. "Not that I'm not grateful, but it was very...bold. And confrontational."

"My brother told me to do it."

I blink at him.

Truly, when I think he can't smile any broader, he keeps doing it. But his cheeks go a little pink. "In my head. I still...I still sometimes hear him like he's here."

I pause and throw my arms around him. "I love you so much more than I will *ever* be able to tell or show you. And I have a feeling he would be exceptionally proud of you right now."

"I definitely am," Odette says.

"We all know I'm turned on," Sheila adds.

Holt hugs me back hard. "He would've adored you."

Is it weird to say I can feel how much that's true? I'm not one to believe in ghosts, but I believe in Holt. "I would've adored him too."

He kisses my forehead. "Let's go have a party."

"And live happily ever after."

EPILOGUE

Holt

BABIES ARE SO SMALL.

So small.

And my little guy—my William Caden Barnes Webster—is barely as big as a rugby ball.

And he's absolutely perfect.

So is his mama, who's sleeping in our bed on our first afternoon home from the hospital.

I should put him down.

Let him nap in the little bassinet we have next to the bed.

But I just can't.

He looks nothing like you, I hear my brother say.

I snort softly and flip him off, mentally of course because I'm holding a baby, and silently tell him to go fug himself.

Doesn't matter if William looks like me.

He's my son. My chosen family.

Just like his beautiful mama.

She's spread-eagle on our bed, taking up the entire king-size mattress.

I can sleep on my back again.

It was the first thing she said when we walked upstairs, and she followed it with an attack of the sobs, then flopped onto the mattress on her back, and she hasn't moved since.

Really should put the baby down.

The Pounders have our first match tomorrow. I haven't slept enough. Need to get my rest so I'm at my best to lead the team. All of my hard work in physical therapy paid off, and I'm fully back.

In top shape.

Ready to lead the team again.

But William won't be this little for long.

He yawns, blinking open bright blue eyes, and my heart melts all over again.

"Hi," I whisper to him.

He screws up his face and smacks his lips like he's looking for lunch, his big blue eyes the only other thing moving in his tiny little swaddled body.

"I love you," I add.

He smacks his lips again.

Fucking adorable, perfect little guy.

The hospital was a zoo.

Deedee was there nearly from the minute we told her William had been born until he and Ziggy were discharged this morning. Roland came by every couple hours. Miranda too. Just a couple of the guys on the team.

Not all of them.

They picked three representatives to come and take pictures and report back to everyone else.

And now we're home.

423

My little family.

Jessica peeks in the door and gives me the stink eye.

That's about the worst she does these days. No more snorting. No more blowing dog drool all over me.

She still gets Fletcher on occasion, which I approve of.

"Want to meet your brother?" I ask her.

She wasn't interested earlier.

Dog still has a little hell-beast in her, and she's never a fan of being home alone for hours on end.

Not that she was alone much.

Goldie and Fletcher took her to play with their dogs while we were at the hospital and dropped her off shortly after we got home.

Jessica inches into the room with more hesitation than I've ever seen in her, sniffing cautiously in our direction.

I squat on the floor, letting her step onto my thighs while she sniffs more.

"Yes, yes, he's a boy," I whisper. "You're gonna have to tough it out a little more. He has a lot of Ziggy in him. You'll love him."

She snorts.

There's no heat to it though.

She knows I'm right.

None of us can resist loving Ziggy, so none of us can resist loving Ziggy's baby.

It's a universal law.

"Is it a boy that Jessica likes?" Ziggy asks.

She shifts on the bed and rolls over to watch us.

Fucking rock star.

Labor and delivery make rugby matches look like a walk in the park.

"I think Jessica's gonna cope," I tell her.

She smiles, and my heart melts all over again.

Just like it does every time she smiles.

I didn't want this.

Didn't want a family. A partner. Kids. Pets.

But I've never been happier in my life.

"Is he awake?" Ziggy asks.

"Just woke up."

He yawns, then stretches his tongue out like he's still figuring out he has a tongue. His little face scrunches up, and then the wail comes.

Ziggy sits and reaches for him, so I scoot onto the bed next to her and hand him over.

"He's so fuck—freaking perfect," I murmur into her hair.

"And he'll only get better," she replies as she holds him to her breast and the little guy latches on. "Until he's a teenager. Then we might hate him for a while. But after that, life will be great. Until he goes to college. And leaves us. And becomes an adult. And—"

She cuts herself off as she starts to sniffle.

"And it's going to be a long, long, long time before any of that happens," I tell her.

"No, it won't," she sobs.

She's not wrong.

But if we've both learned anything in the past year or so —some lessons together, some apart—it's that we still have today.

And this today—this today is beautiful.

Just like she is.

"I love you," I murmur into her hair.

"You're my everything," she whispers back. "Both of you. And the dog. All three of you. My everything."

And of everything I've ever done in my life, being her everything is…well, it's *my* everything.

BONUS EPILOGUE

Jessica, aka an opinionated dog who likes to make sure the men in her ladies' lives know their place

THAT MAN IS GONNA WAKE up one of these days to a *real* dog fart, and he's gonna deserve it.

Do you know what he just did?

Do you know what he just did?

He walked into this house *with a cat.*

That's what he just did.

He was almost tolerable when he left the house this morning, but now—*now.*

Now, he's back, with that weirdo friend of his with the rat across his upper lip, and they're telling my perfect lady mama that they have to keep the cat.

Keep the cat.

The cat that's huddled in a blanket and eyeing me like it thinks *it* will rule this household.

You can think again, cat. That baby that they brought

home a while ago doesn't run this household, so there's no effing chance a *cat* will run this household.

"Are you the boss?" it asks me.

"Am I the boss? *Am I the boss?*" I sneer at it. "I'm not *the* boss. I'm *the only* boss. The bitch-ass boss. The boss above all bosses. And I have these humans trained, so you better figure out your place real quick here, or skedaddle on along."

It smiles. "The humans said you hate them."

I scoff. "I do not *hate* them. That lady you're talking to? She's the best. She gives belly rubs and treats and walks and lets me snuggle. The man holding you finally wised up to the fact that his house was incomplete without her and brought her to me as an offering for my approval. He's such a guy. Very slow. Sometimes inept. I almost have him trained, and I'm not letting *you* mess this up."

It gives me one long, slow blink, and then it yowls like it's in distress, which makes the humans fawn all over it.

Fine, fine, yes.

It looks really bad.

The cat, I mean. Not just the situation.

One of its ears is half-missing. All of the whiskers on one side of its face are gone, like they were plucked out. I can't see all of it because the human man has it wrapped half-way in a towel, but I can tell that it's a short-haired cat, with orange and black fur. I can also tell that its fur looks dull, and the cat itself is skinny.

Like, bad-skinny.

You can see it in the cat's face.

Don't be a dick, Jessica, a male voice that I've heard in my head ever since I came to live here says. *You weren't being cared for well either until you moved in here.*

He sounds like the man in the house, but a little different.

Not as annoying as the human male that I like to test daily.

And in case you didn't know, that's high praise from me when it comes to human men.

The cat yowls again like it's in pain, and all three humans converge around it.

"Oh, you poor thing. We need to get you to a vet," my lady says.

"Goldie knows one. I'll call her," the rat-lipped guy says. "She might do house calls."

"Can we at least give her some water?" my human man says.

The cat smiles at me while I squint at it.

"Are you really a girl?" I ask it.

Who the eff can tell with a cat? I'm not getting up in its tail this early in our relationship. Especially when it'll probably be short-lived.

"Yes, I'm a girl," she says.

Huh.

Interesting.

"You're not just saying that to butter me up?" I ask.

"I'm not that kind of cat."

"What kind of cat are you?"

"The hungry cold kind who saw a guy walking by who looked like he's the kind of nice who'd feed me."

My human lady is hustling into the living room from the kitchen with a bowl of water. "Don't let her upstairs. I don't want her near the baby just yet."

I bark a little in outrage.

We're keeping it?

Just like that?

It's only been in the house for three minutes. This is outrageous.

You were in the house for one minute before you got kept, Jessica, the guy in my head reminds me.

I think back to when I came here, and what I did to test the man, and *fine.*

Fine.

The people who live here are good people who take care of creatures.

They'd probably adopt a stray fish if they found it lying in the road.

I eye the cat again as my lady human drops to her knees next to me.

She was fixing my dinner, and now where's my dinner?

Nowhere.

"Hey, you," she says to me, rubbing me in that really good spot between my ears. "We're not abandoning you if we're taking care of another animal in need. You know that, right? You're half the reason I stayed here when Mr. Crankypants over there got back early from his trip. You're basically our matchmaker, Jessica. We wouldn't give up on you."

"She still hate you?" the rat-on-his-upper-lip guy says to my human man.

"Only occasionally," my human man replies.

I snort.

"It's been three weeks since she's snorted at me like that," he adds.

Because you know Holt's a good guy, that voice in my head says.

It's surprisingly gentle compared to some of the men I knew before I came to this part of town.

"You can be in charge," the cat says to me. "I don't want to be in charge. I just want food and water and a warm bed at night. You look like you'd be comfy to snuggle with. I like snuggles, but I haven't had any in forever."

Same, Jessica, that voice says in my head. *Have snuggles for me. Adopt a cat for me. I always wanted a cat.*

I eye the cat.

Then my human lady, who cocks one ear and rises to her feet.

I hear it too.

The baby's crying.

Naptime's over.

I snort again.

He's such a boy baby.

Jessica's dinner time? He's gonna fuss. Jessica's walk time? He's gonna fuss. New cat in the house that has to be separated from him?

You got it—he's gonna fuss.

"If you let me stay, I can be the boys' pet, and you can be the girl's pet, and then we can all be happy together," the cat says to me.

Huh.

That's not a bad idea.

The boys are tolerable compared to others of the human male species that I've met in my lifetime, but I still don't *like* them.

Maybe they wouldn't try so hard if they had a cat to love all over them too.

"You're not just saying that, are you?" I ask her.

"I don't cross the bitch-ass boss," the cat replies. "I tried that once. And now look at me."

She yowls again.

My human man puts her on the ground next to the water

431

bowl, and she sniffs it delicately like she's afraid it's poisoned, then even more delicately laps her tongue into it.

"Oh my whiskers, *fresh water*," she says, and then she's attacking it like it's a feast.

My stupid heart ka-thumps in sympathy for the feline.

I've been there.

I know that feeling.

If she's lying, you can fart on her too, the guy in my head says.

The mustache guy is hovering between me and the cat.

My human dude is hovering right over the cat, like he's ready to grab her if she makes a run for anywhere else in the house.

But the cat isn't paying attention to either of them.

She's licking the water so fast I can barely see her tongue. Like she hasn't had fresh water in days.

Maybe weeks.

She finally stops drinking, and then she meows softly in contentment and rubs her head against the man's leg. She purrs so loudly, even the humans with their half-worthless ears notice too.

"Shit," my human man says. "This really means I have to keep her, doesn't it?"

"Yep," the guy with the ugly mustache replies. "She rubbed you. You're hers now."

My man strokes her body, which really is small. I don't think she's supposed to be that small. "What do cats need? Litter boxes?"

"I got this one, Captain. You stay and make friends. I'll be back in an hour with a crazy cat dude starter kit."

The cat isn't paying any attention to me now.

No, she's soaking up being petted by the human, still rubbing her face all over his leg.

I sigh and flop to the ground.

So we have a cat now.

"You better keep your end of the deal," I grumble to her.

"He smells nice. I'd like to keep him," she replies.

I eye the man.

He's smiling.

He's smiling like he smiles at my favorite lady mama.

Fine.

Fine.

He has good taste. And I might even admit he has a big heart.

And by the time we all head to bed, even *I* like the cat.

She gives good snuggles.

And even the voice in my head sighs in contentment when the cat purrs against me.

I suppose the human man can live for another day.

Or probably for the rest of my life.

"He's a good one, isn't he?" the cat murmurs sleepily.

"One of the best," I admit begrudgingly. "But don't ever tell him I told you so."

PIPPA GRANT BOOK LIST

The Girl Band Series (Complete)
Mister McHottie

Stud in the Stacks

Rockaway Bride

The Hero and the Hacktivist

The Thrusters Hockey Series
The Pilot and the Puck-Up

Royally Pucked

Beauty and the Beefcake

Charming as Puck

I Pucking Love You

Copper Valley Bro Code Series
Flirting with the Frenemy

America's Geekheart

Liar, Liar, Hearts on Fire

The Hot Mess and the Heartthrob

Snowed in with Mr. Heartbreaker

The Pretend Fiancé Fiasco

Copper Valley Fireballs Series (Complete)
Jock Blocked

Real Fake Love

The Grumpy Player Next Door

Irresistible Trouble

Three BFFs and a Wedding Series (Complete)

The Worst Wedding Date

The Gossip and the Grump

The Bride's Runaway Billionaire

Copper Valley Pounders Series

Until It Was Love

The Roommate Mistake

A Thrusters x Fireballs Mash-Up

The Secret Hook-Up

The Tickled Pink Series

The One Who Loves You

Rich In Your Love

Standalones

The Last Eligible Billionaire

Not My Kind of Hero

Dirty Talking Rival *(Bro Code Spin-Off)*

A Royally Inconvenient Marriage *(Royally Pucked Spin-Off)*

Exes and Ho Ho Hos

The Happy Cat Series (Complete)

Hosed

Hammered

Hitched

Humbugged

Happily Ever Aftered

The Bluewater Billionaires Series (Complete)

The Price of Scandal by Lucy Score

The Mogul and the Muscle by Claire Kingsley

Wild Open Hearts by Kathryn Nolan

Crazy for Loving You by Pippa Grant

Pippa Grant writing as Jamie Farrell:

The Misfit Brides Series (Complete)

Blissed

Matched

Smittened

Sugared

Merried

Spiced

Unhitched

The Officers' Ex-Wives Club Series (Complete)

Her Rebel Heart

Southern Fried Blues

ABOUT THE AUTHOR

Pippa Grant wanted to write books, so she did.

Before she became a *USA Today* and #1 Amazon bestselling romantic comedy author, she was a young military spouse who got into writing as self-therapy. That happened around the time she discovered reading romance novels, and the two eventually merged into a career. Today, she has more than 30 knee-slapping Pippa Grant titles and nine published under the name Jamie Farrell.

When she's not writing romantic comedies, she's fumbling through being a mom, wife, and mountain woman, and sometimes tries to find hobbies. Her crowning achievement? Having impeccable timing for telling stories that will make people snort beverages out of their noses. Consider yourself warned.

Find Pippa at...
www.pippagrant.com
pippa@pippagrant.com

www.ingramcontent.com/pod-product-compliance
Lightning Source LLC
La Vergne TN
LVHW091611080325
805489LV00020B/129